Scribners

Arrogance

Arrogance

JOANNA SCOTT

A Novel

Scribners

A Scribners Book

First published in the United States in 1990 by Linden Press,
a division of Simon & Schuster Inc. First published in Great Britain in
1991 by Scribners,
a division of Macdonald & Co (Publishers) Ltd, London & Sydney

The author is indebted to Alessandra Comini for her two works,
Egon Schiele and *Schiele in Prison*.
The author would like to thank the John Simon Guggenheim
Memorial Foundation, the University of Maryland, and the University
of Rochester for their support.

Reproduced, printed and bound in Great Britain by
Mackays of Chatham PLC, Chatham, Kent

British Library Cataloguing in Publication Data
Scott, Joanna
Arrogance.
I. Title
813.54

ISBN 0 356 19777 8

Scribners
A Division of
Macdonald & Co (Publishers) Ltd
165 Great Dover Street
London SE1 4YA

A Member of Maxwell Macmillan Pergamon Publishing Corporation

FOR JOHN HAWKES

King Nebuchadnezzar

I had made up my mind: any distant city would serve my purpose. So after a full night and part of the next day in a crowded second-class compartment, I was quite fed up, and I ended my journey in Lucca. I followed the other travelers through the station and onto an omnibus, where, luckily, the driver was busy giving his boots a spit polish and did not bother to collect our fares. We remained there in the unseasonable heat, without adding a single passenger, for fifteen minutes or more before the driver drew in the slack reins and raised his whip. At a stop a few miles beyond the station, a group of schoolboys and a clergyman descended noisily, like pale, freckled pebbles tumbling down a wooden chute. I stepped down after them, but when they crossed the street to a small school I turned away and headed back in the direction we had come. My suitcase bounced against my thigh as I walked past one-story stone cottages and un-tended yards overrun with dormant honeysuckle and wild lavender. When I had walked far enough, I turned back toward the school.

A woman met me at the door, and before I could ask she told me "*Niente*," nothing. At first glance she must have taken me for a Gypsy. Her eyes were milky, dull, her auburn hair pulled into a topknot with a few wisps curling angrily about her face. I looked over her shoulder into the narrow foyer, then around at the dirty white stucco and the broken slate along the path. In halting Italian I asked if I could sleep in the garden. She inspected me for a long minute, and I drew my mother's navy sateen shawl tight around my throat. Finally she agreed to accommodate me for a fee, which, if I understood correctly, included neither a fresh towel nor breakfast. The gate would be locked at ten.

She brought me two blankets, which I hid with my suitcase behind a stone wall separating the school garden from the fields. I promised to pay the woman in the morning and left my copper-backed pocket watch as credit. Then I started walking. I walked—for the first time in my life, it seemed—simply for the sake of walking. Eventually I passed through a low archway and entered the old quarter. I would have liked to purchase a loaf of bread, a piece of hard cheese, and some mineral water, but I had only Austrian money, so I sat on the side of a canal, skimming my heels over the surface, my thoughts traveling a twisted course.

It was dark when I rose again. I wandered along an unlit lane that led me to a small piazza in front of a church, and when I tried to press further into the center of the city I kept returning to the same deserted piazza in the heart of the labyrinth. I started to follow the road beside the wall, but I couldn't know whether I was circling the center the far way around, moving away from rather than toward the archway and avenue I sought. I followed a passageway that led through several *campi* to a broader, well-lit street. Of course I had no map.

I heard the sounds of my shoes slapping the cobblestones and stiff sheets flapping on a clothesline. I heard plates clattering and a woman humming. And then I heard another set of footsteps. I didn't turn—I knew that he would be squat, thick-legged, with cracked lips and flattened nose, his cap would be pulled low over his forehead, he would be carrying a faded Spanish leather pouch and he would be drunk. He hissed; they all hiss. I walked briskly, he gained on me, but I didn't break into a run. Near a hooded gas lamp a woman stood alone in the middle of the street, buttoning her sweater. I caught up to her and said, "*Bitte, mi scusa, Signora,*" but before I could make her understand that I had lost my way, the man was beside us, inhaling deeply, combing his fingers through the underside of his beard and grinning, unashamed of his uneven, ash-colored teeth.

He said he would be grateful to receive a kiss from each of us, *un bacio*, here, in the middle of his forehead. The woman shifted her feet to face him squarely, and he closed his eyes in anticipation. She did not move. He blinked, and for a moment I saw what he saw: the pure, withering white blast of her scorn. He was a weak man, easily discouraged. We watched him slink away. Then the woman asked me—in German—why I was out after dark, a young girl alone. (Swiss, wasn't I, or Slavic?) I was Austrian, I told her, relieved to hear my own language and taking her for a friend. I said that I had run away from home because I had ambition and didn't want to waste my life caring for my invalid mother, squandering my youth in a sickroom. The woman said, yes, yes, now where did I want to go?

•

Vienna! Where Imperial Court carriages roll beside rickety cabs furnished with cracked mirrors and tattered lace curtains, where in a crowded outdoor café a common workman might find himself sitting next to the Archduke. Young and old, aristocrats, merchants, students, tourists, and idlers stroll along the Graben and lift their monocles to survey the shapely ankles of a countess or a laundrygirl. Years ago, anyone of fashion was expected to have in his company a long-snouted Pomeranian, its white fur immaculate, its little anus pink and perfumed. Nowadays it is enough to have an emerald-studded walking stick. But don't let that stop you from buying a plump Frankfurt sausage and eating it with your fingers!

•

Egon Schiele, in a letter dated September 1, 1911: "I am so rich I must give myself away."

•

In my haste to escape my mother's illness, I had brought only two blouses, one skirt, two changes of underclothes, and a useless guidebook to my homeland. But on the night I slept in the school garden, I reached a pinnacle of contentment, a delicious freedom earned from exhaustion. I still remember that night vividly: I lay on my back watching the stars, and as the evening wore on the flux of things increased, the sky throbbed and rocked above me, the limp asparagus shoots began to tremble, the earth itself seemed to tip, and soon, despite the cold, the precipitant motion put me to sleep.

I dreamt that I had walked the entire distance from my village of

Neulengbach to Vienna, only to be swept up by a mob stampeding through the gardens of the Hofburg, shouting *"Nieder mit Latour!"* (The war minister, von Latour, was murdered during the uprising many years before. You can go to Vienna and see the lamppost where they strung up his naked, mutilated body.) I tried to keep pace with the crowd, but my feet slipped from under me and I collapsed on the wet grass. Boot heels bruised my back, spurs ripped my clothes and lacerated my flesh, and I thought that I would die if no one saved me. But even in my dream I knew that I couldn't die, not there in the Volksgarten, in the shadow of the Hof. So I closed my eyes, and when I opened them again I saw the steeple of a small baroque church rising above me. I was lying on my back on a strip of cotton attached to wooden poles. The woman carrying the poles at my feet, dressed in white taffeta and a straw hat with a black ribbon, was the mistress of an artist who had moved recently into Neulengbach. At my head, Egon Schiele himself. I knew little about the couple, except that they were renting a cottage in Au on the outskirts of Neulengbach, the people resented them because they lived openly in sin, and the artist invited their young daughters to model for his lewd drawings.

In my dream the hammock swayed gently as the artist and his mistress carried me away from the riot. We drifted through the streets of the Inner City, leaving behind the mob, the clubs and shovels and stones, and eventually we reached the canal. They lowered me from the embankment into a small boat and climbed in after me. As we floated into the middle of the canal, I caught sight of the Prater's magnificent Ferris wheel engulfed in flames.

Soon the entire city was burning, and the heat of the flames felt like the tips of feathers brushing against my face. Eventually I passed into a deeper, dreamless sleep. When I woke, the buds of a nearby forsythia bush were covered with a membrane of dew and the sun's rim, opaque behind the mist, was rising above the edge of the field. Without immediately recalling my dream I felt an inexplicable calm, but as I looked around at the hazy, foreign land and my eyes settled on my purse, I recalled my vague, impractical intentions. I remembered that I had gone to sleep hungry.

I folded the blankets and left them on the doorstep of the school. I didn't bother to change my clothes but merely splashed my face with the brown malt water of a shallow creek. My watch I left to the proprietress. Only on the long walk back to the train station did I remember my dream in detail, how the artist and his mistress had carried me away from the uprising, how we had drifted along the canal while Vienna burned around us. The memory was so acutely real that the emotions of relief and gratitude returned to me. I wanted to find the couple and thank them for saving my life.

·

The cell in Neulengbach, April 15, 1912: A basement compartment with whitewashed brick walls, a single barred slit for a window, the cement floor stinking of urine and mildew, no mirror, one coarse blanket with edges frayed by the iron springs of a bunk, no toilet, no lamp (though to Egon the single orange brought by Vallie provides all the light he needs—he places the orange in the middle of the blanket). Cobwebs dangle from the ceiling, and gold-and-black-striped spiders drop onto the bunk. Egon lets them crawl over the tough heel of his hand and up his wrist. He bunches his sleeves as the spiders make their dainty, high-stepping, feathery way through the hair on his arm toward the elbow.

He pretends not to know why he is here, but privately he knows —they fear his ideas, his honesty. Hardly more than a child himself, he has taken a child's terror and turned it into an adult art. In the dungeon he can do no harm. He kneels on the floor, rubs dust into a puddle of saliva in his palm and with his fingers he paints frescoes on the glutinous walls. He paints the hills to the west of his cottage, he paints a portrait of Vallie and of the fat, bearded guard who delivers his bread and water. As he leaves each image behind to begin the next, the lines dissolve into the brick and disappear completely. But he continues to paint, though he knows that anyone who looks through the keyhole is likely to mistake him for King Nebuchadnezzar on his hands and knees, eating grass.

·

Look around you! At the soldier squatting to feed a kitten a piece of roasted Bohemian pheasant; at the tinman with his burden of mouse-traps, pots and pans, old gravures and stilettos, copper kettles, coffee mills, nails, horseshoes, and handspikes; at the milkmaids dressed in lush green skirts, cotton shawls with red polka dots, dark blue jackets, red silk handkerchiefs and white aprons; at the porters in black tails; at the gnarled grimalkin with her bushels of apples and onions; at the street cobbler hidden in a halo of cigar smoke, dried strings of glue dribbled over his apron. Take a deep breath and smell: plum torte in the oven; sausages steaming in a vat; lime dust sprinkled on the streets; stale wine on the steps leading to a Keller; fresh ink from the presses; sweating horses; overripe pears. Listen: to the old clothes vendors hawking trousers; to the grisettes gossiping and the intellectuals arguing; to the automobiles honking; to the infant's wail and the officer's whistle and the tiny silver bells dangling from the ears of a Jewess. Quaint and modern, austere and florid, chaste and exotic is this alluring paradox, the city of Vienna.

•

While Herr Adolf Schiele lay on his deathbed in the winter of 1904, Egon and his younger sister Gerti sat across from each other on the floor of their bedroom, their knees drawn up beneath long flannel shirts, his bare toes gently pressing upon hers. They watched the toy rocking horse on the bureau tip forward and back, phosphorescent in the moonlight. Egon had been given the horse at the Hoher Markt one Christmas Eve many years ago. He would always remember the magical forest that had sprung up overnight in the old square in Vienna—pine trees draped with bands of colorful tissue, a military band playing, beautiful women wandering about like wild, nocturnal creatures, wrapped in plush furs. He had followed close on their heels and stroked their rumps, his touch so light that these opulent, well-padded ladies felt nothing, and he would have passed that Christmas Eve in a contented dream if Uncle Leopold hadn't caught him burying his fingers in one woman's sable pelt.

"Egon!"

Uncle Leopold slapped his nephew's cheek with a gloved hand, a painless but humiliating blow, and the boy only increased his shame with his hysterical sobs. Another one of Egon's fits. "Not in public!" his uncle ordered. And his mother: "Egon, everyone is watching!" But a child in the throes of despair cannot be calmed by pleas for propriety, and at that moment in order to breathe Egon had to scream. How he despised himself and loved his mother so and was embarrassing her. She begged him to be silent and he wanted to please her but he couldn't help himself, he was a misfit, governed by unspeakable impulses. Lock the door and nail the shutters closed, don't let Egon out!

Egon's father, the stationmaster, had remained behind at Tulln, and it was an old toy merchant who finally placated the boy. "Choose," he urged in his native Czech. Choose between a wooden soldier, a drum, a Noah's ark, a music box, an alpine village inside a glass bubble with soap flakes falling endlessly, a cloth giraffe, a scarlet vest, a miniature rocking horse. Egon squeezed his eyes shut to block the tears, and the toy merchant uncurled his fingers and placed the rocking horse in his open hand.

Since then Egon had asked so many favors from his rocking horse that he no longer bothered to keep track of the results. He couldn't confess his latest wish to his sister—they didn't dare speak aloud, not with their father's insanity trumpeting through the thin wall, incoherent rage broken occasionally by a high-pitched glissando howl, and then the sobs, Egon understood the pathetic sobbing, he knew exactly what his father was trying to say. He reached out to grasp his sister's small, moist hands and silently they watched the wooden horse—perhaps a draft had slipped beneath the window-pane to set the horse in motion, perhaps the vibrations of their father's voice through the wall caused it to rock ever so slowly. Egon yanked Gerti, she leaned back and pulled him toward her. In turn, they raised their feet a few inches from the floor, imitating the seesaw rhythm of the wooden horse, laughing silently, rocking back and forth. Shadows washed across Gerti's face, and Egon was re-minded of the bioscope pictures of a galloping horse; he would have liked to ride a horse in slow motion, bareback.

·

And what about Vallie Neuzil? She would like nothing better than to live in a cottage right here on the edge of the Stadtpark pond, a cottage with walls made not of mud and wattle but of chocolate, a dark, tangy chocolate. How beautiful this city looks today, she thinks as she lazily rakes the wet soil with a twig. How purple, the splotch of color on that duck's wing. And its head, so velvety green. And the ginkgo leaves in the stream beside her—ripe yellow. What sound is more soothing than the gurgle of a stream tumbling over the ledge of a rock and flowing into the Stadtpark pond? Vallie—sixteen years old and nobody's mistress, not yet—has never known a day as soft as today. Soft sounds, soft colors, a soft foehn wind, soft ripples when the ducks paddle across the pond. An old woman on the path behind her scolds a poodle that is frantically trying to

hump the woman's skirted leg. A cluster of ducks glides toward
children who are throwing pieces of bread into the water. Vallie stirs
the soil until it is the consistency of molasses and finds herself thinking about how she will be old some day. The observation seems to
arise from the outside, as though whispered in her ear. She will be
old someday—an unsuitable thought for such a fine autumn afternoon—and as though to provide an analogue for the melancholy
truth, a single duck, completely white, with a pale, almost transparent orange beak, swims out from the cavern formed by a bush's
drooping branches. All the other ducks in the pond are green, black,
brown, the males with two black tendrils curling from their rumps
and a dot of purple on their wings, the females a plainer, sandy
color. The white duck is a mutant, a ghost, shunned by the rest of
the flock. Vallie will be old someday, pitied by girls as lively and
impertinent as she is now; she will be as solitary as this white duck
and as ridiculous as a woman with a poodle clinging to her leg.

But Vallie has felt the doom of age before and knows that there is
nothing to do but shrug off this weighty sorrow and get on with
her life. Perhaps she will be as lucky as her mother and drop dead
before she reaches the brink of old age, will know only this shore
and not the opposite, will sink like a stone into the silent pond and
until then will remain a member of the flock, as beloved as that
female bobbing on the waves made by the male, who courts her
with a jerking dance, paddling in place, arching his neck, plunging
his head again and again into the water. He is rewarded when the
female mimics him, their movements amazingly synchronized—the
sign that she accepts his invitation. With a few powerful strokes he
reaches her, mounts her and takes his pleasure—as the toy poodle
could not.

Vallie is no stranger to courtship, though so far her admirers have
been schoolboys who quickly become more of a nuisance than a
treat. But right now she feels the active equivalent—to want—so
she pushes herself up and heads back through the park, crosses the
Ring, ambles along the Johannesgasse and within ten minutes she is
standing in front of the display window of her favorite confectionery. She likes to examine the chocolates before she decides what to
buy: truffles flavored with pineapple, with orange, with apricot,
with coconut, miniature marzipan fruits and marzipan potatoes and
even marzipan in the shape of mushrooms, a *Haselnuss Wurst* roll,

almond chocolates crisscrossed with white icing, chocolate-covered cherries, pretzels, orange rinds, white chocolate with raisins, bitter chocolate with raisins, milk chocolate, nut clusters, chocolates filled with whiskey, kirsch, gin, and cognac. How to decide?

"Alles?" the woman asks when the two-hundred-gram box has been packed full. More? Vallie looks forward to the day when she will have enough money in her purse to say more and more and more again until she fills a dozen boxes with chocolates. She will start a library of chocolates. But for now she can only motion to the woman to close the box and not to wrap it, for she means to open it right away.

The first chocolate soothes her. The determination to enjoy herself has always been Vallie's main preoccupation, and with such simple desires she doesn't risk disappointment. A box of chocolates and a splendid autumn afternoon—she is too grateful to be selfish. Even though she must work all week in a dress shop for her spending money, even though the city enjoys such perfect weather only rarely, she feels as she walks along that the whole world is a happy accident. She sucks on a chocolate, turns her face up so she can feel the wind against her throat, decides that she lacks nothing. Nothing but company. She wouldn't mind company, she reflects. A handsome duck. An admirer, bearded—yes, she would like to be courted by someone old enough to grow a beard. Surely, with all of Vienna out of doors today, the odds of her meeting a gentleman are in her favor. And then there will be new opportunities in the days to come —more and more and more. As soon as she has swallowed the chocolate she begins to whistle.

•

Egon asked his mother for a dash of coffee in his milk and another slice of bread. Though it was midsummer, he borrowed his older sister's scarf, because an artist must wear a scarf when he paints, and he carried his sketch pad across the field to a clump of evergreens. After climbing to the nest of boughs he had built for himself in the tallest tree, he rubbed curdled sap from between his fingers and stared at the white paper.

Every day that week he had returned to this hidden perch, and the paper had remained blank. But today he felt an inexplicable confidence. He intended to paint the landscape—the brittle meadow grass and patches of clover and gray thistle, the station house with the second-floor window of the very room where he had been born. Yet he couldn't pull his eyes away from the paper, the blank space hypnotic, the rough whiteness a vacuum. Egon sharpened a pencil with the little knife that hung like a sword from his belt and he poised the graphite tip above the sheet. A different artist might have seen the emptiness as an obstruction, but Egon wanted to celebrate the space, the nothing preceding his crude images. To fill the space without cluttering it—this was the challenge.

A tremor passed through the trees, dried needles cascaded like shards of light, and a few landed on the sketch pad propped on Egon's knees. He drew careful lines beside each pine needle, precise incisions, then he brushed the paper clean and began to connect the marks he had made, forming a gaunt, triangular face, square, frightened, distrustful eyes, but not until he drew waves of luxurious hair did he recognize the face as his own. He left the background blank so the flat image of the face seemed to be pasted on a wall, or as he liked to perceive it, fluttering in a chalky sky.

The following Saturday he found his sister Gerti playing by herself in the kitchen, pretending that russet potatoes were a band of Gypsy musicians. Egon told her that if she wanted a present she must meet him behind the house in ten minutes. She gave him a solemn, conspiratorial nod, and he hurried down the hall. When he descended to the yard he was carrying the box containing his seven self-portraits, one made on each day of the past week. He handed that box to the most important person in his life, and she offered him in return a rum-ball she had stolen from the pantry. But when she opened the box and leafed through the portraits she didn't exclaim in wonder and admiration as Egon had hoped; instead her brows slanted, her pout spread into a grin, and she began to laugh so heartily that she had to wipe spittle from the corner of her mouth, she laughed as only a stationmaster's daughter can laugh, vulgarly, Egon thought. Through her tears she must have seen his displeasure but she couldn't control herself. Why did she laugh? Because, she would explain to Egon years later, she thought the caricatures had been designed to amuse her.

Her giddy shrieks attracted her older sister and then their father, Adolf, who considered laughter a transgression. He found his children clustered in a tight circle and he demanded to be told the reason for their hilarity. Melanie held up the top portrait: "Look, Papa, our brother has made a picture of himself!"

Egon remembered the rum-ball in his hand, as soft and formless as a glob of mud now, and when Adolf grabbed the sketch and threw it to the ground in disgust, Egon let the rum-ball fall. The thin band of Adolf's lips between his graying whiskers paled, and Egon, adept at reading the signs of his father's temper, tried to divert his father's wrath from the drawings to himself; he snatched the box from Gerti and pushed his sisters aside, knowing full well that his punishment would increase proportionately to his audacity. So he wasn't surprised to feel his father's fingers around his neck, the blows against his ears—he could endure a beating if it meant protecting his drawings. After all, he had decided years ago that the man who called himself Adolf Schiele was an imposter who had forced Egon's real father into exile. Someday his own papa would return and destroy the usurper.

He knew that his submission infuriated Adolf. He hung like a limp carcass from the man's claws, secretly proud of his own apathy, until his father began to strike him across the face, and then Egon sprang to life, reached for his little dagger and slashed at the tormentor's hand. His father hardly flinched. He caught Egon by the wrist and twisted his arm until he dropped the knife. Then Adolf said, in a voice as furious and awful as the sound of a collapsing bridge, that he would teach his son an unforgettable lesson. Snatching the box from Egon, he strode away, while Egon and his sisters hurried after him. In the kitchen Adolf opened the box and removed the self-portrait that had been sketched on Tuesday; he rolled the sheet into a narrow tube and thrust one end into the firebox of the stove, withdrew it, and puffed until the glowing edge flamed. He held the burning tube with his injured hand, blood trickling into his sleeve; with the other hand he rolled the next portrait and ignited it, and the next, while his wife timidly blotted his wound with a wet rag. Egon watched helplessly, his hatred so immense that he began to relish the emotion. As his father mixed the ashes of the last drawing with the stove cinders Egon felt an odd triumph, a smug, private, pleasurable surge of pride.

Later that same night Gerti crept over to his bed and handed him the last remaining self-portrait, the one that Adolf Schiele had flung to the ground. Egon snatched it from his sister and told her to leave him alone, ordered her to forget about his drawings as well, never to mention them to him or to anyone else again. He lay awake for hours, waiting until his sisters in their beds across the room were breathing with a shallow, steady panting, waiting until he heard his father plod upstairs from the station and close his bedroom door behind him. Egon waited until the floorboards and walls and windows had fallen asleep, then he crept down the hall to the kitchen, where he opened the stove's door and blew on the coals. He stirred the glowing embers until they flamed, and then he set the drawing on fire and watched it burn, marveling at the fluid orange ridge moving unevenly in the dark toward the center of his face.

·

In order for this inquiry to proceed, the authorities in Neulengbach must gather evidence to use against Egon Schiele. So they question the butcher's daughter, for her father has lodged the first formal complaint. They ask the little girl to describe how the artist had first approached her.

According to the twelve-year-old witness, she and her sister had been returning home along a wooded path below the Liechtenstein Castle and the older sister had stopped to look at clusters of ice that dripped like frozen tears from the thorns of a blackberry bush.

According to the butcher's younger daughter, she was trying to convince her sister to hurry along when they heard a crackling noise, like boots rolling heel to toe over shattered glass, and the accused suddenly emerged from behind a tree. Egon Schiele, hidden in his peaked fur cap and brown coat and natty scarf, seemed as sinister to the girls as the shadow of a man cast upon a wall in a deserted *Durchhaus*. The noise as he broke through the underbrush had been so loud, and afterwards the silence covered the world like the snow covered the soil. The accused started to walk toward the girls, and when he was abreast of them, he drew two yellow apples out of the deep pockets of his overcoat. The sisters hesitated, then they each accepted an apple and thanked him and went on their way. The witness bit into hers as soon as the artist was out of sight. It was, she said, the sweetest apple she had ever tasted, the flesh saturated with honey nectar, the skin as crisp as the ice on the branches. When she had finished, she asked her sister if she could have the second apple as well. But the older sister threw the fruit into the forest and ordered her not to tell anyone about the encounter on the path or else they would be punished, the younger sister more severely.

The butcher's younger daughter didn't care what people would think, she had enjoyed her apple. Later that day she returned to the bend in the path where her sister had thrown away the fruit and she searched until her fingers were numb and the sun had disappeared behind the hills. Finally she summoned all her courage and went directly to the artist's cottage—number forty-five in the district of Au, all the girls knew where he lived. She wanted to ask him where he purchased his fine apples. Perhaps he would give her another golden apple, she thought. He seemed to have plenty to spare.

A handsome woman in a silk dressing gown answered the door. When the witness told her why she had come, the woman, Schiele's mistress, smirked and even laughed aloud before she called him. The accused entered the room wearing only thin trousers and a shirt unbuttoned to the middle of his chest. He led the witness into the cottage. It was as warm as an oven in there, and the butcher's younger daughter said so. They laughed again, the two of them, at her expense. The accused agreed to give the witness an apple, but only on the condition that she pose for him. He asked her to lie face down on the floor and pretend to sleep.

Did he order her to take off her clothes? Did he touch her here? Or here? The girl shook her head and refused to say anything more, despite her father's threats. The prosecutor had enough evidence to bring Egon Schiele in for questioning, but after a short discussion with the constable he decided that to improve the case against the artist from Vienna they must find a second witness to support the testimony of the first. They would let Egon Schiele—pornographer, corruptor of children—write his own warrant.

But he had given her another apple, the butcher's daughter announced to her father as they walked home. The artist had kept his promise. She wouldn't be so angry with him if his mistress hadn't tittered at her when she bit into the fruit. And then the artist began to laugh as well, they laughed the poor child out of the cottage. She would never forgive them.

·

Gray hours, April 16, 1912: What is the specific charge against Egon Schiele? They will not tell him. They lock up dangerous men, so he must be dangerous. Look, turnkey, watch the chair, watch it rise in the foreground of the watercolor sketch; with a few casual strokes the artist has made the chair hover in the air. His mattress is infested with fleas, but Egon prefers the bed to the floor. He pinches a flea between his middle finger and his thumb, then wipes the tiny spot of blood on the blanket. A pleasant enough diversion, when he is too weary to paint. If a piece of crushed flea finds its way beneath his fingernail, he lazily cleans his nails with the stiff bristles of his brush. Egon had begged for paper, pencils, brushes, and paints, and today his captors allowed Vallie to give him the box containing his life's purpose. This has been their only concession.

He cannot estimate the time. There are no patterns in his day, no dependable routines. They might wake him from a deep slumber to serve him a dinner of soup and rye bread, and if he does not eat, they will take the food away and give him nothing until he is weak from hunger. Sometimes he hasn't finished one meal before they bring him the next. Since the weak natural light is eclipsed by the soggy leaves that have collected on his windowsill, he must look for other indicators to mark the passage of time. The stubble is rising on his cheek, so he knows the minutes have turned into hours and days. He feels thirsty and calls for water, drinks, and urinates into a bucket, directing the stream in concentric circles just inside the rim. He wonders how many days will pass before the bucket overflows.

He collapses on the mattress, the springs squeaking as he shifts his weight, and he tosses Vallie's orange from hand to hand. Memory would give him temporary freedom, but they have imprisoned his mind and he can't remember further back than to his last bowl of soup. The years behind him have been obscured by this tedious present, where everything is gray; the smell of urine, gray; the fleas' blood, gray; the coarse texture of the wall and the guard's rude voice, gray. Everything, except for his paints. And the orange. He rips open the orange with his teeth, peels it sloppily so shreds of skin still cling to the fruit; he splits the orange and breaks off a ripe segment and sticks out his tongue to receive it. He crushes the piece with his incisors and lets the light of the orange trickle into his throat.

Now he remembers, not automatically, not easily—he has to work to replace the gray with memory—but the light inside him helps to distinguish the forms of the past: *Trieste*. He shall think of

Trieste, the fishing boats with their coquettish French names, the sound of the Adriatic lazily raking the rocks on the beach, and the shattered, jagged lines of gouache scarring the water. It pleases him to think of the vacation years ago with his sister in Trieste, how the gulls, scavenging for food, cried so greedily that Gerti filled Egon's socks with stones in case the thieving birds mistook the wool for crusts of bread. Egon remembers the buoyancy of the water, the heat of the noon sun on his eyelids after he had shipped the oars and laid his head in his sister's lap. For hours they let the rented boat drift aimlessly while they ate oranges and made up tunes for nursery rhymes, singing at the top of their voices.

Drunk from the memory of the Adriatic sun, Egon springs to his feet, arranges his tray of watercolors, takes his favorite red sable brush from the glass of milky water and rapidly defines the forms that he will fill with colors. First he paints an outline of himself, floating, not in a rowboat in the Trieste harbor but on a cot in the Neulengbach cell. He thinks he is painting from memory, but in the finished portrait he has become a sickly relic swaddled in his blanket, with hollow cheeks and wild, glassy eyes—a dying man, he realizes, suddenly fearful of the image and of his own powerful premonition.

Ardent Wishes

I arrived at Vienna's Bahnhof just before midnight, too late to catch the last train to Neulengbach, so I hired a cab to take me to my grandmother's apartment in the Eighteenth District. If she was surprised to see me she didn't show it. I confessed at once that I had run away from home. My grandmother waved her hand to silence me, as though she'd heard as much as she wanted to hear, and she started chattering about her own affairs as she filled a plate with leftovers—beet salad and *Schmalzbrot*. She told me about her butcher, who had just won five hundred kronen in the lottery. She complained about her rheumatic shoulder. I don't remember moving from the kitchen to my grandmother's treasured sofa, and it seemed that I had just arrived when my grandmother was waking me, insisting that I must hurry if I wanted to catch the early train.

When I reached Neulengbach later that day, I walked directly to the post office where my father was sorting mail, greeted him with a kiss and handed him a box of cigars from my grandmother. He demanded to know where I had been for three days. I reminded him that I had planned for months to visit my grandmother, he had given me permission long ago, didn't he remember? It was all a lie, of course. Usually a humble and trusting man, his anger disappeared as I accounted for my absence. He asked for my pardon, explaining that in old age his memory had grown faulty. It was so easy to fool my father. And my invalid mother hadn't the strength or interest to care that the girl attending to her for three days had been a stranger.

At the apothecary on the Hauptstrasse a few days later, two women standing in line behind me traded stories about the artist who wore pointed American shoes. The children who had seen the inside of his cottage said that his walls were covered with drawings of naked men and women doing unspeakable things to themselves. Schoolgirls competed for his attention and considered it a compliment to be invited to model, even if they knew nothing about art. The same month last fall that the artist had moved into Neulengbach, broad-rimmed straw hats like the one his mistress wore bloomed on young heads throughout the village. The mothers had banned the hats and forbidden their daughters from speaking to the couple from Vienna. According to the women in the apothecary, the more intractable girls continued to visit cottage forty-five in secret.

It was then that I made up my mind to introduce myself to the artist. I decided that if he was truly as sensitive and intelligent as the man with the black, probing eyes in my dream had been, he wouldn't be interested in the clownish antics of Neulengbach girls. Rather than hop about like a jackdaw, I would engage him in a meaningful conversation. So on my free afternoon, when my father came back from church and took my place beside my mother's bed as he did every Sunday, I wandered into Au and followed the lane leading up the hill past the cottage. On warmer Sundays during the fall months I had seen the artist working in the pasture adjacent to his yard, and now that the snow had melted I found him outside again, his easel planted precariously in the spongy earth. I approached him and studied the charcoal sketch in silence, and then I cleared my throat and commented on the visionary quality, the absorbing depth in the landscape. He paid no attention to me. So I watched in silence, satisfied simply to be near him, hoping that he would perceive my inner melancholy and find me an inspiration.

I had brought along a museum catalogue, and when the artist looked up at the scenery before him I drew the catalogue from my cape pocket and asked the artist if he, too, would exhibit his paintings in the Künstlerhaus. Only then did he address me. It was obvious that he considered me another ignorant and coarse peasant girl with no aesthetic sense, and though he thought my question stupid, he took great pains to explain to me why the art in my catalogue would have no lasting significance. He spoke of his own art as if it

were a mechanical invention that would change, fundamentally, ir-
reversibly, the way we live in the world. His vanity intrigued me. I
would have liked to feel such confidence. Right then I decided that I
too would become an artist.

As soon as he had finished declaring his doctrine and purpose, he
ordered me to leave him in peace, and I obliged. At least he had
spoken to me, and I was grateful for his attention, even if I had
distracted him from his work and wasted his valuable time.

•

To understand the peculiar magic of this city, you must be willing
to search for charm in any quarter. On to the ghetto, then, the foul-
smelling, noisy ghetto, a setting so repugnant that a brave traveler
will likely find it exotic, even picturesque; a neighborhood where,
according to the famous travel writer Marie Horner Lasdale, memorable treasures may be found. So why not enter one of the
"leprous-colored hovels," as Mrs. Lasdale has described them, climb
the rotting staircase and visit an authentic slum interior? The room
will be cluttered with old pewter vessels, the ceiling covered with a
thick layer of grime. Who knows but that you might find, propped
beside a cracked porcelain stove, an old Jew muttering incoherently
about man's guilt and God's vengeance, the release of death, and the
snake growing inside him, extending from his heart into his veins
and arteries, a single, rubbery coil. When he closes his lids you might
see the membrane pulsating as if some creature were actually slithering behind the sockets.

And if you listen closely to his speech, you would hear how the
old man has confused himself. He tries to ease his pain by comparing
it to a snake, but the reptile has taken on its own life, breaking from
the control of his reason, forcing the old man to believe there is an
actual serpent coiled in his bowels. It will continue to grow until the
man destroys it himself by swallowing a teaspoonful of arsenic or
opening his veins with a kitchen knife.

Don't bother dallying with this suffering ancient—a quick
glimpse, a short meditation upon the plight of the poor, and then
hurry on to see the ten thousand skinned hares strung up in the
market stalls.

•

Chamber of horrors, April 18, 1912: How does Egon measure a woman's beauty? Not by the texture of her skin or the color of her hair; he doesn't care whether he can skim a woman from a bowl of cream or pluck her from a garden, for the most important quality is her fluidity, her freedom of motion. His love of motion compels him to prefer children, to admire them for their limber, spontaneous gestures, for the way they innocently possess the space around them. Whether they are hopping on one foot or waving goodbye, they move like leaves swirling, lagging, drifting on a river's opaque surface toward a firth. Even Gustav Klimt's gilded seductresses do not compare to the girls of the Second District, young, nubile, so slippery and colorful. Egon used to decorate his pubescent darlings with gouache, crayon, gold and silver paint, and, like Klimt, he depicted them as watersprites and gave them the power to breathe underwater. But after Klimt had introduced him to seventeen-year-old Vallie Neuzil, after she had become Egon's mistress as well as his model, his females become bolder, with charged, provocative gazes and a mannered angularity. Sometimes they clutch themselves indecently, sometimes they strain to break out of their black-chalk and watercolor bodies.

In his cell in Neulengbach he thinks of the women in his life: his mother, his sister Gerti, Vallie. He would like to make a huge mural and include them all in it, but instead he finds himself drawing the line that will become the edge of his face in yet another self-portrait as a prisoner. In this one he outlines a distended bulb, which he turns into a fetus's enlarged head with bewildered eyes and lips in an oval —here the fear of death has become the newborn's shock at the infinite space surrounding him.

He falls asleep with this new self-portrait beside him on the bed, the two-dimensional child-man staring at the ceiling, while Egon dreams that he is standing on a grassy bank of the Tulln River, tossing bread to the swans. When he wakes, he realizes that in the dream he had actually been throwing pieces of his own watercolors into the water, and still the swans had greedily devoured the scraps. He imagines how he would slit open the bellies of the swans and extract the bloody pulp and glue it onto cardboard matting.

He is considering this idea for a collage when the door opens and the afternoon guard enters the cell, bucket and broom in hand. Egon tries to recall where he has seen this brute before: perhaps collecting firewood beside the road, or on a Sunday morning, casting his line into an ice-laced stream. Strangers quickly become familiar faces in such a tiny hamlet, and soon they are associated with one's own cyclical moods. The guard makes Egon think of frosted pastures, of the brisk January cold that poured in when Vallie opened the bedroom window for a few minutes in the morning, of pine boughs laden with snow. He orders Egon to wash the floor of the cell, and though his smug tyranny is irritating, Egon feels grateful to have a task, however insignificant. He lifts the brush from the suds and kneels, scrubbing vigorously, contentedly, he even begins to whistle one of the songs from his childhood. He wonders if Vallie has already contacted his sister or his friends in Vienna; they would help him, they might arrive any moment to help him, so Egon is glad to have the chance to tidy his little cavern. He wouldn't want Arthur Roessler to see him wallowing in his own filth.

After the guard leaves, Egon continues to scrub, leaning heavily on the wire brush, churning up a chalky, bone-brown paste. If he continues to apply such force he will scrub a hole in the floor and through the earth below, he will scrub his way to freedom. He leans back on his heels and laughs aloud at the thought of such a fantastic escape, laughs fiercely because he is glad to be laughing. He has a boyish trill, due partly to his habit of biting his lower lip, due mostly to the contradictions inside him: he feels himself to be both young and old, untried and exhausted.

The guard hears his laughter and bursts into the cell. "You call that clean!" he shouts and spits on the floor. "Clean as pig slime!" he bellows, kicking the bucket so a wave of dirty water sloshes over the edge. He orders Egon to scrub the floor again, to keep scrubbing until he can see his reflection in the cement.

·

Egon's mother was raised in Krumau, and Egon often visited this small Bohemian city, though he had no family or acquaintances here and his mother's maiden name had been forgotten. Usually he came with a couple of friends and stayed no longer than a week. He had frequented the few brothels in the city and once, when he was nineteen, he spent an afternoon with a young goatherd, whose name he never learned. Then, in the summer of 1911, he rented a cottage in Krumau because he wanted to paint a picture of his mother's past, and he invited his mistress Vallie along because she reminded him that he was still young, helped him to shrug off his consuming ambition. In the cottage in Krumau, in the upstairs room with dormer windows facing the cottage across the street, Vallie danced naked, not caring that any curious neighbor could look in and see her full breasts, the red tuft of her pubic hair, the firm muscles in her legs; she loved to strip and toss chocolate-covered cherries in the air and catch them in her open mouth. With a loud, sucking noise she would encourage Egon to do the same, and if he tried to draw the curtains she tugged on his arm and reminded him that the world had no reason to bother about Egon Schiele and the saucy girl who shared his bed.

But the residents of Krumau cared too much about this couple—there were rumors that the artist lured children into the cottage and used them as models for pornographic postcards. Within a few weeks of their arrival, Egon and Vallie were warned in an anonymous note that they had better leave town. So on the following day, as the cluster of church bells announced noon, the disreputable lovers walked to the station, their arms linked, while a few old women dressed in black, with kerchiefs wrapped around their heads, stood in doorways and watched the outcasts pass.

From Krumau they moved to Neulengbach, a village only thirty kilometers outside of Vienna. They rented a hip-roofed cottage in the sparsely populated district of Au, and every afternoon, month after month, when the walls were covered with deep scarlet shadows, Egon and Vallie peeled off their clothes and chased each other from room to room.

During one of these romps in early spring Vallie decided that she, too, would be a painter. In the studio she seized a valuable kolinsky brush from Egon's palette, brandished it with a practiced swish and when Egon lunged for her, she swiped red pigment across his cheek. He cried out, "Blood for blood!" and with another brush he swirled blue across her hand. They dueled with colors, they blotched, striped, bruised themselves, until the hues distracted Egon and he grew more interested in the designs than in his own desire. He began to study Vallie with a critical, appreciative eye, the way he evaluated all his unfinished work. His erection softened and he urged his lover to remain still while he painted gold haloes around her nipples, a silver belt around her waist. She continued to dab at him, dotting him with sepia and orange, and when Egon lowered his brush for a moment she took the opportunity to reach for his crotch.

"Close your eyes," she directed, and he surrendered. "Now open them." She had streaked his penis with bright canary green. He wrestled her to the floor, and while he had her pinned on her back he ran his tongue between the lines of color, moistening the pale, unpainted flesh.

But now it was Vallie's turn to spoil the fun; with her hands buried in his hair, her knees bent over his shoulders, she stiffened and wriggled away from him. He looked at her in confusion, followed her gaze across the room to the open door, where a young girl stood on the porch just beyond the threshold. The girl stared back at the tangled pair, mesmerized, for a half-minute or more. Then she tore herself free and fled down the porch stairs, away from the cottage, down the road toward the village center to alarm the citizens about this godless pair from Vienna. Or so Vallie predicted, tucking her tousled hair behind her ears. She chucked Egon on his chin and suggested that they avoid the inconvenience of another scandal and leave before the mob gathered.

But Egon knew that the girl would tell no one what she had witnessed. "I know the little fool," he assured Vallie. "She bothers me when I'm working, she distracts me with her insipid questions. She is a loner," he explained. "A stranger among her own people. She won't do us any harm."

.

What did I see that day when I was fifteen years old and had gone directly to cottage forty-five, determined to ask Egon Schiele for advice about painting? I saw wooden toys, a soldier and a milkmaid tattooed with colors. I saw her smear him with green, I saw him paint necklaces around her breasts. The artist and his mistress were born to decorate and flaunt their bodies, they were given flesh so they could deface it, as children are given scraps of paper and dogs are given cast-off shoes.

Later, while my mother slept, I scratched open a flap of wallpaper where her bedpost had worn it thin and I admitted to myself that I was responsible for what I'd witnessed. I had entered their cottage without permission, intruded into their privacy, I had watched, and I had enjoyed myself. As they indulged in their obscene games, I had discovered my own impurities, savoring most the mistaken sense that I was in control. Until they fixed their eyes on me, that is, and then I lost my power over them.

For a few days I was able to recall the scene in detail—her silky fingers cradling his sex, coating him with paint, the artist circling her body with a single band of silver, both of them kneeling, probing, stroking each other, oblivious to me. But too soon the memory grew faint, the colors faded. And I knew that I would have to return to their cottage, not for advice but to feed my eyes, to watch without being seen.

•

When he was a boy living in the Tulln station house, Egon drew on napkins and tablecloths. He drew steam engines and diesels. With a pencil he sketched the two-truck coaches, the sleeping cars, the piloting and driving wheels, the hopper cars and boxcars, flat cars, tank cars, produce cars, and livestock cars. Beautiful trains.

Stop! signaled Adolf Schiele, the stationmaster. *Proceed at restricted speed.*

Obedient trains. Egon's mother had an ambition for her son: "Egon should study instead to become an engineer, our most ardent wish." But Egon didn't care about the internal machinery. He liked merely to draw the sleek iron surfaces of the trains rolling effortlessly into and out of the station.

Sometimes idle boys from the village would play along the tracks; they would place coins and pieces of fruit on the rail, hide behind the bushes, and when the train had passed they would race for their prizes. The flattened kreuzer went to the winner, the pieces of mashed apple were thrust inside the trousers of the smallest boy, and then they would kick at kneecaps and buttocks in a wild melee, while Egon watched from his bedroom window.

He was watching the day the boys bound a stray cat to the rail with chicken wire. Egon waited, and after a quarter of an hour he heard the locomotive's whistle, which meant a train had reached the closest switchlock and would pull into the station in five minutes. Without his shoes he ran downstairs and onto the gravel road beside the tracks. He didn't feel the sharp-edged stones cutting into his feet, he didn't bother to curse at the shaved heads bobbing behind the hedge. He hurried directly to the cat, knelt and tried to tear the wire loose. As he struggled, the cat sank its fangs into his hand, puncturing the flap of skin between his thumb and forefinger. He knocked the animal's head against a wooden tie as the nose of the locomotive slowly rounded the curve.

The wire had been wound tightly around the hind legs and the neck, and the old tom panted like a bird with a broken wing as it struggled to draw air into its lungs. Such an ugly cat, a quick, bloody finale would be a blessing, Egon thought, slapping the creature again to subdue it. Half a second and it's over, cleaved in two, and there's an end to the winter nights spent curled on top of a pile of broken bricks, an end to the scavenging, to the cruel antics of village boys. The cat's eye was full of hate; Egon had never before felt the force of such unmediated, savage hatred. Why should he try to save this filthy, thankless beast, he wondered, even as he managed to slip the front wire over the cat's torn ear. He pushed the rump through the rear loop, but instead of scampering away the animal crawled forward on its belly, its hind legs dragging, which was exactly how the boys had found it that morning, crippled, crawling along the road. They had meant to kill it mercifully, they would testify to Egon later, rather than to stuff it in a potato sack and have it suffer the slower and more agonizing death-by-drowning.

The cat moved sluggishly, ears flattened against the swirls of dirt and gravel as the train passed. Egon had an impulse to throw the cat beneath the wheels because it was so mean, so craven, it had no right to live. But he abandoned the cat, leaving it to the boys still hiding behind the bush, and he pinched the puncture wound on his hand to clog the thin string of blood. He walked back to the station house, stepping daintily, hunched and scowling, the unnoticed, unappreciated hero of the day.

·

And now, even more than he needs little girls, our hero needs watercolors, black chalk, oils, canvas, pencils, paper, India ink. He needs absolute silence and natural light. By 1911 he has finished the requisite three years at the Academy of Fine Arts and had his work exhibited in the Kunstschau and been denounced as a perverted caricaturist. He has painted his mirror reflection many times over; he has received commissions from the influential Arthur Roessler and has been championed by Klimt; he has left Vienna for Krumau, Krumau for Neulengbach.

In the autumn of 1911 he begins two large paintings. One, *The Hermits,* depicts a pair of cloaked figures who clearly resemble Gustav Klimt and Egon Schiele. The Schiele figure stares out from the canvas, while the blind Klimt rests his head on his companion's shoulder. In the other painting, *The Monk,* a man wrapped in a gray habit sits on a mountainside, his legs stretched out in front of him, his pointed black slippers peeking from beneath the hem of his robe. The face bears some resemblance to Schiele's, but the cheekbones are sharper, the features more delicate. The ridge of mountains behind the monk suggests that his solitude is boundless and impenetrable, and with his arms crossed over his chest he seems to be declaring that he will never be persuaded or coerced to step down from his cliff throne.

Egon has invited his patron Heinrich Benesch and Benesch's son, Otto, who is Egon's junior by a year, to Neulengbach to view both canvases. In the poorly lit room that Egon uses as his studio, Heinrich Benesch is quick to praise the more allegorical *Hermits,* yet he and his son study the other painting for a longer length of time. Egon watches nervously as the younger Benesch chews his thumbnail and the elder combs his fingers through his beard. When Heinrich turns to congratulate him, Egon observes that both Beneschs are ill at ease. The father speaks dryly about the formal innovations, floats his hand over *The Hermits* to show his son the daring use of line and space, explains the technical necessity of applying a strong binding coat beneath a thinner coat—"lean over fat" is the expression he uses. Egon suspects that on the train ride back to Vienna, Herr Benesch will discuss with his son the essence of Egon Schiele's failure.

The night after their visit Egon stands in his flannel nightshirt on the wooded hill behind the cottage. Though it is just past midnight, the darkness seems to be dissolving into a murky slate gray. Egon sets up his easel on the sloping path leading from the kitchen to the garden and he resumes work on *The Monk.* Without making a pencil sketch first, he outlines a chaos of bulbs, he paints bluebells, nightshade, and roses across the mountain background, he trails columbine around the feet of the handsome monk. The cascade of colorful blossoms crowds the canvas like the pattern on cheap wallpaper, and the monk seems to rest in a comfortable interior, waiting for vespers, contented with his life of contemplation, a trifle worried by a passing thought perhaps, but on the whole of a mild, untroubled disposition. Egon fills the sky with haphazard bouquets, balances blossoms on the head of the monk, dabs clusters on his cloak.

Just before daybreak he carries the canvas down the road leading into the center of town, turns off onto an unmarked lane, stumbles uphill over potholes and loose rocks until he reaches an iron gate emblazoned with a rusted six-pointed star and bordered on either side by strands of barbed wire. There aren't many dead buried in this neglected cemetery, and no one will notice a new grave. So Egon tears up weeds, with a flat, spear-shaped stone he carves out a shallow, rectangular ditch and he plants *The Monk* in the fertile soil.

Until dawn he sits with his knees tucked under his chin at the foot of the grave, thinking grimly about how he began with such hope and has accomplished nothing—or perhaps this has been his ambition, to destroy whatever he creates.

He thinks of his early childhood, the first years when he wanted only to make things, to draw, to keep active, and didn't care what happened to his pictures. He remembers one day in particular when he had watched a chained dog turn its snout upward, its thin nostrils twitching, the peach-colored tongue lolling out the side of its mouth. The dog's haunches had tensed, its jaw dropped open, and for no apparent reason, the beast began to howl. Later that day Egon heard the village barber talking about a body found drifting belly-down in the river that morning. Egon understood then that the dog had sniffed death on the wind. He decided that he wanted senses just as acute, so he could smell a drowned man from far away or over-hear the secrets his mother kept to herself or the conversations be-tween the brakesman and the engineer as the locomotive approached the station.

But as the years passed, it wasn't his ears or his nose that gave him power—the more time he spent making images, the longer and bonier his fingers grew; the more incredulous he became, the wider his eyes. "Childlike," his patron Arthur Roessler has described him. But Egon came to believe that with his eyes he could see things invisible to others, with his fingers he could distinguish subtle grades of texture, and with his eyes and fingers together he could make fanciful worlds and realistic portraits with equal precision.

At times, though, he felt afraid of his hands, as if he thought that his fingers had a will of their own and that one day they would betray him, they would uncoil and spring at his eyes like crows plundering a squab's nest, shattering the tiny, vulnerable eggs. So although he always loved to flood his senses, to frolic, to wrap himself in a blanket and roll down a hill, though he lived and worked with an intensity that could only exhaust him prematurely, fear gradually poisoned his pleasure. He was afraid of his hands, his virtuoso hands. Sometimes he wanted to smash his knuckles against a granite block, mangling his fingers permanently. As often as possible, he drew. At first he drew to keep his hands busy, he drew the world that renewed him ("I have become aware! Earth breathes, smells, listens, feels in all its little parts!"); from memory he drew the stern, dauntless faces of the people who had too much control over his life (Uncle Leopold, his mother); he drew trains, painted icons, painted other painters.

Two years ago, when he was living in a single room on the Kurzbauergasse in Vienna, he had begun work on a pair of self-portraits, two lusterless reflections, taking special care to scrape the fresh undercoat with a palette knife, providing a permanent foundation for the surface paints in an effort to make the portraits immortal. Egon never tried to sell the two 1909 *Selbstbildnisse,* and occasionally he takes them out of their portfolio and forces himself to meet the reproaching eyes. With these paintings he thought he had come to accept his fear, to tolerate the enemy inside him. Encouraged by the success of the self-portraits, he had decided to try to produce an image so offensive that even he could not bear to look at it. In the two years since then, he has made his figures increasingly ugly in an attempt to infuriate not his audience but himself. And yet it is only with this new self-portrait of the artist as comely monk, the artist as pious hero, that he has finally succeeded. He would rather look at newly turned dirt than at a flowery, consoling version of himself.

Eine Schöne Leiche

A foul odor clung to the drapes, to the crocheted throw rug, to the blankets in my mother's sickroom. It was the stale, vaguely sweet smell of burnt hair—I can smell it now, even as I remember. Among the daydreams that I allowed myself was this vision: that flames were consuming my poor mother, blue and orange flickering flames, iris flames sprouting from the mattress, and I would reach out my hand and lay my palm flat upon her forehead to make sure that there was no fire, no smoke. There was only my mother and myself and the glass-domed clock that she insisted upon keeping near the bed so she could hear the endless ticking. With an effort she would raise herself on her elbow to check the time and confirm the fact that she was still alive and had survived the night. My presence didn't provide proof enough, nor did the pudding I spooned into her mouth—only the clock, and the ticking that sounded like rats scrambling around inside the walls.

I would sit in the squat, chintz-covered armchair with its lion paws and round-cushioned back, and when I wasn't sleeping or looking after Mother, I embroidered forget-me-nots on linen doilies. As I pressed the needle through the cloth I would let my mind wander. I liked to imagine that the artist and his mistress came to visit me of their own accord because they heard I had talent and they missed the company of their Viennese compatriots, the refined, *haut-monde* conversation. I liked to pretend that I had all the skills and materials necessary to impress them.

But I never pretended for long—my mother's voice would break into my thoughts, dragging me from my better world into hers: "Is it morning yet?" Outside, behind the closed drapes, the sunlight would be leaping in sparks off the snow. But my mother's sense of time had nothing to do with the sun—the hands of the clock determined her condition, and though the interior light of her bedroom hardly altered and the lamp was never extinguished, my mother despised the darkness with a passionate hatred that in her earlier years she had directed toward Jews and Gypsies. She considered the night to be the devil's magic, designed solely to destroy her, "a sphere of dream and spell," she would say bitterly, quoting Goethe. She was convinced that she never slept, that the pain never relented, that her consciousness never released her. I tried on occasion to catch her in her groggy confusion as she woke, to make her admit that she had indeed been asleep only a moment earlier, but she always insisted that she merely had been resting her eyes. So I would plump her pillows, reheat the footwarmers, tuck in the blankets, loosen the stiff collar of her nightgown, give her a spoonful of the syrupy concoction prescribed by the doctor and wash her face and arms. If the diarrhea returned—a thin black discharge, a frequent reaction to the medicine—I would give her a full sponge bath, stroking her shrunken body from her neck to her ankles as if I were combing her hair.

By the first week of April, 1912, I had gone twice into Au—once to seek out Egon Schiele in the fields and show him the Künstlerhaus catalogue, and once straight to his cottage to ask him what I had to do to become an artist. On my third visit I approached the cottage from the south, stepping as softly as I could over the frozen grass. The day was too cold for the artist to work on his landscapes, the clouds too heavy and gray. In truth I hoped to find Egon Schiele and his mistress just as I had left them, lying naked on the floor of the studio.

Standing on a wheelbarrow I raised myself to the back window, peered through the glass, curled my fingers around the sill, pressed my nose against the lower pane. In the deserted room, the easel had been covered with a sheet so I couldn't see the canvas, and my breath fogged the window, obscuring the rest of the room from view. The glass against my face reminded me of the texture of my mother's skin, and as I balanced on the slippery metal bowl I found myself resenting my mother, for she was just like that window, a barrier, a fragile, fogged surface dividing the world into opposite sides. My mother was teaching me how to die—not how to die with dignity or even with speed, but simply how to die. And the canvas was like life itself, shrouded, tempting, positioned close to the window as though to spite me, as though the artist knew I would be visiting that day and wouldn't have the courage to knock at his door.

•

Blue Curaçao, 1903: To Adolf Schiele it is an exquisite, inimitable blue, not a cat's-eye blue, not the blue of a hyacinth or of the sky at any time, neither more blue nor less than the pigment of any visible thing. Blue Curaçao is blue like blood mixed with oxygen is red. A dangerous blue, a voluptuous blue full of promises, an exacting blue that demands payment for the pleasure it provides, a blue that will be forgotten as soon as it is gone, a blue that disappears from memory as soon as it disappears from the bottle, a deceitful blue that tastes like a spoiled tangerine. But the color disguises the taste, so Adolf need only look at what is left in his glass to be tempted again, until, after the final swallow, when only a dusky film remains in the glass and in the bottle, the rancid taste returns to him. And later, his urine splashing against the side of a station seems to him a demonic parody of blue.

Blue Curaçao. The one exotic jewel in the filthy train-station café, the one ornament that doesn't suffer from Biedermeier nostalgia, shoddy craftsmanship, or slow decay.

Every evening in the train-station café at Tulln, a man sleeps slouched in a corner booth, his snores as constant and reliable as the ticking of Adolf's pocket watch. A younger man at a back table writes furiously for a moment, then blows his cigarette smoke against the paper to dry the ink. A white, long-necked porcelain cat with green glass buttons for eyes sits next to the cash register. A ceramic jar covered with dust has a shelf above the sink to itself. And on another shelf, between the anisette and grappa—the bottle of Blue Curaçao, Adolf Schiele's sole pleasure after a long day spent monitoring rail signals and loading and unloading mailbags.

While his wife serves goulash soup to the children, Adolf drinks Blue Curaçao—straight, undiluted—in the smoky café, sipping it at a table by himself. Speech requires effort, and the blue syrup turns him into a creature as passive as the white porcelain cat, so rather than talk to the barmaid who brings him the bottle, rather than complain with her about these corrupt times, Adolf prefers to listen to the man snoring and to stare at the receding blue. Sometimes he stirs the blue with the handle of a knife to make the pliant liquid swill against the glass; sometimes he fills the glass to the rim and touches his tongue to the surface, keeping his eyes open so the blue mutes the taste, numbs his tongue, congests him until he can't even smell the poison.

Marie has never heard of Blue Curaçao. She knows only that her husband comes upstairs after the midnight train with a strange, citrus smell on his breath and his voice congealed, as if his throat were coated with buttermilk. Without a word he will undress and step through the darkness toward the bed and lower his full weight upon his wife as he says her name softly, lovingly, to wake her.

Afterwards she will set Adolf's lamp beside the basin and wash the cloudy semen from the inside of her thighs. The sweet stink of Adolf's breath—she decided long ago—has something to do with his sickness, something to do with their poverty as well, and she has made up a tale to explain how Adolf's sicknesss feeds on his salary, how money is both the cause of madness and the cure. In the story that she tells herself, her husband sits alone in the station café and orders a bowl of stewed coins. He chews the kronen noisily, as a horse chews raw carrots, lips rolled back, teeth clicking. Every night the stationmaster of Tulln eats up his daily earnings and still gnashing, he drags his money-stuffed carcass up the stairs. Thus the glaze coating his tongue. Thus the strange wheezing and rumbling through the night as he sleeps.

Marie has managed to maintain peace in the household, though she fears the day when her son's anger will equal the passion of her husband's madness. Egon grows stronger, Adolf's sanity deteriorates, and someday the two will destroy each other, unless Marie can keep them apart and ensure that they have only a scant acquaintance. If they treat each other with the formality expected of strangers, then they won't be inclined to raise their fists in rage.

On this midwinter holiday, after Adolf has descended to the ground floor to meet an afternoon train, Marie wakes Egon and Gerti in the morning darkness, treats them to a special breakfast of hot milk and *Krapfen* filled with custard, gives Egon his box of colored pencils and tells him to make a picture of his little sister, a portrait of sweet Gerti, with a purple background to match the ribbon that Marie will put in her hair today. The finished picture will be framed and hung in the hall, she promises her son, knowing that the commission will keep him occupied, knowing as well that Adolf would never permit her to hang up one of Egon's pictures, nor would she want to be guilty of encouraging the boy's misguided ambition. But for now Marie has only one purpose—to keep her husband and her son apart.

For most of the day Egon and Gerti remain in the attic, coming down only once to use the toilet—Marie watches them from the first-floor window as the children dash from the back door to the latrine and enter together. When Egon is home on holiday, he and his younger sister are inseparable, and if their attachment to each other weren't so convenient for Marie, she would insist that they find other playmates. For now she encourages their friendship. On their way back to their studio, Marie gives them each an apple and tells Egon that she hopes Gerti in the portrait will be as pretty as Gerti herself.

By late afternoon Marie has lost herself in the challenge of a torn sock and she doesn't look up when Adolf enters the kitchen and stands beside the stove, warming his hands, muttering about the cold and his thankless job. Marie pays no attention to the direction of his plodding footsteps as he proceeds down the hall and climbs the attic stairs to fetch the toolbox. Marie is thinking about the next stitch when her husband finds his two children cowering beneath the rafters, and she has no idea that above her Adolf is ripping a blanket away from his nine-year-old daughter, revealing her naked, hairless body splotched with red. Marie doesn't hear the boards creaking as Adolf pulls his son roughly to his feet, scattering the colored pencils and the pile of failed sketches. She doesn't hear the single, desperate gasp of a sob that rises from Gerti's stomach and lodges in her throat.

Adolf knows that his children deserve to be punished, but his lips set in a skewed, enigmatic line, and he has a curiously pleased look, as though he wants to laugh but doesn't know why. He stares at his daughter while she fastens the buttons underneath the bib of her dress. Then he leads Egon down two flights of stairs to the ground floor, through the station to the deserted café. He takes a seat at his usual corner table, though it is not yet dark outside and he still has to usher three more trains through Tulln. No matter. He has a more important responsibility right now—to his son and to Blue Curaçao.

Egon drinks eagerly, not because he fears his father and not with a boy's swelling pride at being introduced to an adult privilege. He drinks the blue syrup his father pours into the glass because the color seduces him, and soon he forgets that moment of terror in the attic when he thought his father was going to beat him, forgets as well his frustrated efforts to re-create the image of his sister with those sticks of colored lead.

If only he knew how to mix watercolors to produce this deceptive blue that tastes of oranges . . . with the blue inside him, maybe he will intuit the exact proportions of oils and will know which under-coat to use. He has so much to learn about technique—the teachers at the school in Klosterneuburg daunt him with their huge volumes on the history of art, they tell him that he must learn about every notable past artist if he is going to benefit from their experiments and avoid repeating their mistakes.

His father laughs when Egon spits into a clear glass ashtray and swirls the foamy saliva with his fingertip. It seems to Egon that days have passed by the time his mother comes down to the station café to retrieve her son for supper. Anger is the honeybee, Egon thinks dreamily as he watches his mother stride toward the table. And his mother's face is the tired blossom. He sees the fury in her eyes as she looks from Adolf to Adolf's glass to Egon's glass and back to Adolf. But her hands on his neck feel sticky and warm with kindness, and he permits her to lift him by his collar from his chair and guide him across the room, while Adolf trails lazily behind. Egon has shared the blue silence with his father and for the first time in many years he feels a comforting allegiance to him, a lingering amusement, as though an indecent joke had been shared. What was the joke? Some-thing to do with Gerti, or with the stout barmaid—Egon had smelled the perfume wafting from the cleft of the barmaid's bosom when she set the bottle and glasses on their table. But there had been no conversation with his father, no words uttered; their shared, intuited understanding precluded words.

Egon wants to disappear into a cloud of sleep or at least to lie on a bed in a darkened room and to think about the luxurious softness of sleep. His father also wants to sleep, but first he wants his wife.

By now, though, she is busy ladling soup into wooden bowls and wondering about what might have happened if she hadn't broken up the little party in the station café. Adolf tries to pinch her rump and catches only folds of her skirt between his fingers, tries to slip his arms around her waist, but she twists away and sets two bowls on the table. She thinks about Adolf's stewed coins and the money they will save if he eats at home tonight.

Melanie and Gerti enter the kitchen hand in hand. Little Gerti climbs into a chair and begins to pick at a slice of bread, peeling off the crust, squeezing the ball of dough inside her fist. She does not dare look up at her father, whose lips tighten in an odd smile at the sight of his younger daughter, while his fingers curl like snails retreating into their shells. No one, not even Adolf, could anticipate what Adolf means to do until he has already seized Egon by his collar and thrown the boy against the wall. A strange, suffocating silence follows the sound of Egon's head hitting the plaster. He sinks to the floor, and the sob that had been caught in Gerti's throat for the last hour explodes before she can clap her hand over her mouth.

"Leave him alone," Marie Schiele says in a whisper, almost gently. But despite the softness of her voice, it is clear that she is prepared to throw the pot of simmering soup at Adolf or impale his leg with a fork. So while Egon crouches on his heels against the wall, panting like a puppy, Adolf kicks the wainscot beside Egon's head and then careens from the room, pushing Melanie roughly aside as he leaves.

Marie and her children neither move nor speak. They hear Adolf stomping about in the attic, and they all stare at the ceiling as if they expected it to warp and crack from his weight. Minutes later they are staring at him again, as if he were the ceiling beams, as if they were waiting for him to collapse. Gerti is still sitting at the table, Egon huddles in the corner, Melanie in her striped wool skirt and sweater sinks into the striped wallpaper, and Marie stands by the stove. Adolf opens the grate and stuffs folded squares of paper into the coals—the drawings that Egon made of Gerti, Marie assumes. Adolf is burning Egon's work again to punish his son. Not until the last piece of stiff paper falls from Adolf's hands does Marie realize that Adolf hasn't been destroying the boy's worthless sketches but something else, something that belongs to all of them. He has been burning the family's railroad stocks. In his calculating rage, Adolf has unlocked the metal box that he keeps in the attic, collected the titles to the stocks, the Schiele family's sole assets, and he has burned the documents, all of them, including the one that he dropped on the floor. He burns everything before Marie understands what he is doing and tries to stop him.

And though she can rake through the hot coals with her fingers, though she can order her husband out of the kitchen and close her legs to him forever, she will never be able to salvage the part of her children's future that Adolf has destroyed.

.

Some of you might gravitate to the smoking section in the rear of the tram, others to the front section, the *coupé*, where a forest of exotic plumes extends from the ladies' hats. Some of you will wander the streets to admire the jewelers' window displays, others will head for the Kärntnerstrasse to see, of all things, the coffins—extravagant containers unlike any others, decorated with floral carvings and cherub friezes, inlaid with ivory and tortoiseshell. In Vienna they decorate every blank plane or ridge available, and you won't find a more elegant domicile than those secured with golden clasps along the Kärntnerstrasse. Here, the windows seem crowded not with the bleak furniture of death but with huge pieces of marzipan and silky chocolate tortes.

You might choose to spend the rest of the afternoon shopping in stores along the Graben, or you might visit the Imperial Museums to look at, among other works, Dürer's gruesome *Die Marter der 10,000 Christen*. And then there's an à-la-carte hotel meal, the theater, and an unforgettable café dessert (we recommend this Hungarian delight— six layers of mocha cream sandwiched between six layers of cake, sealed beneath a crust of caramel!). But all of you will sooner or later return to your beds and collapse in delicious exhaustion, and you will hardly feel your wife's lips brush against your forehead when she kisses you goodnight.

Wien, glorious *Wien.* You will wake refreshed at dawn, dress quickly and start over again: the coffee and sweet rolls, the sights, schnitzel and beer, opera, caviar, and the Ringstrasse, where day after day the stones of the monuments glint palely in the sunlight, as though the city were already what it longs to be: *eine schöne Leiche,* a beautiful corpse.

•

Egon's friend and patron Heinrich Benesch learns from Egon's mistress that he is in jail, awaiting trial. Benesch, eager to offer whatever help he can to the promising young artist, visits Egon in prison on three separate occasions.

On the first visit to the Neulengbach Rathaus he is surprised to find the basement cell respectably clean, pungent with the odor of ammonia and quite roomy, though Egon insists that the cell is nothing but a sacristy of filth, spitting the word "filth" onto Benesch's boot. The authorities mean to humiliate Egon by forcing him to inhale the stench of his shit. They have given him walls to use as canvases, they have given him a flea-infested bed and a piss pot, and now he is trapped inside his own monstrous, putrid reflection, cowering like a child in a dead mother's arms. Filth. That's what Egon Schiele can make, that's what he is.

Benesch tries to comfort him, assuring Egon that his incarceration will last no longer than the week; certainly a grave injustice has been done but it will be quickly remedied. Benesch knows a young lawyer. No one wants to help Egon Schiele more than Central Inspector Heinrich Benesch does. Benesch—inspector for the Austrian Transport Service and amateur art collector—listens patiently while the young artist curses the authorities, the populace, the guards, curses the dull and ignorant villagers, curses the empire that will not protect its geniuses, curses the God who lets the fields go fallow, the vineyards grow wild. But even as he rages his voice softens, his fists relax because he has remembered his love: not simply his many particular loves—for Vallie, his sister, his fellow artists. He has remembered his love of the natural world, of a balmy sea wind, of slashes and coils of light on the surface of the water, of a sloping pasture on the edge of Krumau at dusk, of the time he walked barefoot in moonlight and felt the Bohemian soil gently bulge and flatten, like the chest of a sleeper. He thinks dreamily of a young boy he once met up in the hills.

One moment Egon's eyes are as definitive, as forbidding as the double barrel of a rifle, the next they are vague, unfocused, and if Heinrich Benesch were a different sort, he would think that the young artist was deranged. But Benesch loves Egon like a son and knows that his strange behavior is just a performance—Egon has as much common sense as anyone his age, and with his powerful will, his dexterous imagination, madness is something that he flaunts and discards, like a paper mask worn during carnival.

A sensitive and efficient employee who has spent his adult life, like Adolf Schiele, in railway stations monitoring the trains, Heinrich Benesch looks toward the most eccentric men for companionship. He met the young artist at an acquaintance's house in Klosterneuburg and since he doesn't have much money, he collects the paintings that Egon otherwise would have thrown out, the ones that don't go to the clutch of loyal buyers who will take anything that shows a naked woman in a compromising position. So Benesch has surrounded himself with the cast-off images made by this outcast artist, he has insulated the walls of his bedroom with the paintings and is starting to be known in Vienna for his eclectic taste and limited funds.

He has come to help. He would like to convince young Schiele to feel ennobled, for it takes great talent to be able to stir the public from their torpor, and whether you earn their applause or their contempt is of little concern as long as you hold their attention. Benesch cannot tell Schiele what charge has been laid against him because he does not know himself, not yet, though he assumes it has something to do with Egon's art. Men with authority and little patience are inclined to label individuals they don't understand as criminal and conveniently dispose of the problem by putting it under lock and key. The Central Inspector doesn't have to inspire in his young friend the pride of notoriety. To Egon, the division in society is perfectly clear: a few will support his art and many will reject it, and if anyone tries to interfere with his work, he will respond just as he did years ago when his father seized his first self-portraits. Heinrich Benesch knows that Egon will act impetuously, violently, with scorn. And with dangerous pride. Egon has spoken proudly about the time he pricked his father's hand with a penknife, and clearly he feels proud when he shouts insults at mankind from the basement of a town hall.

But right now the artist is submerged in his own thoughts: he remembers geese paddling in a uniform V across the sky, sunlight glossing rooftops and bridges and crumbling stone towers in the town of Krumau, a boy's callused hand exploring the contours of his back. Egon replaces the thin natural light with his past; his senses reverse themselves, and he experiences his memories as completely as he has experienced the confining space of prison.

Benesch is fascinated by, even envious of, Schiele's ability to withdraw into his private world, but he knows that an artist who exists inside his illusions, like a face inside a mirror, has no reason to share his talent. Why should anyone bother to dab a wet brush against a canvas when his daydreams are more absorbing than any stretched cloth could be? Benesch tugs Egon's sleeve to jostle the artist from his trance and in an attempt to save them both embarrassment, he begins a sentence halfway through, as if the dialogue had continued between them without pause:

". . . raspberry juice with soda water, if you'd like," he offers, and waits for Egon's reply.

•

In 1893 an outbreak of scarlet fever in Tulln took the life of ten-year-old Elvira Schiele. One morning she vomited on the noodle board, and Egon heard her sobbing weakly as Adolf carried her down the hall to bed. By the next day her face and chest were covered with pinpricks of red, and the doctor came to visit and stayed nearly an hour. It seemed to Egon that he was handed a bowl of beef stew seven times a day, whenever he asked for milk they gave him water, cider, even beer, and if he cried because he desperately wanted a cup of fresh milk, his father would threaten him with the belt and his mother would clasp his little heart-shaped face between her palms, gravely explaining that he could have no milk today, nor tomorrow, he would have no milk at all this week because the cows of Tulln were sick.

Egon believed that Elvira must have had something to do with the fact that there was no milk; if only she would go away, he would surely be allowed to drink a cup of milk. He was forgotten by his parents for hours at a time, and no one chastised him when he pulled a piece of stringy, overcooked beef apart with his fingers or pressed his thumb through a boiled potato. Like a tiny, senile old man, Egon played with his food and made up songs, singing them aloud, but no one listened, no one heard him rambling on about the cow that ate his sister Elvira and the magical cup of milk that was never empty; because the bottomless cup belonged entirely to Egon, he was as esteemed as the Emperor himself: Adolf Schiele carried his son on his shoulders and Marie Schiele baked strudel in celebration —it was a perpetual holiday in the Tulln station house, in Egon's song.

At night, while his parents and aunt and uncle drank black coffee in the kitchen, Egon crept down the hall to Elvira's room. He wanted to sing her the song he had made up, then she'd be sorry she had poisoned the cows. The bedroom door was ajar, and years later Egon would still remember vividly how the moon coated the floorboards with frothy peaks of cream, and how his shoes stuck to the wood as he walked past his own empty bed to the bed where his sister lay, the blanket twisted around her legs, her torso bare, her lush, dark hair spilling across the pillow. Egon will never forget how his sister's face and neck were covered with mealy paste—her own skin, he realized when he touched her, fingering her slack jaw and her parched, protruding tongue. Every breath she took shuddered slowly down her throat while her lungs heaved greedily. When she exhaled, a whistle escaped from deep inside her body. The boy stroked his sister's hair, he ran his finger around the gray, rubbery lips, then he crawled onto the bed and stretched out beside her, his arm slung across her chest so he could feel the air bubbling in her lungs.

He pretended to be asleep when his parents found him, hung limply in his father's arms as Adolf carried him toward the stairs. He and Melanie were supposed to spend the nights during Elvira's sickness on mattresses in the attic, but after pausing at the bottom of the dark staircase, his father continued down the hall to the master bedroom and set his son in the middle of the quilt.

After his parents had returned to the sickroom, Egon opened his eyes and stared at the crescent moon tangled in the net of branches. In a whisper he sang the song of Elvira and the cow. He had damned his sister—he was responsible for her condition, he was the one who had wanted her to suffer. Just as the song described, his father had lifted him high, and now Egon was a potentate enthroned on his parents' bed. The diseased cow would take Elvira away; the curse couldn't be undone. Guilt filled Egon like imaginary milk had filled the magical cup, though not the simple guilt of stealth and petty crime. He realized that he had exceptional power and with the right words he could cause his sister harm. When he heard the strangled sobs coming from her room he wanted to cry with her, but the moonlight had frozen his tears, and without tears he could feel no sadness. He finally fell asleep, his eyes still half-open. In his dreams he relived moments of their life together and mistook the sound of dried poplar leaves and gravel blowing across the train platform below the window for her laughter.

The next morning his mother dragged him off the urine-soaked quilt and sent him to the kitchen to be bathed by a neighbor, a woman with a blemish above her right eyebrow, a huge, brown protuberance pierced by two wiry hairs. Egon stood naked, shivering in the wooden tub while the woman squeezed the sponge, dribbling lukewarm water along his spine. He was twisting his head around, trying to see the woman's magnificent mole, when he heard his mother's scream—a high sharp note that collapsed into a hiccough and evaporated into a silence that should have lasted forever but was broken by a splash as the sponge dropped into the soapy water around his ankles.

The following year Marie Schiele gave birth to another daughter —Gerti—and for months little Egon could be heard muttering strange tunes around the station house of Tulln. He sang with a grave sense of purpose, he sang to ward off evil and to placate the vengeful dead.

A Black City

MY mother: a worn-out *Judenfresser* and invalid. Her cataract spectacles were always propped uselessly beside the clock, and if I leaned forward in my chair I could see a reflecting plane in the lens, a tiny mirror framing my distorted face and the bookcase behind me, the orange flame of the lamp wavering on the edge of the glass like one of my delirious thoughts.

As her condition worsened, I began to watch with the same bewilderment that I have felt standing at the edge of the ocean. She surged and relaxed, surged and relaxed, enacting the haunting rhythms of nature, and it seemed to me that I was on the point of recovering some essential but hidden memory that always resisted me. A piece of forgotten knowledge lurked just beyond my awareness, and no matter how intensely I concentrated, I could not discover what I so dearly wanted to remember.

In a daguerreotype I have of her as a girl she is beautiful, with her tight curls framing her face like a bronze helmet, her lips forming a thin, unusually long strip, her eyes, copper-colored here, as blue in life as melting iron. Indeed, my mother was made not of bone, flesh, and fluid but of fire and metal, so her cancer seemed unnatural to those who knew her, and she fought against the intrusion with astonishing fury. She had always believed strictly in justice: moral justice, social justice, the justice of race and genetic destiny. She was humiliated by her decline—she had assumed that she would follow a logical course through life toward a particular, predetermined end and would die a correct death. During the day she behaved like a rich, petulant woman at the dressmaker's, as if her pain were a poor fit, the wrong size, as if a mistake had been made in the measurements. At night, when the morphine wore off, she would claw at her body that had become a stranger to her, a traitor in complicity with the darkness.

While she could find no explanation for her illness, I could find none for her persistence. Why did the frail, bludgeoned form cling to life, why did the hair follicles continue to sprout, the toenails continue to grow so fast that I had to clip them once a week? Why did she continue to suffer when she knew there was no hope of recovery or remission? And why was I expected to give up my youth to her?

I might as well have wondered why the ocean slaps and claws at the land. To keep myself from wondering, I let myself contemplate that more promising mystery—the couple from Vienna and their perverse games of love. And only two days after my third visit to the cottage in Au, while my mother struggled to fight off a sleep that was nearly death, I decided that the bedroom could not contain the scenes that I wanted to imagine. So I unlatched the window and threw open the shutters—an act, I realized too late, that was as vicious as pouring poison into my mother's ear. The sound of her agony as the cold intruded, the moan, its echo—even now, though so many years have passed, I hear it and am ashamed. Needlessly ashamed, I know, for my mother would never have blamed me. Instead she blamed the night itself, just as a drowning man will blame the water, and she lifted her hands from beneath the blankets and tried to push the cold away. Not until I closed the shutters did she relax—from the stillness of her body I thought she had sunk at once into sleep, exhausted by her panic. But when I looked more closely I saw that her eyes had remained open, even alert, the pupils constricted. But something in her eyes had changed. It was as though her attention had turned halfway around, as though another world inside of her skull, behind her eyes, had become more interesting than the world in front of her. When I finally spoke, apologized for opening the window, she replied in her usual fatigued whisper, "No matter." And then she smiled.

The smile was the sign I'd been waiting for: my mother had passed into the final stage of her illness, and as long as the room remained insulated, unchanging, she needed no one. Far more than I felt pity, I felt a contemptible elation at my new freedom—I could come and go as I pleased. This was the most important thing.

•

Which day?: Egon is to be moved. Without explanation, the warden enters his cage, ties a rope around his wrists and leads the prisoner into the corridor, past empty cells and a room equipped with a gas range, a bed, and a cracked enamel sink, which at a glance reminds Egon of a pregnant woman's belly.

He demands to know where he is being taken, but the warden refuses to answer, using silence to punish his charge, using a friendly grin to mock him. Is there any sort of courtesy that has never been turned to a wicked purpose? Egon wonders. Even the most virtuous girl is dangerous, for virtue turns those who are less pure into worshipers, modesty demands false admiration.

To be aware of the double nature of things and to use this knowledge to his advantage: this is Egon's style, and his obsession with cruelty has provoked condemnation from his friends. But those who know him best understand that Egon is vulnerable, they see the fear in his eyes wavering like undulations of heat above a smokestack. At any moment the world might turn against him, as it has in this year of 1912, trapping him within whitewashed brick walls in Neulengbach. So even though he protests, injustice does not surprise him. Hasn't he expected this—to be dragged, a brute on a leash, down corridors, up dark stairways, across courtyards to the gallows?

His eyes feed greedily on the tilt of the guard's head, on the shaved neck, on the plaster bust of Franz Josef set upon a card table in the foyer, on the old man peddling by on a bicycle. He wants to saturate his mind with a life's worth of images, for he doesn't have much time left. But it seems he is not being taken to be executed, not directly, at least. In front of the Rathaus they are joined by another guard, a stranger to Egon, and the two uniformed men escort their charge along the quiet street.

When they pass a café Egon inhales the smell of fresh-baked bread and coffee, an intoxicating smell, the scent of ordinary, uninterrupted life: a wife opens an oven door, children play beside a stream, molding mud pancakes to fry on a barrel lid, a pig snuffles from side

to side in a wooden pen, bells tied beneath a goat's beard jangle, and
a man's voice reaches to every corner of the house and yard. It is a
foulmouthed voice and can do nothing but compare human industry
to excrement, priests to whoremongers.

"Leave me alone!" the man screams intermittently, needlessly,
because he is already alone, at least until the wife carries a peeled
onion and bread into the room, sets the tray on the bedside table and
tears pieces from the warm loaf, dropping them into his mouth as if
he were a porcelain clown at a fair. Ordinary life. Egon stares grimly
at the cottages, at the fields, at the tar paper hills in the distance, at
the Liechtenstein Castle. So much open space in this suburban district, but not enough room for a slender, iconoclastic artist and his
female companion.

They cross the shallow ditch to the station, and the Neulengbach
guard tugs on the rope tied to Egon's wrists, pulling him up the
wooden steps to the platform, where he drops the rope leash so he
can roll himself a cigarette. Egon senses that he is to be passed like a
slave at an auction from one owner to another. But he doesn't mind,
for here, in a railway station, he is at home. While the two guards
discuss the merits of their respective tobaccos, Egon squats unnoticed and presses his cheek against the cord of steel. He can feel a
faint vibration in the rail, just as he can feel Vallie's pleasure when
he is inside her—first a barely perceptible trembling, then the vaginal walls contract, and she will moan, her voice as reassuring to
Egon as the sonorous whistle of a train. But he always knows long
before the sound, he knows from the vibrations, the rippling, that
an overwhelming force is bearing down. He would like to keep his
face against the rail until he can see the diagonal slits in the bolts on
the locomotive's nose, he would like to unsettle the dull people on
the platform, to cement an image in their minds, something they
would never forget: a mangled face, the skull twisted and splintered,
an eyeball squirting from beneath the wheel and landing on the
guard's black boot, the brains spilling across the tracks. But the
women, of course, would swoon and cover their eyes, and as soon
as the train had pulled forward, the stationmaster would throw a
tarp over the bloody mess.

Perhaps effect is what we live for, he thinks as the Neulengbach
guard jerks on the cord attached to Egon's wrists. Perhaps we live
in order to prepare ourselves for a memorable death: we surround

ourselves with friends who will mourn us, with works that will preserve our names, with photographs to paste on our tombstone. We would prefer others to suffer our death before we have to suffer theirs.

But Egon is distracted from these thoughts by the sight of the iron mallet of the engine easing into the station. Such violence, a strength so much greater than the diminutive brakeman inside—like Egon's strength, leashed to a guard. His skill and vision give him immense power, but now he must answer to ignorant guards, rise when they tell him to rise, eat when they feed him.

The Neulengbach guard prods him forward, steering him into an empty first-class compartment, but it is the other guard who follows Egon, pulling the door shut behind him. As Egon huddles in a corner close to the aisle door, he sees that his rope has been dropped and is dragging like a broken tail—his new escort allows him this small liberty. Egon watches as the man struggles unsuccessfully to lower the window and then taps his knuckles against the pane, shrugging to the other, who stands on the platform, looking foolishly forlorn.

Let them hang you in my stead, Egon thinks, glaring out the window at the brass-buttoned idiot who will spend the rest of his days pacing up and down in front of empty cells, returning home at night to cook his own supper, for surely no woman would tolerate the impotent bastard, no woman would share his bed. Egon gloats as he considers the guard's empty cottage in Neulengbach, his immense solitude, his insignificance.

The man is not worthy of so much attention, Egon reminds himself. He sinks back into his seat, comforted when the train with a series of jerks begins to move forward. He can nearly pretend that he is on vacation or on his way back to Vienna. His good humor must be infectious, for the guard has pulled a pack of cigarettes from the pocket of his shirt and is kindly offering one to Egon, who, with his wrists bound, must use both hands to remove the stick. It slips from his fingers, and he watches the white slug roll across the slats and lodge beneath the upturned toe of the guard's boot. Egon should have been wary—he is too trusting, too innocent, as though he has learned nothing from the deceitful village.

He raises his eyes, expecting to see the characteristic, malicious smirk he has come to know so well, not expecting to see the blade of a penknife pointing at his chest. He cringes against the leather cushion, presses his shoulder to the inner window. He understands: all of a sudden his life makes sense, the puzzle is complete. The same knife he once used to defend himself against his father has been turned upon him. The execution is so correctly designed, so novelistic, Egon thinks with sickening fear as the guard takes hold of his rope bracelet.

The man has already started sawing the cord between his wrists before Egon realizes that this knife is not meant for his flesh. He stares with relieved fascination as the severed threads bristle and the rope grows thinner and finally snaps. He wants to reach for the cigarette now, but the guard has drawn two more from the cluster, and he places one between Egon's parted lips, places the other in the corner of his own mouth, and lights a match. Egon puffs obediently, his hands folded upon his lap. As the guard holds the match to his own cigarette, the train lurches along a bridge over a ravine, the hand wavers, and the flame catches a few wisps curling out from his beard. Gray hairs sizzle, hissing softly. But the fool doesn't notice the singed beard—he has managed to light his cigarette and after emitting a few pungent belches, he smiles contentedly.

Egon forgets to inhale the smoke and lets the ash crumble onto his hands. He doesn't know whether to trust this fossil of a guard or to expect an abrupt end to his short holiday, so he studies the man's face above his beard, where the skin is as gleaming and red as the leather seat, the narrow eyes full of wickedness and laughter. A face quite used to laughter, Egon decides. The man has absentmindedly set the knife on the seat, and if Egon were swift enough he could sweep the blade into his hand and slice the guard's thick jugular. Instead he asks, "Where are you taking me?"

The guard yawns, and a ring of smoke escapes, hovering in the air in the shape of his gaping mouth. "St. Pölten, of course," he replies.

"Why?"

"Why? You want to know why you're going to St. Pölten? There's a funny question," he declares in a voice so infectiously weary that Egon doesn't bother to explain that he has done nothing wrong and has nothing to fear.

·

During the months Egon and Vallie lived in Neulengbach, a new primary school was being built up the road from Au, the bellies of young wives were swelling, the population of the village was multiplying at a remarkable rate. Reproduction had become Neulengbach's primary industry, as though the people thought more children meant profit, but of course it worked the other way—as the cottages filled with cribs, clogs, muddy socks, scarves, wooden soldiers, wooden swords, butterfly collections, rusted keys that fit no lock, and bloodied knees and noses, the parents became poorer and the conversations in the café on the Hauptplatz became angrier. Though the old men publicly blamed the Semitic moneylenders in Vienna for Neulengbach's poverty, privately they blamed the parents for crowding the little village with their sniveling, filthy offspring. Children—like a scourge of rats—were more than just a nuisance. They used up savings and depleted larders, and the only person in the village growing richer was the doctor. The parents themselves blamed their children, disguising their resentment with strict discipline. They hired a schoolmaster who had a holster made so he could hang his paddle board from his belt. They hired a schoolmistress whose long fingernails left scratches on her students' cheeks.

Inevitably, cottage forty-five in Au became a refuge for these fragile vessels, who could take in only so much brutal morality before it began to leak from the cracks. Egon kept the studio well heated, and Vallie always had a box of chocolates to share. The local children had never met two people as spirited and generous as this couple from Vienna.

When they first moved to Neulengbach in the autumn of 1911, after having been chased from Krumau, Egon had been content to draw the landscapes, his mistress, his own mirror reflection, his dreams. But the distant sounds of children hooting and whistling on Saturday afternoons began to distract him, so he took to wandering the sloping paths in the woods below the deserted Liechtenstein Castle. He collected sturdy pronged branches to give to the boys to use for slingshots, he filled his pockets with apples to give to the girls. At first the children were timid and would run from him when he approached them, but gradually he won their trust. The boys tried to impress him with their trophies—dead blue jays and woodpeckers and sometimes even ravens. Egon devised competitions to occupy them: the first boy to kill a squirrel would be emperor for a day, the first boy to collect a dozen birds would win a glass marble. And while they were off hunting, Egon would lead the little girls to his cottage, where they enjoyed the purest freedom they had ever known. They somersaulted across the floor, they jumped from the curled arm of the old settee onto a stack of pillows, they walked in their bare feet, like impertinent cats, across the kitchen table. They wrestled, pinched, bit, pulled hair, and no one scolded them, no one made them stand in a lightless closet or told them that if they cried they would have no supper. It was as fine as being a member of a traveling circus, for the artist encouraged them to romp and shriek, and his mistress even applauded when they walked on their hands.

And then, after they had exhausted themselves and were thoughtfully selecting chocolates from a box, Egon would choose his model. This was the greatest compliment of all for a girl—to be told that she was worth the cost of his paints and paper, worth the time he would spend with her. The other girls would gather silently around the kitchen stove, listening to Vallie tell them stories about ogres and witches, while Egon instructed his young model in the difficult task of remaining absolutely still. The girls liked to hear most about the forests where magical toadstools grew, trees argued with one another, rose thorns were poisonous, and wolves danced on their hind feet. Vallie chewed chocolate truffles as she described how he-wolves gave off a perfume that smelled of hickory smoke and jasmine, how their eyes shone like colorful fish in the pool of darkness around a campfire. While they listened to Vallie, the girls would forget about their companion until they heard Egon humming loudly, and then they would scamper from the kitchen into the studio, where the artist would be snapping his box of pencils shut and his model would be sitting in the middle of the floor, her knees drawn up beneath the pleats of her skirt, her cheeks flushed, her eyes glassy.

The girls wouldn't ask their friend what she had done for the artist, or what he had said to her while he worked; in order for the mystery to remain sacred and compelling it had to be a secret, just as Vallie's tales had to remain unfinished. After a girl modeled for the artist she was never the same, the change ineffable but permanent, the difference important enough to divide the girls of Neulengbach into hierarchical classes: there were those who had sat for the artist and those who hadn't. And there were those who had never even visited the cottage.

Egon understood enough about children to recognize the strength and legitimacy of their sexual desires, but he wasn't prepared for the force of their jealousy. The ones ignored by the artist discovered that they had a new power, a power that grew faster than their mother's bellies. For every invitation extended by the artist that resulted in a pornographic drawing on his wall, for every rumor whispered in the schoolyard, the neglected girls acquired damning facts to pass on to their parents. As the evidence accumulated, the anger of these provincial people intensified—they had in their midst a child molester and his mistress. And though the most intractable girls continued to visit the forbidden cottage in Au, the parents ignored this breach because the public prosecutor insisted that they must wait to strike if they were going to destroy the artist utterly. They waited patiently, with the same prudent, self-righteous confidence that they felt waiting for their children to become adults. Egon made sketches, Vallie told stories, little boys stoned birds, and the parents encouraged the few dutiful girls to tell them everything they'd heard about the artist.

At the end of winter, the parents of Neulengbach were rewarded for their patience. The butcher's youngest daughter, one of the chosen girls who had been inside the cottage and had modeled for the artist, came forward to confess. But not until the following month, when the postmaster told the police that his fifteen-year-old daughter had been seduced by the artist and kept in his cottage for three days and three nights, did the town magistrate decide that the evidence was sufficient. He sent two men, a constable and a municipal officer, to the home of Egon Schiele with the purpose of discovering the exact nature of his work, bringing him in for questioning and confiscating any pictures that appeared suspicious.

•

When Egon was six years old, his father took him to the drill grounds in Vienna to watch the soldiers charging with their raised bayonets and to tour the Arsenal, where fifty-six marble heroes stood grandly on their pedestals. Bored by all the pomp and machinery of war, Egon picked at the dried snot in his nose, but as soon as he saw the Queen of Bohemia's armor he brightened and begged his father for an identical sword and helmet. His father reminded him to be thankful for what he had.

After they left the Arsenal, they crossed the Ring and headed up a busy avenue radiating out from the city's center. Since Egon's father was preoccupied with his own thoughts, he didn't notice that his son had separated a hardened ball of manure from a dung pile and was kicking it ahead of him, dirtying the pointed toe of his dress sandals and white socks. His father directed him to wait outside a shop while he purchased a present for his wife. When Egon was alone he flattened the manure ball with his heel and to his surprise a small, satiny beetle emerged from the filth. He bent down to examine the insect as it crawled across a wide cobblestone—a beetle as elegant as an ebony scarab, with emerald chips for eyes. How was it possible, he wondered, for such a handsome thing to live in such mire?

He laid his forefinger across the beetle's path, and it crawled sluggishly over the log of flesh, not much caring about a destination, just numbly plodding forward like an old refugee woman conditioned to disaster. He put his finger in front of it again and watched it crawl up and over the obstruction. He kept teasing the beetle in this manner, giggling at its stupidity and determination while it climbed to the *ne plus ultra* and descended.

But his happiness was rudely interrupted by a man's thundering voice, and he looked up just as a huge, dilating shadow covered him, scooping him from the ground, smothering his face in starched cotton. The darkness curled over like a wave, and as it broke, Egon managed to squirm loose, so he didn't end up flattened like a dung ball under the man's immense bulk.

Then there was such commotion, hooves clattering, women screaming, and Egon thought this had something to do with the military exercise he had watched that morning—the soldiers, so disciplined in drill, must have gone mad and were stampeding through the city, thrusting their bayonets into whomever stood in their way. Where was his father, and why had a crowd gathered, and what had happened to the poor black beetle? Had it been crushed in the panic?

As he raised himself on his arms, he saw a fashionable woman peering from beneath the black lace pinned to the rim of her hat, and just then someone dug his fingers into his armpits, dragging Egon to his feet. He tried to horse-kick, but the man pulled his hands across his chest, securing him in the straitjacket of his own arms. He struggled, stomped, twisted his head around and attempted to sink his teeth into the man's hand. Then he heard his name uttered in a clipped, opprobrious tone and he realized his father was the one restraining him, while the attacker stood coolly to the side. Adolf Schiele boxed his son's ears and threatened to hit him again if he wouldn't be silent, and Egon had no desire to provide the crowd with more of a spectacle, so he managed to contain his sobs. Adolf handed the stranger a few coins and then he took Egon's hand in his and dragged him away. Egon began to whimper again, he couldn't help himself—the world made no sense. But instead of slapping him, his father lifted Egon into his arms and carried him around the corner, out of sight of the crowd. It didn't matter anymore that his father had punished him unfairly, Papa was Papa and would always arrive in time to save his son.

With his arms around his father's neck, his chin fixed upon the ridge of his shoulder, Egon saw a young commissionaire hurrying toward them. But Egon knew better than to worry now—his father would fend off this wisp of a man and they'd be on their way again. The commissionaire called out, his father turned, and the man skidded to a halt.

"Your package, sir."

Not until his father had dug into his pocket and dropped a coin in the outstretched hand did the fellow lay the brown paper package on the ground, touch his finger to his cap and wheel around again, sprinting away. Adolf Schiele set his son down and brushed aside the strands of hair clinging to the boy's cheeks. "Close your eyes," he directed, and Egon obeyed, bracing himself for a beating. But he heard paper rustling, felt his father place something on his head and he curled his fingers around what seemed to be the wooden handle of a spade. He opened his eyes before his father gave him permission and found that he held a toy sword and wore a bucket-shaped head piece with castellated edges. Adolf saluted the little warrior, and Egon did his best to hide his disappointment—this wasn't anything like Queen Libussa's bejewelled sword and helmet. But to please his father, he stabbed the air with his sword as he had seen the soldiers do with their rifles.

At home that night, during a late supper, he learned the truth about the incident outside the store. While Marie Schiele spooned soup into Gerti's mouth, Adolf explained how their dolt of a son had nearly been caught under the hooves of a fruit vendor's horse. He said he had heard people shout and had looked out the store window to see a man leap in front of the horse and haul Egon to safety. As Egon listened he remembered the beetle. He would have liked to explain that the beetle was to blame, for it had absorbed him so thoroughly he hadn't even noticed the cart approaching. But still he was grateful to the insect. Next time, he promised himself, he would catch the beetle and hide it in his pocket while he had the chance.

•

Where has Egon Schiele gone now? Vallie Neuzil carries a satchel full of raisin buns, but the guard meets her at the door and informs her that the prisoner has been transferred. To where? The man shrugs and flicks his cigarette stub past Vallie onto the street.

For the first time since Egon's imprisonment, Vallie begins to worry about the outcome. Perhaps injustice cannot be corrected so easily. Egon is quick to make enemies, after all, and when his temper flares he lets insults spill off his tongue. The authorities need only to provoke him and they will have whatever evidence they need, if the drawings that they took from the cottage aren't damning enough. Egon would serve himself best if he could manage to act like a gentleman—a record of good behavior in prison would serve as his most convincing defense. His friend Heinrich Benesch has told Egon that he knows an able lawyer, but how can anyone help such a wilful young man? Egon shall never forgive the village of Neulengbach, and no court will pardon a man clearly intent on revenge.

The guard is about to close the door without so much as a civil "Good day," but Vallie catches his eye with a pleading, forced smile. She stares at the fold of skin squeezed forward by his stiff collar, while he measures her with his eyes. If she wants to know where the criminal has been sent, maybe he could find out, depending upon . . . he pretends to give Vallie the option of deciding the terms. Depending upon. Vallie doesn't reply, yet neither does she resist when the guard takes her chin in his hand and turns her pert face up, pressing his lips against hers, forcing his tongue into her mouth. But the disgusting taste of tobacco and garlic are too much for Vallie to endure, and she pushes him off, knocks away the hands that have slipped inside her raincoat.

"You are under arrest!" he calls after her, using the familiar address. "Come back here—you are under arrest!" He laughs heartily at the frightened girl without moving from the doorway.

Five wobbly strides take Vallie around the corner of the prison onto a slate path. She hugs the satchel against her belly and glances over her shoulder to see the slit that was Egon's cell window, half expecting to see his face pressed against the bars and hear him calling after her. For the first time it occurs to her that she may never see Egon again.

It begins to drizzle, and at the bottom of the hill Vallie veers off the path. Without any clear purpose she bundles her cloak around her knees, leaps from stone to stone across a muddy creek bed, climbs over barbed wire and heads into an abandoned pasture, where the grass is still tipped with brown and piles of straw are scattered like corpses across a battlefield. Bramble vines loop around her ankles, tug at the laces of her shoes, but Vallie keeps stumbling forward, her shoulders hunched against the tiny darts of rain. She holds her hat against her chest as she ploughs into the wind—in the city she forgets how malevolent nature can be, notices only the raindrops dripping daintily off gutters and the popping, lascivious gusts of wind that lift her skirts.

She tries to calm herself, but fear has taken hold and her body reacts accordingly, her heart strains to feed her panic. When she sucks in shallow breaths she tastes the saliva of the guard. What crime has Vallie Neuzil committed? She has done nothing wrong; they can't arrest her for accepting an unwanted kiss. And who would go to the trouble of pursuing her across the field? Vallie Neuzil is only Egon Schiele's mistress and had come to bring him raisin buns.

Before she reaches the shelter of the bordering woods, one knee suddenly buckles under her and she sprawls forward, twisting her right wrist as she tries to break her fall, landing heavily on the satchel of raisin buns. She lies inert, and the grass on either side unbends, stands upright, so from above she appears just another pile of straw, just another corpse. She inhales deeply and soon is relishing the sweet smell of damp earth and dung, almost comforted, hidden, no one would ever find her in this fallow acre, she can rest here, die here. Now there is only the throbbing pain in her wrist to disturb her, though even this seems to subside, as if the separate parts of her body were conspiring together, willing her to sleep.

She relaxes, and her memory returns. She thinks of her mother beneath the crust of earth, presses her ear against the ground, for now she wants desperately to hear her mother whispering her name. Like a dreamer, she has lost all sense of what is possible. She gives in to the desire, and it seems to her that this has been the primary propulsion, her fear only an attendant annoyance. When she hears the far-off sounds of church bells chiming she is satisfied, because she knows that the bells are a greeting from her dead mother.

Perhaps she would come to see the absurdity of the situation if she reflected long enough: a smartly dressed girl lying in a field, soaked by the rain and wet grass. But she becomes aware of another presence in the field, as if a gaze could be felt physically. She raises her head to find that she is being observed not through a pair of admiring eyes but through tiny slitted nostrils. A gray mole crouches so close to Vallie that she can see the separate granules of dirt clinging to the snout. It remains still, inhaling Vallie's scent, its sides heaving rapidly as Vallie lowers her arm and with an agile snap seizes the blind rodent. It is the size of a spaniel's paw, weightless in her hand. The black snout pokes out from her fist, and Vallie is careful to hold the animal firmly to keep it from escaping, but gently as well, so she won't crush the fragile body. She can feel the rapid heartbeat, the vibrations penetrating her fingertips, making her own pulse quicken.

From the inside of her body looking out, nothing distinguishes Vallie from the rodent in her hand. Absorbing the heat from the animal, she feels a tightening in her stomach, a faint nausea, and she suspects that she is about to undergo some extraordinary transformation. She remains on the verge, feeling as if someone should notice her, as Gustav Klimt had noticed her when she was only sixteen years old, as Egon Schiele had noticed her the following spring in Klimt's atelier garden on the Josefstädterstrasse.

The swell of anticipation recedes, and she realizes that the mole has stopped struggling, like a swaddled child it seems to have grown used to the confinement. Vallie turns her hand over. As she parts her fingers to look at the mole it twists around and hops off her palm, landing without a sound upon the earth, slithering off, its little rump wagging as it disappears in the grass.

So Vallie is alone again, alone, exhausted, and newly appalled at her condition. She pushes herself onto her knees and staggers to her feet, but instead of returning directly to the road she continues in the direction of the pines. Underneath the trees she flicks away mud and grass sticking to her coat and positions her felt hat so it cuts in a slanted line across her forehead. Though she knows she should feel ashamed of her behavior—from the kiss at the jailhouse to the inertia in the field—she can't help but feel a slightly sheepish pride. Not many girls would have had the skill or the courage to catch a mole with their bare hands. Not many girls would have left the path and run wildly across the field.

She realizes that she is hungry. A girl might forget propriety but she can never forget her appetite, and Vallie remembers with pleasure the satchel full of raisin buns she baked for Egon, raisin buns that now belong, by default, to her. She unties the leather cord and weighs a glazed, lumpy bun in her hand before she raises it to her mouth. Tearing off a piece, she examines the tiny air pockets in the dough as she chews, holding it beneath her nose to inhale the fragrance of lemon. But she smells instead, unbelievably, the fetid odor of fur and animal filth left behind by the mole. She throws the bun to the ground in disgust and removes the masticated wad from her mouth, scoops out along with it something that resembles a pale, tiny bone, followed by pieces of hide and sinewy shreds of gut. It appears that Vallie Neuzil is the victim of a sinister joke, a trick that must have something to do with the prison guard. Or perhaps she is confused. She dredges her throat with her fingers and leans forward, balancing against the trunk of a pine tree. She can trust nothing in this village of Neulengbach, not even the ground beneath her —the shell of earth might crumble, split, it might turn hot as white coals. There is nowhere to hide. What chance does she have? What chance does any girl have who cannot help herself?

•

Schönbrunn, 1915: Egon watches the girl as she tucks her head between her legs and somersaults across the lawn, exposing the pink elastic ruffles of her bloomers; he watches as she picks up a broken spoke from a bicycle wheel and runs toward the cluster of ducks, herding them into the fountain. The old woman scattering chunks of bread scolds the mischievous young sprite, who slaps the water with her stick to drive the ducks into the water streaming from a nymph's pitcher. March winds blow the child's attention to and fro, and in a moment she has darted back across the green mall, moving in sweeping strides as if to pretend that she is a Hungarian skater in an otterskin cap, then slowing to a trot, jerking her head down and snorting; now she is an ambassador's horse shod in gold.

She stops and cocks her head—she has heard a familiar call, or perhaps she has only remembered the sound, but the memory must be louder than a military band, for she begins to wander in widening circles, as if trying to approach the source. Egon notices that her braided jacket has been carelessly patched, with squares of dirty cotton flapping like dead leaves on a grapevine, she wears no stockings, and someone has tied string around her shoes to hold the soles intact. A woman grips her purse as the child drifts by, and nannies lined on a bench glance up from their embroidery to check on their own wards, young heirs and heiresses chasing one another around the basin and the outcrop behind the grotto. No one knows to whom the waif belongs, no one is concerned, since the police are sure to find her before nightfall and take her to the *zentrales Kinderheim,* where she'll stay until someone claims her.

If Schiele had discovered this girl a few years earlier, he might have invited her home and used her as a model, but now he knows better; solitary children are traps, bait set for solitary men—the more helpless the youngster appears, the more dangerous she is. Egon knows that if he approached the child, her screams would cause a crowd to gather and someone would surely recognize him. They would stone him on the spot, or they would have him thrown into jail, and if the authorities didn't tear out his fingernails with their teeth they would see to it that he was transported back to Neulengbach to suffer through those twenty-four days in hell.

Besides, Egon has enough trouble taking care of himself. In the last year he has traveled with his portfolios to Munich, to Zurich, to Györ in Hungary, but he keeps returning to Vienna, the only worthy proving ground as far as he's concerned. Here he peddles his landscapes and portraits to dealers and sells his drawings to nameless fetishists, who expect him to show gratitude for the few coins they drop into his outstretched hand, hardly enough to buy theater tickets and pay for a decent tailor and not enough to feed both him and Vallie. So why should he pity a plump, carefree child when he doesn't waste pity on himself? Pity is expensive, pity belongs to those who can afford to pause and contemplate alternative, luckless destinies. Egon Schiele does not allow himself to pause—thought must result in action, and when he studies any object, whether it be a stone nymph in a fountain or a disoriented child and the curve of her earlobe, he calculates how he can use that image in his work, even considers how much the final painting will be worth. Of course he makes mistakes, and back in his studio he has to sort through his sketches to find a single inspiration. Too often the sights most striking to him at first glance prove worthless when he faces a blank canvas, and he will stand chewing on the handle of his paintbrush as he considers how much time has been wasted acquiring trash, staring, probing, surveying the world without any result.

He wants to train himself to be both frugal and prophetic, to use his eyes with the utmost skill and economy. He knows that children are dangerous; he knows as well that they should have no place in his art. Their soft lines and dimpled flesh, so seductive; their impish, upturned noses, so charming, so dishonest. Egon turns his back to the sickly yellow Schönbrunn Palace, to the ducks in the fountain, to the ravens wobbling beneath the weight of their huge beaks, and to the little girl, who would have walked directly into the water if the old woman hadn't caught her by the shoulder and shaken her, shaken her firmly to bring her back to her senses.

How easy it is for children to dismiss yesterday as a dream and to begin again; children can deny the perceptions of the last hour as easily as the first Emperor of China denied the existence of the past by ordering all the books written before his reign to be burned. Egon doesn't worry about lost children; rather, he envies them the ease with which they replace one interest with another. How resilient their selfish little egos are.

But before he has reached the gate by the parish church, he is chiding himself for neglecting an opportunity. At this safe distance he can admit that as much as he distrusts children, they fascinate him. His obsession had forced him to leave Krumau and had nearly destroyed him in Neulengbach, so now he cannot be too careful— he has tried to divert his interest in children and to disguise his own immaturity with cynicism and hauteur. But others continue to describe him as childlike.

Childlike. Do they mean childish? Puerile? As he is wondering about this distinction, a hack driver without a passenger shouts at Egon to move his filthy ass out of the way. Egon slaps the trotting horse's haunch, and in order to strike at Egon with his whip the driver lets the reins fall slack. The horse breaks stride and begins to canter, and the driver is forced to turn his rage and his whip upon the animal.

Childlike. Egon will soon be standing before the judge again if he cannot restrain himself. He must learn to hide his impulsive half. But he wouldn't paint at all if he did not paint honestly. For Egon, a line reveals only itself and doesn't refer to other shapes—an image cannot contain another image. Egon knows that he holds nothing back in his work—the many parts in his paintings, the barriers, the hoods and capes and mourning veils, replace rather than cover up portions of the naked body. No one will ever lift the cloth to have a peek at the loins beneath.

As he walks through the Hietzinger Gate, he thinks of his *Encounter*, painted for the von Reininghaus contest. The mural, though incomplete, had been included with entries from other competitors in Pisko's gallery. This self-portrait with hallowed saint hadn't won him the prize of three thousand kronen, but it had aroused the indignation of influential critics, who loudly denounced Schiele's vanity and his awkward, primitive figures. After the contest Egon had lost interest in the painting, but during the walk back from the Schönbrunn Gardens he has an idea: he will transform his *Encounter*, he will flatten his painting even further, and he will duplicate himself. He will photograph himself standing next to his self-portrait. Two lifeless, flat, dissimilar Egon Schieles will pose side by side for the camera, each figure pretending to be the reflection of the other. He will show the critics of Vienna that they know nothing about beauty, that their aesthetic laws have no meaning, and though these gentlemen may make claims about this city, they will recognize that its charm is simply a matter of common agreement. Let the workers sweep the streets and cart away the dung and rubbish, let the city celebrate its tapering spires, its palaces, monuments and cemeteries —Vienna would never control the eyes observing her. And it is the artist's responsibility to educate those eyes. Autopsy is the word which perfectly describes this act of looking. Egon hopes that one day the mouths of his critics will open wide in wonder at one of his self-portraits, a string of drool will cling to their beards, and they will laugh not at him this time but at humanity, they will laugh with the gargoyles hanging from bell towers and balconies. Symmetry and perspective, chiaroscuro, balance—all these, Egon Schiele believes, offer false comfort, and a man is truly aware only when he learns to accept, even to delight in the incongruous, terrifying nature of the visual world.

Impatient to resume work on his *Encounter*, he proceeds at a brisk clip, but his circular thoughts lead him around the square, past identical cafés with only one of two kinds of pastries displayed in their windows due to wartime rationing, back to the parish church and the Hietzinger Gate. Not until he feels the gravel of the drive beneath his thin leather soles does he realize he has inadvertently returned to the park.

Well, here is occasion to laugh aloud, at himself this time, at his confusion. He has a sudden impulse to find the little girl and ask her to explain herself: does she have a home, is she hungry, is she an orphan, is she a Gypsy? Egon locates the old woman tossing tufts of bread into the stagnant pool of the grotto fountain, he sees the governesses on the bench, he searches the faces of the children playing tag, but he cannot find the girl.

He grinds his fist into his palm as he scans the mall and the slope above the grotto, he takes a few steps to the left, backs up, walks forward and halts abruptly, as if surrounded on four sides by glass, then glances in distraction at a blind beggar woman sitting on the asphalt path nearby, a dirty gray shawl draped over her head, a man's derby upturned on the ground before her. Leaning against her arm is the child Egon has been so eager to find. The girl sneers back at Egon, as though with spite she will force him to drop a few coins into the hat. The mother's eyelids are sealed closed, slightly distended. Egon has no money to spare, so he walks past and settles on a bench, where he can watch the mother and child from a distance.

But the girl leaves the shelter of her mother's bulk, shuffles along the path toward Egon. When she is directly in front of him she kicks a leg behind her, tips her head back and starts to dance, spins in the wild, fearless way that only children can spin, flailing her arms, turning faster, strands of hair whipping across her face. She staggers onto the grass, slicing the space with her open hands, and topples to the ground.

Irresistible. Egon cannot help himself. He springs up from the bench and hurries to where she is sprawled, the breeze rippling the patches of cotton on her coat, her fists pressed against her eyes to block the sunlight. He touches her lightly on the shoulder, and when she opens her mouth he sees that the entire top front ridge of teeth is missing. With her parched lips she seems a death's-head, an icon of his own mortality. Startled, he draws back as he would from a decaying cadaver that he mistook for someone asleep, but the child clamps her arms around his ankles and refuses to release him. He squats, tries to bribe her with a nub of black chalk he has found in his coat pocket, dangling it in front of her eyes, pressing it into her palm. She closes her fingers around the chalk. Egon pokes her play- fully in the ribs, in her doughy thigh, forgetful of his earlier resolve, glad to be in the company of such an untamed, unwashed kitten after the many months spent struggling to defend his art, participat- ing in secessions, overthrowing tradition. How insignificant his work seems now, how banal. The child's spirit invades his body, and he would like to dance with her, to forget his purpose, to empty his head and dance.

The courtship is quick—when he has drawn a few short giggles from her, he seizes a leg and an arm, lifts her from the ground and swings her in circles. The girl screams with delight, stretching her free hand out as she flies horizontal to the ground. Egon is certain that no one has ever transformed this ragged child into a bird before, and if he is conscious of the danger of this game, he can excuse it as an act of charity: he is giving the child a rare memory of joy. But he doesn't need to justify himself—no police intrude, no crowd gathers to condemn his aberrations, and he winds slowly to a stop only when he is too dizzy to stand upright.

Sprawled on the ground again, the girl covers her eyes with her fists, though she continues to giggle quietly from the thrill of the flight, or perhaps at the foolish man who has wasted his time and his black chalk on her. She tips her head as Egon had seen her do earlier, looks sideways at him, then scampers back to her mother, leaving Egon panting, his rubbery arms hanging limply. He resumes his place on the bench to watch his inconstant friend as she nestles against her blind mother. Her fingers fumble with the blouse but- tons, but the mother remains indifferent to the child squirming in her lap, indifferent to the small, sweating face thrust against her bosom, to the mouth searching for her nipple. Now the child's eyes close as she sinks into her own delicious darkness, and Egon turns his head, unwilling to watch. The child is old enough to bewitch men, but still she survives on her mother's milk. Egon has been betrayed by his own sentiments, he has let the lie of childhood trick him.

Later that afternoon, Egon lies on the ottoman in his Hietzinger studio while sparrows hop along the windowsill, taunting him with chirps that sound maddeningly like the sucking noises of a nursing child. He spits a mouthful of beer into a wooden ashtray. His unsold creations, propped against the walls, watch him with skewed, unseeing eyes, his own reflection in the full-length mirror watches him, the puppets and china dolls on his bookcase shelf watch him. Vallie is visiting relatives in Ragusa, so Egon is alone, as alone as he had been in the prison cell. What is the purpose of unsettling memory, he wonders, admitting that he has no more control over his impressions than he has over the wind. He is a victim to his senses, forced to inhale, ingest, absorb the world. Egon wishes he had the sort of mind that could generalize and relieve him, temporarily, from the tyranny of sight; he wishes he could look at the world without seeing the slashes and divisions, so many minute discordant parts—too many parts, he cannot order them in categories, the quantity has overwhelmed him and now he lies helplessly, his wrists bound, stones on his chest, unable to forget the one image that has displaced all others: blind mother with child.

But he must return to work, prepare *Encounter* and varnish Fräulein Beer's portrait as well, paint his colorful cities, his dead cities, cities of jumbled rooftops and chimneys. If only Vallie were here to serve him a cup of coffee and pass a chocolate from her mouth to his. Or Gerti and her new husband Anton, a saint, Anton Peschka, Egon wouldn't have trusted his sister with any other man.

He pushes open the shutter, scattering the sparrows, and inhales the springtime fragrance of Vienna, modern Vienna. His loneliness is as stifling as a monk's coarse wool robe, and he tries to exhale the nagging memory of the little witch of the Schönbrunn Gardens. But he can't even lift his foot. He would rather be dead than caught in this paralysis of thought, he would rather disperse like vapor, blowing about, condensing on stone facades and blades of grass. He would like to be the blind mother's child.

Yes, the obsession is a sickness. Because "Egon should study instead to become an engineer, our most ardent wish." To work, then, a man destined to die young must work twice as fast. But still he dallies at the window, trying to fill his mind with the faces of friends. He wishes he could visit Arthur Roessler, reliable Arthur Roessler, who appreciates Egon Schiele. But Roessler doesn't appreciate surprises—he prefers scheduled meetings, lacquered invitations, and calling cards. Egon considers dignity akin to beauty, to innocence, to obligation—all lies of class—and if Roessler weren't such a good friend and influential critic, Egon would show him just what "correct" men miss.

This, for instance: he flickers his tongue at the young women standing in the apartment directly across the street from his own. A yellow-frilled, tea-drinking bevy; he will have some fun with them. He can see one pulling a pin from her straw hat, the sleeves on her dress bunched at the wrists, frothy cotton roses sewn on the shoulders. When she tilts her head she reminds Egon of a heron he once saw standing at the edge of a lake, preening its breast feathers. Herons are good omens. He shouts a greeting to her, but it is the second girl crossing the room who notices him. There are only two of them, two proper girls wearing high-waisted, pleated dresses, hats, and hair ribbons. The taller one points at him, the other presses her fingertips against the window, the taller one pulls the other back by the shoulder. They seat themselves on either end of the sofa and begin to talk and laugh with contrived gestures, trying to fool Egon, to prove to him that they are deeply involved in their own affairs.

But Egon cannot bear to be alone, not today, not after what he has seen in the park. He puckers his lips to kiss the sweet wind, calls "Good day" to the pretty girls across the street and disappears. When he returns to the window, he catches them peering in his direction, though they quickly pretend indifference again. Coy ladies. Egon flaps a self-portrait over the windowsill—the artist in a white vest, checkered shirt, his arms akimbo in his characteristic pose. Finally the girls give in and open the window so they may have a better look at what the stranger is advertising. Egon waves a second self-portrait—a gaunt, standing nude with a sunken chest and limp penis. The girls begin to titter at his work, as his own sisters had laughed many years ago. But he doesn't mind, for he wants to amuse them. Their laughter saturates him, helps him to forget everything, and when he sees them wiping tears from their cheeks he knows he has succeeded. "I have so much more to show you!" he calls, and they exchange wondering glances, as if they are too innocent to understand what the stranger means.

·

Slice of life: In the first decade of the current century, in a coffee-house on the Dorotheergasse, a Boston banker and his wife were surprised to meet a distant family relative, an Englishman who lived most of the year in London and dealt in curios and antiques. The Englishman had come to Vienna in hopes of purchasing a particular Füger miniature, but he had been outbid and after a long day wasted wrangling with stubborn Germans, he was grateful to hear his own language, however warped it was in the Massachusetts vernacular. The Americans were vacationing in Europe and had left their three children with a governess in Paris while they traveled through Swit-zerland, Austria, and Italy. They had bought a number of guide-books in preparation for their tour and they were reviewing these when the Englishman hailed them from across the room.

He squeezed his globular self between the crowded tables, tapping on chair legs with his cane, rousing the patrons from their conver-sations and commanding them in his booming, brigadier's voice, in English, to make room for an old man, make room. Once he was seated, the trio announced their delight in unison—to think that they should chance to meet in this corner of Vienna after so many years. They paid tribute to fate, to divine will, to luck, and then they passed on to the next stage—a moment of thoughtful silence while they assessed one another. The Englishman did not know that the Americans were noting the dry patches around his ears and wonder-ing whether the rumors about his drinking could be true. The cou-ple, in turn, did not suspect that their cousin was passing harsh judgment on the wife's matronly, unlaced bosom, thinking how terribly sad life was: men lose everything when the women lose their youth.

But no one let his meditations spoil the gaiety, and at the urging of the wife the Englishman shared her piece of *Gugelhupf.* He scraped small forkfuls of whipped cream from the top of the cake and sa-vored each bite as though this is what he had traveled eight hundred miles for—sublime *Gugelhupf,* not a Heinrich Füger miniature.

Meanwhile the husband had picked up his book about the Austro-

Hungarian Empire and was examining the binding. With his slight, characteristic lisp, he mused, "Doubtless the Italians are inclined toward laziness. But this author maintains that the Austrian-Italians are cleverer than their brothers on the other side of the Alps. The Slavs in the southern regions are a backward people, in contrast, and thus are poorer than the Italians, but being poor they have remained relatively innocent. Their wives are as handsome and proud as you'll find among peasants."

"It's common wisdom that Czech women make good wet nurses," offered the wife, adding, "I've heard that the Poles are like lapdogs—clean, thriftless, generally content, and their women know nothing about housekeeping."

"But for the most spoiled of the fair sex," the husband said ruefully, "the author tells us we must turn to the Rumanian, who leaves his wife free to do nothing but cherish her beauty. Of course, paint and false hair take their toll, and the young Rumanian ladies lose their bloom early in life."

"Such diversity," the wife sighed, stabbing the cake with her fork before it disappeared entirely into her cousin's mouth.

"And the Jews," added the Englishman.

"The Jews," the husband echoed.

The woman swallowed and said, " 'An unhappy, uprooted race!' " quoting word for word, from memory, from the guidebook in her husband's hand. " 'Their most unfavorable traits are terrible want of self-respect and proper pride.' "

The three fell silent for a few minutes. The wife's thoughts returned to her children and to the governess she had hired in Paris—a reserved, aquiline woman who had fallen on hard times. During the interview in the hotel she had worn a mink collar so tattered that patches of skull showed through, and the lips of the rodent were wrinkled back in a frozen snarl.

The husband thought about his bank's senior vice-president—there had been murmurs recently, hushed accusations of embezzlement.

The Englishman looked around for the waiter so he could order tea and perhaps a piece of cake. "You're in no hurry, I hope," he said to the couple.

The husband replied, "No, no," while the wife impatiently dabbed her cinnabar lips with the napkin.

•

Egon Schiele, in a letter to Anton Peschka, 1910: "How ugly every-thing here is. Everybody is jealous of me and underhanded. There is falsehood in the eyes of former colleagues. Vienna is full of shadow, a black city."

•

In 1909, when Vallie first met Gustav Klimt, she had been giving more thought than usual to her prospects, a girl on her own in this great centrum of culture. She was working in a dress shop just off the Petersplatz, she had a room to herself in her aunt's apartment in the Ottakring District, she had even received a marriage proposal from a young altar boy who had swung the incense burner at her mother's funeral. Upon her aunt's advice, sixteen-year-old Vallie had rejected the altar boy and instead found the job selling expensive dresses to corpulent widows and society girls—a respectable job, but within a week the routine had become oppressive, and Vallie decided that she deserved better.

So when the bearded man dressed in a black cashmere cape and a fur cap pulled low over his forehead entered the shop one December night just before closing and without even introducing himself, de-clared that he would make her famous throughout Vienna if she would consent to be his model, she couldn't help but giggle. He waited for her to lock up, and then she let him escort her along the crowded Graben lined with snowdrifts to one of those leather-up-holstered tourist carriages waiting at the Kohlmarkt. As he opened the door, he declared proudly that he was the artist Gustav Klimt, as though she should have recognized his name at once.

She sank into the button-pleated seat in the carriage and glanced at the man's profile between his cap and his beard, decided from his small, alert, appraising eyes that he would make a fine partner in business. This artist stood to profit from her beauty, while for Vallie the exposure would mean an obvious improvement in her station, a step toward independence. At the shop she was forced to remain on her feet all day, ironing, sorting, selling, fastening stays, pinning hems, admiring so many mirror reflections. Now, apparently, it was her turn to be admired.

The artist said that he had seen her arranging dresses in the display

window yesterday and had known instantly that hers was the face
he had been looking for, as if he thought he could make her a star as
widely admired as Katherina Schratt, Vienna's leading lady and the
kaiser's intimate friend. Vallie knew enough about modern art to
understand what was entailed—she would have to stand naked before this stranger, she would have to shiver in the cold for a few
hours. She smiled to herself at the thought of her nude body on
display in a gallery frequented by the same women who came to her
shop; how betrayed they would feel when they discovered that the
girl who sold them their long gowns and sashes and shawls had been
chosen by the artist Gustav Klimt to be celebrated for her natural
beauty, and she thought that if this broad-shouldered, handsome
stranger wanted more than her image, she would give it to him. A
girl who had nothing to lose would do well to follow the example
of Katherina Schratt, or better, of Anna Fuchs, the former scullery-
maid, who was now Anna Sacher, a widow and the owner of Vienna's most elite hotel. Vallie and the artist both would benefit from
the arrangement; she rested her head against his arm to indicate her
willingness.

Soon he was loosening her scarf, stroking her neck with his bulky
fingers, and Vallie didn't object. She eased back against the cushion
and took out a small bag of almond macaroons from her purse. She
offered one to her escort, popped the macaroon into her mouth
when he declined, chewing as he rubbed his knuckles along her
collarbone, and when he reached over to caress her breasts she shut
her eyes so she wouldn't be reminded that the man was a stranger.
She swallowed the chalky sweet and plucked another from the bag.
Surely he hadn't expected Vallie to give in so quickly. He whispered
that all of Vienna would fall in love with her. She didn't remind him
that his promise depended on her consent and she didn't resist when
he removed the bag of macaroons from her hands and set it on the
floor of the carriage.

But then, without a word, he stopped and leaned away from her,
leaving Vallie to wonder if guilt had overwhelmed him, to wonder
as well if she should blame herself for being too accommodating. As
it turned out, he was merely directing the driver to continue around
the Ring, and when he had closed the panel he took off his rabbit-
fur cap. Vallie looked from his bald temples to the white mist outside the window: a sharp wind was blowing snow about in vicious

spirals, and the people walking raised their gloved hands to shield their faces.

Three months earlier the excitable altar boy had bitten Vallie's lip and brought a tiny bead of blood to the surface. So when Gustav Klimt pressed his mouth against Vallie's ear and asked her if she had ever had a man before, she said yes. He pushed her skirt up and ran a fingertip beneath a garter; before Vallie understood what he meant to do he had slid two fingers into her. With his other hand resting against the small of her back, he lifted her off the seat until she was half-standing in the cramped interior of the carriage. Fascinated, she watched the slow plunging motion of his wrist. He guided her down onto the saddle of his hand, and his fingers slipped out when the carriage bounced over a pothole. But he held her steady, covered her mouth with his to inhale any sound that might escape from her. He tasted of mint, not like an old man should taste at all, Vallie thought, and she felt brave enough now to look at him—at the whiskers sprouting from wide pores, at the curve of the nostrils, at the slack, wrinkled skin under his closed eyes. She stared until her eyes misted.

When they finally arrived at Gustav Klimt's apartment, Vallie collected a handful of snow and pressed it against her cheek, cooling her soon-to-be famous face. How life could change so drastically, so quickly, she thought, feeling wise, even nostalgic. How easy for an influential man to lift a poor girl out of the mire. She followed Gustav Klimt into his atelier, and a tall, striking woman in a black dressing robe, her hair knotted loosely in a netted cap behind her head, met them in the hallway. Klimt introduced the woman as Emilie. Vallie stared at the peacock in the rug so she wouldn't have to meet this woman's probing eyes. She wondered why the artist needed a girl like Vallie when he had a woman at home who surely was the most elegant woman in the Empire. Vallie wanted to tell Emilie that half an hour ago she had been a common shopgirl but in the carriage she had been completely transformed by Herr Klimt. Surely the Frau could see the change for herself? Yes, she could see, and Vallie didn't need to hear her opinion: to Emilie, Vallie Neuzil was no different from the rest of the nameless, budding hopefuls Gustav snatched from pastry shops, from dress shops, from park benches and doorways.

"We'll put her in the countess gown," the artist said to the woman without a trace of chagrin, without venom or regret. And to Vallie he said, "A stunning costume, with woven gold and pearl brocade. Priceless. Like you, my dear." He tickled her chin again, leaving Vallie to stare after him, more astonished than ashamed. So she wouldn't be naked after all; she would sit for him fully clothed, as though she were just another conceited hen who wanted to be remembered for her wealth as well as for her supposed beauty. Now she felt the same sense of betrayal that she had thought her customers would feel when they saw her youthful body framed and hung in a gallery on the Schwarzenbergplatz. She would appear not as herself but as someone else, in a borrowed costume. Yes, it was Vallie's turn to be admired, to be fitted and pampered. She followed Emilie into the walk-in closet and watched as the woman searched the racks for the countess gown, a gown as priceless as Vallie.

·

Another day, a May day! They trot around the pen in the St. Pölten prison yard, with the guard as the controlling axle. But control is merely a convention here—clearly the inmates in sheer numbers have considerably more strength than the guards, who fill their hours of sentry duty rolling cigarettes and writing letters to sweethearts. If the prisoners conspired together they could easily rebel. Of course the rifles give the guards an advantage, but weapons wouldn't protect them if the prisoners acted swiftly and brutally.

Egon, however, has grown accustomed to captivity, where someone else thinks for him, tells him when to wake and to sleep, gives him a bucket for his waste, serves him food, and were it not for the absence of color, the monotony of steel gray, Egon might be content to remain in jail. He arrived in St. Pölten yesterday and already he longs to be on a train again. As he jogs he tries to comfort himself by remembering the dark, bottomless crevices below the aqueducts on the Semmering Line to Trieste.

He stumbles along the periphery of the yard in the farting, panting file of men, while the guard slides the loop of his riding crop between his fingers. The packed mud is slippery from the morning drizzle, and once in a while a man's feet slide out from under him and he falls, clogging the tracks, causing the cluster to jam. The guard shakes his crop, cursing the stupid sons of whores while the fallen man scrambles up, and the pack jogs on sluggishly, following upon one another's heels, yelping and spitting.

At first Egon thinks the sounds are the involuntary protests of their bodies, but when one man leans forward and hisses incomprehensibly in his ear, Egon realizes the sounds are directed at him. He ignores the gray-skinned pimps, thieves, and murderers, whose lower lips protrude from the masks of their beards like the moist, pink tongue of a Pekinese. Unwanted brothers. They whistle through their teeth at him, but he jogs with his head down, his fists clenched, ready to strike. The inmate behind clucks at him, the red-haired gnome in front calls over his shoulder, "Your name, man!"

Egon concentrates on synchronizing his limbs, pumping his right arm when he raises his left knee, running flat-footed to keep his pointed American shoes from slipping out from beneath him. These criminals have been hired to drive him mad, to plague him until he cannot stand human company. But he will not go mad, he will outrun them all. Their voices swarm about his ears, converge in his head, and slowly Egon begins to make sense of their demands. They want to know his name, yes, and something else. They want to know why. Why what? Why he has been buried alive in St. Pölten's prison.

Speechless

WOULD I have been so desperate had I known then what I know now? That someday I would leave Neulengbach forever, I would marry and emigrate to America, someday I would wear rubber ankle-boots, white stockings, a thin green cardigan, a brown beret, and I would take my metal cane and go out into the streets and walk for hours. Complacency has been hard-earned—I am proud to need so little.

But in the spring of 1912 I saw another kind of future in my mother's eyes, and the more imminent her death became, the more I needed to be among the living. There was no one in Neulengbach more alive than the artist and his mistress, no one in those few weeks more daring and surreptitious than I. It wasn't long before I took to visiting cottage forty-five late at night, leaving my mother alone for hours at a time, creeping past the closed door of my father's bedroom. Without lighting a lamp, I would find the bottle of cognac hidden in the pantry, take a glass from the cupboard and carry both outside. I still remember how the cognac would turn limpid, with wormy veins of brown illuminated by the moon, and how the cool April air smelled of spring, a rich, musky fragrance. I would spread my cape upon the earth and lean back, supporting myself on my elbows, looking for the stars that had rocked so furiously above the garden behind the Italian school. I would sip the liqueur and scan the landscape for a flash of white that would be a man's beardless face, I would listen for the sound of a woman's laughter. And eventually I would push myself from the ground and set off.

The first few nights I hid from every cat that stole across the road, but by the end of the week, with the moon fat and reassuring, I was humming to myself as I walked. So on the fifth night, when I heard the wagon creaking and the horse slopping through the mud ahead, I didn't bother to hide, for I was sure no harm could come to me.

The woman holding the reins was one of the peasants from the outlying farms who drove in before dawn on market day and spent their profits drinking and dancing at a tavern. I moved aside to let the wagon pass, expecting her to call a greeting. But while she in her colorful red garb radiated light, it seemed that I had been diluted by the air and was invisible to her.

A pair of unsold geese huddled in a cramped cage in the back of the wagon, their beaks tucked beneath their wings, their eyes hidden. A corpulent man lay on his side next to the cage, and I saw his lips moving, not in the rapid, fastidious manner of prayer but more slowly, mouthing a silent song. His eyes caught mine and he rolled onto his belly, staring rudely at me as the wagon passed.

"Princess," he moaned, *"Ich liebe dich."*

Without turning in her seat, the woman raised her arm and as quick as a lizard's tongue the horsewhip uncurled and cracked above the man's head. "Keep your mouth shut," she said.

I waited until the wagon had disappeared behind the rise in the road and then I began to run, slowing only when I had rounded the curve and was out of sight before the wagon rose on the far side of the dip. I pressed on, feeling more foolish than bold now—the peasants had nearly ruined the night for me. But the moon still glowed and the regimental poplars still stood at attention. I had only to follow the public road into Au, to climb onto a wheelbarrow, to steady myself against the windowsill.

A drunken peasant's protestations of love could not compare with Egon Schiele's insult, as it turned out. The artist knew how to shame me. He knew that if he left his drawings strewn about his studio I would see them. He knew that in the darkness I would be able to make out the grotesque, contorted nudes, men clutching their genitals, monstrous, pubescent girls embracing each other. And Egon Schiele knew—he must have known—that instead of indignation I would feel envy, shameful envy so intoxicating and addictive that by the fifth night I would be willing to risk everything.

·

In the city of Krumau, Erwin Osen, Moa, and Egon wandered along a narrow grass island between two strips of flagstones. Erwin and Egon, absorbed in conversation, walked on either side of the slender dancer Moa and leaned across her toward each other to emphasize their points: that an artificial image depends upon an actual image, Egon argued, or that art's single function is to parody precursors, in Erwin's opinion. Moa interrupted to direct their attention to a narrow, cobbled street veering off, flanked by a colorful fruit stand and a bakery. Couldn't they follow that street and find out where it led? Perhaps the bakery on the corner had Erwin's favorite pastry—a flat cake with huge dollops of prune jam and poppyseed paste. Moa tried to tempt him by describing the delights they might find, she moved closer to him and pressed her thin arm around his waist. Moa was already habit for Erwin, while for Egon she seemed an exotic, slatternly girl ready to flirt with any gentleman who tipped his hat to her. Moa and Erwin were lovers, while Egon had and wanted no one—Klimt hadn't introduced him to Vallie Neuzil yet, and his sister and occasional hired girls provided all the inspiration he needed.

"But why do you object?" Erwin asked Egon, ignoring the cajoling Moa at his side. "It is up to us to refine the aesthetic image, so we must work from those who have come before us. A painter's vision is obviously deliberate, while the arrangement of the clouds in the sky is entirely a coincidence. As far as I'm concerned, the language of painting consists of other paintings. Titian might not have been entirely successful with his portrait of Isabella d'Este, but he had the right idea, modeling the portrait not on the Signora herself but on an earlier portrait of a portrait."

"But why limit the sources, Osen? What about these buildings, for instance? Artificial images, planned, designed, constructed from raw stuff. Why not make them your subject?"

"I'm not suggesting that we ignore the world around us. But what we see right now is a random collection, and I am interested in intention."

"But then what about Moa, our exquisite Moa? You would have to exclude her from your list of worthy subjects. Yet I've seen the many portraits you've done of her." Egon lifted his hand to Moa's face, tracing the pronounced cheekbones and penciled brows. She let him touch her, apparently pleased by his interest, smiling like the Moa of Erwin's portraits smiled, inviting, coy.

"In this world there are too many paintings of beautiful girls—not enough paintings of paintings of beautiful girls," replied Erwin, grinning now at his witty formula. "If you examined my Moa's more closely, you would see in every painting a different woman—an Odalisque or Eve or Judith. The real Moa is only the material, like the canvas itself, as vital and as insignificant. But she knows what I mean. My dear Moa is as much a product of accident as that dandelion in your buttonhole."

Egon lowered his hand and flicked his fingers against the drooping weed he had plucked from the garden of their pension.

"Tell me, kitten," Moa said slyly to Erwin, "about your intentions when you make a picture of me, tell what you expect to accomplish, and I will tell you about the intention of my mother."

"Your mother?"

"My mother's intention. My mother knew just what she wanted and she found the man who would give her it. I am not entirely an accident."

"Show me something that has no pattern, no intention behind it," Egon added hurriedly, glad to have Moa's encouragement but determined to remain Erwin's primary opponent. "Name a single object —natural or artificial—that has no design."

This rhetorical challenge only bored Erwin and he waved away the argument, offering cigarettes to his clever lover and to his humorless friend.

"What is free from intention? Or from coincidence, for that matter?" Egon persisted, accepting the cigarette, tapping the end against the heel of his hand. But he had already lost both Erwin's and Moa's interest—Erwin was holding a match for Moa, mischievously jerking the wooden stick so the flame tickled the tip of her nose, and she spit upon it to extinguish the fire. Erwin twisted her shawl around her neck and exclaimed in falsetto, "You will hang by the neck until you are dead, dead, dead!" And Moa, rolling her eyes back so that only the bloodshot whites showed, emitted a strangled plea for help and raised her hands toward the sky.

"Oh, will you stop it, both of you!" Egon demanded. The couple sobered, Erwin lit the cigarettes, and they walked docilely along. But they soon took up another game, this time using Egon as shield and obstacle, grappling for each other's hands, reaching around Egon in order to slap and pinch each other, brazen whelps—Egon couldn't help but wish that he had never invited them to travel to

Krumau with him. Simpleminded, uncommitted Erwin Osen was really the most immature of the Neukunstgruppe artists, the most ineffectual fomenter. He was a dabbler, an uninventive painter, and a spiritless stage performer when he played the harlequin to Moa's Godiva, the fly to her Ariadne, John the Baptist to her Salomé in cabarets around Vienna. A notorious pair—anyone in Egon's circle would be proud to have them as close friends. But Egon had come to Krumau to record impressions, to feed off the Bohemian scenery, to satiate himself with the crude, static images that Erwin held in such disdain. Together, Moa and Erwin seemed barbarians in this sacred place where his mother had been born.

Egon dropped his half-smoked cigarette, crushed it beneath his shoe and announced that he wanted to spend the day by himself.

"I would have smoked it!" Erwin said. Egon picked up the squashed butt and placed it in his friend's shirt pocket, then repeated his intention.

"Wicked boy." Moa caressed her throat as she laughed, a gesture that Egon found at once both seductive and repellent and made him want all the more to be rid of these two. Moa was as treacherous, as voluptuous as any one of Klimt's vipers, and Egon secretly abhorred such civilized, cultivated eroticism, preferring Gypsies to the fashion queens of Klimt's work, preferring the smell of human sweat to mellow, expensive perfumes. His mother had told him about the Gypsies who camped on the outskirts of Krumau—he would find them, he would spend the day watching the men dance and the women sing. So with a salute he kicked his heels together, turned about and started off in search of the Gypsies, ignoring Erwin's sullen rebuke, ignoring Moa's sweet, imploring voice as she begged him to return.

He walked down the street that Moa had wanted to follow, cut through an alley so quiet that he could count the drops of water falling from a drainpipe. He walked along the road leading out of town into the farmland surrounding Krumau; he threw kreuzer to a group of ragged children who surrounded him and tried to reach into his pockets; he declined a ride from a peasant who offered to carry him in the back of his wagon to the next town.

The macadam gave way to dirt, and Egon skipped over a ditch and tramped through a pasture, finding there only a few gaunt, listless cows where the Gypsies should have been. Finally, with his shoes soaked from the swampy field, his knees aching, and his hair pasted against his forehead, he decided to rest in a sloping grove of beech and aspen. Using his leather purse as a pillow, he lay on his belly and closed his eyes, enjoying the warmth of the sun against his back, enjoying as well the dampness in the earth seeping through his thin cotton shirt. In his dreams—rather, in the passive consciousness of half-sleep—he heard Moa's alluring voice whispering to him so softly that he couldn't distinguish the words, and then Erwin's rasping, feverish voice. But Egon couldn't tell what they wanted with him. Now Moa's voice mingled with Erwin's, and from their low barks and sighs he realized that they had been whispering to each other, not to him—they didn't care that he was listening. Or they cared enough to muffle their speech so he would hear only the sound of intimacy and not the substance.

Loneliness and anger roused him, loneliness and anger and frustrated desire, for in truth he wanted Moa, just as he would have gladly shared any of Klimt's lovers. He wanted these women because of their fabricated beauty, their perfumes and painted faces, though for these same reasons they disgusted him.

He woke curled on his side and as he reached inside his trousers to comfort his cramped, stiff penis he heard a shuffling noise nearby and looked up to discover that he was not alone. Squatting on his heels a few yards from Egon was one of the Gypsies he had been searching for—a Gypsy, a goatherd, it didn't matter who he was or what he did, at that moment nothing mattered except the boy's exquisite manila skin and windblown hair, his slight frame, the long fingers intertwined, the wide-set crescent eyes focused on Egon's crotch. Nothing mattered at all except that as soon as Egon pulled his hand from the depths the boy bounced up and started to walk away.

"Wait!" Egon called, feeling brazen suddenly, flirtatious, like Moa. The boy turned to face him. "What is your name?" Egon asked. He was grateful that the boy remained silent, his blank expression unchanged. "My mother comes from Krumau," Egon said in an idle attempt to win the boy's interest and trust. The boy stared again at the bulge in Egon's trousers, but the gaze didn't discomfort Egon, instead the attention of such serene brown eyes aroused him further. This wasn't the first occasion in Egon's life that he had pursued a crop-headed, vulnerable youth. But this time he ignored all the ritual preliminary steps of courtship, he crawled forward on his hands and knees over the wet leaves and with an audacity that astounded him even as he did it, he reached for the boy's hand, missed the fingers, grabbed the cuff of his sleeve instead and tugged gently.

He would never tell anyone what happened in the woods outside of Krumau that afternoon when he had deserted his friends. And neither would this young god of the grove tell, Egon knew. This nameless silent god. Nature's extraordinary gift to him—yes, a gift, Egon believed, for such love wouldn't have been possible otherwise—was to leave a space where there should have been a tongue. The boy had no tongue. Egon found this out only by pressing his lips against the young stranger's lips and sweeping his own tongue through the warm mouth, into the hollow behind the teeth. This perfectly formed youth had no tongue. Egon sat back on his heels in surprise, not at all repulsed, simply amazed, and the amiable boy kneeling in front of Egon opened his mouth so Egon could see the narrow stub wagging between the tonsils.

So it would never be told. With a light wind rattling the leaves and making shadows dance across their faces, they unbuttoned their shirts from the collar down, as if one were the reflection of the other. And then Egon began to move more rapidly, skillfully, pretending to himself that this kind of lovemaking was a casual habit. He caressed the boy's narrow shoulders, stroked his throat, and the boy made a gurgling sound—laughter, Egon supposed. He embraced the naked body that was clammy, slippery, completely trusting, he ran his tongue along the slope of the chest, over the ribs, took the crown of the penis in his mouth and showed what a tongue could do, felt the pulse in the swollen blue vein. Egon swept away the leaves and roughly pushed the accommodating creature onto his back, finally forcing something that was nearly speech from the soundless boy. At that moment terror weakened Egon, he faltered as he realized that he was still in time and would carry the burden of this strange dream for the rest of his life. But he couldn't stop or go backward in time. So he let himself feel a passion comparable only to the love he felt for his sister Gerti, different from that desire, though, because the accident of this sudden passion made the intimacy pure.

It should have been a pure, vivid memory as well, without embarrassment, it should have been a comfort to him when he remembered. Except that the memory was like the boy's mouth—hollow. And though they spent hours in the grove and finally fell asleep cradled in each other's arms, the boy trembling at each gust of tepid wind, when Egon woke at twilight he was alone again—the nameless mute had disappeared forever, leaving behind nothing, not a strand of hair, not a red slipper, not a patch of dried semen on Egon's chin. As he buttoned his soiled shirt and brushed dirt off his purse he couldn't decide which he despised more: the tongueless boy, the memory, or the darkness. Before he left the grove he kicked the leaves and twigs over the place where they had lain together to wipe out any signs of their love, to erase what had happened, as if he could have done this to the memory as well, as if he were preparing to deny an accusation that he knew would never be made.

.

Imagine this: the entire population of Vienna, except for yourself, has been evacuated for one day, and you decide to follow the Imperial Vienna Tour mapped with dotted lines in your guidebook. But quickly you discover that the Danubian capital is not entirely deserted. When you pass through the entrance of that Waterloo of architecture, the Staatsoper, angels salute you, winged Lipizzaner stallions prance; as you wander into the glittering foyers, along the empty, carpeted aisles of the auditorium, across the silent stage where red velvet curtains hang sullenly and the tiers of unlit, ornamented boxes above seem like the backs of hundreds of canvases hung facing the wall, you hear footsteps, perhaps a muffled sigh. Impossible, you tell yourself—you are alone in this baroque interior, alone in the city of Vienna. But the sound of shallow, quick breathing is unmistakable. You remember the story of the architect van der Nüll, who collaborated in the design of the Opera House and committed suicide shortly after his favorite diva refused to perform in this paragon of beauty. Could it be that van der Nüll is still upset? There's no need to linger here to find out—you might as well take advantage of the day and see as many sights as you can. On then, and since you'll want more of the same, visit the Hofburg and the adjacent gardens. Start with the Square of Heroes, where Prince Eugene and Archduke Charles ride ill-proportioned mounts, and continue to the nearby square where Maria Theresa sits eternally on her throne.

You decide to rush off to tour the "Old Steffl" before the crowds return and you have to contend with lines at the taxi stands, with erratic tram schedules and belligerent traffic police. But as you hurry through the Volksgarten, past the inspiring statue of Elisabeth, you see a pigeon alighting on the empress's head. So you climb onto the marble pedestal and try to whisk the bird away. The impertinent bird only stares at you as it hops over the woman's brow, out of reach. It lets a few drops of its berry-stained juice splash upon the ridges of stone hair. Without thinking, you lunge across the empress's lap and seize the bird by its rubbery legs; it flaps frantically, but you have a firm grip and pull it toward you, shifting your hands to clutch its breast, unable to restrain its wings. The pigeon makes strangled, chortling sounds as it struggles.

It is a garbage-fattened, filthy squab. You've never wrung a bird's neck before, and around you in the park there are only the unhelpful statues, useless clutter—a bronze Mozart cannot slaughter a pigeon. You manage to tuck the bird under one arm and to wrap your fingers around its neck. You begin to pull, as if dislodging a stubborn cork, but a pigeon is built more solidly than you had imagined. You relax for a moment, hugging the bird tightly against your chest, and look up, expecting to be comforted by the empress's appreciative gaze, surprised instead to see your own shapeless shadow darkening her face. You confuse the shadow with her judgment.

Ashamed, you fling the pigeon into the air and watch as the dazed bird flutters its wings, glides to the ground and lurches about in confused circles. You climb off the pedestal, duck your head in contrition. But it is obvious that you have lost the immortal woman's respect, though you were only trying to assist her, to rid her of the pest. You don't need anyone to tell you that the statues of Vienna are slow to forget cruelty, slow to forgive.

•

Meanwhile, on the Mariahilferstrasse: After three days spent with her great-aunt and her grandmother in their dreary cottage in Ragusa, Vallie decides she has heard enough fortunes told with tea leaves and cards and she returns to Vienna a day early. She intends to surprise Egon, to creep behind him and throw her arms around his neck when he is propped on his metal stool before his easel, his heels hooked on the lower crossbar, his bony knees jutting up. Such a frail thing—Vallie tries to fatten him with wine, pastry, chocolate, though she might as well be stacking more wood on a funeral pyre. Someday the flames will consume him, and she'll be on her own again. But why should she waste time worrying about the future? Comfort and adventure are all she needs, along with chocolates and something special for her lover. She's brought nothing back from Ragusa, nothing to remind Egon of the sea.

She takes a shortcut through a narrow passageway that serves as a courtyard for a complex of apartment houses. Though she had enjoyed wandering along the edge of the bleak, indolent, icy surf, she prefers to be surrounded by the smells of sauerkraut, paprika stew, stale beer, by the sound of children crying and heels clattering along the pavement. Other girls would avoid this noisy *Durchhaus*, but Vallie feels as though she could enter one of these buildings this moment, climb the stairs, and on the third-floor landing find her mother and friends still gathered around the hallway sink. Insatiable gossips. Vallie had never wanted anything to do with them and would hurry past after calling the obligatory greeting. The apartment she had shared with her mother had two small rooms, and every day except Sunday she would help prepare breakfast and supper for the four workmen who lived in the apartment above and who cherished Vallie as though she belonged to them, bringing her kerchiefs, colorful hair ribbons, and candy. She and her mother had been lucky to have such decent quarters—the workmen slept in bunk beds in a single room and they'd told her that most of Vienna's inhabitants made their homes in the sewers or in trees. Girls like Vallie had special privileges, they'd explained, convincing her that she was innately superior to most other children. Though time and misfortune have tempered her vanity, at heart she remains an aristocrat, believing that she has been blessed with unusual luck and advantages. She might have grown bitter, resenting the workmen for misleading her, but instead she is grateful for their protection and has learned to treat herself as the men treated her—indulgently, lovingly.

So on the expansive Hietzinger Hauptstrasse she stops at a confectionery and purchases a bag of chocolates; she sucks thoughtfully on an orange-flavored truffle as she continues, wondering what she could bring to Egon—something unusual, something that would amuse him. In the window of a Tabaktrafik she sees a pipe with a stem carved in the shape of a buxom woman, naked except for a string of wooden beads around her neck. If Egon were a pipe-smoker, Vallie might have bought him this wooden lady to prove that she understands him.

Sugary saliva trickles to the back of her throat and it reminds her of Egon's taste. An elderly man notices her smile and touches his fingers to the rim of his bowler, but she brushes past him, searching the windows of milk shops and wine shops and bakeries for something special—an orange studded with cloves won't do, neither will a puzzle of an alpine vista. She should have brought back a jar filled with sand and a few ounces of Adriatic water. Maybe her arrival a day early is enough of a gift. Yes, her present will be herself—she will enter the front room without calling hello, she will undress quietly and lie as rigid as a cherrywood pipe stem on the bed, waiting for Egon to finish his work.

She thinks she has made up her mind until she sees a dirty ragamuffin on the curb playing an accordion. One end of a string has been tied around the child's ankle, the other end around the neck of a sleeping kitten. Vallie squats beside the kitten and with two fingers kneads the matted scruff around its neck. How much does the little girl want for the pet? The child silences the accordion, turns up her filthy face and proposes an unreasonable price, but Vallie still feels some pity for the indigent people of Vienna and she willingly counts out her money. The pug-nosed mercenary deposits the coins in her pocket and unties the knot around the kitten's neck—the string, it appears, is not included in the deal.

The kitten, as weightless as a moth on Vallie's hand, blinks drowsily and falls asleep again. It will be dead soon. Vallie has bought a dying kitten for her lover and she will present it to him with this challenge: *as long as you keep this animal alive, you may keep me.* A joke, of course—Vallie has no intention of leaving him, even though Egon has convinced himself that the romance is doomed. If he would recognize that the future can never be more than a dream, he wouldn't feel compelled to make such ominous predictions. But he is convinced that his art thrives upon hardship, so he goes out in search of suffering. Whatever binds Egon and Vallie together, they do not agree about the purpose of life.

She pops another chocolate in her mouth, decides she has walked far enough and looks around for a tram stop. But she remembers that she has spent her change on this furry lump in her hands, so she continues walking, inhaling the scent of almonds this time, associating the smell with Vienna, her own Vienna, really her favorite possession.

When she arrives at Hietzinger Hauptstrasse 101, the sky is a smoky color, the hallway dark. At this late hour it will be easy to enter the apartment unnoticed. But when she presses her ear against the door she hears a voice, Egon's, always so urgent, so dire, followed by the high pitched chatter of a woman: likely his sister Gerti with her husband, Anton Peschka. Gerti, who never looks at Vallie except to nod good day or good night, never offers a kind word to her. Vallie considers leaving and returning in an hour—perhaps the couple would have departed by then. But why should she mind their company? Gerti Peschka puts Egon in the highest spirits, after all, brings him bock beer, sings nursery rhymes for him while her husband smokes quietly in the corner. Vallie has arrived in time, she won't miss the fun. As she flings open the door she blows a flourish through her cupped hand to announce herself, then stops.

The two guests and Egon fall silent, their faces all like the masks of Egon's hideous phantoms, openmouthed, as though about to break into a moan. Finally Egon manages to speak, not with a keening sound but with a tone so ominously polished it seems to Vallie that in the last few seconds he'd made some irreversible decision.

"Vallie, let me introduce you to the Harms, Edith and Adele."

"My pleasure."

Cloth roses hang like dollops of yellow icing on the shoulders of the younger sister's dress. The large-boned brunette nervously brushes her fingertips together as if to remove crumbs and says, "We were just on our way out."

"Please stay," Vallie urges, struck by the girl's obvious guilt. She notices that neither of the sisters wears kohl around her eyes, and their lipstick is a quiet, pale peach. Vallie had used a purple crayon that day. She finds herself savoring Egon's embarrassment, an unfamiliar pleasure.

"Adele and Edith live across the way." Egon waves his hand toward the window. "We've just met," he says, motioning now at the schnapps, as though the bottle provided some sort of explanation.

"Will you join us?" the brunette asks, her brows cresting as she widens her eyes politely. An impertinent guest, Vallie thinks, already feeling dispossessed. Briskly she pours herself a glass of schnapps and transfers the kitten to Egon's hands without a word. The three women stare at the animal weakly licking the knuckle of Egon's thumb. Vallie notices that the kitten's tongue is the same color as the sisters' lipstick.

"Is it sick?" asks the one with the yellow buttercream roses.

"Egon is going to nurse it back to health," Vallie says and adds, "He can do anything, you know."

"So we've seen," the girl murmurs. Though they both appear such fair-skinned *Mädchen,* Vallie begins to wonder if there is a secret impunity hidden inside their demure shells and her interest in them increases. She sits in the chair next to Egon, who remains standing, and she motions to the girls to resume their seats on the ottoman.

"Did you carry the cat all the way from Ragusa?" Egon asks. Without quite understanding why, Vallie tells him yes, that she found the kitten tangled in seaweed on the beach, that she saved its life.

"I can smell the salt air," he says, burying his nose in the matted, sooty fur. The sisters' peach lips part in identical smiles, as if they already suspect that Vallie has told a necessary lie. Vallie swallows the first sip of apricot-flavored schnapps with some difficulty, for it tastes bitter after her chocolates, then she empties the glass in a single gulp. She decides that Adele and Edith from across the street might not be as foolish as she first thought. Perhaps they could be friends.

•

May 2, 1912: In St. Pölten, Egon points out to his patron, Heinrich Benesch, that he cannot prove himself innocent until he knows the charges against him. He is certain, however, that they won't keep him here forever—he has work to do, new paintings to execute. The authorities may delay his success by locking him in this cell, but they cannot interfere with his destiny.

Destiny? A few years ago, Central Inspector Heinrich Benesch had gained an important insight into the notion of destiny and he wants to share it with Egon. He had been riding on a tram on the Burgring beside a military parade, watching the boys in their bucket hats and white gloves, their bayonets raised, the high-stepping Lipizzaner leading the way. Crowds on the street finally blocked the tram, so Benesch had climbed off and found a position where he had an unobstructed view of the colorful regiment.

While he watched the parade, Heinrich Benesch, gentle Heinrich Benesch, imagined what would become of these boys. As the soldiers marched in even columns, the horses pranced, and children tagged behind the troops, Benesch predicted the most predictable destiny for them—the soldiers were marching to their graves, he decided—not a difficult prophecy to make, the only variable being the time between now and then. And suddenly, for a moment, with the sunlight paling the soldiers' chins, the top half of their faces hidden in their helmets' shadow, Benesch saw destiny at work: he saw the waxen, expressionless faces begining to melt, the skin dripping from the skulls, coagulating in thick clumps in the hollow of their necks. As their legs scissored and their heels clacked against the pavement, their faces softened, the eyes and mouths disappearing beneath the folds of melting flesh. These boys were going abroad to a war that hadn't been declared, and none of them would return alive. Of course, if anyone had asked, Benesch would have admitted that they were only marching back to the armory, as they did every week.

As soon as the parade had passed and the spectators dispersed, Benesch leaned against a signpost to steady himself. He had watched Vienna's sons march to their deaths. He had to struggle against the impulse to run after them, and he stood with his eyes closed for a good five minutes or more, trying to figure out why he had conjured up such a morbid vision. Never before had he been overcome by such conviction; yet it had been an oddly satisfying certainty; yes, the presentiment had pleased him. And he had only to realize that he had enjoyed the horror to know that his own desire was the provocateur—desire had transformed the military parade into a funeral procession, an unnatural, mawkish desire. He had seen what he had wanted to see—the death of the Empire—and had mistaken his contemptible wish for a lucid moment of clairvoyance. And now it appeared that his young friend had done the same.

"You confuse your wishes with truths," Benesch says gently. "We Viennese have so few facts and we learn to make do with gossip and rumors. We are poseurs, self-made oracles. What do you really know about the future? You know what you want, that's all."

"I know that I am different, Herr Benesch."

"You hope so."

"My work proves that I am different."

"But you cannot know how time will change you."

"I can feel my future here, in my hands, and here, behind my eyes. If you could feel it too, you would agree with me. I don't belong to myself, Herr Benesch, I belong to you and to your son, to Arthur Roessler, to Klimt as well, to my friends, to strangers, to children who are yet to be born." With that he spreads his arms, palms turned outward in melodramatic mimicry of sacrifice, a gesture that makes it difficult for Benesch to gauge the sincerity of his claim.

Much Too Much

EGON Schiele's mistress, Vallie Neuzil, could play all types, a harlequin with as many costumes as there were men to admire her—sensual, nubile, plump, dexterous, moody, secretive, gentle, sinewy. She would never end up as one of the aged whores who begged at the back door of convents for food, women who had been pointed out to me by my grandmother in Vienna when I was younger, unlucky women who soaked themselves in cheap fragrance and smelled like bouquets of flowers sharing an open coffin with a corpse, women with roan teeth and bellies distended from beer.

At first I had eyed the artist's mistress with fear, wondering whether poverty or loneliness had driven her into his arms. But the more I saw of her—at the market, on the street—the more I became convinced that he was the weaker one. And sure enough, the first time I dared to look through the bedroom window I saw him tucked against her curved body, twitching and moaning in some frightful dream while she slept placidly. Sleep—this was the first picture I would have liked to paint: sleep in its opposite states, troubled and serene, resisting time and forgetful of time, anxious sleep and healing sleep.

As I stood on the wheelbarrow below the bedroom window, something in the artist's dream startled him awake, and he sat up, baffled, rubbing his eyes. In a moment he would look toward the window, see my fingers pressed against the glass—he would leap from his bed and pursue me into the meadow. When he caught me he would use me as my grandmother said Turkish workmen in Vienna used careless girls, and then he would crush my skull with a flat stone so I could never tell anyone what he had done to me. Villain. I watched as he pinched sand from his tear ducts and swung his legs over the side of the bed, one hand submerged in his groin, scratching his testicles, his limp penis an eerie silvery color. Still intoxicated with sleep, he wandered from the room, and I stepped down from the wheelbarrow and crept around the house to the front porch, to the studio window. I waited for him to appear in the room, waited like a coil of wire hidden in a piece of raw meat, waited until the grass began to hiss and rattle from a morning breeze.

"Who sent you here?"

I jumped back, staggered away from the impossible sight of the artist standing before me, a towel wrapped hastily around his middle, his uncombed hair quivering in the wind. I stumbled, fell with a dull thud and scrambled to my feet. Egon Schiele blinked, his eyes glinting like the flash of white on a starling's wing.

"What do you want with me?" he asked softly, and I just stared at him, unable to defend myself, accepting my ruin, accepting as well the cigarette he offered me from a pack concealed in his hand. I let it hang between my lips while he struck a match, then puffed mechanically, my throat sealed so only my cheeks ballooned, and the smoke dribbled from my mouth. I had never smoked a cigarette before; nor I had ever been caught peering through the window of a stranger's cottage.

Clearly he considered me a deranged peasant girl, and I couldn't utter a word to prove him wrong. But I could pull away, which I did when he reached for my elbow. I felt his condescension in his touch as strongly as I had heard it in his voice the day I had brought him the museum catalogue. He was a modern rebel from the city, and I a dated, cowardly romantic, who had been excitedly planning a masterpiece that I would never begin: *Sleep*. I was provincial, puritanical, homely, and he was New Vienna—proud, bellicose, important.

He took a step forward, and I kept my eyes focused on his puckered nipples and the few strands of hair curled on his thin chest. He brushed the back of the hand holding the cigarette box against my face. Instead of the heat of shame I felt bone against bone, his fingers against my skull—a touch without nuance, without meaning.

"At least tell me your name," he said—an objectionable demand, reminding me of my identity again when there should have been no facts, no names, no identities. And right then the smoke reached my lungs. I buckled with a fit of coughing, my tongue as helpless as a wad of cotton in my mouth, saliva beading on my lips. The artist motioned me to be quiet, caught me from behind, pressed his hand over my lips. How would he explain himself if his mistress woke? Naked, having a smoke with a girl from the village . . . I struggled furiously, forgetting my timidity in my need for oxygen, aware even while I tried to peel his hands away that somehow, helpless in his arms, I was in control. But too quickly he released me, and the porch seemed to tilt so I could hardly stay upright. I staggered away from the garden cottage, while the artist called with breathy laughter, a feeble attempt to prove himself superior again: "Wait, little friend, come back! Tell me who sent you!"

Once I had gained the road I settled into an easy jog, the earth leveled to a horizontal plane again, pebbles squirted from beneath my shoes, and my lungs filled with spring, with the good smells of soaked pastures and mulch. He had held me so firmly, yet it had been so easy to escape. The artist had tried to protect his reputation, while I had nearly disgraced him. I savored the lingering taste of tobacco and wondered if his hands had left a mark on my cheek.

•

Trieste: "Situated at the northeastern corner of the Adriatic Sea, seventy miles northeast of Venice. Made into a *colonia* by Julius Caesar, surrounded by ramparts under the order of Octavius." While Egon read aloud, Gerti drew a profile of a bearded man on the compartment window with red crayon, trailing the whiskers from chin to sill. How fortunate that her only companion on this trip was her brother—they had never before been so free, and she felt just like a bride when the conductor came round for tickets. Indeed, by tilting the brim of her straw hat over her forehead she could make herself look older than her twelve years. She was, after all, only four years younger than her mama had been when she married Adolf Schiele and went on a honeymoon to Trieste.

The children were repeating the honeymoon, traveling from Vienna to the sea. When they were waiting on the platform in the station, Gerti had noticed Egon looking proudly at her, as a man might stare at his new wife. But they were brother and sister, not newlyweds, and had begged permission from their uncle to visit Trieste. They would stay overnight in the same hotel where their parents had stayed, perhaps in the same room with bougainvillea-flowered wallpaper and Tiffany lamps. Gerti wondered if her father had held her mother's hand like Egon held hers as they traveled on the Southern Railway toward the Semmering Pass, through the tunnels and round on a viaduct, one hundred and fifty feet above a wide granite-walled ravine. Even with the window closed, the air in the compartment smelled of pine resin.

She interrupted Egon's reading to say that the mountains were so charming, she would like to live someday in an alpine cottage and she hoped it would be a long while before the train began to descend. Egon assured her that Graz was a long way off, Trieste even farther, and in between there would be more mountains to cross, with castle ruins, purple heather, and waterfalls.

When he first suggested the trip, Egon expected his mother to furiously dismiss the idea, but instead she had exclaimed with delighted surprise, clapping first her cheeks and then his. Trieste. He had often heard her speak of her honeymoon in Trieste. After her husband died it would have been a simple matter to arrange a trip, but she preferred worshipping Trieste from afar, through obscuring memory. And now she could travel to the Adriatic without ruining the past—her children would be her eyes and ears, and the old experience wouldn't be corrupted by the new.

Her darling son, her little genius—if only he would listen to her and study to be an engineer, learn the mysteries of machines rather than waste his youth splattering blank paper with paint. Men who understand how to build and repair machines control the world; men who can invent machines control the future. "Why must you make such ugly pictures?" she had asked her son too many times to count. When Uncle Leopold refused Egon's request for money to pay for the trip to Trieste, Frau Schiele argued on her children's behalf, reasoning that Egon would have a chance to ride one of the most magnificent trains of the world—the Semmering Line, built in 1854 and christened by the young emperor himself. Egon should have the chance to experience this extraordinary engineering feat—he might come to desire influence of a much larger scope than his art would ever provide.

But Egon cared more for the as-yet-unseen Adriatic than for the mountain landscape. The sea: only a turquoise tint on postcards, a dull sepia brown in photographs. He hoped there would be a storm that night, and he and Gerti could stand at the window and watch lightning split apart the sky. He had brought a sketch pad, colored pencils, and watercolors—he would draw Gerti rising from the night sea, Gerti carried aloft on the crest of a wave, her nipples as brown as the the buttons on his overcoat, her hair tangled, her thin legs curled under her like the legs of a newborn foal. He would call it *Tide of Youth*.

In the last few years, Gerti had been Egon's most inspiring model. But lately she had begun to change, and Egon realized that soon she would be lost to him. He would never love another as he loved her. Her lids hung heavily, flirtatiously, over her eyes, her pert smile seemed more an invitation than a spontaneous expression of pleasure, and more than once he had found her standing silently in front of a sketch, squinting, as if she were searching for some minute clue to herself.

In the past, whenever he had asked her to model for him, she had undressed willingly, scrambling out of her pleated skirt and blouse and standing obediently in some awkward position, her arms raised, one foot pressed against the opposite knee at a right angle, or perhaps on her hands and knees, wagging her little bottom at him. To Gerti, modesty was a chore, like sewing, like mathematics, that other children learned, while her brother had been her tutor and had cultivated in her an innocent self-love, a naive confidence. But Egon knew that time was contaminating her, estranging her from her body, making her ashamed. Soon he would have to find another girl to inspire him.

He glanced up from his book to watch as his sister licked the fingers of her left hand and added the rim of a monocle to the face on the window. How much time did they have left together before her body became a secret, hidden from both of them? "Wouldn't you like to visit Capodistria?" he asked, simply because he wanted to hear the sound of his sister's voice. But she continued to work on her cartoon without replying, so Egon prodded: "But that's a full day's trip, and we won't have time."

"We shall do whatever we want," she declared. Her eyes met her brother's, and she turned back to the other gentleman, the figure on the window.

She was growing coy, Egon thought. Demure. Insincere. His

Gerti. "They call Capodistria the little sister to Venice," he said, "but we only have one night in Trieste. We won't have time to visit Capodistria."

"We shall go all the way to Rome if we want—we have money and no one can stop us."

"And if we don't return home in two nights, who will Uncle blame? I am responsible for you."

"You can do what you want. I'm going to collect snails, I'll have a hundred snails in each pocket of my skirt before the end of the day. And I won't give you any if you remain in such a cross mood."

How had his little sister acquired this art of coquetry, sheltered in the abbey town of Klosterneuburg? But she was right to scold him —Trieste promised adventure and even if Gerti would eventually reject him, for two days he had her all to himself. For Egon, this honeymoon trip signaled an end, but it would be a glorious end—in place of Gerti he would have an indissoluble memory.

Egon didn't pay much attention to the city of Graz as they passed through, but Gerti pointed at the steep Schlossberg rising over the rooftops, at the ghostly clock tower, at the tulips lined like spectators alongside the train tracks. And beyond Graz there were more hills with ruins and peasant huts, then the bald, glittering cliffs of the coal quarries, and then more mountains with a few pine and larch saplings bristling on otherwise barren slopes.

When the landscape was hidden in darkness Gerti fell asleep, her head propped against the profile on the window. She would be angry at Egon for letting her sleep through the frosted Alps. But he wanted these mountains for himself, these pocked, jagged mountains fixed like broken teeth on either side, the train crawling as quietly, as tentatively as a fly on a sleeping man's chin. And he wanted Gerti for himself. He watched the edges of her nostrils dilating slightly, the mist collecting on the glass over the crayoned lips. In sleep she seemed a child again. He gently removed her hat and set it on the seat beside him.

Hours later he shook his sister awake: "Gerti, we're here!"

"Home?"

"Trieste. Come on now, and don't forget your hat."

"Trieste?" To Gerti, in the haze of her dissipating dream, the train had traveled in a circle from the station in Vienna through a fairytale landscape and back again. She heard compartment doors slam, the wheels of hand trolleys rattle, travelers calling to assemble their groups—the same sounds she had heard at the start of the journey. And the same smells: steam, metal, grimy concrete, urine, cigarettes. Trieste? This station was no different from any station in Vienna, except that here the porters wore work clothes instead of uniforms and the café inside had no tables, so the men stood in a cramped row at the bar, sipping coffee, chattering in Italian. The Italian that Gerti had heard the cobbler in Klosterneuburg speak seemed coarse in comparison to this musical language. Maybe Trieste wasn't any less grand than Vienna, maybe Trieste was a different world entirely, Austria's possession only on paper, in truth Rome's progeny. Gerti had never been—more importantly, had never felt—so far away from home.

The squat, aging buildings outside the station had none of the flourish of the Viennese baroque, but here the colors were more varied, a blur of pastel walls. Gerti wanted to know the fastest route to the water and did not bother to admonish Egon for letting her sleep through the final leg of the trip, for she relished the surprise of waking up such a long way from her demanding uncle and from the cramped room she shared with her older sister. What would she do first? Something criminal, something unforgivable.

Before she could decide, Egon grabbed his sister's free arm and began to stutter her name, just like a flustered beau, Gerti thought, like a fellow with a flaccid tongue trying to declare his love. She shook him off, told him curtly that she hoped their hotel was nearby. But Egon still dangled at the beginning of some unutterable sentence, saying, "Gerti, but Gerti . . . ," her name falling like one dead leaf among a flurry of leaves, among the voices of other travelers hurrying through the doors of the station.

"Won't you, Gerti, please . . . sit for me this afternoon?"

The family artist, their own wunderkind. Long ago their aunt had predicted that he would either die famous or in jail—such a fervent passion must have consequence. And even hundreds of miles from home, on vacation, he thought of nothing but his art. But Gerti had other concerns and she pulled him across the street, crying out to a passing sailor, "Which way to the sea?" The sailor plunged one hand into the red nest of his beard as if he would find a map there. Then he pointed down the main avenue. Gerti released Egon and ran as fast as she could, for she knew the water wouldn't wait for her, and

Egon let her lead the way, certain that by not answering directly she had given her consent, and he could make a dozen studies of Gerti in Trieste—he would show her what she was becoming, how she was changing, he would provide her with a chronicle, a visual testimony of his own observations.

As they skirted the edge of a public garden, Gerti released Egon's hand and reached through the wrought-iron fence to pluck a yellow crocus, tucking the stem behind her ear so the satiny trumpet bounced against the side of her face. The smell of the garden contaminated Egon's mood—it was the stale, hopeless smell of winter, though the spring flowers were in bloom and the Mediterranean sun heated the afternoon with an illusory warmth; the next rain would turn to sleet, flattening the new flowers, and the cold would return. Egon preferred crisp, autumnal colors, honest, practical colors to these ripe shades. Spring—the most deceptive season, and his sister was intoxicated by its false promises.

With the bay in sight, Egon paused to set down the two suitcases and catch his breath. When he found Gerti again, she was already bribing a sunburnt fisherman with a few kreuzer for the use of his rowboat. The fisherman winked at Egon as he approached, his grin suggesting that this young wench must be more than anyone could handle. So Egon moved between his sister and the fisherman, assuming the role of principal barterer, noticing only after he had begun to load the luggage into the boat that his sister had already slipped away and was dashing up a lane cluttered with empty fishmonger carts.

Gerti, as inconstant as weather. Egon waited on the dock for a few minutes, then lowered himself into the boat—they had paid for the use of it, after all. With his eyes closed, the water sloshing below the thin boards, he savored this unfamiliar buoyancy—he had been boating on mountain lakes and along stretches of the Danube but he had never floated on salt water. Thick as jam, almost the color of marmalade. He dipped his hand, leaned over to taste the puddle in his cupped palm just as the boat tilted dangerously, not from his own shifted weight but from Gerti, who was straddling the small bow area. Her arms were full of oranges, and he noticed that she had lost the crocus. She handed the oranges one by one to Egon—if she had stolen them, as he suspected, he didn't want to know, so without a word he accepted the fruit. Gerti untied the rope to the dock ring, pushed off, and Egon manned the oars, the oranges tumbling off his lap to the bottom of the boat.

"Die Freiheit des Meers!" Gerti shrieked, delighted with her mastery of such a poetic phrase, and Egon understood that she meant to refer to the picture he should draw: a boating-at-Trieste scene. *Die Freiheit des Meers!* But he had no interest in artificial lines and colors right now; instead he gave himself up to the motion of rowing, the oars splashing in unison, the tendons in his lank arms tightening as the muscles strained. If he had paused to reflect, he would have cursed his fixed-image art, and if his mother had seen her son completely absorbed in the sport, she would have called his attention to the miracle of mechanical speed: "So why don't you study to be an engineer?"

Gerti listed the sights as Egon rowed: the stack of a steamship behind the breakwater, a fleet of fishing boats, a bright yellow sail, and there, a marble palace further down the coast.

"That must be Miramare," Egon murmured without turning his head.

"Miramare," echoed Gerti. On the train Egon had read about Maximilian of Miramare, who had enthroned himself as Mexico's first emperor and had suffered for his presumption. His gentle wife, Charlotte, had prevailed upon Napoleon and the Pope to help her husband protect his title and though she had won their sympathy they offered no support, so her husband was court-martialed and executed by his Mexican opponents in Querétaro, and poor Charlotte lost her mind. Why would anyone leave Trieste for Mexico, Egon wondered, steering the rowboat toward the stairs that descended to the water and disappeared below the surface. He reached for the edge of the lowest marble precipice, trying to imagine how it would be if he were Maximilian before his lust for power destroyed him and if Gerti were Charlotte before her husband had ever been to Mexico.

His arms felt rubbery, his tongue dry from the salt water. With his knife he pierced the skin of an orange and squeezed the pulp and warm liquid into his mouth, then he threw the fruit into the water and yawned in delicious exhaustion. Meanwhile Gerti secured the boat to a ring on the balustrade. As she collected the oranges from the bilge, Egon tugged playfully on her skirt, yanking down the loose elastic waist an inch. With a yelp Gerti pulled away from him, darted up the steps and cut across the courtyard. A few strollers idly turned their heads to watch her, and a dachshund on a leash tried to nip at her ankles as she rushed by.

She headed for a wooded area adjacent to the garden, and Egon, leaving the suitcases in the boat, caught up and passed her, so that now she was pursuing him, her beloved Maximilian, and they were running away from Mexico, the land of failed republics and revolutions. Some said the heat of Mexico had weakened Princess Charlotte's reason, others said her nervous collapse resulted from her meeting with Napoleon. But today the lighthearted Charlotte had returned intact to Miramare, laden with oranges, laughing as she tracked Maximilian, who hid behind a sycamore trunk and sprang out to frighten her, jostling the pyramid of oranges, causing them to spill onto the ground.

They decided to spread their picnic here, beneath the sycamores and elms, where the shade offered some privacy, making it easier to play their games. To Gerti, they had come to Miramare for a honeymoon picnic and she was a bride, a stationmaster's new wife; to Egon, Gerti was a would-be emperor's darling and they were enjoying their own estate.

"Let me see you now," he cajoled, but she ignored him, brushing away a plump black ant that had begun to climb over the buckle of her shoe. "I want to see you here, in the woods of Miramare." Gerti tossed a pebble at him, and in mock rage he leaped upon her, clawing at the collar of her blouse, forgetting the rules of this game as he tugged at her clothes; like a lusting, selfish emperor he forced himself upon his bride.

But Gerti knew that a stationmaster needed to be reminded of his place. Just as her mother surely would have done, she spit on her aggressive mate and tore the brown curls from his scalp and tried to catch his forearm between her teeth.

Mad Princess Charlotte! She had given up her sanity for her husband's sake, though he had preferred Mexico to his wife. Egon caught the princess by her arms, unbuttoned her collar and wrapped his fingers around her neck, massaging those tender spots behind her ears, whispering, "Miramare," because he sensed the word had magical power, moving his hands over the knobs of her shoulders as she relaxed, unfastening hooks, opening her blouse. Hard little disks bulged beneath her nipples, and he pressed his fingers against them to feel the change. She was smiling now, telling him with her eyes that she would do anything. Mad Princess Charlotte.

If visitors to Miramare had happened to be strolling along the wooded paths that April afternoon in 1906 and had seen the tangle of bodies, they might have tried to rescue Gerti Schiele, beating off her assailant with their walking sticks, shouting for the police. Or they might have turned abruptly, offended by the scene, and hurried back in the direction of the palace.

•

Some day, May, 1912: What has happened to the familiar? Egon is surrounded by degenerates who stare at him with contempt or curiosity or paw at his arms and ask if he has any *Tschiks,* cigarette butts for them to chew. He looks around for help, but the guard on duty ignores his charges—he has sauntered over to the foot of the watchtower and is calling, "Any sign of land, brother?" The guards of St. Pölten carry on this long-standing joke, pretending that they are rogues on a galley lost at sea. Egon Schiele would have liked to pretend that he was riding in the belly of a ship, but fulsome reality presses in, surrounds and traps him in the prison yard. The men want him to confess his crime, and when he tells them that he doesn't know why he is here, that on April 13, a constable and a municipal officer had appeared at his cottage door with a warrant for his arrest and without an explanation, the prisoners laugh their jeering, predatory laugh. Egon looks at the stained, misaligned teeth in their open mouths. These underworld criminals stink like drenched dogs; he stamps his foot to be rid of them.

One inmate with a few tufts of red hair clinging to his freckled scalp points at Egon's American shoes, kisses his fingertips in appreciation and asks if he could have the shoes in exchange for something of his own—for his cell blanket or a postcard of a woman wearing seashells and black boots. Egon threatens him with his fist and the next thing he knows someone has kicked him in the back of his knees. The inmates catch him before he falls and support him by his elbows, lifting him until his feet dangle above the ground.

The circle of tormentors opens, and the guard ambles toward the center. He touches Egon's chin with the whip of his riding crop, moves closer and trails the tip of the handle along Egon's nose. "Is there something wrong?" he asks, peering intently at Egon's ear, curling the whip around his lobe. No one replies. "We don't want any troublemakers," he croons almost seductively. Egon notices that one of his pupils is dilated, the black disk completely eclipsing the iris. This eye moves sluggishly, blind in the Cyclops-head, and the skin around the good eye has intricate crow's-feet from the strain of squinting.

Perhaps he is discomforted by Egon's scrutiny—Egon would like to believe so. With a short guffaw the guard backs out of the circle and returns to his post beside the ladder. The men release Egon, shove him through the hole of their tight huddle, and he feels a brief exhilaration at his release. But the circle of bodies is enclosed by less malleable walls and by a concrete-colored sky. There can be no escape from St. Pölten.

He wanders toward the other solitary prisoner, an old man nibbling food from his cupped hands—raisins perhaps, or shelled nuts. His lips are a deep cherry red, with a bluish hue around the edges. Drawing near, Egon sees that the mound on the man's hand is actually a dollop of mud, which he pinches and shapes into a ball; then he sweeps his tongue around the flattened palm to lick up the bits that crumble off his little sculpture. But the intricate work doesn't completely absorb him. After a few minutes he glances up at Egon and asks, "Here, you! What do you want?"

"I am an artist," Egon confides, "just like you."

The old man erupts in a gravelly howl of delight, and the other prisoners gather to watch this new spectacle, forming a horseshoe around the two artists of St. Pölten. When the madman hiccoughs, the mud drops like a turd from his hand.

•

On New Year's Eve, 1904, Egon's father belched, and the blade of the razor nicked him. In the kitchen Melanie baked apples and Egon tied Gerti to a chair with string, while in their parents' bedroom Marie set the razor on the table beside the shaving mug. The mug had been her present to her husband four years ago, a special gift to mark the turn of the century. Marie had found a potter in a nearby village who agreed to paint a winter scene of the Tulln station house on the enamel, and a capable job he had done, taking care with such details as frost on the windowpanes and lettering the family's name in elegant script. Marie's sister declared it the finest mug in all of Austria, and the potter assured her that the glaze would hold through her lifetime; if any cracks appeared he would reglaze the mug for free.

Marie blotted the blood-laced lather as she reminisced about that special holiday. Sometimes she wished she had never crossed the threshold into this century—the last years had brought nothing but trouble, what with Adolf's sickness and the creditors after him and the strife between Adolf and his children. Still, how thrilling it had been to watch the new epoch replace the old at the stroke of twelve. Marie had sung Bohemian folk songs while her children pranced around the kitchen and Adolf shook a tambourine. Wild as Gypsies they had been that New Year's Eve. Marie sang herself hoarse, and Adolf drank bock beer out of his new shaving mug.

And later, after everyone had gone to bed, Marie had put on her husband's coat and sheepskin cap and slipped outside. The air of the twentieth century froze the mucus in her nostrils, but the cold felt purifying, as if all the dirt of the past had been blown away by winter winds. Everything had seemed brand-new—the snow, the stars, the bricks of the station house—all as fresh and solid as the enamel baked on her husband's shaving mug, and the train tracks were the trail left behind by the potter who had designed the panorama. Marie knew she shouldn't linger in the cold but she couldn't bring herself to return to the house, not when a century had just been born. So she followed the path beside the tracks, her shoes leaving shallow prints in the crust of snow, the sound like a tassel brushing against Adolf's tambourine. That night Marie had felt as though the years ahead belonged entirely to her, as though she owned the century. What would she do with one hundred years? Why, give them away, of course—to her children, to her husband, to anyone who had promise or ambition.

As it turned out, Adolf Schiele had been less ambitious than she had hoped, and only four years into the new century he lost all interest in his affairs. Even as she scraped the razor over his cheek, slicing off the tops of his tiny pimples, drawing more blood, she knew that this time she was grooming him for his coffin. The doctor had predicted that he wouldn't survive through Christmas. But while Adolf had grown indifferent to his life, terror kept him fighting, and that very morning Marie's brother-in-law Leopold had

said, "Our Adolf is finally doing something right." He meant that
because Adolf was prolonging his life into the new year, his family
would be assured a larger pension. Marie thought Leopold's comment vulgar, though as 1904 came to a close she couldn't help but
consider how a few extra kronen would help: Egon needed a new
winter coat, Gerti needed shoes. Even with the higher pension, her
elder daughter would have to keep working at the ticket booth,
unless they accepted the invitation to move in with Marie's sister
and brother-in-law in Klosterneuburg. If only Adolf had gone for
treatment when the lesions first appeared or when his hair began to
fall out in wiry, black clumps, like strands pulled from a horse's
mane. When he saw the hair in his bathwater or on his pillow he
would bellow in rage, and Marie would leave him alone, locking the
bedroom door behind her. She had feared for her children but not
for herself—Adolf had never raised his hand against her and never
would. As docile as his wife was, he must have sensed, even in his
madness, that she would cling to her shred of dignity and desert him
if he ever struck her.

A fine trick he had played, though, letting the disease run its
course—now he was abandoning her before she could do the same.
Still, Marie felt mostly pity for the dying man as she drew the blade
along the ridge of his sunken cheek. Incontinent, delirious . . . no
one deserved to suffer such degradation, and really it would be for
the best if the end came quickly, but not too quickly, of course, not
until tomorrow, January 1, 1905. Seven hours to midnight. For his
sake she hoped he wouldn't wake again. She would have changed
the sheets if she hadn't been afraid of disturbing him, but she chose
to let him lie in his own filth rather than risk provoking another fit.
She dabbed at the soap that the razor had missed. If only he would
expire quietly, in his sleep. She imagined smothering her husband
with the pillow to hurry him through his misery—an ugly thought,
put in her head by the same demon who at that moment took possession of Adolf Schiele, causing him to tremble, imperceptibly at
first, then more rapidly, like water coming to a boil. The convulsion
caused the bed to rock, the headboard banged against the wall, and
Marie, afraid that her children would hear, begged Adolf to be still.
She pinned his arms to the mattress and called out his name. But
then she felt an odd torpor stealing over her, as though all her
strength had been siphoned into her husband to fuel his tremors,

and she collapsed back into the chair, helpless, feeling nothing except a bland curiosity as the body before her succumbed. Beads of sweat gathered on his lower lip and his eyes widened hungrily, as if he wanted to devour the images around him—the ceiling, the candy-striped wallpaper, his wife.

Long after her husband lay still, Marie mistook the blur of her vision for the blur of life, and she recognized death only when Adolf's right eye, askew in its socket, caught her gaze. The first thing she thought was that she would have to find Adolf's Austrian Railway dress uniform, complete with epaulets and dagger. Then she understood what had been lost—unexpectedly, the absence ached, her shoulders folded over, she collapsed into the hole left by Adolf Schiele. Her husband, her name. She had expected to feel some sorrow and a trace of relief, not this engulfing pain for a man she had despised—yes, she had hated her husband, and his last act of spite was to die without giving her a chance to either cure or absolve herself of hatred.

When Melanie carried the tea and baked apple to her parents' bedroom, she found her mother and father staring wordlessly at each other, like gorgons who had turned each other to stone. Marie's elder daughter set the tray on the bedside table and with extraordinary presence of mind she pressed her fingers over the frog skin of her papa's eyelids and lowered them, as she had seen the priest do to her sister Elvira years ago. She asked if she should send Egon for the doctor. Marie didn't reply, so Melanie resolved to take charge of the arrangements; she would delay her own grief and see to it that her father was treated honorably.

But before she reached the door her mother snapped, "I will tell you when to go," in a voice unnaturally fierce, as brittle as Adolf's voice had been. Melanie hung back in the shadows, frightened by the stranger in her mother's chair.

Eventually little Gerti appeared, having been graciously released from her bonds by Egon. And minutes later, Egon arrived, sensing the truth even as he walked down the hall. He found the girls standing beside the bed, Melanie's arm slung over her little sister's shoulders, and as only son and heir to his father's name, he assumed his place next to his mother's chair. He stared at the bars of red on the wallpaper so he wouldn't have to look at the dead man's porous face, the greased curls of his mustache, the ashen lips; he balanced on one leg, folding the other against his bottom, and when he grew tired he sat cross-legged on the floor. His sisters did the same.

As the hour wore on, Gerti's thumb found its way into her mouth, her head sank into her sister's lap, and Egon, forgetting his age, forgetting his newly assumed role as head of the family, wrapped himself around his mother's ankles. Soon the children were breathing evenly, softly, inhaling through their mouths to keep out the smell of their father's death.

Marie Schiele would have liked to sleep. But she wasn't going to allow her husband to deprive the family of their pension—she intended to report to the doctor that Adolf Schiele had passed away at dawn on the first day of the new year. She would keep the gas turned high, the flame blazing behind the grate. The body must be kept warm if she were to collect the money due her. It was 1905. Already the century felt withered, spent.

•

A famous dialogue in Gustav Klimt's atelier garden: Peonies, wisteria, nightshade, bleeding hearts, grapevines, rose trellises. The metallic clatter of a tram on the Josefstädterstrasse. Two wicker rockers, filmy sunlight, a skin of dew. Coffee in hammered silver cups— Hoffmann originals. A calfskin lampshade behind the window. Gustav's bare feet—one crooked middle toe—wool robe, hands tucked into the sleeves, eyes closed, tiny muscles twitching at the corner of his lips. Emilie's hair. A simple wrought-iron bench. A photograph of the athlete Sammer, a gold-plated leaf covering his groin. Silence. Gustav's critical eye turned inward. Where, he is wondering, can one find beauty, Schiller's "lofty serenity and freedom of spirit"? The sensitive clitoris hidden beneath the folds of a woman's skin. The brilliant visceral red inside the vaginal cavity. Emilie's black-and-white robe. Time like water—viscous, slow. Without opening his eyes, Gustav raises the cup to his lips. Emilie and Gustav in the garden. Emilie and Gustav and Egon Schiele.

Emilie: "Who are you? Why didn't you knock?"

Egon: "I want to talk to Gustav Klimt. Herr Klimt, I have come to see, to ask you . . ."

A portfolio of black chalk and watercolor. Gouache on canvas. Leopold at the piano. The artist's mother. Summer nights. Egon masturbating. A forest shrine.

Egon: "Please, do I have any talent?"
Silence.
Gustav: "Much too much."

•

Will Frau Harms permit her daughters to be escorted to the cinema by that good-for-nothing from across the street, the one who has been heard whooping in the middle of the night like an Apache and who spends an hour every day buffing his pointed white shoes? Most assuredly not! But Edith and Adele are old enough to know what proper decorum entails, they won't put themselves at risk. Besides, Egon Schiele already has a lady friend.

"Dear Fräulein Ed. and Ad., or Ad. and Ed. I believe that your Frau Mama will permit you to go with Vallie and me to the movies, or to the Apollo, or wherever you want. You may rest assured that in reality I am entirely different from an 'Apache'!"

Pigeons never chortle so seductively as they do on a December morning in Vienna, tucked beneath a windowsill, their purr like the hum of a coal furnace, the sound as warm as a woman's hands tucked inside an ermine muff, and on the day that Egon will take Ed. and Ad. to the movies he wakes with the pigeons, absorbs their heat, feels an unfamiliar yet pleasurable anticipation. Usually he is too restless to lie in bed in the morning, but today he would like to remain on this sliver of a mattress forever, waiting, listening to the pigeons, Vallie squeezed between him and the wall, her knees drawn up, the soles of her feet pressed against his thigh. He traces the bumps of her curved spine, not worrying that he will disturb her, for Vallie has a great talent for sleep and probably wouldn't wake if Egon pricked her with a pin.

He stares at the ceiling, his hand coming to rest on Vallie's round shoulder, and he tries to invent a comforting fantasy to absorb this urgent and unfounded expectation. He is not sure exactly what he wants, not sure whether his desire involves a woman. Certainly his mistress plays no part. Vallie: not an impeccable housekeeper by any means, nor as quick-witted as he might wish, but as honest as he'd ever find, with an incomparable sense of humor. He knows she deserves better than he can give her—a steady income, a few weeks in a mountain spa, occasional dinners at the Hotel Imperial, a new silk gown. Most of all, she deserves a man's respect. Egon has used her as he uses the rest of the world, always calculating her next portrait, though over the years Vallie has become less an inspiration than a responsibility and would never be Gerti Peschka's equal. Egon still prefers to have his younger sister sit for him.

As he considers this, he comes to understand one aspect of his emotion, as a man might succeed in identifying a single spice in an unfamiliar dish: he feels certain that today he will discover an important inspiration for his work. Perhaps the Harms sisters have something to do with his confidence—Edith and Adele, Adele and Edith —perhaps they are the source of his optimism. Today his success seems perfectly logical, the years behind him preparation for the years ahead, a gradual ascent, no wasted hours. Soon he shall begin his masterpiece.

How simple it is. He feels as though he has lived inside the earth for twenty-four years, sucking juices from tree roots, and suddenly he has woken from his incubation, woken with the pigeons, unencumbered by the present, knowing that the untimely death he predicted for himself was nothing but a fiction, a pompous lie, his defense against the humiliation of age. An obsolete defense. He will grow old, and his reputation will take care of itself.

How marvelous, this grip of space upon his skin, the sound of the birds, the rectangles of sunlight shining like mirrors on the wall opposite the window. Yes, soon he shall begin his masterpiece. And then begin again. His only regret is that he must leave Vallie behind.

•

In the latter half of the nineteenth century, the feuilletonists of Vienna sounded an increasingly bitter and nostalgic note, indicating the resistance of many intellectuals to the unprecedented reconstruction of their city.

"In this age of resignation and melancholy," lamented the typical feuilleton, "we too easily forget our heritage. The virtues of the past are steadily vanishing beneath the wrecker's lead ball. Our musicians entreat us to accept the loss with their sentimental farewell songs, our artists glorify the fantastic and the foreign, our architects celebrate monstrosity, and alchemists pose as scientists. Look at the state of young people today: self-absorbed, atheistic, impetuous, irreverent. What has happened to Biedermeier piety? What has happened to gentlemen like Mayor Lueger, men with golden Viennese hearts and an incomparable knowledge of wines? Why, they are busy dandling in their *chambres séparées* while their sons deflower the daughters of greengrocers."

Vienna had been scarred by nineteenth-century disasters, by the scourge of cholera, by the Stock Exchange *Krach*, by the Ringtheater fire, and perhaps most deeply, by the famous tragedy at Mayerling. In 1889 the double suicide of Prince Rudolf and Marie Vetsera at the hunting lodge of Mayerling attracted international attention, while in Austria the Emperor Franz Josef tried futilely to suppress the truth by censoring the newspapers and issuing an official court version of the incident. Mayerling became a public secret, and the young Prince Rudolf and the girl Marie a public obsession.

Perhaps, to the embittered feuilletonists, Mayerling not only signaled a historical change but also could be held responsible for the decay of morality. Perhaps they blamed Prince Rudolf for influencing the offspring of the city's political elite, for corrupting the name of Vienna, for abandoning his title and his nation. Whatever the feuilletonists thought, for years they were forced to remain silent on this issue, and Mayerling remained a burdensome, festering memory, with many questions unresolved.

Recent generations have returned to that day of January 30, 1889, with voyeuristic passion, speculating about causes and motives and actions. Was Marie Vetsera a victim or a conspirator? What did the Emperor say about the matter to his wife, who appeared publicly only in full mourning after the death of her son? Others may be inclined to wonder about the hours between Marie Vetsera's death and Rudolf's death: what did Rudolf do, alone in the hunting lodge, for the six hours (the coroner's estimate) after he had killed Marie and before he shot himself? What did he think? And what have been the repercussions of those mysterious six hours upon the rest of the world?

Kept Women

IN 1921 I moved to Munich. Egon Schiele had been dead for three years, my mother for nine years, my father lived in a pensioner's home and could not remember his name, and I had married a man who wore a gold-rimmed pince-nez. He accepted a job managing a bookstore on the Schellingstrasse, and we rented the apartment above the store.

One evening in the winter of 1923 we had arranged to dine with friends, and I came down early to browse. My husband was finishing with his last customer, a shrill-voiced woman seeking information on the Avignon popes. Among the display of new publications a certain title caught my eye; I picked up the thin book and turned it over in my hands as if it were a letter to me that I didn't want to open, a letter from a forgotten lover—as indeed it proved to be, a letter from Neulengbach's unwanted artist, published for any indiscriminate eye. I looked up quickly, expecting to see my husband smirking at my discovery, thinking this was a trap he had set, but I found him still attending to his customer. I had never mentioned the Schiele affair to him: the name Schiele meant little to my husband, whose tastes inclined more toward literary and dramatic art.

I forced myself to open the cover, scanned the introduction written by the eminent art critic Arthur Roessler and retired to the rear of the store to read the brief diary itself, an account of Schiele's twenty-four days spent in prison. I became a spy again, probing the secrets of this childishly candid man, trespassing, intruding, at the same time taking offense at this ghost flaunting his agony.

"Soft, timid wailing, screams—loud, urgent, imploring; groaning sobs—desperate, fearfully desperate. Finally, apathetic stretching out with cold limbs, deathly afraid, bathed in shivering sweat." Once again I stood outside his window, surrounded this time by thousands of other readers, all of us gaping at a prisoner alone in a cubicle with only the electric bell above his bed to remind him of the modern world, a world covered in a matrix of pipes, wires, and railway tracks, a world that never slept, never darkened, while Egon Schiele existed in perpetual twilight for twenty-four days.

"I am a human being! I still am, although imprisoned. Does no one think of that?"

In turn bitter, passionate, despairing, pious, the diary was full of lies, false claims, poor approximations. How could anyone have known the man behind that screen of words?

"I, by nature one of the freest, bound only to the law which is not that of the masses."

What law did he mean? "One of the freest," he wrote, asserting his birthright as iconoclast, as rebel, when the very phrase "by nature" suggests the worst prison, the kind that lures the moth into the flue of a lamp or a lemming into the sea. The surest truth is silence. A blank page. An empty cell. Not a cell with Egon Schiele inside, his "place of the damned," as he called it

But Egon Schiele had peopled his prison diary with other characters besides himself. In his effort to find a reason for his imprisonment, he had finally decided that he had been accused of "the abduction of the strange girl," a "strolling young lady" who "asked stupid questions and also had no instinct for the essence of art or for artistic creation." The girl who distracted him when he was working outdoors, the girl whom he wrongly identified as his accuser, the idiot girl: me. Nameless, and now as defenseless against his charges as he had been against the town of Neulengbach.

Eleven years had passed since I'd last seen him, eleven years that had dimmed the obsession. Hindsight is the adult's privilege, and I had come to understand that my love for the artist—and for his mistress—had been a mistake of my youth. But with Herr Schiele's diary in hand, I was the same skinny, foolish girl I had been eleven years ago: a stupid girl without instinct for the essence of art.

I read from cover to cover about his twenty-four days in hell, snapped the book shut, tucked it inside the pocket of my wool cloak and sat down on the piano bench. The player piano had been brought into the shop by the owner to vary the decor and was used more for its ambient look than as a musical instrument. But when I pumped the pedals the scroll began to turn, sluggishly at first, and the piano poked out the opening chords of a Schubert lied.

Strange girl. Stupid. Without instinct. Egon Schiele's judgment would outlive me. At the thought of his triumph, I forced the piano to keep up with my rage, provoking the woman at the desk to whirl around and squawk, "Must you?"

I replied by pumping the pedals harder and the woman turned back to my husband, expecting him to provide some sort of reprimand, but sensed at once a conspiracy between us. Her jaw fell slack, adding a third chin to the pronounced double, and she tottered out of the shop, her gait and figure reminding me of an old-fashioned, squat hackney cab on wobbly wheels.

After the door swung shut, my husband fingered the books she had left behind on his desk and he looked across at me, his spectacles lowered, his gaze both uncertain and amused. Instead of resenting his tolerance, I felt grateful—he was a reserved man and never demanded explanations or apologies.

Later that night, on the walk up the Türkenstrasse from the restaurant, snow began to fall in large, wet flakes, sticking to my husband's eyeglasses, clinging to my lashes. Munich was unnaturally quiet, the silence like that of a void, of a place that had been uninhabited since the beginning of time. Suddenly, inexplicably, I wanted to tell my husband about my infatuation with the artist from Vienna and to give up the book hidden in my pocket. As determined as I had been to protect the memory a few hours earlier, I now wanted to rid myself of it, to pass the secret to my husband even as I related it, so that the romance would be his burden and I could forget it.

But we continued walking, our arms linked, and I only imagined the conversation we might have had. I would begin, I thought, by describing the cottage in Au, built on a low hill, with a view from the yard of the jaundiced-brick Liechtenstein Castle. I would tell him about the artist and his mistress and how I had run away from home when I was fifteen, the first time to Italy, the second time to the artist's cottage. Of course I wouldn't have told my husband everything. Even as I rehearsed the confession, I selected certain details to withhold, the same details that Schiele left out of his diary, details that might have embarrassed my husband, incited needless conflict, and that had no bearing on our marriage. But why bother telling anything, if the few facts provided would have seemed to my husband what the flakes melting on the brim of his hat were to the rest of the snow—random, hardly significant?

·

Kokoschka, Oskar: born 1886, Schiele's senior by four years.

"An Expressionist, he produced a number of semidramatic works, written in a whimsical vein, in which the problems of life were treated in a somewhat loose and vague manner."

Trained at the School of Applied Arts rather than at the Vienna Academy, Oskar worked for the Wiener Werkstätte, as did Egon, and though they both participated in the 1908 Kunstschau, there is no record that the two young artists ever met.

As a child, Oscar enjoyed igniting huge ant colonies with home-made gunpowder and watching the scattered, half-dead ants drag their mutilated bodies over their charred fellows. Ants, he discovered, are extraordinarily resilient and will show signs of life after they have been partially disemboweled, singed, or even severed completely in half. Red ants recover more quickly than black ants, and soon after an explosion the survivors will begin busily transporting the larvae to a new community.

One day, because of his experiments with gunpowder, Oskar was banished from the local park by the mother of two charming little girls, but within an hour the exiled young terrorist, hoping to attract the daughters' attention, was trying to scale the wall separating the park from an adjoining dump. He had almost reached the top of the wall when his foot slipped off a loose brick, and he lost his grip and fell backward onto a pile of rubbish, landing on the bloated, decaying carcass of a pig. A swarm of plump, bottleneck flies rose and eclipsed his vision, the stench of rotting flesh paralyzed him, and he was unable to roll off, unable to cry out. As Oskar remembered it years later—and as he told a group of friends gathered at the Café Museum—the dead pig itself lurched up and sent its burden tumbling down the hill of garbage, with the flies trailing the boy like smoke behind a steamship stack.

"The story of his life," Egon Schiele, at an adjacent table, said in a whisper to Erwin Osen. "His public is the swarm of flies. And I, I am the pig." He raised his glass in a sneering, unnoticed toast to Oskar Kokoschka, his rival and his only equal among the young artists of Vienna. On one side of Egon the dancer Moa searched through her purse for a cigarette. On the other side, Erwin, as usual bored with café anecdotes, absorbed himself by tying cloth napkins end to end.

•

But what is wrong with Egon? He should feel grateful that he has a calling in life, that he doesn't waste time wondering how to fill time. Who can blame Vallie for wishing that she had received a proper education and could spend her days translating novels from the French while Egon brooded about his art? She wishes that she had learned to play the flute. She has always been inept with a needle and thread and she doesn't even own a broom, though occasionally she will borrow one from a neighbor to sweep up the chalk dust that collects in the corners.

But Vallie has never been inclined to complain about her situation and she won't begin now—she'll take her pleasures where she can find them, which is, for the time being, in her frequent collations: a swallow of beer, a macaroon, black bread with a thick pat of butter —these have become her only luxuries. A woman must eat, and Vallie adores chocolate truffles, especially the ones filled with liqueurs; she loves the surprise of flavor as the chocolate cracks between her teeth, she loves the giddy surge after eating half a dozen at one sitting. Food reminds her that she is alive, taste makes her life enjoyable. Though it's true that hunger poses a considerable challenge, and for some people the labor diminishes the pleasure. First the shopping must be done, and at the grocer's, the baker's, and the butcher's there are so few options for the woman who wants to be sure to purchase only the highest quality at a reasonable price. Vallie still remembers the disappointment she would feel as a child when she picked a bruised, rancid cherry from the fruit bowl—the sense of betrayal, the anger, as if a solemn contract had been broken, as if the cherry were her mother's practical joke.

After the shopping there's the long walk home with a heavy basket, and then the food must be put away, only to be taken out again in a few hours and prepared for a meal. And the preparation—a chore that has never appealed to Vallie, though her appetite has grown refined over the last few years. She has to admit that she would like to be pampered and protected, like a dowager's much-loved dachshund, rather than to be completely independent. She doesn't need solitude and open space as Egon does; she has never cared for the country, with its weeds, gnats, goats, pollen dust, manure piles, muddy rutted roads, and of course the peasants—Vallie has nothing kind to say about the peasants. In Neulengbach they sent Egon to jail, and Vallie had compromised herself so she could find him after he'd been transferred to St. Pölten. An indiscreet tickle, a wet kiss . . . the warden was an obese, gap-toothed fellow, about as appealing as a spoiled cherry. He wouldn't even tell her where Egon had been taken—she had to find out from Heinrich Benesch where her lover was imprisoned and when he would come to trial.

The sacrifices she has made. There had been talk in Neulengbach that the charges would be brought against Vallie as well as against Egon, but over the weeks the authorities forgot about her part—or else they decided that she wasn't worth the effort of an inquiry. So Vallie was left to her own devices and until Egon was moved from Neulengbach, she spent every waking hour trying to make his internment more comfortable.

His gratitude afterward had been sincere, even excessive—no one had stood by him as staunchly as his Vallie. Heinrich Benesch meant well, yet when he found out that the charges against Egon involved minors and pornographic pictures, he considered the situation hopeless. Klimt remained in Attersee, and Arthur Roessler hadn't bothered to cut short his vacation at Lake Garda. So only Vallie remained unflaggingly devoted and encouraging during the days of uncertainty, only she had been ready to suffer any humiliation for Egon's sake.

Now that he can afford a studio in Hietzing, he may work in relative calm and doesn't need protection against a censoring public, so Vallie has lost her primary job. But she has proven indomitable before. And after Egon has left to sulk in the streets, Vallie finishes her soup, clears the table and touches up her face with rouge and kohl, for she means to pay a visit to her neighbors, Adele and Edith, Edith and Adele, the two girls who, of late, have been distracting Egon from his work.

Not that she suspects her lover of infidelity. She has stood back on many occasions while Egon admired other girls—virginal, accommodating girls, his infatuation like a lone branch carried along by a creek, lodging against a rock jutting above the surface or in the crook of a felled tree and then swirling on again. The girls who interest him become annoying obstacles soon enough. Vallie knows that to keep Egon to herself she must move with him—from apartment to apartment in Vienna, from town to town, as weightless as a leaf clinging by its stem to a dead branch. Egon's twig. Vallie giggles into her cupped hand as she crosses the street. No one understands his moods and needs as well as she does. It won't be long before he tires of the Harms sisters, and Vallie will have him to herself once again; she will paint him with brilliant yellow and carmine, she will tattoo him, brand him permanently with her signature, carve her initials in his skin.

She climbs the circular stairway and on the third-floor landing she raises the hoop in the lion's brass mouth and confidently claps it against the door. She hears feet shuffling inside and realizes too late that she should have devised a reason for appearing uninvited in the middle of the afternoon. No matter. Frau Harms opens the door, greets Vallie coldly and without waiting for her to speak, reports that her daughters are spending the day in the Prater with the artist . . . what is his name? . . . the Fräulein's . . . her companion. But Adele and Edith had told their mother that Fräulein Neuzil would be their escort. So what was she doing on this doorstep in the middle of the afternoon?

"Of course," Vallie stammers, awkwardly and ineffectively trying to hide her surprise. Of course, the park, the Ferris wheel, peacocks and balloons—she had completely forgotten the date, and on such a glorious day. She begs Frau Harms's pardon and excuses herself, rushes down the stairs and stops to call up from the second-floor landing—she is sorry to have missed Edith and Adele, Adele and Edith: she asks Frau Harms to give them her regrets.

Back at Hietzinger Hauptstrasse 101, Vallie scrapes the sticky residue of a caramel from the back of her teeth with her thumbnail as she thinks about how she has been deceived. At least she has succeeded in causing trouble—Frau Harms obviously suspected the truth behind Vallie's clever evasion. Egon Schiele planned all along to take the sisters to the amusement park without Vallie Neuzil as a watchful escort. Tongues will start wagging, people will speculate about the artist's intentions, they will look askance when young

Edith and Adele walk past on the street. Egon Schiele poses more of a threat to her household than Frau Mama had suspected.

.

A sympathetic if uninventive man, Central Inspector Heinrich Benesch can't help but brood about Egon Schiele, accused pornographer. The newspapers have taken up the story, and now everyone in Vienna knows about the scandal. While bearded men in uniforms interrogate the young artist in a windowless room in St. Pölten, Benesch sits in a corner of an obscure Weinstube with his son Otto, Egon's junior by two years but far surpassing him in maturity. Otto draws his tongue around the edge of his glass and waits for his father to speak. Benesch knows he should carry on a conversation and would like to ask his son about his studies, but the wine leaves an unpleasant, peppery aftertaste, and his own cigar smoke stings his eyes, making them tear. He feels beaten, exhausted. He has tried, however futilely, to help Egon Schiele, but the young artist has shown only indifference to Benesch's attempts, so sure is he that his work will benefit from the infamy of the trial and that in a matter of days he will be free. But this saturnine central inspector is convinced that Egon will spend the next three months—at least three months, probably more—in prison. And if he does ever achieve a posthumous fame, it will be because the public has confused his life with his pictures, preferring his tumultuous biography to his art, obscuring the work with trivial facts. The life of Egon Schiele will sell the drawings and paintings—without the legend the same images would be worthless.

As worthless as Central Inspector Benesch, who has dedicated his life to unerring duty, who is always loyal to his family, to his employers, to the state, always reliable, unassuming, predictable. Vienna is filled with men identical to him—he could easily be replaced. Benesch's single unusual quality is his relationship with the young artist Egon Schiele and now he is about to lose even this. He shifts abruptly in his seat, knocking his glass with his wrist and splashing wine. Otto swabs the table with his handkerchief.

"Father?"

But worry absorbs Heinrich Benesch, and his face, like Otto's handkerchief, is stained, crumpled. He imagines Egon slouching in his chair, dull as the drunkards in the Stube, replying with bored disdain to the volley of questions: place of birth, mother's maiden name, religion. The authorities need this information to complete the required forms so that Egon can be tried, convicted and sentenced to hard labor. Benesch gazes at the man slumped over the table opposite and imagines a prisoner framed by a pyramid of light beneath the single bulb. Someone must suffer for the men who feel nothing, and Heinrich Benesch is ready to accept the burden; he imagines himself in Egon's chair, facing an implacable interrogator. He curls his hands over his spectacles to block the light.

"Father?" His interrogator, Otto. He wishes his son would turn his eyes away. Heinrich wants to apologize but he can't speak when Otto dogs him with that patient, inquiring gaze.

"Father?" Otto repeats, splitting the syllables, pausing between the halves for so long that Benesch wonders whether he will continue. Father—the name of all men with watery red eyes, soft paunches, round, girlish calves, impotent, vulnerable, defenseless men, chalk-skinned inside the cage of yellow light.

And even as he imagines himself in Egon's place in the interrogation room, he knows that Egon would be undaunted by the harsh lights and the questions and likely would be impertinent enough to interrupt with his own demands: may he have a newspaper delivered to his cell, will they let him sleep an extra hour in the morning, and by the way, about the prison fare—would they please requisition some paprika and salt for the cook?

•

egonschiele. EGON SCHIELE. Egonschiele. In the winter of 1917, at a camp for Russian prisoners-of-war in Mühling, Egon hides behind a bunkhouse and blows on his knuckles, which poke out from fingerless wool gloves. On the third page of his sketch pad he tries three different versions of his signature. The E of his forename is the most important letter, and Egon would like to design a perfect shape to lead the rest of the name. The artist's signature is his flag, after all, and it should express his aesthetic principles without detracting from the work—ideally, the viewer's eye should come to rest on the name only after the other details of the picture have been absorbed. Conversely, the name must be effectively startling, even intimidating—precise, aggressive letters will inhibit a viewer from making abrupt judgments.

Near the grubhouse a whistle trills excitedly and is answered by shouts—Egon assumes that some lazy runt forgot to cart the garbage to the pit or to stoke the barracks stove, and now an officer has discovered the crime. If the criminal is found, he will have to polish the kitchen chrome with his tongue. The senior men enjoy humiliating their charges; though this might seem merely another inexact cliché of war, during Egon's short, uneventful term in the army— first at a training camp in Prague, then at warehouses in Vienna, and now here, at a prison in Mühling—he has discovered that men in uniform depend upon such formulas. Everyone has been assigned a part and is thoroughly rehearsed. Egon feels trapped in a dream where he has been cued onstage, the set an amazingly convincing prison, with nothing to indicate that this scene takes place in Mühling and not at a prison in St. Pölten. And of course he has forgotten his lines, or perhaps he never learned them—he can't remember if he's ever read the script. No matter. As soon as his superiors saw an example of Egon's beautiful handwriting they promoted him to the position of camp illustrator, and now they treat him with unusual respect. So while the other soldiers repair fences damaged by the winter winds or scrub the latrines or prepare the meals, Egon is free to roam about the grounds, making pencil and watercolor sketches of whatever happens to catch his eye: the ladder and barrel of a water tower, or a withered Russian leaning against a wall, a blanket wrapped around his head, eyes glowing like tiny windows of a furnace.

Egon doesn't bother to explain to anyone the difference between art and illustration; he merely adheres to his routine, letting the lines themselves determine the image, starting with and then abandoning the original scene. The subject can appear in an infinite number of guises, and the finished portrait depends as much upon the early lines, random hieroglyphs, as it does upon the model. His signature, for instance, is determined by the first impulsive mark that forms the spine of the letter E. The thought of creating different signatures for his different selves intrigues him. But Egon knows that a viewer orients himself by finding repetitions, and no matter how varied his art is, even the most sympathetic critics will concentrate on the similarities between works separated by time, subject, and technique. It troubles him to think that all but the most blatant diversities in his vision will be ignored. A painting illuminated by natural light continually, imperceptibly transforms from minute to minute, and Egon would want his work to be as varied as a uniform block of color that changes hue as the sun moves across the sky.

But he grows bored with his signature. So he turns the next bulbous vowel into a woman's body, plants a roughly sketched figure of a man on top of her and draws similar images across the page. It is difficult to tell whether the men are strangling their mates or making love to them. Modern romance. Egon pauses to turn the plain gold wedding band around on his finger. In his wife's most recent letter, she reported that she was making arrangements to live in a nearby village—she has already contacted a woman who lets rooms near the camp, and soon Frau Edith Schiele would be spending every Sunday afternoon with her husband. In his letters to her, he tells her how at night he tries to conjure his wife in the space between his arms, he tries to transport her from Vienna into his bunk. How desperately he needs to fill the emptiness. He knows that Edith married him for reasons other than love—love will be the consequence of marriage, not the reason. She married him to liberate herself from her mother's control and from the banal competitions with her older sister, escaping into Egon's home as a shipwrecked sailor might find refuge in a cave from storms. If the earth gives way above her, she won't need a gravedigger—that's Edith's attitude. All can be so easily obliterated by war, by accident or illness, just as easily as an image can be wiped out by Egon's paintbrush, so there's no use wasting time worrying about the possibilities. Egon knows that Edith doesn't desire him, not yet at least. But this is the challenge—he will win her love, he will feed her the pomegranate seed and make her dependent on his devotion. Still, he can't help but wonder that such an old-fashioned girl should be so crassly practical in matters of romance, while a girl as modern as Vallie Neuzil once considered him her life's purpose. He still cares for Vallie and had even proposed drawing up a contract that would obligate him to spend two weeks of every summer with her—but Vallie had refused his terms. He hasn't heard from her for over two years; occasionally he imagines her in bed with a man in some fashionable Ringstrasse hotel.

"You there, what are you drawing now?"

Egon does not have to look up to know that this most repugnant of questions has been asked by none other than the Maggot—a dull-eyed, fat soldier nicknamed privately by Egon for his habit of appearing when he is not wanted, as stealthy and disgusting as a worm deep inside a pear.

"I said, what is it you're up to?" demands the soldier, his thick lips parted in a grin, intimating that he's smart enough to know an indecent image when he sees one and can play the game as well as anyone. He waits for the camp chronicler to describe the scenario, but Egon continues to scratch his pencil across the paper without replying. The lines devour each other, and then, magically, distinct figures emerge from the web, sexless figures, one kneeling, one standing with an arm raised, and in the hand a club . . . or whip . . . or ax? The details of the scene remain ambiguous, yet the brutal action is so explicit that the soldier catches his breath and wheels around abruptly. Correctly, he has understood that the drawing is an insult directed at him.

The Maggot's hate is transparent—Egon could narrate his thoughts: a pervert, a convicted child molester, that's what the soldiers say about this artist, who acts as though the world were just a bubble inside his head. Maggot has watched him swaggering his hips as he walks, subtle as a black-haired Italian *puta*. Treated like a kept woman by the officers, while Maggot spends most of the day filling buckets with potato peelings. He'll show the pretty boy what to do with that tight, ripe ass of his.

Egon almost wants to laugh at the poor man's futile rage.

Danse Macabre

ONCE in a while, without reason or warning, our village of Neu-lengbach would fill with music. We all knew the musician—a mad-man who had lived at the top of the church tower for as long as I could remember and received his board in exchange for ringing the hours—and we all tolerated the metallic wailing of his violin, ignored his music as we ignored the sound of rain on the tile roofs. Even my mother didn't seem to notice when the notes seeped through the barriers of glass and wood into her bedroom. But on April 7, 1912, I sat beside her bed and heard in the same melody that I had heard a hundred times before an irresistible invitation. The musician was summoning me, he was telling me that I must leave my home once more and go to the forbidden place in Au.

I had not danced for years, though my grandmother used to take great pains to teach me. On Christmas Day she would wake me before dawn, we would light the kitchen stove, and we would prac-tice waltzing. Though my grandmother would rest her hand on my rump and bind me to her hip, I was terribly awkward. Once I knocked an empty carafe off the sideboard with my elbow, and cut my finger on a sliver of glass. My grandmother bandaged it, and later that day, when my father went to pour the wine, she said that she had broken the carafe in the middle of the night, on her way to the toilet, since no one had bothered to give her a chamberpot the evening before. She fooled my father with her lie, but not my mother, who asked me how I had injured my finger; I didn't answer, and she didn't bother to ask again.

Even my grandmother wouldn't have been able to lead me through this uneven, frenzied waltz—it had no more rhythm than the current of a swollen river. A river, yes, and I wanted to be swept helplessly along, to give myself up to the demonic sound, to whirl through the ballroom of the Liechtenstein Castle in the artist's arms, to brush my cheek against the creamy petals of the camellia pinned to his lapel.

I dragged my hand over the stove top to absorb the lingering warmth as I made my way across the kitchen. It was early, and my father was still playing billiards at the café. I would not be missed. So I walked into the empty street, the cottages on either side of me like beautiful and wicked women, harmless as long as they did not speak and could not see me. Their vanity depended upon light, and in this sodden darkness they could make no comparisons.

Neulengbach, where I was born and where I had expected to be buried beside my mother and father, in the same cemetery with the bell-tower musician—I despised the village for its selfishness. But that night, with the music in my head, a drab rain falling, and a willow branch tumbling along the street beside me, propelled by the wind, I could forgive Neulengbach, I could nearly pity it.

I thought I understood the music then—the madman was tickling his violin to make it laugh, to make it giggle and groan. My admiration for the musician grew, and I stopped to listen more closely to his music, stepped to the side of the road to steady myself, grasped the crossbar of a tall, wrought-iron gate, and held my breath.

I wouldn't have been surprised to see the rats of the village swarming toward the church tower, flanked by a contingent of skeletons shaking tambourines. I wouldn't have been surprised if the village children had streamed into the streets in their nightclothes. But I was caught unprepared by a low, insidious growl that lasted no longer than a single beat before a huge black form threw itself against the opposite side of the gate and seized a piece of my cape between its teeth. I wasn't sure whether I had screamed or if the music had begun again—an unnatural sound, wherever it came from, a tritone wail, the chord like a rod half-submerged in water, broken, misaligned. I pounded at the dog's snout and managed to pull my wrist away. But then the beast dropped to all fours and thrust its head through the iron bars of the fence, clamped its mouth around my knee, the top incisors sinking into my wool stocking.

"Devil!" I tore free, and while the dog bounced behind the fence, I ran down the road into Au, wishing that I had a gun and could put a bullet through the dog's skull, the Kindermanns' hound, the village Argus. Likely the Kindermanns themselves had heard the dog barking, had heard my own screams as well. Yes, they had heard and grinned at the thought of their beast devouring yet another stray cat, thinking about how tomorrow they could gather the bones for Frau Kindermann's stewpot.

I picked up a flat, jagged stone and threw it in the direction of the dog, but the animal kept barking, and the darkness absorbed the rock. The rain bounced in silver, mercury drops, and the mud was slippery beneath my shoes but I rushed on, indignant, craving revenge for all the wrongs that had been done to me in my lifetime. In a minute I was at the artist's cottage. My fists had hardly touched the door before it swung open, and I stood face to face with the artist. He chewed on a spent cigarette butt and looked wonderingly at me.

"I shall tell them you did this!" I cried, thrusting my ripped cape before his eyes.

"What's wrong? Who is here?" The mistress's voice, sharp, inquisitive, rose from the rear of the room. I smelled her perfume before she appeared in the doorway beside the artist. "My dear, come out of the rain! What a poor, drenched little rabbit," she exclaimed, folding my hands between hers. The mistress drew me into the cottage, tugging gently when I balked. Egon Schiele stood with his arms folded, watching in obvious amusement, and the door swung shut behind me, as though pulled by an invisible wire.

•

After the war, after the death of his wife, in the delirium of pneumonia, Egon thinks back over the years to the first night he spent in Trieste with his sister, when Gerti was twelve and Egon sixteen. The sun had long since set when he followed Gerti out to the end of a steel support beam that formed part of the unfinished skeleton grid of a pier, and even twelve years later he still remembers how the water rolled beneath him, the entire volume of the sea sliding back and forth like water in a bowl. His memory is so powerful that the thought of the water makes him nauseous, and he spits a mouthful of acidic saliva into a bunched corner of the bedspread.

It is October, 1918, and Egon is in a bedroom at Hietzinger Hauptstrasse 104, the Harms's apartment. He thinks he is dying; but he has thought the same before, when he was sixteen, balancing two meters above the Adriatic. He had been sure then that he was on the verge of death, about to lose his footing and fall into the sea.

His sister had brought her brother there to frighten him. He hadn't asked her to lead him along this precarious bar, but then he hadn't objected either, and she had decided that she must prove herself braver. On this trip to Trieste, in the Miramare park, Gerti had realized that through the first twelve years of her life she had been deprived of a crucial emotion. Finally she had come to understand what she had been missing—the thrill of danger, that special panic a person feels when time comes close to stopping. Gerti didn't want to leave Trieste before experiencing the passion she had never felt before, the excitement that had always been a boy's privilege, forbidden to her.

When Egon tried to call her back she ignored him, stepped carefully until she reached the end of the beam, crying out, "I'm here!" her voice cut off abruptly as she lost her balance and fell into the darkness. No, not fell—that's not how Egon remembers it. The darkness of the sky came down to her, enveloped her like a huge silk shawl thrown over her head. One moment she was visible—a figurehead bending backwards, cresting her flat bosom; the next moment the curtain had fallen over the place where she had stood. The water lapping was as insistent as a watch ticking in a dead man's pocket, and the harbor lights were the eyes of indifferent spectators. Gerti had disappeared into the night.

"Gerti!"

Even as he crawled forward, Egon knew he couldn't save his sister —what was his strength compared with the power of the sea? The sea had swallowed Gerti. The beam grew narrower beneath his feet, as though made of ice, as though someone had played a terrible joke on both of them, lured them out onto a melting icicle. But still Egon shimmied forward on hands and knees, while the accursed water drowned his Gerti, his baby sister, claimed her completely before Egon could.

"Gerti!"

What the water did . . . it had been a honeymoon of sorts, ruined now. Nothing to be salvaged, nothing left of Gerti but an absence at the end of a steel beam.

"Gerti, please!"

And then the trembling. Egon had never experienced anything like it before. Someone was shaking him, trying to turn him inside out, and he forgot about his sister, cared only about saving himself, clung weakly, nearly choking on his own tongue. But by then he had reached the last section and saw the pale, sluglike fingers on either side of the beam, saw the thin wrists disappearing into striped sleeves.

So she had tricked him, she had made him think that she had drowned, when all the while she had been hanging from the beam like a carcass from a meat hook. Astonished that his sister could be so cruel, Egon wormed back toward shore, ashamed at the tears that came now that he knew she was safe and that the beam could be trusted, crying because he had admitted the desire to himself and would always remember—not how desperately he had wanted to save his sister but simply how much he had wanted her. Crying too because her consent would only have filled him with disgust. Sliding backward along the beam to the beach, with the surf splashing gently; now the lights of Trieste were stars that had dropped from the sky. He was startled to find himself lying supine on the strip of gravelly sand, moving his arms and legs to make angel wings, wondering where the moon could be hiding and why the lights of the city didn't burn off the darkness. But then light was infamously weak, not as weak as sound but too weak to change night into day.

"Cruel Gerti!"

Egon remembers how the darkness made the beam invisible, so his sister seemed to glide to him on outstretched wings, angel wings, as agile and brazen as a gull.

"Why didn't you try to save me?" she had demanded, kicking sand over her brother's outstretched body. "What if I had been drowning? You don't care what happens to me, do you?" She puckered her lips in a coy pout, for she sensed that Egon understood the trick she had played on him. But she wanted to hear her brother tell her how brave she was, how artful, how daring, which he refused to do, for the truth would seem filthy. If he told Gerti how he had felt, she would want nothing to do with him.

Or would she? On this October day in 1918, isn't it Gerti pressing cold compresses against his forehead, Gerti watching her brother die of influenza in his in-laws' apartment, Gerti Schiele Peschka who answers, "Yes, I am here," whenever he calls her name? If he confessed . . . but no, he has nothing to confess, not anymore. He has never forgiven his sister for the trick she played on him in 1906, when she was twelve and he sixteen, a terrible deception, letting him think that she had drowned while she swung from the end of a beam, her feet skimming the surface of the swells.

"Gerti?"

"I am here, Egon. Try to sleep."

Her voice comforts him. If only she had answered that night in Trieste, had said to him, "I am here," then he never would have known how much he loved her. But he lost his little sister for good that night; he will never recover her.

·

The churching of woman: (The Woman, at the usual time after her delivery, shall come into the Church decently appareled, and there shall kneel down in some convenient place.) "Forasmuch as it hath pleased Almighty God, of his goodness, to give you safe deliverance, and to preserve you in the great danger of childbirth; you shall therefore give hearty thanks unto God, and say . . ."

Push, breathe! She cannot, the pain having shifted from beneath the rib cage to the lower abdomen, the infant's head now lodged in the birth canal, unable to slide forward through the dilated cervix, unable to slide back. Marie's toes curl under as each contraction pulls her toward the red howling center, the pain outside the circumference of red like light from the sun, everywhere at once, while the center is a void, producing pain but feeling nothing. If she could collapse into the center all would be as it was before—standing beside the stove, a bowl of steaming coffee in her hands, the train's departing whistle, and her husband behind her, an hour before the next train arrives, her husband's hands slipping inside the bib of her apron—"Now, while the girls are asleep . . ." As it used to be. But at this moment she must breathe, and between breaths she remembers that eventually the center will dissolve. There is nothing incessant in this life, the pain will relent, and later she won't remember the pain, though she will recall how her body went rigid with every spasm, the recollection belonging to a spectator, as though she had been watching with the doctor, standing beside him, staring into the red. She wanted to hate her body for collaborating with the pain, but if she turned against herself she would have no chance of surviving.

"Grant, we beseech thee, most merciful Father, that she, through thy help, may faithfully live according to thy will in this life and also may partake of everlasting glory in the life to come."

Soon the pain will be a son, she will give him a name, hold him to her breast, and feel his own tiny cylindrical chest palpitating as fast as a sparrow's. The child will be outside, separate, and yet closer to her than ever before—he will have suffered with her, miraculously emerged from the terrible center. She will attach herself to the child not with a proud, protective, maternal love but with a stunned gratitude. Even if neither of them remembers how it came to a halt midway and the pain was everywhere, Marie and her son will always understand what they have shared. She will not ask herself why it comforts her to know that she has not suffered alone, she will not worry about the purity of the emotion. She has sense enough to respect this fragile new love. She has heard of mothers who turn away from the first sight of their child, repulsed by the thing that has caused them so much torment. She is lucky to have never felt this instant aversion—for that is the way it happens, they say—a mother's hate spills out all at once and she has to live falsely from then on, pretending to cherish the child she does not want. No, Marie treasures all of her children because they have passed through the center, confirming for her that the instinct to survive is right, is logical, despite the inexplicable pain.

"Grant, we beseech thee, O heavenly Father, that the child of this thy servant may daily increase in wisdom and stature, and grow in thy love and service, until he come to thy eternal joy."

•

Late in the afternoon: Trot, trot, one behind the other. His pointed American shoes are covered with mud. Trot, trot. A humiliating, nonsensical race. Egon imagines painting the St. Pölten prison yard and then cutting the canvas into monochromatic jigsaw grays so that none of the pieces would indicate any three-dimensional object, none of the pieces would be more than a splotch of shadow. Trot, trot. Twilight grays. He wouldn't lend any vibrant pigments to this world, not even a dusting of orange for a forehead. St. Pölten doesn't deserve any gifts from his imagination—all will remain gray, without highlights, without distinguishing traits. The minute parts of a prison have no meaning when they are independent from one another. Egon would scatter the pieces in the wind and leave it to some determined child to fit the scraps together again.

He wishes he had his oils and a clean canvas. Someday he would like to return to Krumau and paint the City Hall—last year he painted it from a postcard he had picked up on one of his visits, but this year he would like to set up his easel in the courtyard at night and paint the facade in darkness. All would be gray, like the prison yard, a lusterless gray, like the streets and buildings in this pleasant town situated on the Traisen, with ten thousand inhabitants, a prebendary church, and a jail.

The man behind him leans forward suddenly and mutters something in his ear. Egon cannot make any sense of his words, so he ignores him, shuts out the voice by composing a letter in his head to his Neukunstgruppe friends. "Dear Comrades—life, as we know, is disintegration." The prisoner at his heels continues to annoy him; Egon can feel the foul, hot breath on the back of his neck. Disgusted, he gathers saliva on his tongue, purses his lips and prepares to turn around and spit. But just then the guard calls "Halt!" signaling the end of their exercise, and the men disperse.

In the yard the wizened, red-haired convict who has persecuted him before nudges Egon in the ribs and asks in a low voice, "Why are you among us?" And because he wants to shake off this annoying parasite, Egon finally condescends to reply: "I don't know, they haven't told me why."

At this, the old man's wiry nostril hairs tremble like a wasp's antennae and his shoulders shake, which seems to indicate that he is laughing, though Egon can't be sure, since the fool makes no sound at all. Then he becomes rigid, his bloodshot eyes widen, and he declares, each word distinct, unmistakable: "You seduced a girl, right?"

So this must be the suspicion of the court. *You seduced a girl.* This is his crime! Finally he knows why he is here—on charges of seduction. He wants to grab the old man's hand and shake it vigorously, he wants to kiss his filthy muzzle and thank him for finally shedding light on this mystery—a tired but appropriate phrase, for the prison itself suddenly seems a haven of light. Egon sees colors where he saw only gray—burnt umber in the sky, ocher streaks on his white shoes, and the old man's lips are livid red. He sees a new world, all because he has learned the reason for his imprisonment: seduction. It will be easy enough to prove his innocence. He had scores of admirers among the little girls of Neulengbach, but this charge must stem from the supposed abduction of the strange one, the girl who plagued him with her stupid questions while he was working outside and then began to spy on him and Vallie. Eventually she had appeared at his cottage one night crying hysterically, claiming that this was her last refuge. The girl had stayed with Vallie and Egon for three nights, including one night with Vallie at a pension in Vienna, until her father had come for her. As he escorted his daughter out of the cottage, the father had promised that the matter would be kept in the strictest confidence, his voice straining nearly to the cadence of an appeal, as though he were seeking Egon's assurance that no one else would ever learn about his daughter's desperate behavior. And because of this promise, because of the father's shame as well, the thought that the girl and her father were his accusers hadn't even occurred to Egon.

Now Egon was certain that the matter would be resolved as soon as the girl provided an honest testimony—he would write to her directly if only he could remember her name. Her father must have rallied Neulengbach for the sake of his daughter's reputation. But wouldn't she be better off if she admitted that nothing had happened to her during those three days, nothing improper, nothing of lasting consequence? There had been no seduction; it was as simple as that.

•

"The dreaming boys," Central Inspector Benesch calls them, these young rebels of Vienna who have seceded from the Secession, rejecting Jugendstil design along with the Academy fogies. Theirs is an art of rejection. Gerstl, the most outspoken, laughed at the priestly Klimt, laughed at Mathilde Schönberg for spurning his love, and in 1908 laughed as he shot himself. Now his work remains locked in a warehouse. The others—Schiele, Peschka, Faistauer, von Gütersloh, Osen—carry on the Gerstl spirit. Considered hoodlums by the classicists at the Vienna Academy, tolerated as difficult though promising apprentices by the Secession artists, called "dreaming boys" by Heinrich Benesch, they pretend to dispense with the past when really all they want is to sign their names on the crowded sheet of history, to secure the respect of their country, to be remembered. Every generation must distinguish itself, and these young men have developed their own distinctive style, distorting and emaciating the turgid, muscle-bound torso so much in favor at the Academy, borrowing contortions and gestures from Munch, Rops, Minne, borrowing brush strokes and settings from van Gogh. The Neukunstgruppe wants to be radically original when in truth they take the logical opposing position in an argument that has long preceded them.

Benesch had hoped that Egon—the most talented of the group—would someday develop a more varied style. Only when he replaced borrowed ideology with his own personal vision would his work mature. The mind is not a trap, and an individual should not look for refuge in polemics devised by a group. Perhaps in prison Egon would learn that art must be more than a self-consoling expression of outrage.

He visits Egon in prison one more time, a week before his trial. Benesch has no doubt that the young artist is guilty of the remaining charge against him—displaying erotica in front of children. (In reply to a letter from Benesch, the examining magistrate told him that the charge of seduction had been dropped.) At any rate, Benesch hasn't come here to discuss the crime with Egon. In a sense, he wants to bid the young man farewell—not so bluntly, of course, he won't let Egon suspect that even his most committed patron has given up hope of his immediate release. But he wants to see the artist before the weight of the judge's damning sentence crushes him.

Benesch finds Egon alone in his cell in St. Pölten, pondering his most recent work, thirteen watercolors painted in Neulengbach, arranged in uneven rows across the cot. Without looking up, Egon says, "I know why I am here," and smoothes the bent corner of one of the self-portraits. Benesch clears his throat, tries to think up a reply to Egon's declaration but decides there is no use talking about what can't be altered. So he studies the watercolors in silence.

He would prefer to see more interesting work from Egon Schiele on the eve of his doom. These anxious self-portraits suffer too much from Egon's tendency toward self-pity and self-advertisement. Obviously the artist wouldn't want to hear his honest opinion, but Benesch still has a responsibility if not as a patron then as a father. Although Egon is not related by blood, he completes the fraction that begins with Heinrich's son Otto; together, Otto and Egon are all that a man like Heinrich Benesch could want—a sober, respectful scholar and a heretical artist—and Benesch has a chance to compensate for his own misdirected life in this pair of opposites.

In St. Pölten, Egon waits for the inspector's reaction to the thirteen watercolors, among them four self-portraits captioned with polemics about the artist's rights. He sucks in his lower lip as he surveys them, his glance snaking back and forth as though he were searching a map for a landmark. Egon wants to give Benesch a sense of place. He hopes that Benesch will identify with the emotions of these watercolor characters. The basis of aesthetic judgment, Egon believes, should be not appreciation but empathy—he wants his viewers to feel what he feels, he wants them to dissolve into his images, wants them to share his desire and pain. And he wants to help them recognize themselves.

Prisoner! In this, the most solemn of the self-portraits, the overcoat takes up most of the space, like the smoke of smoldering coals, and all that remains of Egon is the small, off-centered head with its clenched teeth and frightened eyes. Benesch should understand that the caption is a statement of complex rage. But the inspector simply removes his spectacles and looks up at Egon with a slightly impatient smile, as if he has just been appraising a worthless stone. *I Love Antithesis,* reads a more ambiguous caption. *Hindering the Artist Is a Crime. It Is Murdering Life in the Bud!* declares another.

"You don't think they're any good."

"I didn't say . . ."

"Then tell me what you think. Or don't tell me. I can see your opinion in your face. You're just like the rest of them, a bourgeois coward, more interested in your next meal than in art."

Benesch massages his eyelids with his fingertips, and when the young artist has finished ranting he murmurs, "May I venture to say that these seem . . . they appear to be . . . necessary for you."

"Necessary, yes, Herr Benesch, as necessary as my shit."

"You have been lonely here, haven't you?"

"Oh, but I have this!" Egon mocks, squeezing his crotch. The older man ignores the gesture, tries to find better words to describe the watercolors. "Prayers, yes, these are prayers before they are anything else."

"Prayers, you say?" Egon pulls a brush from a glass of water and pinches the tapered bristles between his fingertips, squeezing the excess liquid with a characteristic flick, sprinkling clouded orange drops across the cement floor. "Chug, chug. You see, I am a machine, Herr Benesch, how can I know what to say to God, how do I know what to believe anymore?" He springs to his feet, smears the brush into a brown disk on the tray and begins to dab at the older man, staining the collar of his shirt, his cheek, his temple, his bald pate, shrieking, "I can't stop myself!" jousting with his little brush, thrusting his pelvis forward. But the stoical Central Inspector remains as still and uncomplaining as a statue while Egon scrawls illegible letters across his cheek and brow.

"I have no thoughts of my own. I am a machine," the artist says, falling back on the bed, his laughter evaporating into a parched cough as his eyes meet the humorless eyes of Benesch, whose face looks like fungi-dotted bark and whose expression forces Egon to recall his debt to the man he has just abused. Benesch has visited him in prison three times, while none of his friends has bothered to make the trip to Neulengbach or St. Pölten, and his sister hasn't even sent him an encouraging note. And what about Arthur Roessler, powerful Arthur Roessler, who has predicted a great future for Egon Schiele? Why won't he use his influence? Because sex crimes are contagious—anyone who has contact with the accused puts his own reputation and career in danger. Egon would have his friends back when he has proven himself innocent; they would raise their fists in protest against the unjust treatment but until then would remain silent, unfaithful Peters. Except for Benesch, sincere Heinrich Benesch.

Instead of hiding his face in his hands and weeping out of exhaustion and gratitude, Egon gathers the quilt of watercolors, pats them into a neat stack and hands them to his patron. Benesch accepts the gift without a word, secretly feeling a greedy excitement at his own inadvertent manipulative skill. Thirteen original watercolors, handsome payment for his frankness.

"This is all I have left to give you," the artist says.

For a moment Benesch wonders if he is being ridiculed, then quickly rejects the suspicion—mockery would never be so generous. And Benesch could not be more contemptible, taking advantage of Egon's despair this way. But he knows that he would only offend the artist by refusing the watercolors—an offering of art should never be declined.

"I'm sorry," he says weakly. "I didn't mean to suggest that they are without merit."

"But they are without meaning. They have no audience. Except for you, Herr Benesch; you will be their audience today. And from now on, as long as I remain in St. Pölten, I will have nothing to do with art. I will wait until I return to the world again before I begin another painting." His voice grows shrill as his conviction falters, and it becomes clear to Benesch that Egon, however meek he pretends to be, is not prepared to accept harsh criticism. Beneath the martyr's intentions lies a recalcitrant, childish pride. Egon wants to be completely visible, always performing for an attentive spectator, so that anything he produces has importance. Benesch likened these watercolors to prayers, Egon likened them to excrement—meanings, in Egon's view, that are close enough to be identical. But Benesch doesn't truly believe that only Egon can appreciate this little patchwork of colors—they deserve a place in any retrospective, he thinks, tenderly balancing the stack on his knee.

"This series has its own importance, whatever you say. There are some interesting experiments."

"But experiment implies the potential for truth, something to be proved or disproved, Herr Benesch, and in here I can't be sure of anything. How can I know that the clock in the square chimes the correct hour or that my drinking water hasn't been poisoned? Maybe I will be summoned for morning exercise tomorrow, maybe I will be forgotten. And how can I be sure that the guard isn't listening through the wall? Perhaps at sunrise tomorrow I'll be blindfolded and shot, and someone else will eat the breakfast meant for me. Anything is possible in prison. You are wrong to call them experiments. But do what you want with them, they're yours now. I won't embarrass myself further, rest assured." He studies the white arcs of his fingernails. "I've heard that the thoroughly crazed ones pluck out their eyes," he murmurs, and then, "Now, if you'll excuse me," indicating that it is time for Heinrich Benesch to leave. The inspector smears the wet script on his forehead with a handkerchief.

On his way out Benesch asks the guard to keep the prisoner in cell eight under close observation, which is, after all, exactly what Egon wants: to be watched, to be the center of attention. The guard accepts Benesch's kronen and offers him a cigarette in return.

•

Sex and Character, by Otto Weininger, published in 1903, was in its seventeenth printing by 1918. An expanded version of his dissertation in philosophy and psychology at the University of Vienna, *Sex and Character* explores concepts of gender, linking masculine to reason and creativity, feminine to irrationality. Weininger blames feminine values for destroying high Viennese culture, for corrupting industry and art. Woman, after all, defaces pristine flesh with her powders and lipsticks, she hikes up her skirts and shows off her legs, woman flickers her tongue, spreads her thighs, struts, flaunts, dances, teases, jilts. Woman—the degenerative impulse. Woman—the dream that causes man to wake in a cold sweat in the middle of the night. Woman locks the bedroom door and throws away the key, watches placidly while man leaps from the seventh-story window. How small and vulnerable the crumpled heap looks from above.

Woman equals Jew, writes Otto Weininger, Jew equals woman. Beware of those who lack, he warns, for they will try to make you effeminate, impotent, and complacent and will surreptitiously plant the seeds of madness in your brain. The feminine, once contracted, is incurable.

•

The night Adolf Schiele died, his son Egon wasn't asleep as Marie Schiele believed. Though he kept his eyes shut tight and his breathing low, he remained awake. Not merely awake; without speech, without any sound at all, he conversed with himself while his sisters slept in each other's arms and his mother kept watch over the body of her husband.

Curled around Marie's ankles, Egon felt as though he were floating underwater, felt at first an exhilarating weightlessness, then an increasing pressure against his ears, as though the atmosphere were slowly compressing. He forced himself to inhale, was surprised to find that he could breathe, and gave himself up to the strange sensation. The smell of his mother's leather shoes comforted Egon, and he rested his head in the saddle between the upturned toe and the laces. What if his mother were the one lying inert on the bed and his father were sitting in the straight-backed rosewood chair, his shadow stretched on the wall from ceiling to floor, pulsating in the candlelight? Egon was grateful that his mother had been spared. And as he thought about the family's luck, he wished he could speak to his sister, wished that she could know his thoughts.

It would be an astonishing perception. But on the night that Adolf Schiele died, it seemed entirely possible that thoughts could be palpable, the words like fish brushing against Egon's skin. What was little Gerti thinking? She was probably begging her papa to come back to her, to wake up and give her a goodnight kiss.

Stop it! Egon wanted to order, but the command dispersed in the liquid silence. He had always assumed that he and his sisters had been united in their hatred of Adolf; tonight, though, he was certain that Gerti, the baby of the family, was thinking fondly of the villain, was remembering how her father used to let her ride on his shoulders. He would gallop along the path beside the railroad tracks, and when they were out of sight of the house he would skip across the ties and imitate the clanking and chugging of a train. When she pulled on his ear he would whistle.

Yes, Gerti was free to remember falsely, but Egon would remember the truth—how his father used to beat him when he found the cigar box empty or his lager depleted, how once he had slapped his son so hard that he burst a blood vessel in Egon's nose. The blood had tasted sweet, not coppery, it tasted like molasses, and Egon wouldn't let his mother plug him with cotton—instead, he hid on the stairs below the cellar bulkhead and made himself drunk with his delicious blood.

If Melanie knew what he was thinking she would scold him. Sensible Melanie. She would insist that Egon's nose had bled not because his father had hit him but because haughty Egon had been walking with his face turned toward the sky and had collided with a tree.

When did he ever show us kindness?

Of course Melanie would defend her father, using as evidence of his goodwill the traditional Christmas cake that he would travel all the way to Vienna to purchase. Melanie, Gerti, and Egon would wait for him on the platform, and he always carried a white cardboard box tied with checkered string when he stepped off the train. And pencils. He always had pencils tucked behind his ear and in his pockets and up his sleeves. Didn't Egon remember?

Yes, he remembered, much more accurately than his sisters could —the black wool gloves on his father's hands, the pale, tubular paunch that hung over his shorts after he had peeled off his damp clothes, the flecks of foam in the corner of his mouth during one of his seizures, the sounds of Egon's pictures flaming in the stove, crackling, like distant applause. And the pencils. It was true that every pencil he owned had been a gift from his father.

He wanted nothing to do with us!

But little Gerti would insist that he loved her best of all, that Papa had told her so himself. He used to let her ride on his shoulders.

Be still, he wanted to say to his sister and to himself as well, for he felt a terrible secret slipping from his control, a secret he had meant to forget. Papa. And a woman. A woman wearing frivolous polka-dot shoes, her face painted with intense colors that practically dripped onto the cobblestones of Tulln. Now Egon involuntarily remembered: a woman in a red gown that clung to her like a huge wet leaf. Egon had been on his way to buy a kilo of flour and was so intrigued by the painted woman of the class rarely seen in Tulln that he had followed her onto a side street. So he had watched his father slip from a doorway and wrap his arms around the woman from behind and cover the back of her neck with kisses.

Did he let her ride on his shoulders? That would be rueful Gerti's question. The idea amused Egon so thoroughly that he had to bite his lip to keep from giggling, and in his effort he clutched his mother's foot more tightly. But still his shameful mirth escaped and filled the air—not with sound but with vibrations splashing against the objects in the room, saturating the walls and curtains. He knew it was a sin to laugh in a dead man's company, but he couldn't stop himself. *He let her ride on his shoulders, and that's not all!* Overcome with boyish delight, he savored his naughty imagination, remembering the polka-dot shoes, the black fishnet stockings and strings of clacking beads.

But as he finally sobered he was surprised to feel the laughter continuing, a resonant, quivering laugh, a voice more powerful and expansive than Egon's, an insistent laughter that had no single source. It leaked from the molecules of air and from the pores in the walls, it pounded against Egon's skull and in a minute had slid away into silence. Only as it gave a final vicious chuckle did Egon recognize his father. Polka-dot shoes. Lusts of the flesh. Egon tried to seal his ears, but now there was nothing to block—the laughter had already returned to the corpse, and the air was still again.

Adolf's son cowered beside Marie's chair, stunned, his mouth parched, as though the room were filled not with water but with cold ashes. He clung to his mother's leg as he would have held a huge column in an earthquake even as cracks began to spread across the marble. He had been disrespectful while his father lay on his deathbed, and Adolf had punished him, had ridiculed him thoroughly. So Egon retreated to his private world, vowing never to let his thoughts have such consequence again.

.

Nothing ever went right for Egon Schiele, whether he was working on a study for *Agony* or a self-portrait. Easy enough to make a trick photograph and overlap negatives to reproduce two Egon Schieles standing side by side. But try to make a duplicate image with watercolors—there's more than trickery required. At first the paper was too dry so it wouldn't absorb the colors, and then it was too wet and began to wrinkle; the colors trickled along minute grooves and collected in putrid green puddles, and the water he used to rinse the brush turned his reds to rotting brown. Forming the defining curve of a bloodshot eye was a hopeless matter.

Egon's new wife wended her way across the room to where Egon was stationed by the window, the same window from which he had waved self-portraits to court the Harms sisters seven months ago. Edith had hoped to move to another district as soon as she was married, but Egon had finally been accepted into the army and in a few days would begin training in Prague. While he learned to handle a bayonet and to fold a cravat for an arm splint, Edith would have to continue meeting her sister every afternoon at the café on the Maxingstrasse, across from the parish church.

She set down the breakfast tray and positioned herself so Egon could greet her without having to move off his iron stool. After kissing her quickly on the forehead, he twisted around to face his easel again, lifting the demitasse and sipping as he studied his failure, licking his lips to dull the sting from the hot liquid.

"I dreamt last night . . . ," Edith said in a strangely stilted voice that trailed off, almost as if the words didn't belong to her, as if she were reciting and had grown bored with the script. She squeezed herself between the stool and a card table to sit on the windowsill, searching for activity in the room across the street as she waited for Egon to ask about her dream, but instead he muttered something about portraiture, an impossible task, God knows why he had chosen the despicable medium of watercolors.

"It's like painting with piss. Disgusting work. Excuse me, Edith, but I need to be alone." He paused to sip his coffee, and Edith curled two fingers inside the collar of his shirt to reassure him.

"Think of this picture as a mathematical problem," she said. "In order to solve a problem you must first decide how to look at it. Maybe you aren't looking at it correctly."

What did Edith know about "correct" perception? Still, Egon tried to reconsider the work before him, to reflect upon the scope of the project, to think of the formula, as his wife suggested—the divisions, the split, two equal halves. Or multiples, twins, integers. No, neither halves nor twins, not mirror images—the two portraits of himself must be different, and the difference between them would reveal the variations in his personality. How foolish to think that he should copy a photographer's method and superimpose two identical portraits to create an illusion of doubleness. He wasn't after a trick of illusion, he was trying to express his impressions and wanted to show himself as he saw himself. With distaste he remembered how he had superimposed his photographic image onto his mural, *Encounter;* he considered it now just another lie. In this new double portrait he would describe the vast divisions in himself. But he could not proceed too quickly, he must make sure the work took shape slowly, laboriously, that he did not ruin the image in his enthusiastic haste. His brush swished at his side, spraying flecks of water across the floor, while he stared at the problem before him.

Though Edith knew that Egon was too involved in his work to pay much attention, she wanted to tell him her dream anyway. "We were staying at St. Wolfgang's—Mama, Papa, Adele, and me," she began. "We were attending a dinner given in honor of the actress

Katherina Schratt. But when we sat at the long table her place was empty, and the waiter stood on a chair and announced that the actress must be found or His Eminence would have every guest at St. Wolfgang shot. The next moment I was running up a mountainside, it was night, but the phosphorescent snow made the path as visible as if it were reflecting sunlight. I had no shoes, and the frozen ground cut my feet, and I stopped from time to time to dab at the blood with my muff. Then I saw Mama running between the trees, and I called out for her, but either she didn't hear me or I had been mistaken, for she kept running and disappeared into the forest."

Edith remembered how in her dream the echo of her voice was absorbed by the trees. She watched the quick, casual strokes of the brush as Egon painted an eyebrow.

"Then I saw a wooden shed through the trees. Somehow I knew I would find the actress there. When I pulled on the door it fell off its hinges and crumbled like a frozen pastry shell. There were two stalls inside the shed. It was easy enough to tell where Katherina Schratt was hiding because she had slung her mink collar over the top of the stall door. I said to her, 'We've been looking for you, come out now, Katherina Schratt. Katherina Schratt!' "

Egon's hand jerked back. "Edith, please!"

"Forgive me, I didn't mean to startle you. But it was such an odd dream, so terribly vivid. I'll try not to think about it. Another coffee?" He nodded, and she returned to the kitchen without telling her husband the end of the dream—how the stall door had swung open, revealing the stage actress, Franz Josef's paramour, sitting on the toilet, chewing her arm, actually devouring herself, licking the bloodied stump of the elbow, pulling at it the way Edith's father will tear at a gristly chop. Edith had nightmares long before she married Egon Schiele. But though they were difficult to forget and certainly affected her moods, they were no more than minor irritations. They happened to her, as marriage had happened to her, as lovemaking happened to her, as every emotion that a woman was supposed to feel over the course of the day happened to her.

•

Isn't Egon the man about town these days, escorting Edith and Adele, Adele and Edith to the cinema on Thursday evenings, taking them boating on Fridays, promenading through the Wurstelprater with a girl on each arm? Of course he always asks Vallie to join them, but she declines, refusal being the only dignity left to her. How trusting, how complacent she has been, but no longer can she pretend that Egon's new interest is an accidental digression, no, this time he's chosen the wrong turn down a dead end, and no quick coup d'oeil will set him straight. Any day he'll announce which of the sisters he prefers, but Vallie knows already that she will never have him back, so she spurns his conciliatory promises and contracts.

This morning, though, she feels particularly clever, her confidence occasioned by the holidays. She will buy a veil and a purple feather boa from an old clothes dealer to wear with her dress. True, she will have to march in the All Saints' funeral procession without an escort tomorrow, for Egon has decided to flee the festivities and is spending the weekend with his mother in Klosterneuburg. But because of the war there won't be too many rascals grabbing the fleshy knobs of her hams as she walks through the cemetery— maybe she doesn't even need an escort. Besides, she won't have to follow Egon and his friends to some dreary coffeehouse and spend the night listening to them argue about the latest artist's almanac, when in her opinion the only worthy reading these days is the personal advertisements page in the daily paper: "To the lady in the Central Café who handed me a copy of *Neue Freie Presse* the Tuesday past. I would be grateful to return the favor. Box 475."

Vallie wouldn't mind if a gentleman pursued her through the personals, for she has grown tired of Egon's Neukunstgruppe companions and wishes she had livelier company, someone she could take to see the cherubs along the balustrade of the Kinsky Palace, those plump marble dolls whose antics made her laugh aloud in the cavernous hall of the palace, where she had gone alone one day. When no one was watching, she had deposited a chocolate in the open mouth of one of the stone darlings. Actually, Vallie has more than a few splendid memories collected from days when she has been left to entertain herself; she'll survive on her own.

She walks past Egon's easel on the way to the kitchen, and Poldi, the kitten, now a hefty, inveterate creature, darts between her feet. Vallie's slice of black bread slides off the plate, landing butter-side down on the watercolor stretched on the card table to dry. She peels the bread from the paper, too late, alas, the butter has left a grease

stain on Fräulein Adele's mouth and cheeks. Poor Fräulein. Vallie
grins at Adele Harms, but her smile disappears as soon as she considers that on Monday she must answer for the damage done. Poldi
nudges her heel and Vallie angrily pushes the kitten away, her good
mood spoiled now, her prospects as meager as they ever were.

She decides she does need company after all, if the holidays are
going to be salvaged. Nearly anyone will do, yes, even greasy-
lipped Adele Harms and her little sister, Edith. They're within
shouting distance, so Vallie need go no further than the window,
which she unlatches and cranks wide.

"Ladies!" she calls, cupping her hands. "Sweethearts!" She catches
the epithet in the bugle of her hands, letting only a hum escape. But
no one in the Harms's apartment hears her, or perhaps they do hear
her and simply won't acknowledge the improper salutation. Vallie
has decided upon her entertainment, though, and she isn't easily
dismayed, her persistence being of the steady, unyielding, oxen sort.
So she reties her bootlace, covers her hair with a faded print handkerchief, slowly fastens each wooden button of her gaberdine coat
and even sets out a saucer of milk for Poldi.

"Over beyond the village," she sings to herself as she mounts the
steps of the building across the street, "stands the hurdy-gurdy
man." Inside she leans forward over her toes to keep her boot heels
raised above the marble stairs, for she doesn't like to hear her own
footsteps clacking, their echo returning like the steps of someone
following her.

Edith Harms answers the door, and after they kiss Vallie says,
"I've come to see if you and your sister would like to walk with me
in the procession tomorrow. I'm all by myself for the next few
days. We can take the tram to the Kärntnerstrasse this afternoon
and shop for clothes and bouquets." Vallie knows the sisters would
prefer this fashionable block to the ghetto; they are yellow-ribbon
and lace-collar virgins, while Vallie is feathers and secondhand velvet, a fashionable though somewhat dated demimondaine with
a taste for macaroons, marzipan, and other delicious things,
including, of course, those intoxicating chocolates filled with
liqueur.

Edith turns from the door, leaving Vallie on the landing. Vallie
hears her speaking in a hushed voice to her sister, who answers
sharply, "Invite her in!" So Edith returns and ushers Vallie through

the anteroom into the typical parlor of this typical Viennese family: daguerreotypes propped on the spinet, two chairs with backs carved in the shape of a lyre, a fringed pouf, a settee, oriental dishes hanging on the walls, and the deceased grandfather's portrait above the mantle—a bearded, unsmiling patriarch, wearing the light blue Hussar's jacket and pink trousers of his rank and regiment, his sheathed saber arcing above the painting like the plume of an eyebrow.

Adele greets Vallie with a warmth that bears traces of condescension, but Vallie counters with the suggestive smile that a man will use on potential chattel, and in this contest the peach-lipped Adele proves weaker than the watercolor double back in Hietzinger Hauptstrasse 101.

"I've just put on the coffee," she says nervously, using this as her excuse to retreat into the kitchen.

"Please do," Edith offers when Vallie indicates with a glance that she would like to sit. There is an awkward silence while the younger Harms apparently tries to decide whether or not she should keep her visitor company. She takes a step forward, draws back, then excuses herself, explaining that Adele will need her to carry the tray. So she too disappears, the nervous bird, certainly no mate for a rough man like Egon, Vallie thinks, considering the situation objectively. Adele is better suited, though she lacks Edith's pubescent beauty, always a temptation to Egon, Vallie knows; little sprites with round chins and turned-up noses have an advantage over Vallie Neuzil, who because she can't afford the creams and cosmetics, will someday have potato pancake skin, bleeding gums, and swollen veins.

She hears the sisters murmuring in the kitchen, expects that they are deliberating about the "oughts" of the situation—ought they to treat Egon's mistress kindly or coldly on this unannounced visit, ought they to use the best china or would their parents disapprove? And this shopping spree that Vallie has proposed—would it be rude to decline? What excuse could they use? Vallie can only imagine their trite perplexities and doesn't much care what they think of her. She can't help but feel triumphant when prudish girls show their discomfort, for that means she has jostled their sluggish little minds. By puckering her lips into a fish-kiss or hefting her bosom and inserting her fingers beneath her blouse to rearrange her chemise, Vallie can unnerve them, provoke them to imagine her in the act, latched to the spigot, as it were, her back arched, a single bead of sweat sliding along her collarbone and between her breasts. She can have such fun with a drab *süsses Mädel*—now she has a pair of doves to tease.

In preparation she yawns, stretches her arms and dances the rose-lacquered fingernails of her right hand along her left arm, remembers then that the sisters didn't even offer to take her coat, remembers as well the filthy kerchief on her head. She stuffs the kerchief into a pocket. She hangs up the coat in the anteroom and notices a bowler and black cape on one hook of the coat stand, waiting for the father to return. The Harms household clearly expects much from a gentleman, but they won't have one in Egon—his shoulders are too narrow for such a voluminous cape.

Someone has left the key in the front door. Without thinking about her purpose, Vallie gingerly extracts the key and slips it into that moist secret place, the cleft of her bosom, her composure shaken only for a moment when she hears the cups rattling in the kitchen. Since smoke veils a woman's guilt, she helps herself to a cigarette from the pewter box, lights it and puffs greedily, focusing as she smokes on a banal sculpture on the side table. The cast-iron soldier leans down from his horse, his arms embracing the iron maiden, who stands tiptoed on a rock, her lips soldered to her lover's in an endless farewell. *Rubbish*—that's Vallie's opinion. Sentimental rubbish, she thinks, and Egon has fallen under the spell.

"Mama and Papa are visiting our grandmother in Grinzing," Adele announces as she carries in the tray. Edith tags behind, empty-handed, her lemony curls drooping in oddly meticulous disarray, as if held in place with shellac. They both stop short when they see Vallie with the cigarette. Vallie, Egon's concubine, as unwanted in their household as a stain on the Persian rug. Their delicate nostrils quiver, and Vallie can't help but smile at their discomfort. She spurts out a small, quivering smoke ring, dabs the tip of her cigarette into the distending circle as she says, "I helped myself, I hope you don't mind," gesturing to the cigarette box and statue. "I have been admiring your art."

The lie floats behind the screen of smoke, and the sisters wait for both the smoke and Vallie's words to disperse before they move again, each into a chair, so Vallie has the settee to herself.

"Lovely boots," Adele says in an effort to compose herself, mimicking her mother's condescending, admiring voice. Edith hands a cup of the mocha to Vallie.

"Kid leather," Vallie says, more adept than Adele or Edith at shrugging off superficial praise. "They were almost new when I bought them, though it's true that I have to stuff tissue in the toes to make them fit just right."

Adele's lips, Adele's peach lips, curl into a faint sneer—second-hand shoes, how unfortunate, how disgusting, really.

"I paid the old Jew with kisses."

"Do you travel much?" Adele asks quickly, and Vallie begins to give up the hope of provoking these sweet girls—she should have dressed the part, worn her flapper's dress with its tinsel-weave and wrapped a feather boa six times around her neck.

"We went to Geneva a few summers past—Edith, Mama, and Papa . . ." Adele continues without allowing Vallie to reply. The elder Harms has a full repertoire of tedious subjects and she launches into an account of a visit to a foundling hospital, a monastery, the quay where Empress Elisabeth was stabbed by an anarchist in 1898.

"Luigi Luccheni," Edith comments dreamily. "Luigi Luccheni, that was his name—the man who plunged a file into the empress's bosom. We saw the bench where he had sat. He sat all night sharpening his file, waiting for the sun to rise, waiting for the steamboat crew to begin swabbing the decks. He sat all morning waiting for the boat to make its first tour around the lake, rubbing his file against the block, swish, swish, waiting until the quay was quiet and the two women were crossing the street."

"Edith, I doubt Fräulein Neuzil cares to rehearse the tragedy with you."

"A file, you say? That's what he used?"

"He punctured her heart—and she didn't even know she had been wounded. She walked up the gangway of the steamship and col-lapsed." Edith palpates her own bosom, indicating the location of the fatal wound.

"The horse chestnuts were in their second bloom," Adele says, obviously irritated by her younger sister's melodrama. "Geneva is the Eden of the continent. Have one, Fräulein?" She pushes the dish of pastries across the table, and Vallie, always interested in a sweet with a hidden filling, is pleased to see that along with the apple strudel there are two delicate cream puffs. She chooses the larger of the two, bites into the side, and the pastry crackles, flakes floating like wafers of soot onto the table, the floor, Vallie's lap. In an effort to keep the bulb intact she stuffs the entire pastry into her mouth and tries to chew. But the puff is so swollen with filling that it explodes, and rivulets of custard ooze out the corners of her lips and down her chin. She wipes her face with the back of her hand, remembers herself and reaches hastily for a napkin, knowing that their awe and fear of her is dribbling away with the custard filling.

"Yes, I remember. Switzerland had a second summer in the middle of November," Edith says, a courteous, well-timed diversion, giving Vallie the chance to finish swallowing the cream and pastry and to cover her mouth with the napkin.

"And it had even snowed the week before," Adele adds.

"I remember that unusual fall, too." It is Vallie's turn. She twists the napkin into a tight spiral as she speaks. "Egon and I lived in the country for nearly a year. Perhaps he has told you about it, so you know about his arrest the following spring. An unfortunate affair. Spending three weeks in jail for letting the little girls of Neulengbach peek at his naughty pictures." As she offers this brief history she ripens with confidence again, for she realizes that they don't know all they should about the handsome, eccentric artist from across the street, and though the current Vallie Neuzil doesn't matter to these girls, though they have no respect for this intruder, the Vallie Neuzil of the past will always come between the Harms sisters and Egon Schiele. A few ineradicable memories give her the advantage.

"Filthy pictures and a filthy mind—that's what they said about my dear boy," she taunts, stressing the possessive.

Edith's brow furrows as she considers the scandal, and Vallie senses at once that this little sparrow is already in love—the expression on her face indicates the terrible fact: Egon's scandal will have as much importance and no more than a scar, a pale, puckered knot hidden beneath a collar and tie. Yes, this forgiving bird intends to take Vallie's place.

Adele, on the other hand, clearly doesn't want the family name tainted with rumors of scandal. She stirs her mocha thoughtfully, tips a spoonful of the lukewarm liquid back into the cup. "We are sorry to hear this about Herr Schiele," she finally says, spitting out the bitter words, hastily sipping the mocha as if to wash away the taste. "We never realized . . ."

"And we do not care!" announces the younger sister, slapping her leg for emphasis, a peculiarly masculine gesture, Vallie thinks, noting the disparities between the sisters. "We do not care," repeats Edith, with quiet finality.

"I doubt Mama will allow us to . . ."

"Mama and Papa will never know." Edith's lips are set, welded with contempt. Vallie feels obliged to divert the swelling dispute, though she is fascinated by this glimpse of secret resentments and would like to see more. Perhaps another time.

"I prefer the city to the country," she says. "The only electric lights in Neulengbach were in the Rathaus. I would like to visit all the great cities of the world before I die. But I won't travel if I can't travel first class and wear silk gowns and dine on oysters and truffled pâté, just like Katherina Schratt."

"Who?" Edith asks, sullen but always politely inquisitive.

"Katherina Schratt? You have never heard of her? Why, you know the name of the empress's assassin and you don't know the name of the empress's rival? Astonishing! Do you never go to the theater?"

"We go to the cinema. Herr Schiele has taken us to the cinema twice."

"You have never heard your father speak of the beautiful Katherina Schratt, never heard your mother say jealously that Katherina Schratt is too old for the stage, too corpulent, too awkward? Katherina Schratt, Franz Josef's paramour." It was just like Vallie to unintentionally bring the conversation round to that interesting topic—men and their mistresses. Every hotel has its row of *chambres séparées* and every man has his mistress. Gentlemen will continue loosening their neckbands and embracing beautiful women who scoff at the matronly title of "Frau." The wealthy virgins of Vienna had better accept this fact as a matter of course.

"If Katherina Schratt wants to start a collection of, say, human feet, Franz Josef would have his own left foot amputated and then order the people of Vienna to do the same."

"About that procession tomorrow," Adele says abruptly, returning to Vallie's earlier proposal. "My sister and I are expected to keep our parents company. You see, we have promised to spend the holiday with our relatives. We are joining our parents in Grinzing."

"Then you don't want to come shopping on the Kärntnerstrasse today?"

"Another time, perhaps."

Vallie looks at Edith for her own decision, but Edith is staring at her feet, apparently still contemplating the wilful Katherina Schratt. Then Vallie notices Edith's slippers, white satin slippers, graveshoes so thin that the bulges of her corns show, so fine that they seem to reflect the mottled light angling off the wallpaper. A simple, unobtrusive pair compared to Adele's brocaded flats or Vallie's tie-boots, and Vallie finds herself feeling envious—she would like to have such graceful, simple shoes.

"Another time, yes," she says, eyeing the remaining cream puff, forcing herself to resist it. When she stands, the stolen key slides from a vertical to a diagonal position inside her chemise, and it takes a concentrated effort for her to remove her coat from the coat hook, tuck it under her arm, and thank the Harms sisters for the mocha and the pleasant tête-à-tête.

"Another time," she echoes, and bids them adieu.

Another time, yes, when the devoted Catholics of Hietzing aren't marching to the cemetery with their props of candles and colored lanterns, when families aren't competing for the crowd's admiration by dressing up the tombstones of their relatives with nosegays and wreaths, when the old women aren't keeping their all-night vigil, moaning invocations to the dead. Even today, All Saints' Day, children dressed in black follow on their mother's heels, pinching and kicking each other, receiving a sound slap on the ear from their mother when they let out an irreverent giggle.

Vallie will have to march without an escort or companion. Another time, perhaps, she will shop with Edith and Adele, watch them buy ribbons, cloth roses to pin on their dresses, and satin slippers, slippers as rare and enticing as a cream puff on a Viennese dessert tray—though she herself is only twenty, Vallie covets the slippers and the small feet inside them; she covets Edith's youthful, diminutive figure. The sisters have never heard of Katherina Schratt, while Vallie has worked in a dress shop and has endured the insults of Vienna's haughtiest matrons just so she could purchase standing-room tickets at the Burgtheater. But that was before she met Egon

—with the little money he earns from commissions, and with some help from Herr Benesch, they have been able to go to the theater or the opera at least once every fortnight, though lately he has been wasting his growing income on courtship. Soon Vallie will be forced to return to work.

But who knows what might befall a girl with Vallie Neuzil's wits? With luck she could end up as rich as Anna Sacher, who began chopping vegetables in the kitchen of a hotel, married the hotel's owner, inherited the hotel when he died, and now spends her days drinking champagne, buckling tiny satin saddle-jackets on her pug-dogs and smoking cigars. Vallie would agree to marry anyone if the man in question could make her rich. More likely she would engage herself to a slick spendthrift who would simply disappear one day, leaving her with his debts, and she'd turn into another lady green-grocer like the fictional Frau Sophie Pimpermuss of the newspapers —a wry, sensible character, with a mustard-colored mustache on her upper lip and elbows that look like the hocks of an elephant, or so Vallie imagines.

Youth—this is a girl's most important asset, and Vallie's is fast being diminished by her propensity to eat more chocolates than are good for her. She should use her childish beauty as a dowry while she still has time, find someone to provide for her in later years when she becomes portly and the skin beneath her eyes starts to sag. The child-wife is in fashion in Vienna, and soon Vallie will be ob-solete. Eventually, nature will play its cruelest joke, transforming her back into a child at the end, shrinking her, weakening and con-fusing her, until she is nothing but a tiny, babbling, smooth-gummed creature spending the days cooking noodles for her cats, a roomful of cats, a cat in the cupboard, on the counter, on the sill, beneath the bed, a cat in heat, cats humping, cats sleeping, a cat stalking across the threshold with a sparrow in its mouth, one bro-ken wing dragging along the floor, two tiny feet sticking out like toothpicks. Vallie knows how a cat must relish the sound of the bird's hollow bones cracking between its teeth. Bird feet. Dainty, petite bird feet.

The idea comes to Vallie like a memory, an astonishing, long-forgotten memory. It has something to do with the latchkey against her bosom, slippers, and birds—an idea so shameless that she looks around her, half-expecting a passerby to sense what she is plotting.

But everyone is in a rush today. Even the hefty woman with raven feathers in her hat hurries so quickly that her poodle can't keep up with her, and the impertinent thing locks its legs, sits back on its haunches, so the lady must tug the leash while the pooch skids along the sidewalk like a sled on dull rusted runners. No, not a soul suspects that Vallie is a sort of criminal in her own way, secretly planning an action that will, temporarily at least, paralyze her enemy.

Art Is Dying

SOMETHING sweet. Something warm and sweet—a cup of hot chocolate and I'd feel like myself again, the mistress promised, and I nodded, glad to have her sympathy, comforted by the scent of her perfume mingling with the smoke from the wood stove. At last I was inside cottage forty-five, sitting across from Vallie Neuzil, our knees practically touching. The artist stood behind her and submerged his hands in her hair as she spoke, pulling back the skin of her forehead so her eyes opened wide. Though I guessed at once that Vallie couldn't have been more than a few years older than me, I felt more backward, more helpless and virginal than I would have if I were the girl embossed in profile on the ivory cameo pinned to her dress.

But hadn't she seen me before? Vallie wondered aloud. Hadn't I been—been where? Vallie had met so many Neulengbach girls, she couldn't keep track. "The village is overrun with pretty girls," she said. "The village is . . ."

"Your village of Neulengbach," the artist interrupted, his voice flattening, as if he were talking in his sleep, "I don't trust it."

"And yet he refuses to return to the city," added Vallie. "This village—"

"Tell me: what do your people do after they have finished with the day's work? What do they think? Whenever we come near, they stop talking," Egon Schiele said importantly, hefting his shoulders, his questions implying that he and his mistress were—deservedly—

the main topic of conversation in our little village. He turned toward the kitchen, walking with his back slightly arched, the way young children walk when they are making fun of adults.

"I'm never going home," I announced. "I would rather die than return home. There's nothing for me there." In response, the mistress leaned forward and ran her finger around the curve of my ear, murmuring something about a poor little rabbit lost in the storm, a tender, soft thing who had fled into the world, to strangers. But I was safe here, yes, no one would hurt me, I could stay as long as I pleased. She lifted my chin with two fingers and searched my eyes, her smile suggesting that together we could resist this despotic artist. Then she followed him into the kitchen, leaving me alone in the studio, alone in the room that until that moment I had only seen from the outside and once from the threshold. I heard them whispering—arguing, I assumed, about whether to treat me as a foundling, a trespasser, an enemy, a fool; I heard him persuading her that I would only do them harm and her conceding, both of them dallying in the kitchen, I suspected, in the hope that I would be gone when they returned.

There was little furniture in the atelier—two chairs with bent, tubular legs, a cheap pinewood table, a settee, easels, a full-length mirror. On the top shelf of the single bookcase some porcelain dolls with rosebud lips were turned this way and that, all gazing off in different directions, all amused by some private, obscene joke. Beside them a puppet magistrate with a gray robe and floppy felt hat sagged against a pile of paintbrushes and mangled tubes of paint. On the shelf below, half a dozen toy horses made of glass, wood, and marble stood haunch to haunch. The table was covered with pencil sketches spilling out from portfolios, chalk studies of mouths, noses, clusters of arms and legs bent in unnatural angles, and propped on the easel was a finished watercolor of a girl with peach-colored flesh, pulling her dress over her head. Brown drops of paint had been spattered across an old cowhide rug. The window was black, opaque, and any face on the opposite side would have been invisible. In those few minutes alone, I made up my mind to stay, though I kept my eyes lowered when the artist and his mistress entered the room again. She carried a tray, upon it three cups filled with steaming milk and a bowl of powdered chocolate. She had smoothed her hair behind her ears again, and he had tucked his tie—striped, with tiny silhouettes of ballerinas between the lines—into his high-waisted pants.

"Keep me here at least for this one night. I will go to my grandmother in Vienna tomorrow," I begged before they could speak, before they could order me away. "I will leave Neulengbach forever. This village, it is bewitched, you know. The old hunchback woman who lives in the basement below the apothecary knows spells to drive people insane. She used her magic on the musician in the bell tower—they say that it's because of her he won't come down. Have you heard his music? He plays most every night, through winter and summer. And there is Hopping Karl—you must have seen him hopping up and down the street. It's said that Hopping Karl can make your hair turn white with his spittle."

"Ah, your cruel village," the artist said. "Old women are witches, strangers are insane, and your toad Karl, he'll give you warts."

I wanted to say, *He's not my Karl!* I wanted to say, *I'm not like the rest of them.* Instead I merely pleaded, "Please, just let me stay with you one night."

But they had already made a decision—I didn't need to beg. "You can stay with us," Vallie Neuzil said. "We won't send you away. And don't mind him—he doesn't mean any harm. You're a sweet child."

At that, Egon Schiele fixed his squinting, haughty eyes on me. I understood at once what the artist and his mistress had decided in the kitchen. They would keep me for the night, and they would see how willing I was, how shameless, how eager. I would make myself useful. But as soon as I realized what they wanted, I remembered as well what I had come for: to watch—simply this—as if they were a moving picture, grander than life. To watch, just as the girl in the picture was watching, silent, unchanging. A girl wearing boots, her brown dress hiked over her head.

The artist polished his front teeth with the tip of his tongue, and his lips parted in a smile, as though the porcelain dolls had shared their joke with him.

•

" 'On each national holiday a joint toast to art and science is proposed; perhaps they mean one and the same to the idiot. But they are deadly enemies. Where one of them exists, the other flees . . .' "

Egon quotes from the small volume entitled *Art is Dying,* by Victor Aubertin. "Rubbish, yes?" he goads, and Anton gingerly taps his cigarette against the ashtray in reply. "What are our choices? Aubertin versus Burliuk. The Four Horsemen versus the Blaue Reiter. You and I must choose the New Art and learn its principles— construction drawing, graphics, the treatment of the plane and its intersections, an equilibrium of perspectives. Scientific principles. Because of science, we can see stars that we never knew existed, we can examine the geometry of a hair follicle, we can see the threads inside lines. Victor Aubertin is dying, Egon Schiele is dying, Anton Peschka is dying. But not art—art is our purest expression of death, and death never dies. For this Aubertin despises it. And he blames science for mankind's helplessness."

Anton mumbles in uncertain agreement.

"We are vessels for the spirit, precious, fragile, doomed vessels," Egon continues in his inspired passion. "When we are gone someone else will contain this liquid, this life-soul, and if no once accepts it then the spirit will drain into a tributary, flow into a quiet lagoon and evaporate. But sooner or later the immortal spirit will rain upon another capable man."

Anton Peschka fills his mouth with beer so he won't have to contribute any wisdom. He never quite understands what Egon is talking about when he expounds upon the nature of this inviolate world-spirit and the artist's privileges and responsibilities. But Anton tolerates Egon's mystical polemics, attributes it to the mix of thick Bohemian blood from his mother and thin, blue northern blood from his father.

"A man who says that art is dying wishes he was an artist. A man who says that science has degenerated into devil's play wishes he was a scientist. Men who lack any power of invention are the ones who condemn the inventors."

"They fear change," Anton adds limply.

"They tell us that we are unscrupulous and vulgar. They call us aesthetes, hedonists, decadents, perverts!" Egon cries, his voice rising a pitch with each word. But his shrill hysteria doesn't break through the din in this cramped tavern, and not one of the burly, bulbous-nosed hackdrivers on nearby benches takes his eyes off his stein to stare at the young rebel. Nonetheless, Anton rests a hand on his friend's wrist in an effort to calm him. Pederast. Corruptor of small children. It is 1912, Egon's trial is only three months behind him. He should be more cautious in public places.

"Vessels for the world-spirit," Anton coaxes, and Egon's voice drops to a low, fierce growl. "We are gifted; we must make use of our talent," he says, and Anton nods protectively, paternally. Egon's convictions make him so vulnerable to attack. Anton lets his eyes wander across the low ceiling, where the pipes have been painted a creamy white and water stains mar the plaster. Of all the Neukunstgruppe artists, Egon has been the one to suffer most from the critics' ridicule. In turn, he is more bitter and more idealistic, continually regenerating himself with his megalomaniac belief in the artist's mission. Anton doesn't share Egon's pretensions—as far as he's concerned, art is a profession and Anton Peschka an employee. Ideas, he thinks, have the same effect as tobacco and alcohol: in moderation they won't hamper the next day's work, will even help to increase a man's enthusiasm, but in excess they will impair. He sips the dregs of beer and studies Egon's slender fingers curled around the handle of his mug. Egon should learn to treat his ideas less severely, to spend less time worrying about the impact of art upon the public and more time working. Anton appreciates Egon's younger sister all the more, playful Fräulein Gerti, who has her brother's quick intelligence without his ambition and who knows how to make the best of daily life.

Egon could stand to learn a few things from his sister, Anton reflects as Egon parrots the Blaue Reiter polemic about the importance of mathematics, the potential of algebra, how certain numbers invoked in secret combinations have magical powers.

·

Little People's Paradise Hour: Parents, don't be dissuaded by those who try to convince you that Vienna is no place for a child. Bring your little ones along and see for yourself! While you're waltzing at an authentic Viennese Fasching or celebrating your anniversary with champagne and *Tafelspitz* at a hotel restaurant, Vienna will entertain your children for free. Forget the troubles at home, forget your debts, forget your remorse and forget your sons and daughters, who, rest assured, will be safe.

The Vienna that most tourists come to know is the famously jubilant, witty, debonair Vienna who wears a velvet-lapeled waist-

coat and a polka-dot bow tie. But there is another Vienna, a less
visible city, a potbellied, ashen Vienna with a Kris Kringle nose,
clopping about in wooden clogs, a Biedermeier Vienna who belongs
to the little people. How strange it is, how miraculous really, that
the children of tourists are able to find the unmarked theater in the
Leopoldstadt where no one over the age of twelve is allowed, not
even the Biedermeier man himself. How independent and determined these young foreigners become when they search for secret
plays and masques. Any commissionaire knows that when the children set off for the theater in the Leopoldstadt they are, like Or-
pheus, as good as dead, at least for the evening. So he will pass the
time in a noisy Keller, waiting for the show to end before he returns
to the hotel.

And you should do the same. Your children will be rapt spectators, their anticipation erupting in bursts and squeals as the puppets
do what puppets are supposed to do and knock one another over the
heads with shovels or dance together or marry in an extravagant
ceremony where the bride wears an organdy gown and rides away
in the arms of the groom on a flower-bedecked tableau vivant float,
followed by eight Imperial Court attendants on horseback. And
while you dine on beef broth with liver dumplings, your children
can watch the reenactment of a miracle, as an empress gives birth to
a son. The miniature bed will be facing away from the audience, so
the children won't be able to see the infant slip out from between
the puppet's legs, but the event will be narrated by the State Chancellor puppet in whatever happens to be the common language of
the audience. He will stand at the opposite corner of the stage and
curl his mustache around the spindles of his fingers as he speaks.

"The little prince grows up into a frail young man. He learns how
to stand with his arms raised while his valet buttons his uniforms
and smoothes the tassels of his epaulets, he learns how to dance and
how to shoot and how to welcome ambassadors to the palace. But
he is frequently sick and always anxious, so he drinks champagne
laced with a special medicine to help him sleep and declares himself
to be the most nervous man in the most nervous century."

The children applaud when the Crown Prince raises his champagne glass to his lips and slurps loudly. They stop when the royal
puppet faces the audience and begins to clap at them, as though they
are the spectacle. But when an unseemly sound escapes from the

Crown Prince's fundament, the children know that they have every right to laugh. And so they do, while the puppet bows appreciatively. Then he disappears below the stage, reemerging seconds later with a woman at his side.

"The Crown Princess," the State Chancellor announces as a fiddle hidden behind the curtains launches into a rondo and the stage fills again with counts and countesses. Puppet waiters file by carrying miniature platters of pheasant stuffed with *pancetta,* pâté with juniper-berry sauce, artichokes and white beans, cheese strudel, rum babas, and poppyseed cake. Soon the clamor from the young audience drowns out the narrator's voice, for this is their celebration too, and if they can't sample the delicacies they can at least sing and bounce in their seats in time with the music. Until the music stops, and the stage is silent.

"Happiness never lasts forever," the Chancellor warns. The flames inside the gauze hoods of the footlights flicker ominously, and a few children cover their eyes with their hands.

"The most nervous man in the most nervous century meets the most nervous woman."

The children hold their breath as a lady wearing a pale blue organdy dress with yellow appliqué ascends from the black depths behind the stage and faces the Crown Prince and Princess.

"Will the nervous woman curtsy to the Princess? Or will she prove herself ill-bred and impertinent?"

The other puppets turn to watch, waiting with the children and the Chancellor, waiting for history to be altered. In a flurry of organdy and lace, the anonymous lady curtsies, the Crown Prince and Princess nod, and as soon as the wife turns her back the Prince embraces the beauty in the pale blue gown; the curtain descends.

During intermission the theater remains dark. Children murmur excitedly about possible outcomes—surely someone will die, but who? And by whose hand? Bags of gingernuts appear mysteriously, and each child helps himself before passing the bag down the row. Soon the sound of their crunching fills the room, their jaws moving in synchronized rhythm. The children swallow quickly when the rustling begins offstage.

The State Chancellor slips out from behind the curtain, pinches the handles of his mustache, and says, "Voilà!" as the curtain rises behind him, revealing a bedroom with glowing candelabra and thick

satin drapes covering the walls. Pinned to the drapes are six miniature porcelain eagles with outstretched wings, deer antlers made
from pipe cleaners, and a tiny, furry marmoset.

The children shriek and applaud the inventive set. The State
Chancellor raises his hand to silence them. "The nervous man at his
hunting lodge," he announces.

The Crown Prince bobs up, wearing a pleated silk dressing gown.
The nervous lady appears on the opposite side of the stage and
approaches the Prince, who takes her hand and leads her to a table.
As soon as they have seated themselves the valet enters, carrying a
platter of cold venison and a bottle of champagne, and he is followed
by the Prince's driver, who perches on a stool and begins to sing a
melancholy song about a dying tree on the bank of the Danube. The
valet stands beside him and claps in time to the song, and the children join in. When the song is over, the driver and the valet depart,
leaving the lovers alone.

The Prince and the woman fall into each other's arms on the
canopied bed, and the Chancellor goes about the room making sure
that the doors are locked, snuffing the candles until the stage is as
dark as the theater, the silence broken only by coughing in the back
row. The children strain to make out the figures onstage but in the
darkness they can't distinguish the dining table from the bed, the
bed from the bodies of the lovers.

After a minute or so there is a sudden flash, the pop of a pistol,
the smell of sulfur trickling into the audience. The children continue
to sit in silence, waiting for the next shot, for a scream, for the
Chancellor to explain what has happened, but the only sound is a
clock chiming at regular intervals to let them know that time has
passed. Finally the stage begins to brighten, the gaslights come on
one by one with a hiss, and the Chancellor announces, "The following morning."

Purplish, opaque smoke from the pistol makes it difficult to follow the quick sequence of actions. The Prince has sat up on the bed,
positioned the night table so the mirror faces him, and he holds the
pistol above the mound of blue cloth that is, the children understand,
all that remains of the lady. The Prince presses the pistol against his
temple. Most of the children close their eyes so they only hear the
shot and smell the smoke, but when they blink again they see the
Prince slumped against the nightstand, his wooden face shattered,
covered with dripping crimson.

Some of the younger children start to whimper, one little boy sobs with a sudden, honking sound, other children start to cry, and some run toward the exit. Their hysteria is compounded by the voice of the puppeteer behind the tiny door of the bedroom, along with the sound of splintering wood as a spoon-sized ax breaks through the door's panels.

If anyone chances to be walking past the theater at this hour they will witness an extraordinary scene: dozens of children scattering like billiard balls as a bearded man dashes between them, catching them by their collars, lifting them up while their chubby, knickered legs peddle in the air, setting them back down facing in the opposite direction. Some of the children bump against his knees, but he has only to take them by their shoulders and point them toward the First District and their hotels. In a matter of minutes the square in front of the theater is empty. And if it happens—as it usually does—that a few dazed stragglers wander back, the Biedermeier man will take them by the hand and lead them to their hotels himself.

·

May 4, 1912: After twenty-one days in jail, Egon is learning to manipulate pleasure with a careful strategy of delay; he has decided that he prefers to anticipate rather than to remember his meager satisfactions, so at mealtimes, while other men raise their soup bowls to their mouths, Egon sips pristine spoonfuls of broth, leaving the noodles behind, eating them only when he has drained the wooden bowl entirely and has already soaked up the fat glazing the sides with a crust of bread. This way he divides the meal into three courses, and division always makes a poor man feel more prosperous. Nothing matters as much to Egon these days as a full stomach and an occasional smoke. He realizes how easy it would be for a week to dissolve into a year, how a man sentenced to a life term will forget conventional time—a prisoner's sole purpose is to find a few delights in the monotony, so he must reassign values to things, adapt his likes and dislikes to available materials.

A lesser pleasure for Egon, really just another strategy of waiting, has to do with a peculiar band of light that appears on his cell wall for a quarter of an hour most afternoons. The ends of the line are bent, the curve marked enough for the line to be called a crescent. A crack in the closed shutter lets in the light, and Egon likes to catch the shard on the back of his hand so it splits his skin.

His cell in St. Pölten is airier than the basement cell in Neuleng-bach; this cot has no lice or fleas, and he has only to call for the guard when he needs to use the toilet at the end of the corridor. With a little ingenuity a man could learn to live tolerably well in St. Pölten. But Egon's trial has been set for Wednesday, and since he is sure to be acquitted, his efforts are limited to his procedure of eating soup, to the little game he plays with the light on sunny afternoons, and to the act of defecation, which he puts off until he cramps, letting the excrement collect in the coils of his gut so that those few minutes on the toilet will be that much more satisfying.

But his internment will end soon, he'll be a free man before the end of next week, the false charge of seduction dropped; Egon's most intimate self remains unaltered, unaffected by prison, and in this way he stays an oddity among the inmates. Even the guards seem to sense that he won't remain in St. Pölten for long—no one takes the trouble to introduce himself, they have stopped bothering him about his supposed crime, and in the yard or at meals Egon is content to watch the men smoke and listen to their chatter. Early in the day they are full of ingenious ideas—one man has designed, in his head, an efficient, steam-powered cider press, another can tell you how with pipe cleaners and human hair you can build a block and tackle strong enough to lift a horse. In the morning the men are taut with plans, their faces pinched, their eyes alert, but as the day progresses they argue with faltering intensity. By the end of the evening, after supper, their mottled eyelids are lowered in boredom, and they speak only to beg for or to proffer cigarettes.

The prisoners earn up to two hundred kreuzer a day doing odd jobs around the yard, and they use their money to purchase anything from tobacco to roast veal at the prison commissary. Newcomers who haven't received their wages yet are offered charity by the sullen, corpulent cook. A thimbleful of beer or coffee, a cube of ham, an extra ounce of bread . . . At first Egon accepted these with the same enthusiastic gratitude he would have shown to a waiter after a memorable meal, but he received only a gummy sneer in return. Though no one explained, he sensed soon enough that this cook didn't want thanks, for he did as he pleased and didn't care to have any prisoner treating him like hired help.

On the first morning that Egon accepts his extra portion of black bread without a word, the cook reaches across the table and tops off the crust with a slab of cold bacon. Unlucky for both of them that Egon will be gone within the week, or at least that's Egon's thought as he carries his tray into the cafeteria. He sits on the end of a bench beside the red-tufted dog who had revealed Egon's supposed crime to him, and the old man's gaze settles on Egon's hefty slice of meat while he continues with his lecture on congenital differences between the convict and ordinary men.

"It's the jaw that gives us away—generally sharp and prognathous. And a head either too big or too small."

He is interrupted by a younger, squint-eyed prisoner sitting across the table, who adds to the list, "Twisted noses. Ears as big as saucers."

"And scanty whiskers," a third voice says.

"A marked etiolation of the skin," continues Egon's learned neighbor, still staring at the bacon. Egon tears the strip into unequal parts and places the smaller piece on the old man's empty plate, but instead of stuffing it into his mouth as Egon expects him to, he leans back on the bench and lights a cigarette, his eyes unfocused now as he continues. "We have a pallor due to long cellular containment," he says wisely. "But I don't go in for the theory that we're all born blanched and ugly. Speaking from experience, I can say we exercise a power of fascination over the ladies. We're a class apart. Anyone here able to blush? It's a registered fact, eighty-four percent of us don't know how to blush."

He flicks the cigarette over his plate, and the ash falls, crumbling on the fatty membrane of the bacon. Obviously used to controlling the discussion, he tests his power with a long pause, waits for someone to break the silence. But no one speaks, so eventually the old man belches into his fist and goes on. "We have a particular kind of astuteness. Vanity is largely present, and I cannot attest to an overlarge capacity for remorse. No one here cares much to look back upon the damage done. And about our documented insensibility to pain, well, we have proof of that, don't we, boys?"

"We have Peter!" someone shouts.

"Peter!" the men chorus, and from an adjacent table two men lift a stocky inmate by his arms until his feet are dangling above the floor.

"Peter!" the men cry once more, and Peter good-naturedly salutes them with a puffy, fingerless left hand. But the racket in the cafeteria immediately brings in two guards, as though Peter were the sign that this herd needed to be rounded up and sent off for an hour of exercise.

"Up with you, go on," the guards grunt, beating sticks against the wall. "Go on, now." Egon rises with the other men and follows them out. As they enter the muddy prison yard, the old man who had held court at the breakfast table catches up to Egon and signals him with a characteristic hiss.

"They used to let us shave ourselves," he says, his breath fogging in the damp morning air. "Until the day they passed the razor to Peter. When they came round again Peter passed the razor back, along with four bloody fingers in his crucible. So that's why . . . but here, your neck is as red as Peter's fingers, you're a blusher. Boys, we have a blusher among us!" His voice rises a pitch as he heralds this novelty, St. Pölten's principal exception, the only modest man in the crowd.

·

Three years before Egon Schiele is charged with corrupting minors and detained in prison for twenty-four days, he sits in a lecture hall in the Vienna Academy of Fine Arts. An adolescent boy stands naked on a dais, his back turned toward the students. Professor Griepenkerl directs the boy to shift his weight to his left foot, then with a pointer calls the students' attention to the resulting folds of skin above the pelvic region. As the students arrange their paper on their easels, the professor asks them to consider the rise and fall of classical art, from the outstanding advances of Minoan primitivism to late Hellenic frivolity. He asks them to recall the muscles and ribs of the Parthenon Dionysus, the Lapiths and Centaurs of the Ionic friezes, the robes of the headless *Head of the Procession*. He warns his students to shade with precise cross-hatching and avoid blurring the subtle gradations of the body's landscape into an undifferentiated flat surface. Full figures, depth, dimension—these are the illusions an apprentice must master.

"Such perfect proportions," he says, drawing a rectangle in the air with his pointer, framing the model's shoulders and back. "The eye follows the movement of light and shade. The human figure is most pleasing to us in its absolute symmetry—beauty depends on symmetry, just as truth depends on logic."

The professor, well known for his arcane polemics, is praised by many students for his thorough, if conservative, critiques, and he lectures with the rambling intensity of a solitary man so involved in some problem of intellect that he unwittingly speaks his thoughts aloud. Usually, no one pays much attention to Professor Griepenkerl when he pontificates. But today a small group of students listens carefully—these are the youngsters, led by Egon Schiele, who have been voicing increasingly hostile views, and now they sit with their arms folded in defiance.

Rather than challenge them directly and disrupt the rest of the class, Griepenkerl chooses to ignore them. "As Greek society became corrupt, so did its art. Sculptors came to prefer disheveled old market-women and little boys strangling geese to the gods and goddesses of high antiquity; petty human melodrama replaced the ideals of humanism, and soon no one could distinguish between ugliness and beauty." He removes his pince-nez and rubs the lenses with his handkerchief, taking the opportunity to scowl at the rebels with his misty, nearsighted eyes, rebuking without actually confronting them. It has been a decade of rebellion, of chaotic images and ideological fervor, of artists who spit upon the past. The professor feels obligated to preserve the options for the next generations, to let young men choose for themselves between tradition and ignorance. Oh, he has heard the argument—Wickhoff telling a hall full of educated men that with their second-class minds they think modern art decadent because they cannot face modern truth. Easy enough for an antihumanist sycophant like Wickhoff to champion any passing trend. "Equality of all eras in the eyes of God" is a notion that leads only to confusion.

The professor continues with his lecture, advising his class to resist the paganism of the French artists, droning mechanically on, more eager now than his students for the hour to end so he may retire to his studio and work on his portrait of Elisabeth.

But even as he speaks, one of the upstarts across the room bangs his fist against the wooden box chair, knocks with a steady, thumping defiance. In a moment a second student has joined the first, and then another and another until the clamor from that mutinous corner of the room becomes so loud that the professor is forced to halt midway through a sentence. He approaches the mutineers, his pointer raised. The students stop knocking and look around uncertainly, until the irreverent Egon Schiele begins to snicker. Griepenkerl has no choice—he brings his pointer down sharply on Egon's bony shoulder. But this only incites the class, and their laughter is like the first chord of a symphony. The boy on the platform finally turns around, his hands crossed over his groin. But when he sees that he is not the object of ridicule he too begins to laugh, and his shadow on the screen behind him ripples, as though the screen itself were being shaken.

"Stop it!" Professor Griepenkerl demands, his face lined with fissures of white from the effort of self-restraint—he is a man prone to heart ailments and has been warned by his physician to avoid losing his temper. "Stop it this instant!" But the knocking continues, the laughter continues, so the old man, keeping his eyes level though his twitching lips betray him, marches between the rows of easels, tapping the floor with his pointer like a blind man with a cane. At the exit a draft makes the hairs of his beard quiver.

He slams the door behind him and leans his full weight against it in case anyone tries to escape. He fumbles in his vest pocket for his keys. "That's right, keep on, young devils, laugh as loud as you please. No one can hear you," he whispers as he locks the door. He stands straight, counts slowly to ten to control his breathing and walks with admirable composure down the empty corridor.

•

What is this? Vallie Neuzil creeping through the Harms's dark apartment on a late Sunday afternoon, straw basket in hand? She tests the weakness of the boards beneath the carpet by pressing down the pointed toe of her shoe and listening for the creak. Only when the front foot rests fully on the carpet does she drag the other forward.

Rain drips from the building's projecting entablature, the drops pinging like sharp, pizzicato notes of a cello as Vallie makes her way to the parlor window, kneels on the settee, traces the velvet roses on the upholstery with her fingertips, carefully keeping her shoulders lower than the sill so if Egon happens to glance up from his easel he won't catch Vallie staring at him from the Harms's parlor window. But the precaution isn't necessary, for he has left his canvas to dry, gone to the kitchen to make himself coffee or simply to warm his hands, and in his place on the stool sits the kitten Poldi, a foreleg raised over her head as she cleans the secret pockets of fur with her tongue.

Vallie tries to imagine herself as the cherished daughter of Herr Johann Harms, with intact hymen, waiting by the window, waiting for a man to ask for her hand in marriage, the prospective groom being the artist from Hietzinger Hauptstrasse 101; yes, Egon Schiele will deflower little Edith Harms. Vallie knows what Edith wants and what Egon has promised because she has just read through the most recent entries in Edith's diary. She knows that Edith already considers Egon her possession, as though he were for sale and Johann Harms could buy him for his daughter, whatever the cost.

There had been other girls who had wanted Egon for themselves. In Krumau and then in Neulengbach, pubescent darlings would follow him back to the cottage, where they would take turns posing for him. But though the peasant girls might have inspired him with their starved, inexperienced sensuality, they couldn't match Vallie for exuberance—she knew better than anyone how to have fun. Still, in recent weeks Vallie has felt ancient, peevish, a burden to her lover. She stained Egon's watercolor portrait of Adele Harms with butter, took money from his coat pocket so she could buy chocolates for herself, and when Egon left a torn sock draped discreetly over the edge of the bureau, Vallie didn't mend it as she used to do. If only Gustav Klimt hadn't believed in him, then Egon wouldn't have received so many commissions, Vallie and Egon wouldn't have been able to afford the Hietzinger Hauptstrasse apartment, and they never would have met Edith and Adele, Adele and Edith Harms.

Well, Vallie isn't one to waste away lamenting a failed affair—she is determined to stay cheerful, mischievous, inventive. You wouldn't find just anyone wandering uninvited through the apartment of a well-to-do family while the family is away. It takes a special kind of girl to sneak into a bedroom, to find the younger sister's diary and to read two weeks' worth of entries penned in careful script, only to remember where she was and why she had come when the cuckoo in the hall announced the half hour. Vallie had hurriedly replaced the diary in the desk drawer and then had tucked two pairs of Edith's precious silk slippers into her straw basket, shoes as milky and pure as Edith herself. Yes, no one compares with Vallie Neuzil. She left the four larger pairs that belonged to Adele so the younger sister would suspect the elder, and then she snuck from the room and now is merely increasing the risk by kneeling upon the settee, pretending to be her rival, pretending to feel what Edith Harms felt when she wrote in her diary: "E. will be my husband, but will A. ever forgive me?"

Most of all Vallie feels hungry, a symptom of any number of indistinct desires, and with the object of treating the symptom she tiptoes into the kitchen, illuminated only by one window's smoky courtyard light, finds what she takes to be a pastry box on the counter, tugs at the string, finally tears it with her teeth and opens the lid to discover a lilac plant inside, a lilac plant made out of green and lavender silk, as soft as the silk of the stolen slippers in her basket. Vallie closes the box angrily, as if the plant had been some-one's joke, and now she pursues her original purpose, looking in cupboards, fingering bottles, spice jars, wooden canisters until she finds a bag of chocolate mints—not her favorite candy but they will do. She presses her thumbnail into a soft disk to check its density, then pops two in her mouth, one in each cheek, making a smacking sound as she chews, like a toothless old woman eating poached pears.

Between the sound of the light rain falling in the courtyard and her own masticating effort she doesn't hear the knock at first, and when she does hear it she tries to ignore it. But the third round of knocking, more impatient than before, clearly means that someone wants to enter the Harms's apartment. Vallie sinks to the floor, hugging the basket like she holds fat Poldi at night when Egon is away. She has to remind herself to breathe. With her lips pressed together the chewed candies bulge beneath her cheeks, and Vallie tries to control her breathing by counting to herself, counting slowly from one toward one hundred, five hundred, whatever it takes to dissolve the fear. Before she reaches seventeen she hears footsteps on the stairway. Or is that just the rain dripping onto the windowsill? She'll gamble that the visitor has left—she cannot bear to remain in the apartment another minute—so she steals out of the kitchen, creeping guiltily like the thief she is, out the front door and into the deserted hall with its mosaic tiles radiating from the wrought-iron railing that encloses the stairwell. Descending the stairs two at a time, she reaches the street just as the Harms's cuckoo slides out of its tiny gabled closet.

Last month Egon might have asked his mistress where she has been, but this month he has too many other concerns to care about

Vallie's afternoon excursions. She finds him stretched out on the ottoman, museum catalogues scattered on the blanket around him. Vallie knows better than to engage Egon in a conversation when he has his mind on museums; she knows his opinion—that the museums of Vienna are nothing but tombs, with only dead art on their walls. Nor does Vallie care to talk to him, not now, with Edith's slippers hidden in her straw basket. She hides the basket in the back of the closet, covers it with a black tasseled shawl, though if Egon had any interest at all he would ask Vallie what surreptitious crime she had committed, what she was trying to hide. Luckily, Egon doesn't ask. He hasn't even noticed that Vallie's face has grown rounder, her breasts bloated, as if she were with child, which she knows is impossible, since Egon hasn't touched her for over a month and Vallie's attention has been wasted on Poldi, on various culinary treats, on silk slippers.

In the kitchen she lights the front burner of the stove, watches the flame narrow and contract. The ever-present slogan of the day comes to mind: "Save the Wife Her Time and Care: Cook with Gas." The flame is mesmerizing, almost inviting. Each prong of fire has an inner flame of blue, Vallie notices, a blue like the veins in Egon's neck. She likes to touch those veins, pressing gently to make indentations in the little worms. Egon's neck. What would he do if she touched his neck today? Would he pull away? Vallie wouldn't be able to endure the rejection, but even more than she fears his response, she cannot stand the terrible wanting, not now, after so many days alone, after the last grueling hour in the Harms's apartment.

So she returns to the studio and without a word kneels beside the ottoman, her elbows propped on the cushion, the same culpable elbows that fifteen minutes earlier had been propped on the sill across Hietzinger Hauptstrasse. She combs her hand through Egon's luxurious hair, tugs gently to free her fingers from a tangle, smoothes his cowlick behind his ear, traces a circle with her forefinger on his temple, presses the vein running from his ear to the channel beside his esophagus. Egon's beautiful neck. Tenderly she pries his lips apart and pushes two fingers into his mouth so she can feel the warm, gluey surface of his tongue. Vallie has forgotten that she left the burner on; she has forgotten that Egon has proposed secretly to Edith Harms.

It seems that he has forgotten too, for he has put down the catalogue and is pulling her forward. Vallie's tongue replaces her fingers in Egon's mouth. She straddles him, and his right hand wraps snugly around her waist while with the other he reaches under her skirt and follows the crevice of her plump bottom.

It would be a satisfying reunion, but Vallie suddenly remembers the slippers in the straw basket and then remembers the stove and soon is wishing only that Egon would finish. He squeezes her breasts, pulls with his teeth at a nipple, and she tries stimulating him with her grinding pelvis to an early climax, thinking all the while about how it would take just a short gust of wind—the stove flame would lick the frayed hem of the curtain and the fire would spread up the grease-stained wall, across the ceiling, into the studio. Egon's unfinished and unsold work would be destroyed.

Except for Vallie's little theft, it turns out to be an unexceptional afternoon; there is no fire, and Vallie prepares a simple supper of rotwurst and sauerkraut. Egon leaves as soon as they have finished eating, since he has promised to meet Anton for a game of billiards. He invites Vallie to come along but she declines, insisting that there is something she must finish—a feeble lie, Vallie never has work to do, they both know that.

Mirror Reflections

MY grandmother: proud of her station in life, proud of the few red streaks left in her gray hair, proud of the lime green sofa with the head of a turbaned Muslim carved in each arm. She acquired the sofa on credit in 1908 and finished paying for it in 1911. That winter, when my mother's health worsened, my grandmother invited us to Vienna to celebrate the purchase, and since my father knew his wife wouldn't be able to endure the thirty-kilometer ride in an unheated train, he gave me permission to go alone.

If I caught my grandmother in the right humor, she would let me touch the veins on the back of her hands, veins like bloodworms, swollen, satiated. I had watched her trap spiders in jars and set them free in the geranium box outside her kitchen window; I had watched her crown her head with an artificial braid—a bright red acorn of a wig—and had held a hand mirror opposite the dressing-table glass so she could admire the bun from the back. She belched and farted with considerable force, and more than once I saw her throw a flowerpot out the window at a cat.

As a young girl I thought daytime Vienna was made up of grandmothers like mine, a city of abandoned women, a city where widows came to dwindle and die. My grandmother, widowed at twenty-five, had moved to Vienna with her young son from a village outside of Salzburg and had become an army officer's mistress. The liaison lasted for years. My father maintained that the colonel to whom his mother referred with such affection was her uncle. My grandmother kept the colonel's portrait in a small oval frame above the mantle—the portrait had been painted by a street artist in Rome, and my grandmother said that when she won the lottery she would send me to Rome to have my likeness done.

Months before the artist moved to Neulengbach, months before he and his mistress had become the controlling passion of my life— I visited my grandmother and her sofa in Vienna. She made me tumble about on the velveteen sofa, made me lie and sit and balance my supper plate on my knee. Though I usually prepared my bed on the windowseat overlooking the courtyard, she insisted that I spend the night sleeping on green splendor. So she spread the blanket over me and kissed me goodnight, content with her life now that she owned the sofa and had a guest to enjoy it; she could ask for nothing more.

When I heard her shallow, gurgling breaths coming from the bedroom (thanks to the colonel, my grandmother had two spacious rooms and a kitchen all to herself), I moved to the windowseat, where I could look at the building across the courtyard. I searched the windows, hoping to see men in armchairs sucking on meerschaum pipes, women holding music scores or winding long feather boas around their necks. How desperately I wanted a glimpse of the other Vienna, nighttime Vienna, when the old women slept and the hidden, nocturnal population planned their revolutions, smoked opium and drank expensive wine. I had read about their demands for reform in newspapers and had heard my father call them traitors.

In a second-story apartment a tall, blond-haired woman wearing a blue dressing robe circled the room and disappeared from view. I had seen this woman on other occasions running an ivory comb through her hair. The other rooms were sealed with shutters or heavy drapes, except for an open third-floor window that was curtained with a ratty gauze netting. Inside I could see a basket of bread set out on a table and a long-handled knife stuck in the loaf. I waited for someone to enter the room and slice the bread.

I must have fallen asleep. In the middle of the night I was woken suddenly by the sound of heavy glass shattering, as if a bookend had been thrown violently to the floor, and through the curtains I made out a figure of a man bending beside the table, apparently reaching for an object that had fallen. Then I noticed the jerking motion of his elbow and realized that he must have been thrusting at or pummeling something beneath him. I sat up with a start just as someone unseen in the room extinguished the light. From the darkness arose one brief, vicious exclamation: "Forty-seven, son of a whore!"

I remained awake for hours, trying to convince myself that nothing in the scene had been unusual. An impatient man had merely stooped to retrieve something that had fallen beneath the table—his hat, his glove, a slice of bread. As the night wore on, I decided that I had dreamed the incident, an explanation that became more convincing after I had dozed and woken again and fallen back into a light slumber. I woke a third time at dawn and returned to the sofa. Soon afterward I heard my grandmother in the kitchen. She brought in our tea and sat beside me, lovingly shaving the green hide with her fingernails.

I hoped that my grandmother might mention the incident herself, if it had actually occurred outside of my dreams. But we drank our tea in silence, and then she offered to accompany me to the station. In the few minutes while she was gone from the room I resumed my place at the windowseat—I could see the knife still planted in the loaf of bread, the round-backed chairs pushed against the table in the empty room. I wondered whether I should contact the police, though I had little to tell them: maybe a murder had been committed, maybe not. They would advise me to come back when I had something significant to report. Besides, whatever had happened last night couldn't be undone, and I didn't want to disturb my grandmother's peace. She was an accepting woman, pleased with herself and with her possessions.

On the way to the station we stopped at a kiosk so my grandmother could buy her weekly lottery ticket. She used the date of my birthday, my age and the number forty-seven for the final two digits. Why forty-seven? Why had she chosen forty-seven? I demanded. Because that was the day's lucky number, she could feel it in her brittle bones, she said with a shrug, and what can a woman trust if she can't trust her intuitions? If I believed in nothing else, she hoped that I would have the courage to believe in my intuitions.

•

"Hard labor, hard fare, and a hard bed." By 1917, this is what soldiers and prisoners alike write home to their wives and fiancées to describe life in the prison camp in southern Austria. No need to stimulate the higher susceptibilities of the inmates, this camp isn't maintained to improve the men who come in, unlike St. Pölten's prison, where inmates had jobs and exercise and even work incentives in the form of bonuses that they could spend at the well-stocked commissary store. Here, in the camp for Russian prisoners of war, captors and captives alike are simply waiting for the war to end. Except Egon. Egon had avoided induction until 1915, but once the army had caught up with him, once he had been fitted for a uniform and given a number and a title, he discovered that the war —or at least war as he experienced it in a military training camp in Prague, warehouses in Vienna, and the prison in Mühling—was not the brutal affair that others claimed it to be, and if, as they said, most of the world had been destroyed, then he'd help to restore the world when the war had ended, and he'd make sure that the future improved upon the past. But for now it is his job to record this insignificant corner of history, to sketch the camp, the officers, the soldiers, and inmates. Egon has all the time he needs to work on his art, along with willing models—hollow-cheeked, hopeless Russians who sit on the frozen ground breaking open pine cones and chewing absent-mindedly on the bark.

Ever since he spent twenty-four days locked up in Neulengbach and St. Pölten, Egon has considered prison the most adequate standard metaphor to describe life, and now the metaphor has become literal again, except this time he is only an observer, free to visit Vienna at least twice a month, free to stay with his wife in a nearby boardinghouse on weekends—not free to resign his post, of course, but luckier than the doomed boys in the trenches. Prison is a source full of inspiring faces, pinched, angry faces and faces as serene and pale as death masks.

He walks along the outside of the compound, examining the snow clinging to the barbed wire, and he thinks to himself about how his life is structured by repetition and variation, like the fence with its unequal lengths of wire and interrupting knots. A man's potential for feeling is limited by the range of emotions available to him. But nature modifies old experiences, just as the snow transforms this prison into something new. There had been no snow in the Neulengbach courtyard in 1912, nor in St. Pölten. Add to repetition accidents and coincidences—these arouse and alter a familiar mood, making the world or a barbed-wire fence seem unfamiliar, even beautiful.

Seem. He wishes Erwin Osen were here to argue with his use of this vaporous word; he wishes Anton Peschka were here to listen to him while he speculates. Is. Edith is waiting for him in a local boarding-house—he can be sure of this, at least. So he leaps on the side platform of a passing milk truck that is one of the few motorized vehicles not owned by the military, grips the handle of the door and with his other hand salutes the driver through the window. This milkman is bound by wartime etiquette to help out a common soldier, to give him an extra pint of cream, a hard-boiled egg, or a ride into the village, is compelled as well by his provincial indignation to drive recklessly, steering directly into potholes, taking the curves at a dangerous speed and crossing the railway tracks without slowing. But Egon enjoys the man's fury as much as he enjoys the February wind slapping against his face and the speed of the truck and the bumps and dents in the road. He doesn't even notice that he has bruised his knuckles until he has hopped from the truck and started to walk the short distance down a lane to the boardinghouse.

He hangs his coat in the anteroom and finds his wife, as he expects, curled in a wing chair beside the fireplace, the cat Poldi asleep on her lap. Edith doesn't trust her sister or anyone else to take adequate care of Poldi, so when she travels she carries the cat in a picnic basket lined with damask, a tiny window cut out of the lid. Egon leans over his wife from behind, kisses the side of her neck, folds both his hands over her breasts while she holds the startled cat to keep it from bolting. With Poldi trapped in her arms, Edith leads her husband upstairs to her room.

Repetition: the slow ritual of undressing in the dark (and Egon insists on this same ritual, first undressing his wife, unwrapping the chiffon scarf, unbuttoning the blouse, feeling her skin chafing against his clothes. And then being undressed). The texture of her hard nipples, the silky vulval flaps, the lids of her closed eyes. And the tastes of saliva, a residue of soap on her thighs, her milky secretion. And then to enter—to pump, dig, thrust, the motions instinctual, almost mechanical, all personality forgotten. Edith, Vallie, Vallie, Edith.

He has heard this sucking sound before, countless versions of the same sound. Wet bellies rubbing, separating. A nursing child. Sparrows. A goatherd on a hillside above Krumau. He loves to love, he loves the pure desire first, the object second, and though the quality of desire is surely influenced by the object at hand, his love of desire —his need to feel and his appreciation of this feeling—does not change. His friends say that he has married well—Edith is a Hietzing girl and stands to inherit a considerable amount. But his motives for marrying were much more selfish than the conventional impulse to secure a fortune for himself: he chose Edith for her constancy, chose to invest all his love in her because of her innocence, chose to marry her because he knew she would never betray him. He couldn't trust Vallie, not in the same way; her devotion to him had become a burden in the final months, and her resentment grew in proportion to his indifference. Vallie let herself grow fat to spite him. As her eyes sank into her doughy face, as her chin receded into a thickening neck, her love for him became vicious, and she would tease and seduce him until he was drawn to the same bloated body that had begun to repulse him. Afterwards he would feel contaminated, and for weeks he would have no desire for a woman. But eventually the primary desire, this love of love, would become unbearable, and he would be driven back into a woman's arms, into a prostitute's hovel, back to Vallie or, if he could compose himself and endure the trifles of courtship, to the Harms's apartment across the street.

Now he has to teach his wife the pleasures of a feeling she has denied herself. Only when Egon has finished and is resting his head on her belly does he consider that again Edith felt nothing more than the friction of skin against skin. How to teach her to yield, to want the intimacy—this is the challenge, and her resistance makes her all the more suitable for a lover as ambitious as Egon. He will solve her as he has solved his drawings and watercolors.

Variation: the curtains are drawn to keep out the light poking through chinks in the shutters, so Edith and Egon must crawl about on the floor among the shadowy blocks of furniture, fumbling for their clothes while the cat springs at their fingers. Edith complains that she has lost her panties and her stockings. Egon manages to make his way across the room and he unlatches the window, opens the shutters to let in daylight so Edith may see where her clothes are —the panties draped over the knob of a bedpost, the skirt and blouse in a heap on the rug, Poldi batting at one of her pale gray silk stockings that extends like a tail from the end of the mattress. The other stocking is on Egon's head, pulled down over his face, flattening his features into a ridiculous caricature. He cocks his heads and hisses at his wife, wiggling his fingers, extending the tip of his tongue through a square in the lace.

But Edith won't allow herself to laugh; rarely do her husband's childish antics amuse her and never does she force a laugh out of respect. It had been easier, much easier, to clown with Vallie Neuzil. Egon removes the stocking from his head and hands it to his wife, and as he watches her pull it over her leg he thinks about Vallie, wonders where she is right then, wonders whether she is still alone.

·

To "lieber Egon," from Herr Benesch, May 3, 1912: "Please, whether or not you will benefit from an old man's advice, I beg you to read this letter through. If at the end my words only serve to irritate you, then go ahead and make confetti of these pages. But first give me a chance. I only want to help.

"You probably know that the more serious charge of seduction has been dropped, but the accusation of corrupting schoolchildren remains. I do not doubt your guilt. It is clear to me that your immorality has a noble purpose, and that you love children reverently, piously. But unlike devout women who can do nothing but rub their rosaries when they kneel before an image of the Infant Jesus, you express your complex love by making images. I have watched you draw the face and body of a young girl, I have seen how, as you form the edge of the angular hip, you force the rest of us to see the child as you do. But no judge will sanction your methods. Surely you understand why children are the most valuable members of society and thus subject to the strictest protection. You admired simply, benevolently, but you admired disrespectfully as well and saw in innocence a disturbing, arousing sensuality. The judge will have no sympathy for your aesthetic principles. You can insist that children, too, have erotic desires—you can tell the court that your methods are justified since, in the end, you merely want to show people the truth about themselves. Artists should have as much freedom as physicians, for their intentions are just as worthy. But the most sincere artists do not propose cures. And when they ignore the prohibitions and take advantage of an inattentive society, they will be punished.

"I have seen the sketches in question. You are sure to be convicted. Why, then, haven't I waited to send this letter until the trial is over? Because I don't want my words to seem hastily contrived, I don't want you to think that I am offering condolences. No, I write to you now with the certainty that you will pay for the transgression, and I want to help you prepare for the difficult months ahead.

"When the judge sentences you to hard labor, it will feel as though he has stolen a piece of your future. But if you were my age you would know that at the beginning of his career every man must lose his freedom. How appropriate that your affinity with children forces you to give up your own childhood once and for all. You are like a new father, displaced by your offspring. Responsibility for another becomes a father's principal concern, and you are responsible for your work. Don't forget that responsibility, in one form or another, is shared by all capable adults and is always, in some way, a prison. You might argue that most men can abandon their work or their family, while an actual prisoner risks being shot if he tries to scale the wall. And I would reply: a man can never escape his memory. The science of psychology is based on this fact. In a matter of days your sentence will be announced, and you, like the rest of us, will have to accept that fate. Yes, accept your fate, my young friend, do not waste time despairing. You have said yourself that you are a genius with a mission—so don't neglect your art, or your unrealized potential will become a torment to you. And if the finished work disgusts you, if you consider it an utter failure, do not destroy it. Shortly after we first met I wrote to you and begged you to save every scrap of paper that bears a mark from you, I begged you to keep whatever you considered worthless. *Stove equals Benesch,* I wrote to you, and I repeat it now: stove equals Benesch. So please, before you set anything on fire, remember me."

.

In 1907, while the rest of the household slept, Marie Schiele, nearly three years a widow, fastened the hooks of a sequined collar around her sister's neck and led the way down the staircase. From the hall closet she took out her own and her sister's felt hats, and though her sister protested, insisting that she really didn't mind walking to the train station alone, Marie said that she would enjoy the exercise. On the street the women linked arms and strolled through the empty streets of Klosterneuburg, across the main square and down the narrow stone steps behind the abbey. At the station Marie kissed her sister on both cheeks, and her sister—always so reserved and cryptic —curled her black-gloved hand and signaled for Marie to leave.

They knew too much and too little about each other—this was the problem, Marie thought as she climbed back up the abbey steps. She believed that her sister was going to Vienna not only to shop for a new dress, as she pretended, but to meet a man, a clandestine lover. She sensed the truth from a certain severity in her sister's manner. Though her sister shared her house with Marie and Marie's children, she refused to share her secrets.

And Marie, in turn, didn't speak to her sister or to anyone else about how she, too, suffered from a shameless desire, how she loved a man who belonged to another. And he loved her—she could tell from the way he followed her with his eyes, eyes like those of a caged parrot, slate-colored and alert. Marie Schiele, widow and mother of three, loved Leopold, her brother-in-law. She was sensible enough to keep her love hidden but not strong enough to do what any upstanding woman would do and leave the Czihaczek home, leave Klosterneuburg altogether and lease an apartment in Vienna, perhaps near the Academy where seventeen-year-old Egon was studying. If she moved to Vienna she would be able to see her son daily and to have some influence over his career. But what would her daughters do? Leopold had succeeded in finding a job for Melanie in Klosterneuburg, and in two years Melanie had replaced another girl as the chief bookkeeper at the train station. Now she had a windowless office and an adding machine to herself, and Marie knew she couldn't persuade Melanie to leave the job. Besides, her youngest, Gerti, received a fine education here in this quiet abbey town where the only unmarried men were celibate. Marie Schiele had married against her parents' wishes when she was sixteen and she didn't want her Gerti to make the same mistake. Her daughters needed her. But in the face of Marie's treacherous love for Leopold, no excuse, not even the welfare of her girls, should have justified staying on in Leopold's suburban home. No excuse, except the love itself.

She pulled the clapper of a bell outside the door of a bakery and startled herself with the noise. The upper half of the door opened, and Marie ordered a loaf of bread from the baker, asked for a dozen eggs and a pint of cream as well. The baker slapped his hands together to shake off the flour before he accepted her money. She held the warm loaf beneath her nose, inhaled the rich, yeasty smell as she walked. She would make breakfast for her brother-in-law this morning, a breakfast more sustaining than the tasteless *Semmel* and jam her sister usually left on the table for anyone to snatch on their way out. Marie had always wanted what belonged to her sister—she was willing to admit that the fueling impulse behind her passion for her brother-in-law might well have been envy. But if an emotion so petty were indeed the source, this still didn't degrade the love itself—no, her passion was pure, tender, and innocent because she hadn't and never would act upon the desire.

In the Czihaczek's home again, Marie hung her hat over the wooden knob at the bottom of the banister and listened to the sounds of movements above: wire springs of a mattress creaking, feet shuffling, water splashing, a drawer sliding open. Egon was visiting for the Easter holidays but he would probably sleep until midday, and Melanie, who had the morning free, would also take advantage of the time by remaining in bed. So it was either Gerti or Leopold. This morning Marie wanted to have the coffee made before the family descended. She would spoon the applesauce into bowls and slice the black bread, tear the centers from inside the crusts and fry an egg inside each slice. Leopold would be surprised and grateful for her effort.

Marie broke the first egg into the bread's hollow center, listened with pleasure to the spits and pops, watched as the egg white set and the yolk became firm and lost its brilliance. Grease collected around the edge of the crust, and Marie scraped at the brown foam with a spatula to coat the rest of the pan. She added another slice, tapped another egg against the side of the pan and widened the crack with her thumbnail. But as soon as she dropped the egg a streak of yellow slid out from beneath the bread, and when she lifted the slice to push back the escaping egg the yolk puddled, making a soggy mess. Marie wanted to trap her love for Leopold, to contain it, but whenever she thought about the love it began to leak out, just like the egg. Passion had relentless cunning. In the right light anyone could see the stain of her guilt—Marie had tried to keep her secret to herself, but impossible desire will ruin the most virtuous woman, the truth always reveals itself in a stuttered apology and retreat, in disingenuous laughter, in tears.

She hunched forward to enclose the gap between her body and the solid warmth of the range, and in this awkward posture Leopold found her when he came into the kitchen. He cleared his throat to gain her attention. Unnerved by his entrance, Marie hastily flipped both slices of bread without wishing him good morning, scooped up the piece with the intact egg and placed it on a plate. She would keep the tattered egg for herself, though she had overcooked it and had to scrape the surface of the pan to free the burnt bread. Another pat of lard, a piece of bread, an egg. Now there were tears in her eyes, she couldn't help it. Leopold surely sensed what she felt. Tears were an unambiguous sign.

"Marie?" He stood beside her, curved his flattened palm from the top of her brow along the stiff waves of her hair. She wiped her eyes with the bunched corner of her apron as his arm slid under her matronly bosom, he murmured her name again, but she refused to look at him—her eyes had told too much. And with his eyes, red-rimmed, freckles dotting the lids and the drooping pockets of skin below, he would try to tell her how much he wanted her. In that moment of weakness and temptation, Marie realized that through the last hour she had been more deliberate, more devious than ever before: walking with her sister to the train station, buying the bread, preparing breakfast—every action had been directed toward this verging intimacy, and now Leopold seized the opportunity. They were alone. He drew her unresisting body against him. But the embrace was still too friendly, too casual—until she declared her love aloud, he would disguise his emotion with fraternal concern.

And so Egon, barefoot, his shirt unbuttoned, found his mother in his uncle's arms. What in the first instance he took to be adultery quickly appeared to be only benign compassion—if they were trying to hide something his uncle would have begun blathering some nonsensical excuse and his mother would have insisted that nothing had happened, nothing at all. Instead, Egon watched as Uncle Leopold cordially kissed Marie on both hands and announced that he would finish making breakfast, if she would permit him. Perhaps Egon's mother had been suffering from one of her fainting spells

and Uncle Leopold had arrived in time to save her from collapsing
—yes, that must have been it, just a well-timed rescue. If Egon had
reached the kitchen before his uncle he would have been the one to
save Marie.

Still, as he took his seat at the table, he felt the discomfort of
someone who discovers too late that he is an intruder. Leopold was
the provider, the master of this household, and Egon had to beg
money from him to pay for school, for supplies, for a trip to Krumau and someday to Paris. Egon desperately wanted to visit Paris,
such a serenely confident city, noble, feminine, or so Egon imagined. Paris streets were a tapestry cluttered but not overwhelmed
with colors, intrigue and romance behind every dormer window,
while most of the sights of Vienna—from the monuments to the
Biedermeier coffee cups—had been designed to express and instill
national pride. In Vienna the only kind of romance possible was the
decadent, brothel kind. This morning Egon's mother had the maroon, pouting lips of a Second District girl. Or was it simply the
nostalgic frown of a middle-aged widow who knew that her best
years were behind her? Not even three years had passed since Adolf's
death, and Marie had recovered quickly—too quickly, in Egon's
opinion, for he had come to believe that his father's tyranny was a
symptom of his illness, that the man had been a victim and therefore
not responsible for his sudden fits of rage. Egon wished that he had
understood this while his father was still alive, that rather than resentment he had felt sympathy and hadn't been so eager to provoke
him. And now, though he would never forget how his father
scorned his art, Egon wanted to pay tribute to Adolf—not with a
portrait of the dead man but with representations of victims: dying
martyrs, gaunt male nudes, abandoned children.

Egon believed that his mother should have found her own method
of worship, she should have cherished the memory of the man who
had fathered her children, her mourning should have lasted longer.
Only a few months after Adolf's death, Marie had sold all her furniture, including the two Venetian champagne glasses that had been
Adolf's first anniversary gift to her. She probably would have liked
to sell her children as well, completely erasing the last two decades
of her life. It pained Egon to hear her abrupt, vigorous laughter as
Uncle Leopold told her how yesterday he had seen a woman step
off the train, preceded by three Negro servants who carried her

trunks, and how on the woman's head was the most unusual hat he had ever seen, a hat sprouting a forest of cloth ferns and miniature palms, with a stuffed cockatoo perched on the peak.

The smell of burning fat filled the kitchen, but neither his mother nor Uncle Leopold noticed—Leopold was too busy frying eggs and telling stories, and Marie too busy laughing. Uncle Leopold refused to give his nephew money to travel to Paris; Uncle Leopold had kept Marie from experiencing any ennobling sorrow after Adolf Schiele's death; Uncle Leopold was like a blood brother to Marie—they understood each other, teased each other, caressed each other with innocent affection. But Egon had enough experience to be suspicious of the ostensible innocence of sibling love and he couldn't help but fear that he would lose his mother, that she would become a stranger to him, as his little sister Gerti had become a stranger. Egon had reconciled himself to the changes in Gerti, had even come to enjoy the estrangement, for the mysteries of her maturing body continued to arouse him, and though she no longer permitted him to touch her as he had in the park at Miramare, she still posed for him, and he was able to create substitutes for Gerti with his pencils and brushes —all the bulging knuckles and knees, the bony rumps, the breasts belonged to him. His mother belonged to Leopold, as an adoring sister if not as an actual lover. Marie had found in him a replacement for Adolf, while Egon would remain fatherless for the rest of his life. Some days his loneliness overwhelmed him and he would press his hands against his ears and shut his eyes as if to keep out the desolate fact of his father's absence.

It might be possible, though, that Uncle Leopold served as an absorbing diversion and kept Marie from looking elsewhere for love. As his uncle bunched his sleeves to his elbows before he cracked the next egg, Egon considered the possibility that this commanding, gray-haired transportation official might not be such a threat as he had assumed. In his grudging generosity, Uncle Leopold had kept the Schiele family solvent—they needed little more than what he gave to them: lard, a slice of bread, an egg.

Uncle Leo sprinkled the egg with a pinch of salt, something Egon preferred to do himself. Marie poured applesauce from a huge jar into a bowl, and in a minute Egon's breakfast was before him. His mother ran her fingers through her son's hair, gently separating the tangled strands, and stopped only to pour his coffee. Egon didn't question these abrupt kindnesses—he merely wondered why his mother had been so slow in attending to him. Didn't she think her son a genius, after all? Hadn't she been convinced by him that with his formidable talent he was as unique and accidental as a two-headed sheep, and like any freak must resign himself to being a spectacle? Martyrs, saviors, and emperors were spectacles, and Egon comforted himself by identifying with them, but he felt even more affinity with the world's monsters—though he wanted to be admired for his honesty, it seemed inevitable that he would provoke only fear and disgust.

Last year his mother had bought him a full-length mirror, virtually making herself Egon's accomplice. Yet this year, even while she continued to believe in his potential, she had lost interest, wrote to him less frequently, spoke to him less intimately. But Egon felt more at peace with himself when he was petted, praised, spoiled by someone who had complete faith in him. Such unstinting faith made him a stronger artist.

"I thought you'd sleep until noon. After all, it's your holiday," his mother said.

"I never went to bed," he announced. "I worked through the night." He had taken a candle, pencils, and a sketch pad into Gerti's bedroom and had made a series of portraits of his sister sleeping, something he had wanted to do since he began living alone in his small atelier in Vienna: to catch the body completely relaxed, unaware of its audience, was a feat possible only when the subject slept. Egon's little sister had posed unwittingly through the night, and Egon could demonstrate the extent of his commitment by revealing that, for the sake of art, he had gone without rest.

But Uncle Leopold wanted to compete with his nephew and intruded into the conversation, announcing that he too had stayed up all night. "But it was worry, not work, that kept me awake. Not a wink of sleep, and nothing accomplished." He said this without irritation, indicating that his ability to lose sleep over sundry anxieties was itself a source of pride. "Not a wink of sleep," he repeated, and sure enough, Marie turned from her son and asked with concern that was at once both maternal and flirtatious, "Why, what could be making you so unhappy?" He massaged his temples with his thick forefingers, rubbed his eyes to show his exhaustion—an artful, deceptive pose, thought Egon. Poor Uncle Leopold.

"What do you have to worry about?" Marie persisted. "It isn't money, is it? I could find work in town, or take in sewing. Do you need money, Leo? Tell me the truth."

"I need . . . ," he said, sliding his body into a chair, ". . . to stop letting others take advantage of me. But it's not even their gratitude I want. Loyalty, that's all I ask for; any man would expect as much."

It was the last part of his brief, inflamed speech that provided the necessary clue for both Marie and Egon, and while Marie wiped the stove top to hide her sympathy and love for this neglected husband, Egon felt a less troubling pity replace the scorn. He could admit to himself, without irony, that Uncle Leopold was indeed poor, despite his high-ranking position as a railway bureaucrat, despite his attractive wife and spacious home. Poor Leopold was bored and he disguised that boredom with the indignation of a lonely old man, as if age could offer any sort of consolation.

With Egon home on holiday, Marie had hired a professional photographer—she wanted a picture of the family before her children were completely grown. When the photographer arrived, Egon asked for a special portrait of himself with Uncle Leopold. Marie was delighted with her son's request. While her daughters waited inside for their turn in front of the camera, Marie stood next to the photographer in the yard, directing her son to straighten his shoulders and her brother-in-law to tip back his hat so his eyes wouldn't be hidden in shadows.

But filial sympathy proved hard to sustain, and Egon's enthusiasm began to ebb. The linden trees dividing the yard from the meadow were infested with crows, he noticed; they perched on the highest branches and glided heavy-winged, like black swans, from tree to tree, carrying on their own business, chattering, laughing, scolding one another and ignoring the people below. The crows made Egon aware of the absurdity of the whole operation: while the photographer pretended to trap time, the carrion birds ignored time altogether. The scorn that Egon had earlier directed toward Uncle Leopold now found a new object in the photographer, who was clearly a novice, judging from the way he fumbled with the tripod and lens.

A short, robust man, not quite corpulent, clownish in his attempt at solemnity—with his silence he tried to impress upon everyone present the seriousness of his endeavor, a seriousness that irked Egon not only because of the mocking crows but because he saw himself in the earnest photographer. He thought about his friend Anton Peschka, who considered art no more valuable than the work of a common laborer. Perhaps Anton's humility made him a better man, but his paintings suffered from his low aspirations. A cobbler or a pastry chef who considered himself an artist would undoubtedly be more accomplished at his trade than the man who wanted merely to finish the day's job and head to the nearest Keller. An Austrian artist must recognize and accept his superior status or he would end up as dull as those Biedermeier painters of sentimental rubbish. At first Egon had been too much of a darling himself, trying to please his professors at the Academy with monochromatic landscapes and interiors, and he had received the highest praise. But in recent months he had become something shat by the devil, or so an indignant Griepenkerl declared after examining Egon's preliminary sketches for a self-portrait. Surely his work had improved as his convictions became more passionate.

But then there were the crows, whose nonchalance was a taunt, a mockery of all artistic effort. And the photographer was a ridiculous bumbler. The zealousness of the man embarrassed Egon, and before the photographer could take the picture, Egon snatched his uncle's derby and ran across the yard. While his mother shouted after him to stop his mischief at once, Uncle Leopold, poor Uncle Leopold, recovered from the surprise of the theft and thrust his walking stick in the air. He took off in pursuit of his impertinent nephew, banging his stick against the trunks of the linden trees, causing the crows to scatter like dust and to resettle in more distant roosts.

Near the neighbor's barn Egon threw himself into a haystack, shut his eyes and began to snore with a loud rattling. He heard his mother's voice, heard as well the wheezing pant of an old man, and when he opened his eyes he saw Uncle Leopold collapsed at the bottom of the haystack, hands crossed neatly over his chest, eyes closed. Uncle Leopold, burdened, bored Uncle Leopold, was clowning like a reckless youth.

Not until Marie caught up to them and called for the photographer to hurry along, to bring his camera and to catch this rare picture, did Egon understand that Uncle Leo was frolicking for Marie's sake alone, competing with his nephew for her admiration.

The photographer came toward them, the wooden legs of the

tripod catching in a grassy ridge, throwing him off balance so he nearly fell. The two Schiele girls bunched their skirts around their knees and scampered like thin-legged whippets behind him—they had been watching from the house and didn't want to miss the fun. The females gathered around the haystack, as if Egon and Uncle Leo were some marvelous exhibit at the zoo; Gerti pursed her lips and blew kisses instead of throwing peanuts, the photographer prepared to capture the captured beasts on film, and the comforting smell of hay made Egon forget about the competition for his mother's affections.

"You'll both ruin your good clothes," she said, and then, "Egon, give Uncle Leopold back his hat." When the photographer moved behind the camera the group fell silent, all respecting the sacred effort now. Sound implied motion, and a photographic image depended upon utter stillness. Death, sleep, and the inanimate world made the most dependable subjects, Egon knew, so he tried to remain immobile for this hired imitator—a good model should hardly breathe.

Once the image of Uncle Leopold and Egon in a haystack was fixed on the film, they could push themselves off the huge cushion of hay, let the women brush their lapels, and return to the Czihaczek home. Egon and Gerti walked together, arms linked, and Gerti clicked her tongue at the repulsive sight of a crow feasting on the entrails of a dead squirrel. The squirrel must have fallen as it leapt from branch to branch above, and now its eyes were open, as if it were alive, paralyzed from the fall, watching as the crow took a piece of rubbery gut in its teeth and stepped backward. Egon would have liked a closer look, but Gerti pulled him away—she didn't want such a repulsive sight branded in her memory. Better to gaze upon puffs of clouds in the sky, purple cabbages in the vegetable garden, roses dripping from the trellis. Did Egon want a glass of lemonade? she asked. Gerti would make it for him. Would he help her shop for a new purse that afternoon? She hoped he would give her advice.

But right then Egon saw his mother bend her head until it was nearly resting on Leopold's shoulder. "Uncle Leopold!" Egon called, leaving the squirrel, the crow, and Gerti behind. His mother's head bobbed up guiltily at the sound of her son's voice. "Uncle, I have to talk to you," Egon said firmly as he drew near. "It's about my allowance. You don't give me enough. I need more than bread and water to survive." He assumed his most unsettling expression, stared first at his uncle then at his mother with his lips slightly parted, eyebrows arched, head turned so that he peered out of the corners of his eyes. He had practiced this expression endlessly in the mirror when he was alone—he knew its effect.

Self-Portrait
Masturbating

IN 1937 my husband and I moved from Munich to New York. He spoke French, German, and English with nearly equal proficiency and was able to support us with his work as a translator. In Munich a difficult pregnancy that ended in a miscarriage had left me unable to bear children, but during our second year in New York my husband's brother sent his young son to live with us. I was glad to have company. I would wake the boy at dawn, and we would spend an hour or so at a nearby playground before the other children arrived, bouncing a rubber ball against the wall of the school. At the end of the day I would meet my nephew at the gate and take him to a coffee shop for a glass of milk and a powdered doughnut filled with strawberry jam.

Those were my liveliest years in America. After the war my brother-in-law moved from Vienna to Los Angeles and took his son with him. Since then my main responsibility has been to keep myself occupied. I have few friends and spend much of my time proofreading my husband's translations. But two weeks ago my nephew, a bearded, middle-aged man now, visited and invited me to accompany him to a show at a New York gallery. I suppose if my nephew hadn't been so insistent I wouldn't have gone to the show at all and I wouldn't be telling this story.

Among the few visitors that weekday morning one couple caught my attention. They wore ankle-length raccoon coats and wandered through the rooms as if they were browsing at a fish market, vaguely disgusted and amused by what they saw. They paused in front of a series of self-portraits by Egon Schiele, and their laughter came abruptly, the man's first, as though the woman had reached over and pinched him. "Would you let this guy shine your shoes?" the man drawled, and the woman hooked her arm around his, giggled stupidly and pulled him into the next room.

In one self-portrait, painted in 1911, the year before his imprisonment and trial, the artist's blotched, bony fingers rest on the cushion of his genitals; in *Female Nude,* from 1910, the artist is sketching his model from behind—she braces one hand on her hip and appears both facing out and with her back turned, indicating that all three figures, the artist and the woman from front and back, are reflections in a mirror. There were also landscapes—thunderstorm mountains, harbors, cities—and there were other nude studies. But soon I was too preoccupied to pay much attention to the art, disturbed not by the pictures nor even by the laughter of the couple, but by the sense that a crucial piece was absent from this show.

I found my nephew gazing out a window at the garden below. I kissed him and told him that I had just remembered an appointment with my doctor and must hurry. Before he could protest, I was already heading toward the elevator.

Why in New York are the sidewalks so high, the gutters in the street so wide? I must walk slowly through the streets—these days I feel my age most when I am walking. But even as I walked toward Broadway, the young girl I had been in Neulengbach walked with me. I tried to convince myself that though Egon Schiele had found his fame, I had the advantage over him. He had made it across the ocean, yes, but as a shoeshiner, while I had escaped quietly, blending into the masses of immigrants. Few people noticed when I left Europe, fewer cared when I arrived here, and the anonymity that once made me desperate in my own country has protected me for over forty years on the streets of New York. Years ago I was just another nanny taking care of a child, now I am an elderly woman with a maroon beret, nameless, though not ignored entirely—there are panhandlers on my block who single me out, and the waitress in the coffee shop on the corner knows me well enough to bring my coffee with extra cream before I order—but in general I am left alone, and I have come to relish the peculiar kind of solitude that can be found only on these busy avenues.

Though there were cracks of blue in the sky that day, a cloud directly overhead suddenly filled the air with wet snow, and I escaped into an empty restaurant. I sat by the window at a table still covered with the last diner's breakfast dishes, lit a cigarette and ordered a beer from the waiter. He tied the strings of his apron before he piled the dirty plates in the crook of one arm, and with the other hand he brushed crumbs and ashes onto the floor. Outside, people stopped under the dripping awning to wipe the lenses of their glasses or to draw a quarter from their trench-coat pockets for the newsboy. The sky darkened quickly, and the snow changed to driving sleet.

During my first night in cottage forty-five, I had let Egon Schiele draw my portrait. Eyes closed, hands folded on my lap, I listened to the sound of pencil against paper and to Vallie Neuzil's pointed nails against her skin when she scratched her wrist. As the minutes passed I lost all sense of caution and unfastened the top two buttons of my blouse. With my eyes still shut I unfastened a third button, for I assumed this was what they wanted, but Egon Schiele kept working with indifferent ease, and every time I opened my eyes, Vallie was adding spoonfuls of cocoa to her milk until the drink was the consistency of soft toffee.

It must have been hours after they had extinguished the lights and gone into their bedroom that I finally allowed myself to move. As my vision adjusted to the darkness, I could make out the few solid shapes in the sparsely furnished room, the portfolios and easel, the watercolors pinned to the walls, the two empty chairs where Vallie Neuzil and Egon Schiele had been sitting. I made my way to the door, opened it a crack and slipped outside, into the bottom stratum of a cloud resting on the earth, the fog like a gauze net draped over the cottage. Right there beside the porch I chose a patch of ground and squatted like a dog. How defiant I felt as the steam rose, not only because it was a scandalous thing for a girl to use a stranger's yard as a toilet but because it seemed that my escape had been successful and I could finally claim my youth without guilt.

Back inside the cottage, however, I lost my youth as abruptly as I had found it, discovered that the artist had taken it from me, as photographers steal the souls of primitive peoples. Two stiff sheets ripped from the drawing pad were propped against the spine of the chair, and when I reached for them I knocked a pencil off the seat. I hesitated, afraid that the brief clatter would have woken the artist and his mistress, but no sound came from their bedroom. So I brought the drawings near the grate of the stove and blew on the embers until they cast sufficient light. On the first sheet the artist had drawn various parts of the female anatomy—legs that were too thin and sinewy to be mine, hips that were too narrow, armpits and sunken buttocks. On the second sheet he had concentrated on a single sketch of the naked corpse of a girl packed into a coffin, her shoulders hunched forward and her legs folded beneath her. He had sewn her lips shut with tiny slashes of a pencil, and her nipples were the same size as the coins over her eyes. With the fingers of both hands she pulled open the flaps of her vagina.

The girl in the coffin looked nothing like me. Egon Schiele must have thought the drawing finished, for he had signed his name in the lower right-hand corner, the thick, compact letters bordered by a square, the signature like another body squeezed inside a tiny box. For a moment I considered feeding the drawings to the stove and fleeing from the cottage. But I had nowhere else to go and wasn't ready to return home, so I replaced the drawings on the chair and spent the rest of the sleepless night on the settee.

In the restaurant on Broadway so many years later, those sketches appeared in my mind as vividly as the pictures I'd just seen, and I heard the scratch of the artist's pencil as clearly as I had heard the laughter in the gallery. I couldn't fool myself: my pride in my youthful self, then and now, has been ill-founded—except for checks and legal documents, I have never signed my name to anything. How satisfying it would have been right then to carve my initials in the table with the tip of a hairpin. Instead I decided to make a worthwhile portrait to replace the sketch by Egon Schiele. So I paid my check and wandered out into the rain, searching the crowds for someone who had nothing better to do than to listen to a presumptuous old woman prattle on about her part, her small role, in history.

·

Some people see only Vienna's mask of pinched-lipped asceticism, but there is still plenty in this city of dreams to satisfy the hedonist. Behind one door you will discover the magic casks that are never empty, behind another door you will find the famous notions shop

where you can buy, among other items, all sorts of proven aphro-
disiacs. Don't be surprised if, at the end of a modest side street in
the heart of the respectable First District, you see opium smoke
leaking from a keyhole. If you have an interest, push aside the
beaded curtain in the entrance of any cabaret and you will learn why
the dancing girls of Vienna are renowned. And somewhere on the
Linkstrasse, if you can find the brass door knocker in the shape of a
mermaid, don't hesitate to tap it three times against the plate; when
the young girl answers, tell her that you are looking for Frau Wolf.
Frau Wolf. Say the name slowly, insinuatingly, as if you were utter-
ing the name of a legendary criminal, give the girl your hat and cape
and let her lead you by the hand into the salon full of tufted furniture, potted jade trees three feet tall, and gas-jet chandeliers, the
flames like jewels glimmering through the fog of incense smoke.

Be prepared to wait, since Frau Wolf believes in the importance
of anticipation and won't hurry to meet even the most eminent
client. When she finally slips into the room and tugs on your beard,
be sure to demonstrate your generosity by discreetly transferring a
few banknotes from your pocket to the open drawstring purse hanging from Frau Wolf's sapphire-studded belt.

Frau Wolf: the aptly named grand madame of Europe. She wears
her hair in a bun, the knotted braids as black and rubbery as strands
of licorice. When she smiles, she slides the tip of her irresistible red
tongue across the front of her teeth, and the caked makeup below
her eyes cracks, the wrinkles beneath the clay like a hundred tiny
fault lines. Kiss Frau Wolf's rheumatic hand and state your wish: a
robust creature with supple thighs, a pliant, slender thing, a brunette, an Asian, a virgin. Frau Wolf keeps an extensive supply, so
your selection is only as limited as your imagination. Or perhaps
you will need help to decide: like a procession of priests bearing the
viaticum, Frau Wolf's working girls will move across the parlor,
each girl sliding her tongue over her teeth (the suggestive smile is a
trademark of the house), each begging silently to be selected. Frau
Wolf watches you intently, waiting until your eyes come to rest on
one lovely face. Only then, at a nod from the madame, will the
other girls retreat into the back rooms and your Egyptian princess
step forward, seating herself upon your knee.

Over the years, many of Frau Wolf's famous clients have died
from disease, suicide, or assassination, but the institution has en-

dured. It is said that the madame keeps a diary and has been collecting notes for an exhaustive memoir to be published posthumously. But in dark corners of cafés, in the corridors at the Hofburg, in boxes at the Staatsoper, it is whispered that the Linkstrasse house of pleasure will burst into flames as soon as Frau Wolf's infamous heart stops beating.

.

May 6, 1912: "A scandal," Egon writes in his diary after he learns from Heinrich Benesch's letter that he is being held not on false charges of seducing the hysterical Neulengbach girl but because of his most recent erotic drawings. He has been in "investigative detention" for three weeks, the last seven days at the St. Pölten prison in this airy private cell furnished with a writing table, a candle, and a washbasin on a cart. He is not allowed to send or receive messages. Benesch must have bribed one of the guards to deliver his letter.

Egon dips his pen into the inkwell and continues: "An almost unbelievable crudity!" He has been charged with corrupting minors, as if his drawings were intended solely for the eyes of the children who frequented his cottage, as if children were innocent, devoid of all sexual desire. Adults must insist that sexuality is linked to procreation in order to sanctify their secret pleasures, but Egon has shown the fools that pleasure has nothing to do with reproduction. So now they are persecuting him for his honesty, pretending that the future of their children is at stake.

Egon had turned his back on Vienna's art world, where attacks on him launched by notable critics had pleased the Academy professors and amused his friends; true, he doesn't lack support from a few devoted patrons, but he has no real disciples. When he was only eighteen he had been commissioned to design clothes and posters for the Wiener Werkstätte after striking up a friendship with Gustav Klimt. He had helped organize the Neukunstgruppe revolt and had been the principal author of a letter demanding radical reforms at the Academy. The dealer Pisko had already shown some of his oils and watercolors in his gallery. But it is clear to him that no one of any importance—not Klimt, not Roessler, not even Heinrich Benesch— recognizes the revolutionary implications of his artistic mission.

In Vienna, art has to create its purpose. The haberdashery peddlers, the Spanish riders, the bargemen, the innkeepers—all have their purpose in the city, all labor by rote. But an artist works without any prescribed function and has to convince the people that there is value in his projects. The Secessionists are popular because they delight in frivolity; even the more inventive artists in the Klimtgruppe are the equivalent of supreme pastry chefs: their confections provide the upper class with a pleasant contrast to Vienna's main course of grandiose, neo-baroque churches and government buildings—and to the bland fare of the workers' quarters in outer districts. Gustav Klimt had been subversive in a mischievous way, shocking the bourgeois public with his huge *Philosophy* full of naked, emaciated women painted for the *aula* of the university, but wealthy matrons can still depend on him to execute their flattering portraits. Egon is alone in his determination to offend the people, believing it to be the artist's rightful purpose to deflate the lies of ornament and sentimentality. Every line he draws is like a thrust, a penetration, and each dab of paint an ejaculation. Don't the Viennese swallow gallons of the warm, salty cream in their *séparées,* their brothels, their spas? Yes, Egon has given them his semen to drink, pure, undiluted semen. And to be undiluted in Vienna is to be unwanted, shunned, deliberately ignored.

But the children of Neulengbach hadn't ignored him. They perceived his honesty and were eager to be shown the truth about themselves. Yet could it have been the children who had testified against him, providing the evidence that the adults needed to authorize a crucifixion without breaking the law? Few adults had entered the cottage since he and Vallie moved to Neulengbach. Heinrich and Otto Benesch visited occasionally, and Marie Schiele came once, accompanied by her sister and brother-in-law. Uncle Leopold had been outraged by the dozens of sketches strewn about the cottage, lying belly-up like dead fish on floors, tables, chairs, and he had refused to stay for dinner. Egon hadn't seen his uncle since then, but he had recently written to request a loan in addition to his monthly allowance. His uncle hadn't replied.

More than likely, then, that the traitor is Uncle Leo, who must have believed it to be his duty to warn the villagers of Neulengbach about the pervert living in their midst. Uncle Leopold. It is a deductive proof based on obvious facts—in a cell in St. Pölten, Egon comes to blame and despise his uncle, and though there is just as much contrary evidence, Egon holds fast to his conclusion. His mother, he thinks angrily, must have conspired with her brother-in-law or at least given him permission to denounce his nephew. And where is Gerti, why hasn't she contacted her brother? Neither his friends nor his family have come to his aid. True, Vallie and Heinrich Benesch have tried to cheer him, but they suffer from a certain dullness and insensitivity, so Egon remains an oddity to them, adored not in spite of but because of his eccentricities. The last time Benesch had visited St. Pölten, Egon swore that he would have nothing to do with art as long as he remained in prison. And now Benesch has sent this letter, advising Egon to accept his fate and stay true to his calling.

But acceptance is the curse of mankind. Acceptance and its stultifying mate, habit. What if Egon resists when the guards try to drag him from the courtroom after the judge has sentenced him to prison? What if he snatches the gavel and with one powerful strike splits the judge's bald head wide open? Then one of the guards will be forced to shoot Egon Schiele. With any luck, a photographer will be present to take a picture of Egon Schiele's bloody, bullet-pocked body slumped over the rail of the defendant's box.

But to lose his body, to lose all sensation for the sake of being remembered . . . he thinks of his father's corpse. Death is only degrading, more shameful than old age. Despite Egon's masochistic fantasies he knows that he won't choose suicide—better to sneak quietly away from civilization and leave behind an absence, a mystery. This is the surer way to drive his enemies mad: with an impossible puzzle. And if he is to find a secluded place, he must first escape from St. Pölten.

Escape. The idea soothes him with its promise, giving him the surge of confidence that he feels when he finally has an inspiring study and can begin work on a canvas. He will escape from St. Pölten with the help of one of the guards. The old constable who fetched him from Neulengbach could probably be tempted with a few kronen, but Egon hasn't seen him since he arrived. So he must make do with the night sentry, an earnest, blond-haired youth, the only guard who refuses to let the men smoke in their cells. Egon will try to seduce him. He recalls the Bohemian mute, and how the boy's eyes had conveyed his complicity. Egon will stare at the young guard just as the Krumau goatherd had stared at him, and when the guard enters his cell Egon will introduce him to this dangerous, secret love. Afterwards he won't even need to threaten blackmail—the boy will be desperate to save his reputation and avert the potential scandal and will help his seducer escape through a water-closet window.

How easily a man can change his fate—Heinrich Benesch is a slave to the Empire and refuses to recognize his right to freedom. Egon will show him how, like women and clever children, a powerful man can gain his freedom using the skill of seduction.

Yet even as he comforts himself with this plan, he knows that he doesn't have the courage to act so boldly, not here. The convicted thieves and murderers around him are always ready to beat aberrations to pulp. No one needs to explain to Egon that the sons of Adam resent Eve, that men in prison assume they are protected from her by the walls, and if they find traces of Eve in a fellow inmate, if they hear the unmistakable appeal of the canny witch in a man's voice, then they will expel Eve by crushing the imposter.

So just as Benesch explains in his letter, Egon has no choice but to resign himself. As long as he prefers life—and it is clear to him now that he will always choose life over the embarrassment of death—he must obey the authorities, and eventually time and history will reward him for his patience; enlightened individuals of the future will recover his name. He rests his chin in his hands and breathes deeply, feeling as wizened and wise as St. Jerome. To work, then; he will begin a new series of self-portraits and temper his polemics, as Benesch. The only caption on his next watercolor will be his signature.

But he cannot work. He had wrapped his paper, pencils, and brushes in brown paper and given the package to one of the guards, asking that the materials be locked in a drawer for as long as he remains in prison. The guard will expect a generous bribe from Egon before he returns the package, and although Egon has enough money to buy new paints and brushes, the idea of this last injustice overwhelms him. It doesn't matter to him anymore that he may spend his life in prison, it doesn't matter that he will be persecuted for his frankness, but the necessity of buying back his materials infuriates him. St. Jerome disappears and in his place is a man not unlike the young Adolf Schiele, hands clenched around the metal frame of his cot, bottom lip hidden beneath his upper teeth. He inhales sharply through his nose. Now he must pay for his stupid, histrionic gesture. In a sour mood he gave away his soul. What is it worth to you? the guard will ask, facing Egon through the barred window in his door, flicking the ash of his cigarette onto the floor.

A voice at the end of the corridor startles him, ordering lights out for the night. Egon snuffs the candle with his fingertips, and the light takes with it the clarity of his passion. The lamp just outside his door will burn all night, providing at least enough light to keep Egon from stumbling against the furniture when he paces his cell floor, as he does every night to warm himself. In the darkness he no longer cares about the greedy plebeians who control his life; he cares only about the chill that cannot be diminished with a ream of blankets. So he stalks back and forth in his cell, his chin resting against his chest, his hands drawn up inside the baggy flannel sleeves of his nightshirt, trying to exhaust himself and to forget about the cold. He walks decisively—six steps ahead until his toes rub against the baseboard, six steps to the opposite wall—determined, after these hours of useless meditation, to accomplish something. Falling asleep would be enough.

•

Vallie dips her pinkie into her coffee and with a shoveling motion she makes little waves that splash against the side of the cup and send drops onto the green tablecloth. She stares contemptuously at the cup so that she won't have to see the pity in her lover's eyes. Two weeks ago Egon had disappeared from the Hietzinger apartment, taking with him only a single suitcase, a box of paints and brushes, palettes, a few stretched canvases. She didn't know where he had gone, though she liked to think that with any luck he had wound up in some provincial jail after they had caught him piercing the hymen of a twelve-year-old schoolgirl. Instead of returning to the apartment and offering a decent apology for his absence, he had sent her a letter, instructing her to meet him at the Eichberger Café next Wednesday afternoon. She didn't want to meet him, for she knew he would have no surprises. But at noon today Vallie had put on her Makart-imitation hat—a relic snatched from a ragman's bin, complete with cloth flowers—and since she was early she kept walking along Hietzinger Hauptstrasse all the way to the Gloriettegasse, hoping to catch sight of Katharina Schratt as she passed her residence.

At Gloriettegasse 9 the blinds were drawn as usual, so Vallie had turned around and headed toward the Hietzinger Gate and the parish church. She hadn't worshiped formally for over a decade, but as she entered she crossed herself with practiced ease. She chose a pew in the middle of the church, knelt and prayed for courage and direction. She prayed to the Holy Ghost, for He was more likely than God or Christ or the Virgin Mother to provide some miraculous vision that would help Vallie face her future. She looked around her. A sexton arranged votive candles, collecting the melted stubs of wax in a cloth bag. A young mother wheeled a baby carriage up the aisle and waited for her turn in the confessional. Old men and women were scattered in pews, some with their heads tipped in prayer, others staring at the gilded angels hovering above the altar.

Half an hour later the Holy Ghost had still offered nothing to guide Vallie through the rest of her life, so she dragged herself out of the church, feeling neglected, useless, until an automobile carrying two infantry officers backfired on the street in front of her. The driver didn't flinch, but the startled officers clutched the side doors and ducked their heads. A trivial event, but Vallie realized at once that she had found her sign: shots, soldiers, war. It was 1915, and heaven was calling her to do her part, to bind wounds and read poetry aloud to the men whose bodies had been shattered—legless, hopeless men who had been pulled alive from trenches and condemned to life; now she knew what she must do—she would join the Red Cross, she would wear a white apron and spend all her waking hours in a hospital. Vallie had heard Egon and his friends mocking the war effort, raising toasts to the marriage of medicine and weaponry, laughing about how mankind, that ingenious species, invented a new, powerful explosive for every new vaccine. But this was just the nihilism of unpatriotic cowards, and the thought of them merely made Vallie more determined.

But as soon as she had seen Egon sitting at the wicker table in the Eichberger Café she had forgotten her resolution—the present fell like a cloak over her head, and she could hardly catch her breath when Egon pressed her hand against his lips.

And so they sit here now, in silence, neither of them willing to speak first. Except for a couple whispering in the corner and the women chattering behind the pastry case, the room is quiet. In these suburban cafés one practically needs permission to speak, Vallie thinks, composed enough to feel irritable. She shifts restlessly, and the woven straw of the seat crackles. Finally she says, "I have better ways to spend my time," and tucks her purse under her arm, half-rising from the chair before Egon catches her by the wrist.

"Please. I want to talk with you."

"You want to talk, then talk—you're not made of stone. What have you done to your hair, by the way? It looks different. You look different."

"I haven't changed."

The people in the café rustle in unison, as if a wind has blown across the surface of their placid faces, and Vallie closes her eyes and soaks in the swell of meaningless noises: spoons clank against china cups, a chair scrapes across the floor as a man stands up to leave, a woman's charm bracelet jingles as the baubles brush against the table, water hisses through the coffee machine, the cash register door opens with a whir and ring. And the smells of fresh coffee, bread, a dowager's perfume soften Vallie's pain. This is one of the few cafés in all of Vienna that still serves fresh cream, despite the stricter rationing. When Vallie takes a sip from her cup she feels as though she were drinking the scene itself, as though all the images and sounds and smells were tumbling down her throat.

When she meets Egon's eyes again, the force of memory displaces the present, and Vallie remembers with discomforting lucidity the pleasant sensation of wet paintbrush bristles against her skin. How can he sit there and not remember? Yes, he is a stone, just as blood-less and stubborn. Vallie clutches her purse again, but before Egon makes a move to detain her she announces, "I just want something to eat. You didn't leave me any money, and I'm nearly dead from hunger." She exaggerates, of course. Egon had left behind his liquor and his cigarettes, and anyway Vallie can always find the means to purchase chocolates.

Though the pastry case is nearly empty, Vallie has trouble decid-ing between custard and poppyseed filling and finally chooses two pieces of the poppyseed strudel. She tells the waitress to add the cost to the gentleman's bill, leads the way to the table and stands aside while the waitress sets down plates, folded napkins, and glasses of cloudy tap water.

Only when Vallie is spreading the napkin on her lap does Egon finally speak. "Edith had a dream the other night," he says, but already Vallie has heard enough. She thrusts the fork into the crust that crumbles instead of flakes, evidence that the baker used lard rather than butter. "She dreamt that she was hiding in the closet of our apartment . . ."

Our, he says, as if he and Vallie still shared something.

"She watched you through the keyhole. You were sitting on the floor, a pair of kitchen shears in one hand . . ." Egon hesitates, as if he wanted Vallie to finish the sentence for him. ". . . And in your other hand," he says, pausing to sip his coffee, "you held one of Edith's satin slippers."

"Lies!" shrieks Vallie, slamming the butt of her fork against the table, and the heads of the strangers pivot to look at the impassioned girl and the man who has provoked her. Vallie doesn't doubt that Egon is lying to her—not about the slippers but about Edith's dream. He has fabricated the dream so he can make the blame more vicious, he will accuse Vallie of stealing Edith's slippers without admitting that two weeks ago he had found those slippers hidden in the closet. He wasn't brave enough to confront Vallie directly—he had simply taken the slippers from the basket, packed a suitcase while Vallie slept and left the apartment. Their apartment.

For two weeks she has lived alone in the prison of Egon's mind, surrounded by his canvases and sketches, and though she has wanted to burn everything that belongs to him, she has resisted. Egon has a talent for making passion seem a ridiculous parody of itself—over the years he had made hundreds of caricatures of Vallie. But if she burned those portraits or any others, he would transform her in person as he had transformed her on paper, turning her into a sentient caricature, humiliating her with his powerful, calculating smile. So Vallie hasn't touched a single canvas or sketch, not even to turn it facedown upon the table. She has endured the images that Egon left behind as she endures the stares of strangers when she raises her voice in the café.

"Lies!" she repeats, and tears off another forkful of strudel, thrusting it into her mouth. Lies, caricatures, insults—Egon has made a career out of debasing others, and the critics are right to condemn him. For five years Vallie has given herself to him, given her youth to this charlatan. Now she wants her old self back—if she can't destroy the pictures then she wants to destroy the memories, begin life again as the girl she was before Egon interfered. The affair with

Egon Schiele seems now like one long practical joke, and what began as a reluctant love has become a parody of romance. She hates him, but even this potent hatred doesn't satisfy her, doesn't give meaning or coherence to her life. She wants to spit out the hatred and feel nothing, taste nothing, remember nothing, she wants to stop thinking about revenge.

She chews the piece of pastry savagely without swallowing until it disintegrates entirely, the sweetness seeping up into the roof of her mouth and sliding over the back of her tongue. She takes another bite, sucking the pastry as if it were a sugar cube.

Egon has been breaking his strudel apart with the edge of his fork and he continues to play with it as he mumbles, "Edith and I are engaged."

"And what do you want from me? My congratulations? My consent? Go ahead, marry her, and I promise I won't tell her about your peculiar interest in little girls. But your sweet wife will grow up, and you'll grow bored with her, too. You'll find another innocent darling for yourself, and someday there will be another trial. Next time I hope they lock you away for good!" There, she can spit out the hatred with slurred, ugly words, she need only remind him of his predilections. "Little girls become big girls," she says slowly, for she wants to impress upon him the full impact of the truth.

"Be quiet!" he whispers. "I'm trying to tell you that we still have a chance. I don't want to lose you. I'll take you to the theater, to the mountains, to Trieste, we'll have our own honeymoon."

"You are an idiot!" Vallie speaks haughtily, bolstered by Egon's desperation. So he doesn't want to lose his mistress. So he realizes that such a free-spirited, modern girl like Vallie is a rarity. So he regrets his commitment to the morose Fräulein Harms and senses that marriage will be a tedious job. Too late, Egon Schiele, you are about to become respectable. A feeble veneer. Someday he'll forget himself and he'll be caught with his hands wrapped around his swollen cock, surrounded by a dozen wide-eyed children. Portrait of the artist masturbating.

"I've drawn up a contract," he says, unfolding a piece of paper that he has taken from his pocket. "And I'll ask Edith to sign it. We'll spend two weeks together every summer, just you and I. Edith will have to accept you." Accept her? Vallie's saliva turns sour in her mouth, and she leans forward to bring her face close to Egon.

She collects saliva on her tongue, draws moisture from the roof of her mouth, from the inside of her cheeks. Edith will have to accept her? Accept her? A contract will make Vallie legitimate? Her rage is so immense that her vision blurs, she can hardly see Egon's eyes and is unable to aim until Egon stammers, "Please . . ." The sound of his voice gives her a target. She spits, empties her mouth of the disgusting taste, whirls around before Egon can reach for a napkin, leaves him to pay the bill.

People murmur in restrained astonishment as she stalks out of the café, and Vallie continues to savor her own amazement at her courage as she hurries up the Hietzinger Hauptstrasse. In an unanticipated reversal, she has come out the victor and has sealed up five years with a climactic, unforgettable memory: a poisonous kiss. She has succeeded in spitting out her hate. Now she can devote herself to a neutral cause, she can become a Red Cross nurse and piece together foolish, battered soldiers; she will earn their respect and perhaps even their devotion. Who knows? Vallie might even find her future husband in a hospital ward. But while she walks, a film of the rancid saliva collects on her tongue again. She dabs at her lips with her handkerchief, discreetly forces the gluey saliva into the folds of the cloth. At home she will drink that strange blue orange-tasting syrup that Egon keeps in the kitchen cabinet—if that doesn't rinse the awful taste from her mouth, nothing will.

•

Two and a half years of marriage didn't change Edith Schiele; she still had nightmares, she still preferred to be alone and she still forgot to sign her husband's name. Not that she wasn't a devoted wife— anyone who knew her would testify to this fact. For months she had been following him from one assignment to another, from Prague to Vienna to Mühling, and now that the war had nearly ended and they were living in Hietzing together again, Edith was pregnant.

She didn't want to tell Egon, for she would rather have him notice the change in her. Odd, that he hadn't suspected the truth yet, he hadn't even noticed that lately she was sleeping twelve hours a day. She hoped that a baby would change her permanently; even if she never learned to feel like a wife inside, she would feel like a mother. She wanted to feel different. Everything around her was different. She sat on a chair facing the window, stared dreamily at the brown-

edged sycamore leaves as she thought about the war's effect: aristocrats who used to distinguish themselves by ambling along with
their shoulders slightly stooped, their heads bowed, now hurried off
each morning to the Wienerwald to gather wood for fuel while their
sons hunted rabbits and squirrels to put meat on the table and their
wives threatened one another with knives over a spilled cup of black-
market sugar.

Shortly after their wedding on June 10, 1915, Egon had been
summoned for his third army physical, and this time the military
was willing to take even those with a weak constitution and a doctor's excuse, so he was declared *tauglich,* fit for service. Egon and
Edith had hardly had a chance to be husband and wife before he was
shipped off to Prague. While he waited for Edith to join him there,
he wrote to her about the hardships of military training, the rotten
cabbage soup, the horsehair mattresses, the horrid uniform that had
been issued to him: red pants, shoes with canvas uppers, and a sky
blue jacket with a stain of blood on the breast pocket. The jacket had
been stripped off a dead soldier. But when Edith arrived in Prague,
she was impressed with how robust and athletic her husband had
grown in just a few weeks. That beautiful city worked upon Egon
like a fortifying wine, putting a blush in his cheeks, filling him with
optimism.

His spirit had improved proportionately. On their way across
Karlův most one evening they had spotted a mouse cowering against
the wall of the bridge, and Egon's hand had come down as fast as
the blade of a guillotine—he had caught the mouse, held it in his fist
while he blew on the frightened animal to warm it, and he'd set it
free on the Mostecká. The old Egon wouldn't have bothered to save
such a pathetic creature, but the new Egon, Soldier Egon, had fallen
in love with the world, wanted to touch, to caress everything he
saw. Every time Edith visited him she would hear the soldiers inside
the exhibition hall laughing as if they were drunk, and war to her
began to seem an inexplicable paradox, where mood and reality
rarely matched. The young recruits in Prague were as cheerful as
their wooden imitations in toy shops, yet the newspapers reported
casualties of ten thousand in one day. Edith wondered why the
soldiers didn't mutiny, why they clapped and sang when they were
carried off in third-class compartments to the front.

Luckily, with the help of a few influential friends, Egon was assured of remaining in the ranks of the *Tachinierers,* those privileged military bureaucrats who fought the war from the safety of their desks. He spent that winter escorting Russian prisoners of war to and from Vienna, and he was allowed to sleep at home. In 1917 he was assigned to a prison camp in Mühling, where, despite the cold and the filthy conditions, he was happiest, with nothing to do but fill his portfolio with drawings of dying Russians.

By the spring of 1918 he was back in Vienna, working in a food warehouse, stealing cigarettes and schnapps for himself and Edith. Though an armistice couldn't have been far off, and many soldiers were already back in civilian clothes, the breadlines were longer than ever; in Berlin, Germans hunted down Austrians, dousing them in kerosene and setting them on fire; in Budapest, insane soldiers killed prostitutes by biting them in the neck. Edith feared peacetime more than she feared war. But she did sense a giddiness in the air, as if behind the curtains of every drawing room haggard men and women trembled with the laughter of anarchy and exhaustion. And when they weren't laughing they scurried off to the toilet, because the ersatz coffee made of barley caused dysentery and the Viennese would rather suffer intestinal discomfort than give up their beloved hot drink. During the war, people refused to talk about the progress of the war, except when an acquaintance had been killed, and then they would only speak up to ask, "Where?" and "How?"—as if hearing these details made the death sensible. And now the Austrians wanted to bury the memory of war with their dead. The newspapers had nothing to say about the traitorous Czechs and Hungarians, but feuilletonists were full of speculation about Austria's future: would Austria unite with Germany? would the Emperor Karl go mad like his father? and when would the Bahnhof ticket booths stay open more than a few hours each day?

The Schönbrunn residence, abandoned by royalty, had been turned into an orphanage, and a few weeks earlier Edith had woken in the middle of the night to the sound of children crying. It was a muted, distant sound, and when she raised her head from the pillow the crying stopped, so she decided that she had only imagined it and soon fell back into an uneasy sleep. But her dreams that night were full of emaciated, blistered children, who sat with their backs against a brick wall, and their wailing grew louder until Edith woke again. By then the sky outside was a smoky blue, and the crying she had heard in the dream was just the cat Poldi on the sidewalk below the window.

Later that day she told Egon about the crying children, and he looked at her with intense curiosity, as though he too had heard the sound in the middle of the night but had convinced himself that the voices began and ended inside his head. The next day Egon brought home an extra loaf of bread from the warehouse, and the following morning he took the loaf with him when he left for a meeting with Pisko. Though he hadn't explained, Edith knew that he intended to give the bread to the orphans. In recent days Egon had been bringing home extra provisions—rice and cabbage and bread—and the surplus and more had been going to the hungry children: Egon delivered the stolen food to Schönbrunn and left little for Edith and himself.

Such a sensitive, *tauglicher* soldier. There were times when she understood him intimately, when she could read his eyes and see his secret timidity and his anger, one contrary emotion fighting to dominate and subsume the other. But too often she felt that she hardly knew him, that the stories he told were lies, that even his name was a pseudonym, and that his family and friends all conspired to hide his past from her. This distrust had been aggravated by the rough way he handled her when they made love. He took her when she was just drifting off to sleep, mounted her roughly or pulled her on top of him and entered her with almost cruel precision. But he slept with his arms around her—the strength of his grip proved that he still loved her. Perhaps he meant to punish her for not returning his love.

But Edith preferred not to think about such things, or about the other women he had had before his marriage, or about how he had considered avoiding the draft by injecting himself with a special kind of liquid soap that would have made his testicles swell and given him the symptoms of gonorrhea—artists, he had said, were too important to be sacrificed to war. She preferred to think about the man who gave bread to the Schönbrunn children or spent all day working on the lips of her portrait, as if everything depended upon the vibrancy of the hue. She was flattered by the painstaking care he took with a painting that he had promised never to sell. Perhaps this was the most important difference between her and Egon's former mistress: he never put the portraits of Edith up for sale.

It could be, though, that this distinction made the mistress more valuable, Edith reflected, and she absentmindedly scratched her fingers on the thin wooden arm of the chair to attract Poldi's attention. The cat left the puddle of sunlight where she had been dozing and languidly sauntered across the room, bumping her hindquarters against the legs of the easel, rubbing against the baseboard and then against Edith's shins. She pulled the cat onto her lap and inspected the fur around its mouth, looking for the flecks of dried blood that she sometimes found after one of Poldi's nocturnal hunts.

As she kneaded the folds behind the cat's ear, inducing the soft, opiate rattling, she thought about Vallie Neuzil, such a pitiful creature in some respects and yet so completely in the world. Egon said that Vallie had even ridden a bicycle through the Prater. Edith had never learned to ride a bicycle—her mother had prohibited her girls from learning any sport because bicycles required graceless movements and gymnastics enlarged the hand. Edith couldn't help but fear that one day Egon would come home and inform his wife that their marriage had been a terrible mistake, that Vallie Neuzil was the only girl who belonged in his life.

Vallie had disappeared from Vienna during the war, but now that the war was over, what would keep her from returning to her former apartment and stealing Edith's slippers, Edith's cat, Edith's husband? Oh, Edith had too much time to herself these days, that was the trouble. Too much time to worry about the many unlikely possibilities. Soon she would have to fuss over a child—motherhood was all-consuming, and Edith wouldn't have a spare minute to entertain these hysterical notions. Edith had no doubt that Egon wanted to be a father. Why else would he care so much about the orphans of Schönbrunn?

In this sedentary manner, with her moods rising like wind, spinning furiously and veering off, Edith passed the rest of the morning. When she heard the church bells tolling eleven o'clock, she pushed Poldi off her lap. After so much thinking and so few conclusions, Edith felt irritated by the mystery of her husband and while she pulled her hairbrush through her hair, she opened the lid of Egon's rolltop desk. She had looked through his papers often enough and knew what to expect—if he minded he should have kept the desk locked. The postcards interested her the most, for there was usually a goading, humorous message scrawled by a friend on the back. But today, in one of the drawers, she found something even more interesting, more revealing: a photograph of her sister, taken here, in Egon's studio.

Edith brushed her hair back behind her ears as she examined the photograph of Adele—who was dressed only in a petticoat and high-laced boots and sat in a chair with one leg bent across the knee of the other, so the naked thigh above the garter was prominently displayed. Her head rested on her hand, her expression was both surly and seductive. There were two other photographs: Adele leaning forward so the bodice of her petticoat fell away from the skin and the groove of her cleavage was visible, and Adele in the chair with legs spread, her hands resting on her knees, the lace hem of her petticoat drooping in discreet, creamy folds across her thighs.

So this must have been why Adele hadn't been inclined lately to go shopping with Edith and their mother. And this must have been why Egon married into the Harms family. In one sister he had found a faithful Hausfrau, in the other he had an uninhibited, thoroughly contemporary girl. Adele, *liebe* Adele.

Edith arranged the photographs as she had found them and closed the rolltop, put on her pale yellow wide-brimmed hat and stopped in front of Egon's mirror. She had thin, refined lips, dark, melancholy eyes, but a square chin and large nose flawed the face significantly. If Egon found a more inspiring model in her sister, who could be blamed? They had kept the photography session a secret, but Egon hadn't bothered to hide the products. Indeed, if he left the photographs in his desk he must have wanted Edith to find them. Should she have felt angry? Jealous? Betrayed? Was it possible that her husband and her sister were having an affair? Egon could have married Adele, but he had chosen Edith to be his wife, in spite of her inhibitions. Or because of her inhibitions. Adele, like the mistress, served only a transient purpose.

By the time that Edith had left Hietzinger Hauptstrasse 101 and was crossing the street to her parents' home for her usual midday visit, she had decided upon the one emotion she would allow herself to feel in these circumstances: shame. She felt a dignified, reasonable shame, a shame that comforted her with its certainty, a shame not for herself, but for her sister.

Stigmata

ON the second day we took the train to Vienna. I sat beside Fräulein Vallie, who chattered endlessly about dress shops and hat shops, confectioneries and bakeries, while Herr Schiele, his back toward the front of the train, portfolio on his lap, looked out the window at the ugly countryside that seemed like a crude English landscape painting sealed in a green varnish, covered with dust. Why, I wondered, had this couple moved from Vienna if they had such disdain for provincial people? What value was our sullen land to an artist so preoccupied with the death and decay of the human body?

Preoccupied—at best. But by then I knew that the artist was nothing but a pornographer, his mistress no better than a common harlot. I had worshiped them because they were despised by the people of Neulengbach and because their stylish bravura made them invulnerable. Judging from their clothes, they didn't lack money. I couldn't have said how much men paid for pictures of girls lying stark naked in coffins, but I had seen Herr Schiele slip the unflattering drawing of me into his portfolio that morning and I had no doubt that such pictures were in high demand. With his glowering eyes, silk scarves, and pointed white American shoes, he matched my idea of what an artist should be. To live so well he had to make a profit from his work, and to make a profit he had to prostitute his art. The people of Neulengbach were right about this urban dandy and his mistress: they were dangerous, corrupting influences and deserved to be punished.

From the dream I had in the garden in Italy to the nights spent spying on cottage forty-five, all seemed part of a secret plot, with the drawing of a corpse the final goal. Now Egon Schiele had another picture to add to his portfolio, but I had a witness's authority. On the train to Vienna I decided to confess to my father that I had spent a night with Egon Schiele and Vallie Neuzil. I would describe the sketch and I would let my father avenge the wrong that had been done to me. By the time we had arrived at the station in Vienna, I felt solidly virtuous, even pleased with my decision to return to Neulengbach on the next train.

I hung back on the platform, letting the artist and his mistress walk on. The next minute I would have fled from them, disappeared into the crowd, but just then he kissed her on the forehead and passed through the gate, while she turned to wait for me. She would escort me to my grandmother's, she announced when I caught up to her. We would stop for lunch at her favorite Hungarian restaurant and we would talk about my unhappiness, or I would talk and she would listen, every girl needs a sympathetic friend, she said, stroking my nose with her bent finger. Egon's business would occupy him until the following morning, she would stay in a hotel, and eventually I would go to my grandmother's. But we weren't in any hurry, were we? We might as well become better acquainted before we parted.

Her tone of voice, insinuating, kind, took me by surprise, and I wasn't able to resist. So just as I had been about to betray Fräulein Vallie and her lover, she drew me back, taking my hand in hers, leading me through the station. Even then, as we walked down the stairs to the street, I decided that my father and the people of Neulengbach could wait.

•

Binoculars, 1909: Egon should have spent the money from Uncle Leopold on paint and canvas or at least on a nourishing dinner, but instead he bought a pair of binoculars that he had seen in a display window of a pawnshop. Although they weren't quite new, the shopkeeper maintained that they were of the highest quality and guaranteed Egon a full refund if the binoculars proved faulty in any way. Egon was almost nineteen years old, already a regular at the "Café Nihilism," as the artists disdainfully called Loos's Café Museum. He would drink schnapps and listen to the Wiener Werkstätte artists scorn their bourgeois patrons, the same devoted patrons who enabled these craftsmen to afford their expensive cigars. Egon didn't dare accuse the men of hypocrisy but he did bring his binoculars to the café and while the artists smoked and stabbed at the air with their cigars to emphasize their words, Egon examined them through the lenses, studied magnified sections of their bodies detached from any familiar context.

The focus disoriented him so much that he couldn't aim the binoculars and sometimes he couldn't even identify which part of the body he was looking at. With the fingers out of the area of vision, the curve of a hand draped over the arm of a chair looked like an elbow; a beard could be interpreted as the back of a young man's head; the tuft of a widow's peak on another man's pate could be mistaken for fronds of a potted fern.

How ridiculous the body appeared in fragments. But even more ridiculous were the insects Egon saw when he turned his binoculars around and looked backwards through the lenses. Little men are too weak to be proud, Egon thought as he observed them, and so they are vain. He admired these artists—Klimt, Moser, Hoffman—who were dragging a reluctant Vienna into the twentieth century, yet they also frustrated him, and Egon would have liked to ask them to look through the binoculars at him so they would recognize his difference and his importance. He would lead Vienna beyond the twentieth century, beyond the Secessionists' simple, logical lines and byzantine patterns. There were other alternatives to gaudy baroque than these rational designs. Van Gogh was an alternative. Hodler and Munch were alternatives. The Klimtgruppe valued these foreigners, but they didn't worship them with sufficient reverence and were unwilling to revise their own styles in any radical way. Klimt even refused to paint his self-portrait. Egon had entered the art world of Vienna when he was young and tractable, easily influenced, and he considered his pliancy not just a quality of youth but an advantage. "There is no new art," he had written in a draft of a manifesto for a show at Pisko's gallery. "There are only new artists."

Egon was a new artist, a new hunter using lines as his weapons, killing images in the world and smearing blood on his face. He lowered the binoculars and scribbled on a napkin: "I am a hunter. I prey on the world." Oskar Kokoschka had written a play, *Mörder, Hoffnung der Frauen,* performed the year before at the Kunstschau, and his success and notoriety made Egon jealously determined to create his own literary outrage. So he had begun to record his significant thoughts and to arrange them in verses. The next poem would begin: "I am a hunter." It was a serviceable metaphor and might inspire powerful illustrations.

Without bidding his friends goodbye, Egon slipped from his seat and out of the café, leaving one of the wealthy Werkstätte designers to cover his bill, as he often did when he was short of money. On the street Egon stalked images that he could dislocate with his binoculars, focused first on the window of a Ringstrasse tram. Magnification made the picture grainy, especially with the object so close. But Egon could still make out the nose and painted lips of a passenger, a woman. They were beautiful lips, thin, with the crevice below the nose ending in a slight peak in the upper lip, reminding him of his sister Gerti. As he looked at the lips behind the window he decided that he had been wrong about the impersonal quality of these binocular images. In fact, he would have liked to kiss those lips.

He lowered the binoculars to see the whole face as the tram began to pull away from the stop. The young woman was staring furiously at him—she probably had been staring while he had been examining her lips. Her beautiful lips. But when he began to run along the sidewalk to keep up with the tram, she turned her face away, and the ribbons hanging from the shoulders of her dress looked like rivulets of paint streaming down the inside of the glass.

"I am a hunter," he mouthed jauntily, giving up the woman, raising the binoculars to his eyes again. He was excited now by the way pieces of images could take on new meaning, and he realized that the primary purpose of a pair of binoculars was to reveal secrets. What city had more secrets than Vienna? He walked on, stopping to examine a chunk of peeling, dead bark on a molting sycamore, the rusted spear of a wrought-iron fence, chestnuts in a vendor's roasting tin, a man gazing out the window three stories above a bank, tapping his cigar against the sill. With his binoculars Egon could even see the crumbled ash. There were secrets in the cigar ash— secrets of greed and impotence. There were secrets in the granite blocks of the building—chips, ruts, cracks in the mortar. And there were secrets in the beard of the worn old man who lived from dawn to dusk every day inside a cramped magazine kiosk on the Schwarzenbergplatz. The binoculars showed Egon how the reflexes of the city were constrained by secrecy, by guilt, they revealed damaged skin and stone, gray hair and paunches. Through the lenses Vienna seemed overwhelmed by bulk, as though the citizens thought they could hide inside their buildings and inside their flesh. But they couldn't hide from Egon and his binoculars. He would track down the revealing images and smear their blood on his face and let a howl rip from his throat.

The black border of the iris. The dust of hair on a boy's chin. A muddy boot. Flowers in a woman's hat and the shadow of her parasol propped against a bench. Beer foam clinging to the sides of a mug. A watch chain. Moss growing in the crevices of paving stones sloping into the Danube Canal. The tip of a billiard cue. A kerchief wrapped around a Gypsy woman's head. Stenciled letters on a street sign. A leaf, a pile of manure, a lemon rind in the bottom of a glass.

Details. Blotches, callouses, grooves, bulges. All lines were significant and always existed independently, even when joined or crossed by other lines to represent something as intricately designed as the caboose of a train. The binoculars transformed the world for Egon, and the thrill of this new perspective was so intense that he couldn't wait to return to his studio. First, though, he needed refreshment, so he turned around and headed toward a small café he had just passed, went inside and with the binoculars hanging from his neck, he took a seat in the back room.

He unfolded a napkin and flattened it with the side of his pencil, intending to draw the things he had seen through his binoculars. But without the glasses against his eyes, the girl in the tram wasn't just lips to him anymore—he could only imagine the profile of her face. And when he thought of the cigar ash, he pictured the figure of a man in the third-story window. When he thought of a gouge in a stone he saw the entire facade of the building. So it was the binoculars, not the images, that had lied. Binoculars could magnify and abstract revealing details, but Egon had to have the entire composition in mind before he could begin to draw: he had to imagine a Madonna and Child, rooftops in Klosterneuburg, a woman with a black hat, before he filled in the details.

He ordered a schnapps from the waitress and looked down at the paper napkin. This was a familiar indifference, the same pernicious boredom he had felt in his figure-drawing class with Griepenkerl at the Academy. Without waiting for his drink he rushed out of the café, dropped the crumpled napkin in the gutter and hurried on, the binoculars bouncing against his chest. They had given him a new perspective, an impossible perspective—he couldn't draw the details he had viewed through the magnifying lenses without drawing them in context, and starting with the larger image meant shrinking the parts until the details were indistinguishable. Medieval artists had inflated symbolic details without changing the size of the encom-passing form, and a few ambitious artists today were taking a similar liberty. But it was not a freedom Egon sought, and he couldn't help but wonder whether he had overestimated his receptiveness to other styles. At eighteen years old, he wanted merely to refine his work; he would resist any radical changes.

The binoculars flew over his shoulder and thumped against his back. He slowed to a walk, unwrapping the string from his neck. The more violently expressive the line, the better, as far as he was concerned, yet he wasn't willing to break the rules of proportion. Rules. How he detested them, and yet he had just caught himself refusing to experiment. The binoculars—feminine, seductive, illu-sory—suddenly seemed to him responsible for his confusion, and he turned down a street that would take him across the canal to the Second District, to the shop where he had bought the binoculars.

As he approached the shop the front window looked dark, the shop abandoned, and immediately Egon assumed that he'd been tricked by a charlatan who wasn't a shopkeeper at all. But clouds overhead turned out to be the trickster this time, darkening the street and turning the glass an opaque gray. When he stood directly in front of the window, he could see the mannequins that had been there before: a boy wearing lederhosen, a belted jacket, a felt hat, and a girl in a plain dirndl dress. At their feet were scattered odds and ends—watches, brooches, hatpins, and replacing the binoculars on the velvet cushion was an adding machine.

The cowbell jingled as the door opened, the shopkeeper looked up from his newspaper, and Egon set the binoculars on top of the glass case.

"I want my money back," he said as firmly as he could, for he expected the shopkeeper to resist.

"They are broken?"

"Give me my money."

"But you must tell me what is wrong with them; perhaps they can be fixed."

"There is nothing wrong with them. Sell them to another fool."

The man stood up stiffly and brushed his fingers through the underside of his beard. "There is a crack in the lens? The focusing knob has jammed?"

"I told you, there is nothing wrong with them."

"So you keep them for two days and when you have no more use for them you return them to me? What if all my customers returned the items when they had no more use for them and then expected their money back?"

"You promised to refund my money if I wasn't satisfied."

"But if your dissatisfaction has nothing to do with the binoculars . . ."

"It has everything to do . . ."

"You should have known before that you had no use for them."

"Give me my money!" Egon said, his voice shrill and cracking.

"I will not!" The skin above the man's graying whiskers was scarred with pocks. Egon didn't need binoculars to see secrets on the surface of his body, the gap where a front tooth was missing, his bony hands resting flat on the counter.

"I will buy them from you," the shopkeeper said softly.

"How much?"

"Three kronen."

"But I paid ten!"

"So it costs you to borrow."

"Typical Jew!" Egon whispered. The man blinked, his face calm but his chest swelling as he inhaled. "If you won't . . ." Egon stammered, realizing at once that he didn't know how to finish the threat. "If you refuse . . . take the damned binoculars, then!" he said. But the shopkeeper remained unmoved, unforgiving.

Egon backed toward the door, bumped against a miniature plaster cast of a Corinthian column, steadied it, whirled around and groped in the dim light for the door handle. Outside again, he hurried along the street and as soon as he had turned the corner he thought he heard the sound of breaking glass, a sound that made him imagine a pair of binoculars lying on the street amidst shards of the shattered display window. He glanced behind him to see if anyone was rushing toward the shop, but the few people on his side of the street ignored the sound. Perhaps Egon had been mistaken and had heard only what he wanted to hear. He couldn't force himself to return to the shop and see for himself; he wouldn't give the man that complete a victory.

·

"Gerti!" Egon calls from his bed, the same bed where Edith had died of influenza three days earlier and where Egon would soon succumb, one among Vienna's thousands of epidemic victims in the autumn of 1918. Klimt had died eight months earlier. Egon would be next. But right now, in his mind, he is lost again in that arcadian city, Trieste, where the evening air was saturated with the smells of frying fish and tar and a perfume as voluptuous as that given off by magnolia petals floating in a bowl of water. In 1906, Gerti had teased Egon relentlessly—first with her slim body, then with her feigned drowning—and twelve years later Egon calls from the delirium of his fever for his little sister to come back. "Gerti!" But every time he starts to shout, the name drops to the back of his tongue and chokes him; instead of filling with air his esophagus becomes clogged with fluid, and he feels as though he were drowning.

Gerti has left his side, and the hands that turn his head on the pillow and scoop the mucus from his mouth belong to Adele Harms. Adele, who is not Gerti. Adele, who is not Edith. The epidemic snatched Edith away, along with her unborn child. Egon sat up through the night, drawing his wife's placid face that glistened like larva in the candlelight. Death had never seemed so sensible before. To Edith Schiele, death was a release, an improvement. Egon had been a widower for less than two hours when he sent a message to a friend, a sculptor, asking him to come at once and make a mask of Edith Schiele—Egon intended to hang his sketches and the death mask on the wall above his bed—but now it looks as though the mold will be made from his own face. He fell ill before the sculptor arrived, and the ghost of Edith is tugging at his ankles, pulling him beneath the surface of the Adriatic. She had been so serene as a corpse, after always looking so troubled in life. But since they had buried her, since she had entered that gray, monotonous state where she existed only in other people's memories, she must have discov-

ered how much she loved her husband. A cloying woman now—
Edith Schiele cannot bear to be alone. If only Gerti would give him
her hand and lift him out of the water onto the cold metal spine of
the pier. If only she would sit in the chair where Adele sits. Adele,
who is neither Gerti nor Edith. It is October, 1918, Edith is dead,
and Gerti has grown bored with Egon's suffering and returned to
her own home, to her husband and her little boy. Egon wishes the
pneumonia would make him forget the two women most important
to him—Edith tries to drown him, Gerti has left him in the care of
his in-laws.

In Trieste the beach was damp, stained by the retreating tide, but
warmer than the night air, and Egon closed his eyes while his little
sister kicked sand over him, like a cat covering its waste. On the
grounds of Miramare she had let him touch her breasts, as small and
hard as apricot pits. Sweet Gerti. On the skeleton of the pier she had
forced him to recognize how much he loved her and to purge himself of his desire. On the beach she had buried him. He had remained
as still as the best-trained model while his sister declared him a pig
and a coward who would have let the ocean swallow her before he
dipped his toes into the water. And then she abandoned him—as she
has abandoned him today.

The water sloshed against the hulls of anchored steamers, slack
ropes beat on furled sails, the bell of a buoy clanged irregularly.
Egon had never felt so alone before. He wanted to lie between beach
and sky in this exotic honeymoon city until the tide came in, he
wanted to feel the fingers of the water creep tentatively over his legs,
draw back and reach for him again, he wanted to let the current
carry him into the depths. How his sister would mourn him. The
pain and guilt she would feel.

Influenza is like the Adriatic, gentle and seductive at first, lapping
at his feet then with a surge lifting up and folding over him, filling
his mouth, choking him.

"Gerti!"

Twelve years ago in Trieste, Egon had pledged himself to the sea,
but the tide kept draining away from him, and eventually he grew
bored waiting to drown. So he had stood up, shaken out his shoes,
and walked along the beach, taking long strides, scraping his heels,
leaving ruts in the mealy sand that filled with water. From the harbor he headed back to the Piazza Grande, where gas jets in elegant

wrought-iron cages filled the square with quivering shadows. Egon turned onto the side street that led to his hotel, wondering as he walked whether Gerti would have asked the manager for a separate room, not much caring whether she had, feeling calmer now that he was surrounded by buildings, remembering his talent, his life's purpose. By the time he reached the hotel he had decided that his despair on the beach had been merely an experiment—an artist should toy with the most dangerous taboos but he must never let himself be distracted from his work. He must guard against his own excesses, translate his desires into images. Civilization depended on those images. Gerti had tricked him into taking awful risks, had invited him to touch her, had prompted in him the idea of suicide. But an artist should learn to defend himself against pernicious influences. Pleasure must be subordinate to inspiration, with no time wasted, no unnecessary lines on a canvas, no superfluous words spoken, no friends who are neither artists nor patrons, no lovers who will not strip and pose for him. An artist's vanity was his privilege, and though such solipsistic pride provoked envy in others, he must accept his isolation.

As Egon waited for the porter to open the door, he told himself that vanity made loneliness endurable—even an artist with uneven talent who was willing to devote himself completely to his work should be allowed to feel a bloated pride, the windfall of dedication. Every kind of fanaticism protected itself with vanity. It is not only a privilege, he decided as he climbed the three flights of carpeted steps, it is a necessary weapon.

He ran the fingers of both hands through his hair before he entered the hotel room; he closed the door behind him and leaned against the wall, waiting for his eyes to adjust to the darkness, listening to Gerti's shallow breathing. She was pretending to be asleep—Egon could hear the slight gasp as she tried to slow each inhalation to a slumbering rhythm. Such a conniving girl. Egon made his way through the darkness to the dressing table, sat on the metal stool and watched the shadowy silhouette of Gerti swell and deflate. She was close enough to touch again, and her body worked like a powerful magnet behind the barrier of the family name. An artist had to live inside the box of his signature, and no one, not even his sister, should be allowed to distract him from his work. He would never touch Gerti again.

Attracted and repelled, Egon found himself wishing that the

mound beneath the sheet would stop breathing, would stop moving entirely. And then, in the dazing kind of moment that exists outside of time—a gap that is both an instant and an eternity—Egon entertained himself with a fantasy: he imagined throwing himself across her inert body, mounting his sister's corpse, pictured the scene just vividly enough so that when the fantasy vanished, he had no doubt about what he had daydreamed. And the next moment, when he was back in time again, the knowledge of what he'd done—or of what he'd imagined—produced an acute pain, his skull seemed ready to burst from the pressure, and he lowered his head to his knees, trying to hide beneath the shield of his arms.

He had not realized that he was moaning aloud until he felt little Gerti's fingers on his shoulders. "Egon?" The pitch of her voice, the inquisitive cadence, the appeal were more than he could bear. "Egon?" she repeated, and as he struggled to answer he began to cry. Gerti stroked his back in the open-palmed, tentative way that a timid girl might pet a pony's withers.

"I am so tired," Egon said, as if this were reason enough. And maybe exhaustion was the simple cause of what he would later refer to cynically as his Trieste fit. He felt so tired of life, unable to contain his criminal desires, exhausted by his ambition. And Gerti, as though she were older than him, much older, as ancient as a grandmother with velvet skin and blank, glistening eyes that could see into the future, did not question him at all, did not even speak his name aloud again. She helped him move from the chair onto the bed, wiped his face with the loose cuff of her nightgown and continued to stroke his back until the shuddering stopped and he lay still, not quite sleeping but drained of all despair. How wise and sensitive Gerti proved herself to be that night, respecting Egon's emotion, demanding no explanation, no confession, sensing, somehow, that speech would destroy him.

Finally, in the honeymoon room in the Trieste hotel, Egon did fall asleep, inhaling the smell of Gerti's hair, his arm tingling beneath the weight of her head. His sleep was unbroken, without dreams— a healing sleep. But when he woke the next morning, the sheet tangled around his knees, Gerti was gone. Though Egon groggily remembered her sympathy during the night, he couldn't help but fear that somehow she had discovered her brother's unnatural fantasy and had fled in disgust. Perhaps he had talked aloud in his sleep.

He plunged his entire head into the fresh water in the washbasin, rubbed his hair dry with a hand towel, and without changing his clothes he went downstairs to the dining room. The only person there was a stocky Italian wearing workman's clothes, staring out the window as he sipped his coffee. Egon took a seat at a table across the room and waited for someone to bring him his breakfast. He would ask the porter casually, innocently, if he had seen a young girl leave the hotel earlier that morning. Perhaps Gerti had left a message for her brother; perhaps she expected him to join her.

But he didn't have to inquire because long before he received his breakfast Egon heard laughter, at once recognized the staccato squeals and rose from his chair so he could see past the workman through the window to the garden terrace, where Gerti was straddling a granite sphinx while another girl—Egon recognized her as the daughter of the proprietress—pulled on a rope bridle that had been tied around the sphinx's head. Switch in hand, Gerti giggled as she lashed the stone haunches. Egon wanted to run out to the terrace and embrace his sister, who was a child again, immersed in a harmless game, but he didn't want to break the delicate trance of make-believe. So he watched her through the window, glad to have his little sister before his eyes again. If only he could invent fantasies as utterly comforting as this terrace scene, he thought.

If only he could invent fantasies as comforting, he muses again as Adele dips a cloth in a bowl of rubbing alcohol and returns it to his forehead. If only he could bring back Gerti as she was in childhood. If only he could dream himself to health. It is October, 1918. Egon Schiele is twenty-eight years old. He still has work to do, commissioned portraits, invitations to exhibitions. He could grow accustomed to living without his wife; he could even learn to live without his sister, he thinks with the ineffectual stoicism of a dying man, telling himself that the memory of her straddling the sphinx on a terrace garden should be enough. He has Adele, after all. Adele Harms, as brazen and willing a model as Vallie Neuzil had been. Adele, who is neither Edith nor Gerti. Adele, who is not Vallie. He decides wearily that when his health improves he will ask Adele Harms to be his wife.

•

The pressing question of the day is this: should Heinrich Benesch go alone to the trial in St. Pölten tomorrow or should he ask his son

Otto to accompany him? He is pondering the matter in his small library; a leather-bound book of Japanese stencil-cuts lies closed on his lap. He plans to hand the book to Egon Schiele, convicted pornographer, corrupter of children, as the constable leads him from the courtroom back to his cell. But Benesch worries that Otto will resent his father's expensive tribute to the young artist, though of course Otto wouldn't complain aloud. He never complained in the past when Benesch gave Egon and Vallie twenty or thirty kronen for "absolute necessities," and he didn't offer any judgment when he heard that the money had been spent on an expensive meal in a restaurant and tickets to the Burgtheater. Still, Otto must feel some jealousy, even if he doesn't admit to it. So why bother subjecting the boy to the embarrassing affair? Heinrich would rather have his son beside him when the artist is sentenced, but he knows it would be cruel to force Otto to sit there in silence while the charges are read and Egon publicly denounced by the examining magistrate. Silence—this will be the most difficult requirement of the hearing. Heinrich Benesch will be unable to help, unable to testify unless the judge deems him a necessary witness, which is an unlikely prospect, given the fact that the police have over a hundred of Egon's drawings in their possession and have no need for further evidence. Central Inspector Benesch has been a vocal supporter of Egon Schiele, defending his art to resistant critics in Vienna, intervening between Egon and Arthur Roessler when the compulsive young artist insults his influential supporter, even writing a condemning letter to the municipal authorities of Prague after they had ordered Schiele's watercolors to be removed from the walls of an exhibition hall. But at the hearing in St. Pölten he must sit on a hard bench with the rest of the gawking public, unable to do anything at all.

Benesch has no question about his own responsibility—he has heard from Anton Peschka that Klimt advised Schiele's Neukunstgruppe friends to stay away from St. Pölten, for the presence of other surly, sophisticated young men would only incite a provincial judge. And Klimt has decided that his notoriety makes him a dangerous ally, so he will remain in Attersee. Arthur Roessler is vacationing at Lake Garda, and Gustav Pisko won't close his gallery for the day. Which leaves Henrich Benesch to serve as art's sole representative among the uneducated folk, an unknown and powerless representative, the one man there and probably anywhere—other than Egon himself—who understands the extent of the damage the country has done to itself by imprisoning this artist, who is as much a prodigy as he is a troublemaker. Austrians believe in protecting their children and see Egon Schiele as a threat when in fact he is just a child himself and should be nurtured. Of course the boy will make mistakes. In Benesch's opinion, the self-portraits among the "Neulengbach Series" are mistakes, the images straining to win the viewer's sympathy, to force him to feel the artist's torment with a simplistic rendering of agony and the aid of a slogan: HINDERING THE ARTIST IS A CRIME!

Future audiences will want challenges and enigmas, not self-righteous polemics, Benesch thinks to himself, glancing from his armchair to the closed ledger, the apple, the pens and stationery on his writing desk, realizing with a start that his last letter to Egon was just what he deplores in Egon's prison series—a remonstration and cajoling lecture, as inappropriate as it was well intended. Benesch wishes that he had never sent that letter. He would be more useful to Egon if he didn't offer advice so readily, if he remained a dependable, accepting audience. Who is he to try to influence the young artist? Why, he is nothing but an old man, a father, a reliable inspector for the Austrian Railway, who hasn't held a paintbrush since he was a child. He removes his spectacles, runs the fleshy tip of his thumb along each eyebrow, smoothing the hair, feeling his age around him as if it were a shirt drenched with perspiration clinging to his skin. Who is he? Central Inspector Heinrich Benesch, railway inspector, amateur collector, and Egon Schiele's most devoted friend.

Then influence should be his right, he affirms, puffing a little in his chair from his private argument. A man must be allowed his opinion, and every supporter has the right to try to influence his protégé, to offer his eyes to the artist, to make a Janus head with the artist and to keep watch over the unpredictable public while the artist faces the mirror. Kokoschka refers to his models as victims, which is just what Egon Schiele has made of himself—a victim, helpless beneath the force of his own gaze. Such troubles he brings upon himself, even as his reputation grows. Just last week Benesch heard the architect Wagner announce that Egon Schiele would be invited to show at the important Sonderbund exhibition in Cologne next year. Yet only a few months have passed since the Archduke himself was overheard telling his secretary as he left Pisko's gallery: "No one may learn that I have seen this filth." Powerful men like Klimt, Pisko, and Roessler champion the young artist, powerful men like the Archduke Franz Ferdinand would like to run a sword through his heart.

And yet, despite his need for fame, Egon found such controversy unendurable and chose to live among the children of peasants, a refuge as treacherous as an enemy's bivouac. Peasants know better than the hostile critics of Vienna how to trap the fox that has been plundering their coops—if anyone can ruin Egon Schiele, they can. Unless, of course, Egon follows Benesch's advice and turns his cell into an atelier. The key to happiness is work, Benesch believes, and the peasants know too well that by taking a man's work away from him they take away his life. But Egon's work belongs to the future, not to the present, and certainly not to the inhabitants of Neuleng-bach. Although he warned the young artist in prison that the promise of the future is a mere dream, a parched man's watery mirage, Benesch has no doubt that Egon's prediction is accurate: only in the future will his work be adequately appreciated. In this matter alone Heinrich Benesch, collector of fine art, allows himself a degree of irrational prescience.

But the question remains: should Heinrich Benesch bring Otto to St. Pölten? When Benesch thinks of Egon Schiele's historical importance, he has to admit that a rare opportunity has been provided for his son, a chance to witness a symbolic event long before the significance is understood, and he concludes that a trip to St. Pölten will mean much to Otto in his later years.

Satisfied with his decision, Benesch reaches for the apple on his desk, bites into the dented side and chews slowly, delighting in one of his few secret pleasures—the taste of a bruised apple. Tomorrow he will wear his finest black suit and lend Otto one of his silk hats, his wife will pack a dinner of cold sausage and the flat Turkish bread that has lately become Otto's passion, and they will catch the eight-o'clock train. Already it seems like a holiday.

.

In the Austro-Hungarian Empire, the principle of irreducible sovereignty remains unchallenged. But not for long. While the working man lives in unheated barracks and his naked children play in puddles in the street, princes chase roebucks across Hungarian estates. The masses will rise up someday—the court knows that its supremacy is as feeble as its Emperor, so close to death that the eager Crown Prince had to rush to reach the end first, and the aristocracy enjoys its final days with the pathetic pleasure of a condemned man smoking his last cigar.

Yet for now, what a sight the servants make as they tally a shooting party's plunder. Thousands of hares, partridges, pheasants, stags, a few wild pigs, all heaped at the edge of the garden, only the plumpest and youngest animals plucked from the mountain of carcasses to feed the guests, the rest left for local peasants, who sneak onto the estate in the middle of the night and fill their burlap bags with as much as they can carry, leaving behind a diminished pile that in summer swarms with lice, maggots, and flies and is eventually burned by some assiduous gardener, or in winter lies buried beneath snow, only to emerge and start to rot again during the spring thaw. When the breeze carries the stench from the deserted estate to the village, the peasants, giddy with hunger, remember the aristocrats from Vienna, the music, the feasts, and they take to drinking their beer in huge gulps that make their eyes tear, they sing and dance, pretending that they are aristocrats, and some become so drunk that they begin to believe they really are aristocrats. Night and day they celebrate—neglecting their fields, surviving on nothing but beer and potatoes—until the aristocrats return unannounced, riding from the local train station in a parade of fiacres, the men wearing kid-leather boots and belted hunting jackets, the stout ladies in silk and lace, looking so deliciously useless. Winter parties are the most fantastic of all, with midnight suppers in the frozen pine forest that put the festivals of the peasants to shame. Hundreds of torches turn the long corridors between the pines into icy halls, and a field covered with a patchwork of muslin serves as the ballroom. A string orchestra plays, champagne is drunk, and young counts strap antlers on their fur hats and boast of their day's kill, while their wives gather around a table laden with roasts and stewed fruits, nuts, pancakes, and pastries.

Of course as an ordinary tourist, you won't be invited to a shooting party on a Hungarian estate. But if you happen to spot a group of aristocrats sitting in the Sacher's outdoor café in the Prater, pause for a minute, study them carefully—they are used to such attention

—and reflect upon their fate. They wear the feathers and furs of their prey, and like those wild animals, their beauty is entirely defensive. With their diamond tiaras as sharp as teeth, their beards like claws, only their own kind will readily approach them. With their ebullient colors they blend into huge tapestries and oriental rugs, and with their fleet of automobiles they are difficult to catch.

But someday they will be caught, their backs will be broken, bullets will lodge between their temples, and they'll be left in heaps at the edge of a garden to freeze, to thaw, to rot. Unlike the wild animals, the aristocrats anticipate their doom—they move in jerks and starts, their eyes twitch uncontrollably, and their laughter builds to a hysterical pitch. More and more of them are following the example of Rudolf and choosing suicide; many have gone willingly to remote sanitoriums; one delicate young lady even began to bleed from the palms of her hands during a late supper at the Imperial Hotel. The waiters stood aside as the husband helped his wife out of the restaurant, and not until they saw the handprints of blood on the tablecloth did they deduce what had happened.

•

The only difference between a portrait and a painting of a human figure is a proper name, Egon concluded in 1911, the day after he returned with Moa and Erwin Osen from his trip to Krumau. Seated nudes, reclining nudes, dead mothers, girls wearing striped stockings and black hats, standing against a colored background—all were Egon's creation, shapes without identity, inspired by models, perhaps, but in their final form unrelated to their source. As soon as he labeled a face with a name, though, the picture became a replica of the individual who existed in time.

At the home of the industrialist Oskar Reichel, Egon had the chance to study Kokoschka's drawings and Gauguin's brilliant canvases. With these works as his inspirations, Egon taught himself to emphasize the independence of contiguous shapes by using stylized gestures, flattening the illusion of depth without sacrificing a sense of bulk and motion. And during the few days in Krumau, Egon made good use of Erwin Osen, turned him into a figure bearing little resemblance to the real man yet still expressing his essence, his "life-spirit," as Egon liked to say, better than Osen could in his own theatrical performances. In the hotel room, while Moa looked on,

Erwin Osen had willingly stripped and assumed a range of contorted poses for his humorless friend. When Egon returned to his studio at Alserbachstrasse 39 in Vienna, he brought with him a half-dozen crude sketches, and two days later he finished a watercolor painting of Erwin Osen, which he considered one of his best paintings to date. Egon had mastered a singular trick—he had created in his study of Osen his most convincing phantom yet, a figure who was both living and dead, a figure caught and frozen in the middle of a violent Saint Vitus' dance, a named figure—a portrait—and at the same time an anonymous male nude, who seemed carved from wood, sallow and rigid.

The paradox of death in life, of life after death—this was the root of terror, and phantoms were the supreme representations of terror. Egon unclipped the painting of Osen, the paper still damp and pliant, and with a flick of his hand he tossed it into the center of the room because he wanted to make sure his uncanny Osen could dance, could spin, could float in the air and land on one leg. The paper, heavy with paint, settled gracelessly, painted side up, and slid across the floor. But it was enough of a flight to please Egon. He reached for the picture and kissed the space in front of the paper.

Yet coupled with the joy of his success he felt an increasing disappointment, as though he were asleep, dreaming, and still aware in his dream that the vision wasn't real and wouldn't last. Yes, he had painted a phantom, snatched the invisible presence from the air, given it substance and a life in death, but the figure that appeared supernatural to its creator would seem merely unnatural to the rest of the world, Egon knew, and his necromancer's magic would never be appreciated. Just as awareness will eventually rouse a dreamer, Egon's awareness diminished his pleasure until he felt that he had failed miserably. Wasn't it better to lock the door to his studio, a single room with dirty plaster walls and bare floors stinking of oil paints and turpentine? Wasn't it better to remain inside, never waking from the dream of art, surrounded by phantoms, confident of his success? He had turned Osen into the ghost of Egon Schiele. He would turn everything he knew into a ghost, he would summon their faces from memory and bring them to life. It didn't matter whether anyone else recognized the magic. He would begin, he decided, with the mute from Krumau—he would make the mysterious boy his own again. Life in death.

He sat on the edge of the table, closed his eyes, covered his face with his hands. Five days had passed since that languid afternoon in the hills of Krumau, and he could still remember the touch of the boy's callused fingers on his arms, his lips pressing against the knot at the top of his spine, the kisses that were impelled more by curiosity than by affection, a drop of semen dripping from the boy's penis onto Egon's tongue. But despite the force of the memory, Egon could not recall the boy's face, could not even remember the color of his eyes. The image had been erased when he kicked leaves over the patch of ground where they had held each other, two strangers, so trusting that they had fallen asleep in each other's arms, phantom boys, dead now, both of them.

Egon could remember the face of his older sister Elvira, though she had died when he was only three. He could remember the face of his father, of his teachers at Klosterneuburg and Krems, he could even remember the face of his first Ottakring prostitute and could describe them all as accurately as if he were looking at photographs. But he had no image of the boy he had loved so completely and so briefly less than a week ago. His mind remained full of obstinate memories, every banal and detestable thought that had ever entered his consciousness lay in hibernation and would, he believed, return to him someday. But he had lost the image of the boy from Krumau.

At least he could still remember the touch, and he caressed his shoulders to remind himself of the sensation, afraid that he would lose this memory too, that the experience would disappear, as his first self-portraits had disappeared when he was twelve years old, stolen by his father, swallowed by the stove. Death in life. Egon Schiele—a phantom of himself, a gray, porous replica of all the Egon Schieles who had lived in the past, all obliterated by time.

He existed only when he had company. Alone, his emotions simply repeated themselves, like a top that kept spinning after the child left the room. He needed to be surrounded by people. Most of all he needed tractable models, so he wouldn't have to rely on memory; he needed faces that originated outside of himself. Now that he had forgotten the face of the mute, he realized that he could never again create even an approximate image. The boy proved as elusive as a round square.

Since he couldn't begin a drawing when he had no image in mind, he decided that the portrait of Erwin Osen was adequate work for a day. Egon's phantom would stay in the studio, while Egon would wander the city like a tourist, searching for unforgettable sights, tracking down impoverished children with squinting, red-rimmed eyes wounded by light. Images sustained Egon as food sustained others. Eventually he would have to discipline himself to grow used to seclusion—only in solitude could an artist imagine freely—but for now he was too young, too full of energy to accept the stringent conditions of art. With all his polemics about creation, he wanted only to escape from his studio and roam the streets or play billiards with his friends or find a willing Bohemian goatherd.

He had grown bored with himself. Even as he walked he felt lazy, passive; he wanted merely to be entertained by the sights and didn't much care about using what he saw, not today. He bought a *Salzstangel* to eat as he strolled along the Lerchenfelderstrasse. But the noise of streetcars irritated him and the smell of goulash stewing in huge steel pots over barrel fires sickened him, so he retreated to a café. He picked caraway seeds from between his teeth and lingered over a schnapps, smoked a cigarette, exchanged a few mundane words about the fine weather with the waiter.

Half an hour later he was walking again without any destination in mind, when he looked up and found himself at Josefstädterstrasse, not far from Klimt's atelier. And since the city had become more of a nuisance today than an intriguing spectacle, he decided to pay an unannounced visit to Klimt, as he had done with such successful results four years earlier. Since their first meeting, the older artist had invited Egon into the prestigious Wiener Werkstätte, had included his paintings in the annual Kunstschau, had recommended Egon for commissions. And yet even as Egon's gratitude and respect increased with all these favors, Klimt had changed in Egon's eyes from a dignitary, a high priest of modern art, to a harmless if pugnacious clown, becoming both more of a friend and more of a rival.

Egon entered through the side door that opened into the public courtyard. From behind the wall of Klimt's garden came the trill of a female voice, the clang as a fork touched a pewter plate. As usual, Klimt had visitors; surely he wouldn't mind another. Egon walked straight through the apartment to the kitchen door that had been left slightly ajar and that hid him sufficiently so he could see the girl in the garden without being seen by her.

She sat on a bench, her legs folded beneath her like a foal, stark naked except for a yellow band around her forehead, making her red hair bulge like the edge of a fluted bowl. On the bench beside her was Klimt's white-masked cat, and the girl was trying to tempt the cat to take a piece of sausage from her fingers, scolding it in her childish voice when it refused. The girl was small though amply curved, slight not exactly in build but because she hadn't reached her full height yet. Against her face, freckled and round, the rest of her youthful body seemed as smooth as soap, pale, the skin of her belly making two narrow creases as she leaned over, her pubic hair as red as the hair on her head.

Klimt, a man who wished for nothing more than what he already possessed, usually shared his wealth with his indigent apprentice, but he had kept this treasure to himself. Without moving from the doorway, Egon resolved to steal the girl from Klimt, who had left her alone and unprotected. No easel was set up in the garden. It appeared that Klimt could afford to keep his models like pets, just as he could afford to accept the tea set, a gift from Hoffmann—Egon would have been quick to sell at least the platter and probably the cups as well to support himself.

The girl cut another disk from the sausage, plucked it off the plate with her fingers and dropped it into her mouth as though to spite the cat. As she chewed her gaze wandered. Her serene features hardened when she spotted Egon at the door. With a yelp she leaped up and reached for a robe that had been draped over the arm of the wrought-iron bench.

"Go on, get out!" she cried, squatting behind the bench. Egon laughed aloud, for she was speaking to him in the same tone of voice she had used with the cat. "He'll be home soon," she warned. "Don't let him find you here."

"But I've come to see Herr Klimt. Or that was my intention. Now that I've seen you, I think I would prefer your friendship to his."

"And I'd prefer to be alone, if you please," she said, her fury weak, even coquettish, Egon thought, so he felt encouraged and took another step into the garden.

"If you please," she repeated, clutching the robe against her.

"How much does he pay you? But it doesn't matter, I'll pay you twice as much."

In reply, she pelted him with a fistful of dirt and pebbles, but her anger still seemed playful, her indignation too coy to take seriously. "I wear expensive gowns. I don't pose like this." Even as she defended herself she let a corner of the robe fall away from her chin, revealing the slope of her breast, and her lips in a pinched line seemed about to break into a smile. Egon wondered how he might provoke that smile, but before he could say anything more the girl stood up, casually drew the robe over her shoulders, and as she slipped her arms into the sleeves Egon had one full and satisfying look.

No longer the sweet, modest girl of a minute before, now apparently indifferent to his gaze, she picked up Klimt's cat, nestled her nose in the fur, absorbed herself so thoroughly that Egon wondered whether he should leave and return some other time. But he didn't move. And finally, still looking at the cat, she said. "You're not as old as the rest of them."

He wasn't certain whether she was speaking to him or to Klimt's cat, but he didn't want to ask—he would risk the chance of ever winning her interest with such a stupid question. Instead he took another step toward her and reached out his hand, began massaging the folds of fur on the cat's throat because this was as near as he dared to come to the girl. He asked the inevitable question, a question always so full of implications—"What is your name?"—at last coaxing a smile from her, though not an answer. She remained silent. Apparently Egon would have to wait for Klimt to return before he found out anything about her and could continue his pursuit. Rather than feel irritated by her silence, however, he appreciated the enigma, studied her from this close distance just as he had watched her from the doorway, confident that he would secure her for himself someday, waiting for Klimt so he could challenge the older artist, at the same time hoping that Klimt would be delayed so he could continue to relish the mystery of this red-haired, impish darling who would, in a matter of hours, belong to him.

Unforgettable Impressions

FRÄULEIN Vallie never took me to my grandmother's that day in Vienna. We sat in a restaurant until eight in the evening, washing down cabbage rolls with beer, and Vallie, in nearly every respect my opposite, soon put me at ease. At her urging, I talked about myself; I muttered and protested and shook my head. I grew so animated that I knocked over a vase that the waiter had placed between us, spilling water and daffodils across the table. When Vallie exclaimed I did too, I yelped so loudly that she fell silent and gave me a bemused, cocked-head look. I knew what she was thinking: to her I appeared a suffering, humorless girl, as doomed as my invalid mother, so my spirited voice must have seemed startling, like the sounds that would come out of the "Electrocution Extravaganza" boxes at the Prater, where, for a few kreuzer, you could touch a live wire and feel the shock.

After it had grown dark outside and the waiter had placed a candle on our table, Vallie suggested that at this late hour I come with her to the hotel—we would go to my grandmother's the next morning. I told her that I would gladly spend the night in a hotel, as long as I could pay her later for my share of the bill, for I had brought no money with me.

"Egon will pay," she said, tugging on the drawstring of her purse. "Egon will pay," she repeated, lifting out a gold coin, waving it above her head to catch the waiter's attention.

The pension, a five-story brick building with bow windows and

a granite ivy frieze, was a short walk from the restaurant. Fräulein
Vallie clapped the door knocker at least ten times, explaining as she
did so that the owner, a widow of Russian descent, was nearly deaf,
but the rooms were clean and spacious and priced reasonably
enough. The creature who finally met us was not what I'd expected:
as small as a ten-year-old child, slightly stooped, with straight black
hair hanging like curtains on either side of her smooth, ruddy face.
She might have been thirty-five or seventy-five. Her speech was
lisping, slurred, her tongue fluttering uncontrollably across her bottom lip, and her eyes were opened wide, full of curiosity and affection.

She greeted Vallie with noisy kisses, kissed me as well, told us
how lucky we were, the best room in the house had just been va-
cated, but we must be careful about turning up the gas. Had we read
in last week's paper about the unlucky man who lit a cigarette in a
pension in the Ninth District and blew out the side of the building?
God would make the final decision, of course, but there was no
harm in caution. The mistress consoled the worried woman with a
promise—if we blew up her beautiful building we would buy her
another, grander pension. "Egon will pay," she said, pressing the
woman's hands between her own.

As we climbed the staircase to the first floor, the widow leading
the way, raising herself one step and stopping to rest, mounting
another step and stopping again, she told us that she had been born
and raised in this same building, she had given up a career on the
stage to work here after her father died of tuberculosis. She had
married a carpenter for practical purposes, but he had fallen from
the roof shortly after their wedding, so now she managed the building alone. She would give up her life before she gave up the deed to
the pension, she vowed, clutching the banister to lift herself onto
the landing. And then she merely pointed down the hall toward an
open door and turned immediately to begin the slow descent.

So for the first time Fräulein Vallie and I were completely alone,
in a room with a small wall lamp burning weakly, a basin on a cart,
a brass bed. She collapsed across the wide mattress and motioned
me to sit on the edge of the bed, which I did. She removed my hat
pins, untwisted my hair, reached toward the top button of my
blouse, then thought better of it and lay back, remaining silent for
so long that I thought she had fallen asleep. I stared at my ugly,

square-tipped fingers, unsure of what to do with them or with the rest of my clumsy body.

Finally I found the courage to kick off my shoes and lie beside her, so close that the currents of her breath ruffled my hair. She smelled of talcum, of beer and garlic—the pungency unnerved me, and I wanted most of all to know what to expect; I became so tense with waiting that when she finally did speak her voice took me by surprise, and I flinched.

"Trust me," she said. "You don't trust anyone. You must learn to trust me." She slid the back of her hand along my cheek, just as the artist had the night he caught me peering through the window of his cottage. I thought of that night, recalled as well the day he had laughed when I brought him the Künstlerhaus catalogue, pictured in my mind his rude graphite portrait of me, thought of the artist and his mistress covered with tattoos, the artist sleeping, the artist laughing. No, I couldn't trust him, I would never trust him. And I couldn't trust her either. I was just a filthy, dull-witted peasant girl without a future.

"Leave me alone!"

"Leave you alone?" she echoed, her voice suddenly condescending, venomous. "There's not much more that I can do for you. If you want a separate room we can surely arrange it." As she took off her hat and released the clasp of her coat collar, she pointed out that we had not yet solved the problem. I had come to their cottage penniless, homeless, friendless. There was nothing else to do but to deliver me to my grandmother's, she concluded, dispirited now, regretful. "Nothing else to do," she repeated. "First thing in the morning." And she took from her bag a square of silky material that unfolded into a soot-colored, neck-to-toe nightgown.

From where I sat on the bed I could look at her out of the corner of my eyes, or I could look straight ahead at her reflection in the wardrobe mirror. But when I turned my back to her I discovered a third image, the mirror image reflected in the window, distorted by the glass, the flame inside the bowl of the lamp like a bulging rib, Vallie Neuzil's naked torso as misshapen as a piece of wet clay pulled from either side. For the instant that the image existed whole in the window, before she pulled the nightgown over her head, I wanted to grab hold of it, to pull the reflection out of the glass. I had wanted, I realized after she lay back again and the image disappeared, to catch the reflection, to keep this version of Vallie Neuzil with me forever.

As soon as I had lost the vision, my thoughts turned back to the previous night. It didn't take a great effort to understand that what I had found disgusting in the artist's rendering of me was merely ridiculous. Egon Schiele had drawn what he had seen. In a certain light, viewed from a certain angle, I—like Fräulein Neuzil—appeared ridiculous. And the challenge, I finally realized, was to laugh —not with scorn, not with shame, but with delight.

How I laughed that night, laughed with heaves and sobs. I think I laughed myself to sleep. Fräulein Vallie must have sensed that I wouldn't explain what I found so amusing, for she didn't bother to ask. Most likely, she didn't even wonder.

•

Who has the greater capacity for sorrow, Vallie asks herself—man or woman? Who has the greater talent for evil, man or woman? Who is more adept at cruelty? Who is more resilient? Who feels less remorse? Who is closer to God? Who has the greater potential for pleasure, man or woman? Who has stronger bones, sharper eyes, thicker blood? Vallie parts her knees and inserts two fingers beneath the elastic of her underpants, pulls the fingers out again and examines the blood, carmine red, as Egon would say, oily, with a vaguely sour smell, like lemon rind. Women bleed, and the blood must mean something. Women are perpetual invalids. They are lakes. They are cows or goats or camels. Women bleed because they are being punished, they bleed because they are overflowing with life, they bleed because they are infected.

Vallie wipes her fingers on a rag that smells of turpentine and she ponders the dresses, the skirts, the blouses already folded in neat stacks on the bed. Her possessions. Herself. Now that she is alone again, she tries to keep her mind busy, to hold private conversations, asking and wondering in her own simple way. Before she met Gustav Klimt she had thought little about the differences between men and women. But the first time that she had sat for Gustav in his atelier, wearing one of Emilie's dresses, pressing her lips together and raising her chin slightly, according to the painter's directions, she had become aware of her body as if it were the dress itself, made by and for someone else, a poor fit, hers only by virtue of the fact that she had been born female. In the years that followed, as she was passed from Gustav Klimt to Egon Schiele, from Egon into this abyss of loneliness and ineffectual anger, she grew into the dress and now has grown too large for it: the stays have snapped, the seams ripped; she blames the dress for everything. Because she is a woman. Because she is a woman. In Vienna, perhaps in the rest of the world as well, everything begins and ends with this fact. Because she is a woman.

Who is luckier? she wonders as she packs her two suitcases. Egon seems luckier—he has more control over the direction of his life. Or does he? He has delayed conscription for the moment, but sooner or later they'll snatch him and button him inside a soldier's uniform, as Emilie buttoned Vallie inside the countess gown. Maybe someday, after Vallie has been trained as a Red Cross nurse, Egon will be injured in the trenches and he'll be brought to Vallie's hospital ward, where, with a satisfying vengeance, she'll stick the needle in his bottom while he stares helplessly, swaddled in blood-soaked bandages.

Though she finishes packing in fifteen minutes, she isn't ready to leave the Hietzinger apartment. Here she and Egon lived in considerable comfort for many months—with a gas range, walk-in closets, a porcelain tub, hot and cold running water—until the Harms sisters began tapping on their window across the street. She pours herself another glass of the Curaçao—she had the first fortifying drink as soon as she arrived home after meeting Egon in the café. On the table three of Egon's sketches lie undisturbed, all of them versions of the drawing Egon had been working on before he left: in each, two girls rest together, one sprawled across the other's lap, naked, while the one beneath is clothed and has a ridiculous ragdoll face. Vallie can find herself in neither of the figures, so her gaze wanders away from the table and walls, away from Egon's pictures, to the window—the sky a pasty white, the new leaves a nearly implausible brilliant green, as if each leaf had a flame burning inside the tiny stem.

She comforts herself by thinking about her childhood, when it didn't much matter that she had been born a girl instead of a boy. She was stronger than most other children her age and often called upon to initiate and lead their games. Her favorite was coach and horses. She would drive, while a young boy named Josef would play an agreeable steed and wouldn't even cry as the other boys did when she used her whip. All drivers used their whips, especially when their passengers were famous actresses or French counts. In winter she would steer Josef up and over the mounds of snow piled by tireless shovelers on either side of the street, she would lean back on her heels and let him pull her across the icy flagstones, and she would reward him with a handful of snow, holding it for him as she would have held oats for a real horse.

Another game she especially liked was to dance for the one-legged pensioner, keeping time to his hurdy-gurdy tunes—at the end of the hour he would give each child a kreuzer and advise them to spend their money on a lottery ticket. If they began betting on the lottery at such a young age, they had a better chance of winning at some point in their lifetime, he explained. Vallie and her friends would take the coins to the nearest lottery kiosk, where they would buy a chocolate bar instead.

Vallie had started at a Catholic school but was expelled after she punched a boy in the throat, sending him into a convulsion—she couldn't even remember his name or how he had provoked her, but she could remember that she had been sure the boy would die as she watched him thrash and foam. She had felt a twofold amazement— at his suffering and at her own murderous power. Her mother hadn't even beaten her when Vallie gave her the letter from the schoolmistress, but Frau Neuzil did have one of the workmen upstairs take a smoked ham to the boy's home that evening. She sat in a rocking chair rubbing her hands together as though to thaw them during the hour that the workman was gone. When the workman returned with the report that the boy had suffered no permanent injury, she said nothing, simply kept rocking and rubbing her hands. She spent the night in the rocking chair—Vallie found her asleep the next morning.

Vallie had never liked school anyway, and her mother was glad to have her at home to help with chores. If the workmen all had inciting words of praise for her maturing body, their interest had something to do with their age, and though she had to chop and cook and sharpen her bartering skills at the market, she attributed her duties as a daughter to the special circumstances—her mother didn't have much money, after all, and if Vallie had been born a boy, poverty still would have required the same sacrifices.

Everything changed the day Vallie found her mother unconscious on the kitchen floor. Within a month, Vallie had been sent out by her aunt to work in the dress shop, where she learned about the importance of a shapely bosom and skin as flawless as the silk that covered it. So she began to take care with her toilette, devoting an extra hour each morning to her hair and face, saving her money so she could afford cheaper, simpler versions of the same dresses she sold, until she could compare herself with satisfaction to her wealthy customers. And then Gustav Klimt had entered the shop, vowing to celebrate her beauty. Because she is a woman.

Now the upper half of her body tilts and sways, as if in time to an inner music. She feels as though her life is behind her, and she must walk away from it toward the only end possible, just like the clown Fürst after the finale of his routine in a *café chantant,* when he turns from a mimic into his true self, just another tired old man with gray sidewhiskers. She must leave behind everything that matters: the quiet of Hietzing, the sense of home, her youth, depicted here on the wall in one of Egon's last watercolor paintings of her, wearing orange undergarments, one knee raised above her chin as she pulls on a skirt. She once heard Herr Benesch admiring the watercolor for its driving, centrifugal force. Strange, then, that Egon hasn't sold it or at least given it to Benesch. The painting is not one of her favorites but surely she could make a profit from it.

She pinches her bottom lip between her thumb and forefinger, glances nervously around as if there were someone in the empty room who could have overheard her thoughts. But it is easy enough to console herself: Egon owes her for the years she devoted herself to him; a single painting is a small price to pay. So she places the unframed picture between two pieces of matting board, wraps it in brown paper and twine, straps the package to the side of her suitcase, and she is ready to go—not to the end, she tells herself as she hauls the two suitcases, the stolen picture, and three hat boxes to the door of the apartment. No, not to the end but to a different life. Her fate depends upon her ingenutiy. She clucks for Poldi, but the cat remains hidden, probably to avoid a useless farewell, Vallie thinks with wry admiration. A sensible animal. The cat will plague Egon and his new wife with recollections of his former mistress. She is leaving the cat behind as a perpetual remonstrance.

Until she sells the painting, Vallie can afford only public transportation. The tram arrives just as she approaches the stop, so with all her luggage banging against her leg, she hobbles toward it as fast as she can, ignoring the jeering boys who cling to the rear platform and ride for free. On the tram Vallie stands by the back window, watches with pleasure as the forward jerk dislodges two of the boys. They tumble onto the street and scramble up, unharmed for now, but how their ears will smart after their mothers box them for dirtying their clothes, Vallie thinks. And how alone and frightened the third boy must feel, still holding on. When the tram finally slows at the next stop he drops away, and Vallie taps the window to let him know that she has seen everything. But he is too stunned to notice or perhaps too proud to acknowledge her.

It takes her over an hour to reach the Während novelty shop where her mother used to pawn jewelry. The ancient woman behind the counter doesn't recognize Vallie—so much the better. Vallie decides not to introduce herself. She unwraps the picture slowly, loosening the twine without tearing it, smoothing the package with the flat of her hand, taking advantage of the inherent suspense, inciting the woman's curiosity until the shopkeeper can't stand it any longer and pushes Vallie's hands away, snipping the string with scissors. But instead of a gasp, the watercolor painting elicits only a shrug, and without any comment she offers Vallie five kronen for the picture, hardly enough for one night in a decent hotel. Vallie begs her to reconsider. She knows the artist, she swears that men have paid hundreds for similar works. But the woman merely picks up a feather duster and swishes it over the glass case of a mantle clock, so Vallie begins to wrap up the painting, mumbling that she will take it elsewhere, a threat that does little to arouse the woman. Vallie tries one last imploring look. Surely, if the old woman has any compassion . . .

"Eight kronen," the woman says, "for the picture and the hat." The hat? The Makart imitation on Vallie's head, Vallie's favorite prop? She would like to spit in the old woman's face, just as she had spit at Egon, but instead she removes the hatpins one by one, strokes the cloth petals of the irises before she lifts the hat off her head and lowers her eyes so the woman won't see how distraught she feels at this paltry act of abnegation. The witch's hand reaches out and rakes the booty to her side of the counter. Vallie hears the rattle of change and when she glances up again she finds, beside the piles of coins, a small metal butterfly brooch, the veins on the wings outlined with sequins, the eyes black chips of glass.

With her new fortune in her purse, a feather hat on her head, the butterfly pinned to the lapel of her raincoat, Vallie treats herself to a ride in an automobile. As the cab driver turns onto the Ring, Vallie thinks with melancholy amusement about that ride five years earlier in the carriage with Gustav Klimt. She hasn't decided where she will stay for the next few nights while the war office is finding a place for her in a Red Cross hospital, so Vallie orders the driver to continue slowly around the Ring until she tells him to stop.

How brown Vienna is at springtime, she thinks. Brown-stained, like the pads between her legs. The streets, soggy with mud and manure, fill her with sadness. In a moment she is crying, a handkerchief pressed against her mouth so no sound will escape, her shoulders jerking as though from a rough, jolting force, as though the wire springs in the seat had broken through the upholstery and were throwing her forward at each pothole and bump in the street. Vallie hasn't cried like this for years. The sorrow must be purged, every muscle in her body strains to release it, and at the height of her pain she unclips the butterfly from her coat and presses the pin against her lips, tastes the acidic metal of the wings, presses her tongue against the sequins just as she did once when she was a young girl and her mother was about to take some jewelry, including this butterfly pin, the very same, to the Währing pawnbroker. *Kiss the butterfly goodbye, Vallie.*

The shopkeeper will never know how rich she has made her last customer. Vallie dries her eyes and soon is breathing easily again, thinking with satisfaction about how she has taken advantage of the Währing spider. This cheap pin is worth more to Vallie than a hundred of Egon's paintings or a hundred original Makart hats.

Only later, in her hotel room in the Josefstadt, does Vallie consider that perhaps the shopkeeper had recognized her and had returned the pin intentionally. But Vallie dislikes the old woman too much to believe that she is capable of any act of kindness. So she convinces herself that the woman gave her the pin for the same reason that a tavern-keeper will pour an extra *Viertel* for a new customer or the host of an opium den will refill a pipe for free: to ensure that she will come back. But Vallie will never return to the novelty shop, for now she has everything she needs.

•

"Unforgettable impressions! No passport formalities!" So the advertisement claims, luring the parasites of Europe away from their con-
cert halls and salons, away from their roasted squabs, their
champagne and caviar, to the enormous cemeteries of Vaux, the
battered Verdun landscape, for a two-day, all-meals-included tour
of the war zone, a tour arranged for wealthy women and old men
who think of the war as an exotic show worth witnessing firsthand
—the thing is to be able to say that you have seen it.

This advertisement, clipped from a Swiss newspaper, promises to
give tourists a close-up view of history, a series of unforgettable
impressions. To most of civilization, war is a spectacular show, a
sort of *cinématographie,* with hell as its setting. While the majority of
the bourgeoisie must be content to read reviews of the battles in
daily papers, a few can afford to purchase box-seat tickets.

Egon has heard from soldiers about shell wounds, gas grenades,
and liquid fire, he has heard descriptions of a few of those unforgettable images. And in the Basel newspaper he can read about how
fascinating a battlefield is when viewed through the window of a
luxury automobile. "You receive in the best hotel in Verdun a lun-
cheon with wine and coffee, gratuities included." These, then, are
the options: to be a spectator or a participant in the burlesque. But
Egon refuses to be awed by the war or disgusted by the vulgar
advertisement. From the barbed-wire enclosure of the prison camp,
he thinks of this war as a disease and wants most of all to avoid
contamination. He must survive. He will do anything to survive. So
he avoids contact with the artillery generals and staff physicians who
visit the camp, for they carry the germs of war. When he sketches a
haggard, dying Russian he keeps his distance. And when the men
gather after supper to trade news of the front and outdo one another
with their tales of atrocities, Egon retreats to a chair in the corner,
where he smokes cigarettes and lazily sketches the impassioned faces
of his fellow soldiers as they experience trench warfare vicariously,
through violent anecdotes.

After the promotional trip advertisement has been stuffed by an
unamused lieutenant into the stove, Egon leaves the room, goes out
to breathe the night air that stinks, even in winter, of slops and
sweat. There is no avoiding the filth of man inside a prison, Egon

knows. He would like to paint the stench with creamy brown gouache; he would like to design his own promotional trip poster that smells of war—yes, the stench would educate the bedazzled ladies and gentlemen of Europe, they'd finally comprehend the true nature of this war if they could only smell it. And the poor fools in the trenches would recognize that their war isn't nearly as grand and endless as hell, if they were confronted with Egon's version.

Most of all he would like to smell ink on his fingertips again. Turpentine. Glue. Pure dammar. He is tired, bored, like the Russian prisoners who exhaust themselves with the effort of waiting. They know they will be released someday, if not from the camp then from their lives, so they have nothing to do but to stare off into space, breathing in the stench of themselves. Six years earlier, in Neulengbach, Egon had compared his prison cell to the trap of hell: self-made, total. His youthful rage amuses him now that the world is full of self-proclaimed martyrs. Hell is an ennobling idea—a man who thinks himself in hell considers himself more valuable than other mortals, for he knows he will be spared the agony of dying.

To paint the color of the frozen sky, Egon would mix only iron black with the gum. To paint the wrinkled ground dusted with snow, he would apply a mosaic of browns and then tint the areas between the color spots with brilliant orange. When he stands still he hears the walls of the prisoners' barracks breathing. Yes, he would like to paint the sounds and smells of this camp. He will find a way to entice the naive senses awake with his images, to make his audiences smell and feel and hear, to overwhelm them with his images, not simply startling the eyes but absorbing his viewer entirely, making him smell, making him dizzy with the motion of the lines, making him feel the colors against his own skin, as Egon feels the darkness.

It is nearly midnight, February, 1918. Egon stands in the middle of a courtyard, silently pledging to draw up plans for a museum when he returns to his studio—a living museum full of new art, not a mausoleum. He will write to Klimt and ask him for advice—a deferential letter will please the old master, Egon knows. But he has sent two letters to Klimt in the last month and has yet to receive any reply. Perhaps Egon has offended him somehow. He will drop in on Klimt during his next visit to Vienna. Hopefully his next visit will be permanent. The war will be over soon, and to Egon defeat seems of little consequence. The war will be over, the plague will end, and Egon will go on with his work. He closes his eyes and breathes slowly, in rhythm with the walls, forgets about the awful smell and inhales the world-spirit, stands in the cold for nearly a quarter of an hour, saturating himself with the night.

But when he finally retires to his bed his throat is sore, his lips chapped. As he clutches the blanket around his neck he realizes how foolish he has been, exposing himself to the winter. The war isn't over yet, and the air remains impure. In the passion of the moment he had let down his guard. He makes himself cough in an effort to expel any germs that might be trying to penetrate the fragile tissue of his lungs. What if it is too late? he thinks, staring at a crease in his pillowcase. What if he has already been contaminated? What if the war claims him as its victim in its final days? What if, what if, what if.

Tomorrow he will request a leave so that he can spend the night with his wife. Only his wife can cure him. She will give him a sponge bath, wash off the smell of war, wrap him in a Turkish towel, make him coffee and lie with him, wiping out once and for all, as his paint brush cannot, the "unforgettable impressions" of war.

•

It is not enough to praise Vienna's entertainments, her baroque churches, her restaurants and opulent hotels, her markets, her bakeries, her Keller and taverns, her alleys and parks, her people, her royalty. It is not enough to describe the sights of this plutocratic capital, from the ghetto to the Opera, from "Old Steffl" to the Ringstrasse. The printed words don't change, while the city will transform itself before your eyes. At one moment Vienna will seem to you a rocking stone upon which history is perched, at the next moment the city will be as inviting as a rocking chair, a place where you can forget the relentless passage of time. We hope, then, that we have convinced you to leave behind all of your maps and guides and to venture out on your own—you won't really know Vienna until you lose yourself in the city for a day, for a week, or for an entire season.

But now, as we set you loose, we are obliged to end on a more somber note. As stalwart as the city appears, as muscular and vibrant and clean, Vienna is inexplicably rife with germs. Some say that microscopic parasites cling to the tip of every flower petal in every garden in Vienna, others that the foehn winds carry in mortal infections each spring. Travelers are vulnerable, and the ladies the most vulnerable of all. So our last word to you is a warning: *beware*. Wash your hands before you eat, wipe the toilet seat before you sit. *Beware*. We hope that the frail sex who lacks, as Weininger explains, any *principium rationis sufficientis*, pays particular attention to this advice.

•

Egon's dream. May 7, 1912: "The stroke of your pencil," explains Griepenkerl in Egon's dream, just as he had years earlier in the actual class at the Academy, "creates a friction, forcing graphite particles into the web of fibers. Whether you apply paint or ink or lead to the paper, remember: you are always damaging your ground. So you must think before you make a slapdash mess of the surface, you must consider the effect you want to achieve. If you are using oils, you must anticipate the density and strength of the binder in your paints; the great masters of the past understood the reactions at work, but these days artists rely on specialists to prepare their materials. Modern artists are servants to their medium, they have no sense of chemistry."

So I am here, Egon thinks in his dream, while the professor rambles on about different grounds, varnishes, and the blasphemy of controlled illumination. Here, not in the St. Pölten prison on the night before his trial but in the Vienna Academy of Fine Arts, with its marble corridors, lecture halls, and tall windows smoky with soot. Everything is exactly the same—his dream merely repeats that first class, and he feels the identical excitement that he felt before, when he was sixteen and—as a matter of course—had been sent by his teachers at Klosterneuburg to the School of Applied Arts in Vienna, whose administrators had directed him to the more prestigious Academy; there he had passed the entrance examination and had been admitted despite his young age. His mother, bewildered by the opinions of so many learned men, let Egon do what he wanted. How easy it had been to move from the Gymnasium to the Academy, as easy as boarding the train in Klosterneuburg. How easy and how incredible—to Egon the short ride had seemed to take forever, the tram that carried him halfway around the Ring took longer than forever, and the night spent tossing and turning on his bed in the rented room secured by his uncle was almost more than he could bear.

And now, asleep in his St. Pölten cell, Egon sits a second time in Griepenkerl's drafting class, and again he carves his name into the soft wood of the desk so he won't have to look up and exchange glances with the other students. But suddenly the professor is dismissing the class, though the hour hasn't ended, and at this point the dream diverges from the actual experience of the past. They would begin their study of male anatomy the following day, Griepenkerl announces, closing up his notebook, his impatience obvious. Clearly, this fat, churlish professor considers his students a hopeless lot and his teaching a waste of time. And since Griepenkerl represents the Academy to Egon, the school transforms itself in that moment from a sacred place full of secrets to a dank warehouse where the students are so many worthless mannequins.

For as long as he could remember, Egon had wanted to be an artist, to live in a garret and to wear stylish shoes, but now—in his dream—his ambition falters in the face of the Academy's indifference. Egon might as well have enrolled in a school for would-be engineers, so uninspired does he feel. If he had more courage he would take his month's allowance and run away to Paris. If he had more confidence, he would bring his portfolio to the Wiener Werkstätte and ask for a place in their next exhibition. Instead he puts his sharpened pencil back into his breast pocket and trails behind the other boys out of the classroom.

In the next segment of this lengthy dream he is dining alone in a dreary café. As he chews a tough piece of meat, he reads a newspaper article about a lawyer who never returned from an appointment with his manicurist. The lawyer's decapitated body was found a week later in a coal bin in an abandoned building. The police had no suspects. The story of the crime helps to revive Egon's excitement somewhat, reminding him that he has left behind his cloistered childhood once and for all. To succeed he would have to conquer this vicious city, to conquer it he must know everything about it, he must study the city as he would study the human body in tomorrow's drafting class. He will begin with the streets in his own Second

District, he decides, scraping up the last of the cream sauce, licking it off the dull edge of his knife.

And the dream accommodates: now he stands in front of a bill-board, and a girl—her face vaguely familiar, though he doesn't remember how he knows her—brushes against him, excuses herself and pretends to read the billboard. Then, without a word, she slyly lifts the pencil from Egon's pocket, hikes up her skirt and inserts the pencil between her garter and thigh. Egon follows her as she walks jauntily away. Sixteen years old in the dream, he has never visited a brothel before, and only today—his first day alone in Vienna—has his virginity become, if not his shame, then an impediment to his art.

The girl, who calls herself Mademoiselle Eveline though she has no French accent, leads him into the dark, tiled loggia of an old apartment building, not at all the gaudy parlor that Egon expected, and he sees no sign of anyone else as they climb to the third floor. He does hear doors opening and closing, the sounds like a racking, persistent cough. In contrast to the excitement he felt entering the lecture hall in the Academy, he feels simply a need to act with convincing sophistication, to disguise his virginity, to do whatever the girl wants him to do, to pay whatever she asks him to pay. He prefers, as he always has within and outside of his dreams, more forbidden pleasures. He prefers his sister Gerti to Mademoiselle Eveline. She should learn to keep her lips together instead of letting them shrink back over the gums, revealing a set of crooked teeth. As she unlocks the door, Egon reaches under her skirt to find his pencil, caresses one thigh and then the other, but the pencil has disappeared. He pushes her angrily away—she has spoiled the game, he must start over and find another girl, a more honest girl. But now, inside the room, Eveline kneels down on the floor before him, giggling, pulling at the buttons of his fly.

And then he has skipped to another hour, perhaps to another day, to the same room lit with a single overhead bulb, with the same girl, Eveline, who sips champagne while Egon sketches her. She collects a mouthful of champagne in the bubble of her cheek, and when he orders her to swallow, she purses her lips and expels little spurts, until Egon reaches forward and taps her on the shoulder with his pencil. So she resumes her position, arms folded to prop up her breasts, her mouth open in an ugly sneer. Though she wears no hat, in the sketch Egon props a huge hat on her head, shadowing her face like an open parasol. Feeling especially mischievous, he adds to the girl in the sketch a medal of good conduct, hanging the medal prominently on a string around her neck.

How will Egon pay Mademoiselle? He hopes to pay her with the money he earns when he sells this drawing. He has heard about artists who pay their bills in expensive restaurants by making hasty sketches on the backs of cardboard coasters. When will he be famous enough to do the same?

Before he has finished the drawing he hears voices in the hall, and the door is flung open. The room fills with men, Vienna's eminent critics; Egon doesn't recognize any of them but he can predict what they will say—they are all solemn and patriotic in their public opinions, prurient in secret. Eager to see the work and to condemn it, they crowd around Egon, blocking his view of poor Eveline, who begs someone to bring her a robe.

Though the sketch is unfinished, in the silence before judgment has been pronounced Egon hopes, as he always does, that they will find some value in the drawing. But a single, curt observation delivered in utter disgust is all the other men need. "The medal of good conduct!" exclaims one man, and this enrages the rest—Egon Schiele has given a medal of good conduct to a common prostitute.

"A crime!" someone declares.

"Appalling!"

"Tasteless!"

"Surely it is meant as a harmless joke," a friendlier voice proposes.

"The work itself is facile," another man says, nearly shouting to be heard above the murmuring crowd.

"Not worth our time," adds another.

Egon presses his hands against his head, plugs his ears with his fingers, wanting desperately to wake up, for by now he has just enough awareness to know that this is only a dream. *Only*. A gratifying word. But he can't force himself to wake up, not yet; he must wait while the men file out of the room, discussing among themselves what they will have for dinner. Then he must listen to Eveline's embarrassed tittering, he must watch the champagne seep from the corners of her mouth. He thinks so many things at once: that the medal has no meaning—the circle merely complicates and at the same time unifies the whole composition; that he didn't decide upon his subject—she chose him; that the drawing isn't even finished yet; that he has so little experience, he is young, he will improve.

Please understand, he pleads to no one, alone now in an empty room, a cell, he realizes, for he has finally escaped from the dream, escaped back into prison, and as the dream fades from memory he feels only—yes, a gratifying word—he feels only relief.

History Indeed

VELVET, she explained, made a girl's feet look ungainly. Black satin shoes had already gone out of style. And did I realize that three hundred million birds were killed annually for their feathers? She preferred flowers—real or cloth imitations. Silk rhododendrons were especially convincing. When she went cycling she liked to wear her aviation culottes. Flat canvas shoes with cork soles were good for bathing. And nothing compared to a coat lined with swan's down.

This was the substance of our conversation during the last hour that I stayed with the artist and his mistress in cottage forty-five. We had returned from Vienna the previous day, and since then they hadn't asked me when I would leave or where I planned to go. By the fourth morning I began to hope that I would become a permanent fixture in the atelier. I provided company for the mistress while the artist worked; before they woke that morning, I had even washed the kitchen floor and swept the porch. The trick, I knew, was to make myself invaluable. When the thought of my invalid mother and my unlucky father crossed my mind, I would tell myself that soon I would write to my grandmother, explaining everything, and she would find a way to make up for my absence. Perhaps she would even come to Neulengbach and take my place beside my mother's bed.

But my new life proved too precarious to last through another day, and just as Fräulein Vallie went to fetch her cushion to show

me her collection of hatpins, an elderly man made his way up the
front path to the cottage. With his face partly hidden by his turned-
up collar and his hat, I didn't recognize him at first—or I didn't want
to recognize him. Herr Schiele looked up as Fräulein Vallie entered
the room with her pincushion in her hands, and their eyes followed
mine to the window.

Without a word Herr Schiele carefully laid his brush on his palette,
and he and his mistress went to meet my father at the door. I retreated to the kitchen, where my father couldn't see me from the
threshold, but where I could hear him as he tried to catch his breath.
My father didn't bother to return the artist's greeting—he said simply that he had heard from neighbors that I was hiding here, that he
had already filed a complaint with the municipal authorities, that
unless Herr Schiele returned me at once to my family, he would be
arrested for seducing a minor. The artist replied calmly that I had
come to his home in a hysterical state, I had begged for lodging, and
Fräulein Vallie had seen to it that I was treated with utter respect
during my visit. Nothing improper had occurred. My father said
that he would let the police decide what had occurred.

And then I heard no more, for in that instant I went through the
sort of transformation that should only happen in a dream—I lost
control of myself without losing awareness, watched my hand reach
for a pair of scissors lying on the table, watched, feeling nothing
except an infinite weariness and a vague fascination as I raised the
shears and stabbed at my wrist, watched as my arm jerked away,
uninjured, watched as I positioned the scissors again and slashed
through the air, barely pricking my wrist at this second attempt.
The little spurt of blood was enough to bring me to my senses, I
saw what I had tried to do and began to scream, I screamed simply
to hear myself scream, to reclaim control after that brief madness,
and the force of my voice threw me backward. I stumbled against a
corner of the table and fell.

They found me sprawled on the floor. My eyes must have told
them that there was no danger, for instead of a frantic effort to save
me from myself, the artist, the mistress, and my father could only
stare at me, all of them more embarrassed than startled. Sickness
embarrasses. This was why I fled from my mother. Now I had
become the embarrassment, and after a moment's hesitation only
my father approached me.

My poor father. He wanted so much to live an uneventful life, fulfilling his responsibilities at the post office, supporting his wife and child, attending church on Sundays. And his humble ambition had brought him here, to this infamous cottage decorated with pictures of naked men and flat-chested children, his own mad daughter lying at his feet. I'll never know the extent of his disappointment, for he never spoke of it. But I could see the shame in his face as he bent toward me, the usual look of serene determination replaced by a puckered, bewildered expression, as though he were trying to deny what he saw. The question "Why?" hung on his lips, yet he didn't ask it, he didn't utter a word as he removed the scissors from my hand and wrapped his handkerchief around my wrist. I suppose we both knew that nothing needed to be said. Most importantly, he didn't recoil from me as the artist and his mistress did. Instead my father overcame his disgust, helped me to my feet, assured Herr Schiele and the Fräulein that we would not trouble them again and led me out of the kitchen. They kept their eyes averted, unwilling to look at me or even to bid me goodbye. I didn't blame them. Sickness embarrasses, madness is infectious—they were too convinced of their own importance to risk catching my despair.

As I walked through Au with my father, I thought I had left cottage forty-five and its tenants behind forever. I even imagined that I had accomplished whatever I had set out to do, and if I felt cheated as well, I sensed that my father's loss was greater than mine. At home again, I entered my mother's bedroom, kissed her on the forehead without waking her, tasted the familiar, salty, perfumed skin and settled in the armchair.

This, then, should be the end of my story. However, my father didn't bother to withdraw his complaint against Egon Schiele, provoking the investigation that led to the artist's arrest. Even after my father told the police that I wouldn't testify, that I had no reason to testify, and the authorities had reluctantly dropped the charge of seduction, the prosecutor had enough evidence to put Egon Schiele in prison. And I had the opportunity to see him once more, three weeks later, sitting on the bench for the accused in the St. Pölten courthouse. My father gave me permission to go to the trial, virtually insisted that I go—with breathy indignation he said that I would understand what kind of man this Egon Schiele was, that I would want nothing more to do with him once his character had been thoroughly examined and exposed by St. Pölten's magistrate before an assembled crowd. But neither my father nor I knew that I would serve as an essential witness, though I wouldn't be called to testify. The authorities already had in their hands a record of my visit; the drawing told them everything they needed to know.

·

The Family—*oil on canvas, 1918:* Edith would never sit for him in that position, not without her clothes on or her hair fixed, not with her shoulders drooping, a deep crease between the folds of her belly. He didn't bother to ask her. And he didn't dare ask Adele, since a few weeks ago Edith had confronted her older sister about those photography sessions and had told Adele exactly what she thought about the pictures snapped with the little Kodak Egon had borrowed from Anton Peschka. So for this painting of husband and wife, Egon hired a professional model to use as the wife, a rather slovenly girl with a stocky build. The defining lines practically drew themselves, and after he had a penciled figure, Egon could concentrate on mixing pigments to create a sort of stroboscopic effect. With colors he wanted to give a sense of light flashing in intervals across these bodies, his own body included.

He dismissed the model before he had finished painting the wife and began his own self-portrait. He was the husband squatting ap-ishly behind the wife, one arm resting on his raised knee, the other arm bent across his chest, his fingers scratching lazily just below the joint of his shoulder. He wanted to give a sense of a start-stop motion, so the figures appeared both fixed in their poses and caught in the midst of life, scratching themselves, breathing, sighing. Husband and wife.

He was applying a second, more muted orange to his skin tones one day when his sister-in-law appeared at his door. Edith had gone shopping with her mother for the afternoon—Adele must have known this. She held out her hand for Egon to kiss and said that she would gladly have a glass of schnapps, if Egon offered, though she reminded him that she wouldn't allow any photographs to be taken; her sister didn't approve. Only after they had drunk together and had laughed about Edith's parochialism and Adele had bidden fare-well to Egon, kissing him directly on the lips, did she share the secret with him: Edith was pregnant. If he had been a more attentive husband, she said with a shrug, he would have noticed.

Alone again in the studio, Egon began at once to paint his unborn son into the picture of the squatting couple. When Edith returned an hour later he glanced up from the painting just briefly enough to assure himself that there was no difference in her face or figure, no evidence that he had overlooked. So he focused again on the family portrait—his family—smearing the brush with flake white, paling the child's face with impasto strokes. His son deserved skin as delicate as top cream, long fingers with which to scratch at his chest, just as his father scratched, and a shock of brown hair, brown as his father's hair was in life, not a ghostly blue-brown, as it was in the painting.

"Why do you make such ugly pictures?" his mother had asked him more times than he could count. Heinrich Benesch had recently advised Egon to try to vary the mood and colors of his paintings. "You have grown fond of that melancholy orange pigment," he had observed. "Too fond, perhaps?" Arthur Roessler wanted Egon to spend less time looking in the mirror and more time on commissioned portraits. But Egon's work had been selling with remarkable speed despite the war; he had finally been allowed to take off his uniform and return to his apartment; and the death of Klimt six months earlier had matured Egon, had subtly refined his style as well, at least in his own opinion. Yet even his friends had grown tired of his suffering and were tactfully urging him to wake up from his perpetual nightmare, to reimagine the world.

Conception. Remarkably, he had conceived—his son would be the beginning that his friends wanted, his son would reassure them. So while Edith made coffee, Egon fattened the cheeks of the infant, swaddled the body in a patchwork quilt, intensified the red hue of the lips. His child would never feel his father's agony. His child would believe in a reality that was impossibly good. The eyes were the key. Egon gave the child wide, wondering eyes, eyes that would never see into his father's world. The infant would serve as the father's recantation, an admission that Egon could conceive of joy, despite his obsession with pain. He made the parents suffer in the usual way, mottled them with the melancholy orange pigment, gave them morose, exhausted expressions. Egon didn't spare them as he spared the child.

Ever since he had been a child himself and had made up a little song to curse his sister Elvira, Egon had been afraid of his disquieting prophetic powers. Sometimes it seemed to him that simply to envision something meant to conjure it, and he couldn't help but fear, in his more superstitious moods, his own caricatured self-portraits. He tried to depict authentic emotions in his art, he tried to be honest, yet the finished images were always dangerously different, representing not the man he was but the broken man he would become. The dreaming mind, Egon believed, could see into the future; when he worked he was dreaming, and when he woke from the dream of art his premonitions surprised and disturbed him. Earlier in his career he had been proud of his ability to turn his models into phantoms, but now he wanted to destroy all the images in his work that foretold death. He couldn't control his prophetic powers, just as he couldn't control his dreams.

The Family would have to remain unfinished. Egon had already doomed the husband and wife, giving them diseased yellow skin. And he had made the child, his beautiful cherub, too gentle, too perfect—this child could never be born. So Egon gave up on the portrait before he had painted in the wife's feet or finished with the child's plump legs, and he resumed work on a more restful likeness of Edith, begun months earlier and put aside.

When Edith herself finally informed her husband that he would soon be a father, he tried to act surprised, but it was clear from her sad eyes—melancholy eyes—that his response disappointed her. He could have been more enthusiastic. He could have offered encouraging words.

In the days that followed, as the influenza epidemic of 1918 swept through Europe and the last germs of war reached suburban Hietzing, Egon tried to convince himself that the portrait of his would-be family must be burned. But he couldn't bring himself to destroy it, not yet. Instead, he finished the portrait of Edith and brought it to Gustav Pisko, who sold the painting to the Austrian state for 3,200 kronen. With this money—more than he had ever before received for a single work—Egon decided to take Edith to Trieste, away from the epidemic, away from the family portrait. But the curse worked faster than he expected—Edith's throat became inflamed before Egon could even begin to make arrangements for their trip, and her confinement made escape impossible.

If divination is a gift of God, as believers maintained, then in his art Egon misused the gift: he condemned his wife to death by imagining her dead. He had done the same to Klimt, Osen, Vallie, and too many others to count. Now he had only to fill his sketch pad with illustrations of the dying Edith Schiele, biding time until it was his own turn.

•

Normally, before any criminal trial, a closed preliminary hearing is held, in which the prosecutor presents the evidence and the magistrate determines the status of the case. But the Schiele scandal has attracted so much attention that the examining judge decides to open the door of the courtroom, turning the initial hearing into a mock trial, with an audience but without a jury. Corrupting children is a serious charge, so serious that the judge sees no need for the accused to speak in his own defense. The people of Neulengbach have been only too patient with the pederast living in their midst. And not only has the defendant used their children as subjects for his obscene pictures, but he insists on proclaiming himself Vienna's premier artist. The prosecutor reveals that Egon Schiele sells his pornography for three hundred kronen a drawing, an outrageous price, even for a canvas by a legitimate artist.

Heinrich and Otto Benesch arrived early enough to find seats in the second row of the courtroom. They assumed that their presence would reassure their friend, but Egon didn't glance at them once during the proceedings—instead he kept his gaze fixed on the judge, his eyes just like the blazing, feline eyes in his unsettling portrait of Eduard Kosmak. By the end of the day, Heinrich Benesch almost admired the undauntable judge. His final speech suffered from too much moral outrage, perhaps, but any element of passion helped to enliven the trial, which had been, on the whole, only tedious. A shame to destroy a valuable work by Egon Schiele, though the artist himself hardly seemed to care—he had even grinned as the judge set the drawing aflame. At least the symbolism of the judge's misguided action had resonance and would be debated by the feuilletonists in tomorrow's papers. And the sentence proved more lenient than Benesch expected—twenty-four days in prison, which Egon had already served during the investigative detention. So the law took from him one drawing and twenty-four days of his life, not an unreasonable fine by any means, considering the charge. Now they have reason to celebrate.

While Egon collects his belongings from his cell, Heinrich Benesch, Otto, and Vallie go on ahead to a local beer garden recommended to Vallie by one of the court clerks. Herr Benesch has grown a little light-headed from the tension of waiting—in the rush to catch the early train that morning he had forgotten the cold supper his wife had packed for them. Surprisingly, Otto showed more interest in the trial than his father did. The boy had listened intently while the prosecutor spent nearly an hour presenting his array of proofs: oral proof, testimonial proof, instrumental proof, conjectural proof, "which together provide a complete proof," the lawyer had announced proudly, turning away from the magistrate's oak table to the audience in the courtroom, "and complete proof is always the objective in penal crime." Perhaps, he had added, the oral proof—the defendant's confession—should be excluded as evidence. The defendant had already admitted to making the pictures in question, but he wouldn't admit to the specific charge of corruption. Even disregarding the defendant's testimony, the three remaining proofs, including witnesses, documents, and presumptions, would leave no doubt in anyone's mind that the man accused was guilty.

Yes, how attentive Otto had remained, even while the prosecutor's most sympathetic listeners shifted restlessly and some even left the courtroom for a breath of fresh air. Good Otto, always trying to gain wisdom from his experiences. Well, the Schiele affair is finally over, and if nothing else Otto has learned something about loyalty. Heinrich Benesch has stayed loyal to Egon Schiele, and the artist has stayed loyal to his work. Benesch wishes that the prosecutor had avoided discussing the money issue, since the huge prices Egon puts on his work do suggest a complexity of motives. But on the way out of the courthouse, Otto asks innocently why genius must always be misunderstood, indicating that he has remained indifferent to the business aspects of Egon's career.

Heinrich Benesch isn't blind to another more pressing danger, however. Egon Schiele poses a new problem, this time in the person of his mistress, Vallie Neuzil, a charming if uneducated girl. On the walk to the beer garden, Herr Benesch senses from Otto's nervous chatter that the girl interests him more than she should. She reminds Benesch of one of Toulouse-Lautrec's colorful vamps, not the kind of girl a young scholar like Otto should pay attention to; Otto, a would-be art historian, should limit his attention to an artist's rendering of such women. If Herr Benesch is being unfair to Fräulein

Vallie, then he can justify his fears as a father's natural concern. He must protect his son and while he doesn't mind Egon Schiele's immoral conduct, he won't have Otto taking up with a common shopgirl. Perhaps Otto should have spent the day at home studying, Benesch thinks as he listens to the clicking of Vallie Neuzil's boot heels on the cobblestones. Heinrich Benesch had been eager to offer his son a glimpse of history, but in truth the dull, predictable trial of Egon Schiele hardly deserves the label of history. While Otto complains about the judge's misguided attempt to publicly censor the artist, Fräulein Vallie seems to consider the entire day a farce and keeps breaking into subdued giggling, not bothering to explain what, exactly, she finds so hilarious.

The crowded beer garden is enclosed with canvas-covered trellises. Heinrich Benesch would have preferred a coffeehouse with windows and potted ferns, but he leads the way to a table and as soon as they are seated, he asks politely whether this digression in their lives has left Vallie and Egon short of money. She responds with her typical innuendoes, assuring Herr Benesch that they have enough to make do. They owe their landlord two months' rent for the cottage, but Egon has arranged another show with Pisko in May, and in the past few weeks they have received letters from Carl Reininghaus and Oskar Reichel—commissions, Vallie hopes. Or condemnations. They are addressed to Egon, so she hasn't opened them. But somehow they will find the money they need. Herr Benesch offers to help them cover their back rent; Vallie refuses. He doesn't have much money on hand, but he would be pleased if the Fräulein would accept a small gift; Vallie shakes her head violently. At the very least, then, he will pay something—he can't afford much —for the thirteen watercolors, the "Neulengbach Series," as Benesch refers to them, that Egon gave to him last week. With the gift so politely disguised, Vallie finally agrees to accept the money from Herr Benesch.

The trouble with this young lady, Benesch thinks to himself as he takes out his wallet, is that even the most abstinent gentleman cannot help but imagine unspeakable things when he looks at her. Her casual habit of gently pinching her full lower lip between the nails of her thumb and forefinger, the thin painted lines where her eyebrows should be, her tendency to pull up the sleeves of her blouse to her elbows or to fiddle with the satin-covered collar buttons—

even these insignificant gestures seem designed to inspire a man's imagination. Benesch counts out twenty kronen and glances at his son to see if Otto disapproves. But the waitress has arrived at their table, and Otto is pushing aside an ashtray to clear a space for the steins of beer. So Heinrich Benesch proposes a toast to Egon's freedom, Otto seconds with a toast to Egon's genius, Vallie laughs, and they clink glass and guzzle.

The tangy lager soon improves Herr Benesch's mood. He decides that he has been worrying needlessly about his son. Otto, with a disposition as mild as Heinrich's, would never become lovesick for a girl like Vallie, not, at least, without his father's approval. Through two rounds the friends of Egon Schiele celebrate his release without him, and though admiration for the artist is the only thing the three have in common, their conversation becomes animated, even playful, romping through all sorts of disparate subjects that have nothing to do with Egon Schiele. They speak about the poor quality of the beer they are drinking, "Handsome Karl" Lueger, automobiles, cigarettes, perfumes ("Who ever said that a woman smells best when she does not smell at all?" Vallie teases, holding out her wrist for Benesch Senior to sniff). With the Fräulein in their company, they don't have to worry about awkward silences. Otto decides that he is hungry, Vallie scoops up a handful of sawdust and offers it to him, he swipes at her in feigned annoyance, and she blows the sawdust onto his lap. So full of spirit, Heinrich Benesch thinks to himself, smiling at Fräulein Vallie, understanding better than ever what Egon sees in her.

Somehow they get onto the subject of bullfighting, and Otto, who has traveled to Spain, asks his father how this barbaric ritual ever came to be transformed into a sport. The cruelty, Otto says, is not in the act of slaughtering the bull but in the rules of the game— the bull has no chance against his competition, yet the crowd pretends that the contest is fair. "But bulls have a nasty habit of goring people," Vallie points out; thus they must be punished for their incompatible natures. Better a bull in the arena than some sweet, harmless creature. "Do animals weep?" she wonders aloud, her eyes unfocused as she considers this question, until a familiar face abruptly appears in her line of vision.

"Gerti!"

With her hands fluttering excitedly, young Gerti Schiele explains

that she came by herself—against her mother's wishes, of course—
to see how her brother would fare today. She had sat in a back row,
for she didn't want Egon to know his sister was watching. She
thought she might make him nervous. But where has he gone? A
man at the courthouse told her that he'd sent her brother's friends
here. Wasn't Egon a free man again? Or had she misunderstood?

Benesch assures her that Egon would be joining them soon. He
slides closer to the wall and motions Gerti to sit beside him. The
watchful waitress brings another beer, and the friends toast again to
their favorite martyr, with Gerti clucking in slight annoyance at her
brother's predilection for scandal, Vallie adding. "He couldn't have
done it without me," Otto grinning stupidly, Benesch thinking to
himself that young women are so much more independent than they
used to be.

Just then, as if on cue, the gate to the beer garden opens, and the
friends look up, expecting Egon Schiele but seeing only an old beggar man in a tattered overcoat and huge galoshes that slap like flip-
pers against the floor as he circles the room, his hands outstretched.
He stinks of stale urine, and the customers keep their backs to him
when he approaches, no one gives him money, and from the way
he passes in such stumbling haste along his route, he doesn't seem
to expect their charity. Vallie, Gerti, Otto, and Heinrich turn to face
one another again, but the beggar must have identified them as
promising targets, for he stops at their table and holds out his hat.
They try to ignore him, but the old man refuses to leave them alone,
and since his stench makes him difficult to forget, Heinrich Benesch
drops a few conciliatory kreuzer into his hat, a hat spattered with
holes, as it turns out—the coins fall to the floor, and with a groan
the man lowers himself to his hand and knees and begins raking
through the sawdust for his lost fortune.

If they weren't waiting for Egon, Benesch would take the young
ladies elsewhere. In his frantic search the beggar crawls underneath
their table, looking up skirts, no doubt. Benesch blames himself for
the situation, but he doesn't know what to do and merely mutters,
"Poor fool," trying to guard his dignity with condescending pity,
the pity a poor mask for the disgust he feels. Here is true degradation. The treatment Egon Schiele received in the courtroom today
cannot compare to the groveling desperation of this old man.

The man is still scratching beneath the table when Vallie cries out,
"Dog! He has his hands on me!" in a voice loud enough to be heard

above the din, and while she lashes at her assaulter, men at nearby tables break into rude howls of glee, cheering on the beggar. Heinrich Benesch finally rouses himself and comes to Vallie's aid, catching the old man by his belt loops, dragging him out from beneath the table. He raises his foot and is about to give the beggar a furious kick in the jaw, but Otto cries, "Father!" It is a warning, a reprimand, enough to bring Heinrich Benesch to his senses. So he lifts the man to his feet and drags him by a frayed lapel to the gate.

"Next time . . . ," he begins, but the threat trails off, for there, standing just outside the entrance, is Egon Schiele himself, with his hand clapped over his mouth, barely holding in his explosive mirth.

"Herr Benesch . . ." Egon can hardly speak, he is so full of laughter. But he can stuff a handful of coins into a deep pocket of the old man's overcoat and then give him a comical salute to send him on his way. These two, apparently, are conspirators: the beggar had been working for Egon Schiele and must have been instructed to molest Fräulein Vallie. Egon Schiele, wunderkind and devil. Benesch is too appalled to speak. Egon lifts his suitcase, rests his other arm on Herr Benesch's shoulder, and together they walk into the beer garden. Benesch stands aside as Gerti and Vallie leap up and cover their noble hero with kisses.

"Did my friend introduce himself to you, by the way?" Egon joshes as he takes a seat.

"Your friend?" Gerti is confused. But Egon merely gestures toward the gate, and Vallie Neuzil understands what Benesch has already perceived—that Egon had commissioned the old man to treat her indelicately. Unlike Benesch, though, Vallie doesn't take offense. "His friend," she echoes Gerti. "His friend. You're the dog, then!" With that, she throws her arms around her lover and nibbles at his ear.

"We met in prison," Egon explains, unable to give up the joke yet. "He's an artist, too." The group, Benesch excluded, join in loud guffaws, their laughter like a bubble of glass around them, protecting them from the stares of the hostile, provincial people. As he watches the youngsters, Heinrich Benesch disapproves enough to wonder whether the residents of Neulengbach had been right to object.

Marie's favorite tale? Why, "The Wise Peasant Girl," of course, about the girl who takes off all her clothes, wraps herself in fishing net and lets herself be dragged by a mule to the palace. Neither naked nor clothed, neither walking nor riding, neither on the road nor off the road—the girl fulfills all these conditions simultaneously, and the king makes her his queen. Marie told the story many times over to her children because she wanted to teach them the importance of cleverness. "In this world it doesn't matter if you are strong or handsome or wealthy, if you are not clever," she would warn them and then would repeat the story to demonstrate this truth. Though the children usually fell asleep before she finished, she wouldn't stop until she had told the end of the tale, for this was her favorite part, when the queen outwits the king a second time. The king, finally fed up with his shrewd wife, orders her to return to her peasant hut, but he allows her to select one treasure in his palace to take home with her. She chooses him. Thus she remains a queen for the rest of her days.

Marie raised her children as well as she could, tried to teach them to be obedient and to be clever. Her eldest, Melanie, turned out to be the cleverest of all and has been able to support herself without the help of a husband. Egon might have become clever, if he had lived longer, though he never paid much attention to Marie's story of the wise peasant girl and insisted on making the same mistakes over and over, committing the same sins, feeding his ravenous vanity with lies through his short life. Gerti, on the other hand, always tried with endearing if futile persistence to stay awake to hear the conclusion of the tale, and though she didn't gain much from the effort, when she herself became a mother she asked Marie to tell the story to her son.

So again Marie Schiele found herself in the midst of narrating, on a visit to her daughter's household in 1921. Her grandson, little Anton Schiele Peschka, played with his pocket torch, shining the light on Marie's face while she spoke, pressing it against his hand to illuminate the skeletal web, pointing it into the cave of sheets propped up with his knees.

Marie had told this story so many times that she could let her mind wander away from the words. She had reached the age when she felt compelled to account for the years behind her and had much to occupy her thoughts. The children were her achievements. Therefore, the achievements of her children were her responsibility. Her grandson, a pert rascal with sharp, squirrelish features, comforted Marie, made her feel that if the younger generations hadn't actually improved upon the past, at least the best traits of the family had not been lost. Her grandson had the chestnut-colored eyes of Marie's brother, who had drowned when he was eight years old and she was twelve, and though the idea of reincarnation belonged to pagan religions, Marie believed that family resemblance must be more than just a coincidence. She hadn't spent so much of her life in mourning garb for nothing—a year and six weeks in black crepe for her husband, six months apiece in silk and lace for her parents, her daughter Elvira, her son, her brother-in-law, and occasional months in half-mourning for more distant relatives. The black of mourning absorbed the dead as tar absorbed the heat of the sun, and survivors carried the burden of those who had died before them. No wonder Marie had developed a hunched back—with so many lives to harbor until they could return to the world, as her brother had now returned in her grandson, she was like a woman perpetually enduring the final weeks of pregnancy, and she looked forward to her own death as she had looked forward to childbirth. She trusted her daughters to shelter the ghosts that she had sheltered, to take care of her own spirit as well. Women, she thought, were more reliable than men in this respect.

But Marie considered herself a pious Christian and was as troubled by the sins of the past as she was comforted by time's continuity. Her husband had been her shame and in order to preserve him, she had to remember everything—his love for her, his infidelities, his violence, the slow deterioration. Her brother-in-law Leopold had become her shame, for though they had never committed any sin against the flesh, they did not hide their desire from each other. Her son, too, had become a cross to bear in his short life and remained her shame after his death. He had left a legacy, all the thoughts that a young man should learn to keep to himself were displayed in his offensive pictures. Sometimes Marie thought she even recognized Gerti in those faces, though she couldn't be sure and never dared to ask her daughter whether she had posed naked for her own brother; Marie simply didn't want to know. Mother and son had had little contact in his last years; Egon hadn't even invited her to his wedding. But though the art collectors of Austria had seen to it that his work would be preserved, Egon still belonged to Marie, whether she wanted him or not. If only he had studied to be an engineer.

She had reached the climax of "The Wise Peasant Girl," the moment when the king decides to send his wife back to her father's hut; her grandson had stopped playing with his light and was making those chomping, sheeplike noises that children often make just before they fall asleep. But Marie continued with the story, thinking as she narrated that she had spent these many years just as her grandson had spent the past hour, in meaningless, distracted employment and then in sleep, and all the while there had been a voice describing everything she did, filling her mind with memories. Memories helped an aging widow like herself make sense of the world, just as fairytales helped a child.

And yet, when she reached the happily-ever-after and fell silent, sat absolutely still, listening to her grandson breathe, she found it nearly impossible to believe that she had been alive so many years, that she herself had once been a child. In the darkness of the bedroom it seemed to Marie Schiele that there was only here and now—the past belonged to the dead, and the dead had been absorbed into the night's own crepe mantle. The present would end only when the darkness absorbed Marie, too, and until then she would remain acutely aware of the great, senseless gulf surrounding her body. With her story of the peasant girl, Marie had sounded to her own ears like a chattering milliner, speaking simply for the sake of hearing her own voice. What good did the story do for her grandson, if he hadn't even listened?

Perhaps simply the sound of the voice, the soothing drone, was all that mattered. Marie listened, and now, instead of hearing the child breathe, she concentrated on the voice that described how an old woman sat beside the bed of a little boy while the wind splashed in great waves against the house, rattling the windows. The voice told her the simple story of her life, comforted her by putting the facts in their proper places, just as her weekly confessions comforted her. Confession guaranteed absolution—this certainty was the reward of faith. And didn't a woman who had suffered as much as Marie deserve a reward? It would turn out all right then, she decided, tipping her head against the back of the chair, closing her eyes. It would turn out all right, as long as she kept no secrets.

Anything Goes

AT the beginning of his presentation the prosecuting lawyer submitted five drawings to the judge and then pointed a trembling finger at the accused. The lawyer was evidently so overcome with indignation that he could hardly collect himself enough to begin. Meanwhile, the St. Pölten judge absorbed himself with the sketches on his table and didn't seem interested in the argument. From where I sat I could see Egon Schiele's profile and I took the opportunity to observe him at length. His eyelids were coated with a buttery crust of red, as usual he was clean-shaven, his fingernails were filed in smooth, feminine ovals, and he had a canker at the side of his mouth. From time to time he would rub the heel of his palm over his front teeth.

I had overheard a woman beside me predicting ten to fifteen months of hard labor for the artist, though justice would be served, she said, only if he were locked away for the rest of his life. This same woman kept offering me peppermint drops during the trial, insisting with a jerk of her shoulder until I accepted. Vallie Neuzil was blocked from my view—I had seen her walk in alone just before the trial began. There must have been others in the crowd who had come to support the artist; I wondered about their relationship to him, wondered whether they believed in him as passionately as he believed in himself or whether they had come to the trial because they owed him a favor.

When, in his speech, the lawyer referred to the poor children of

Neulengbach, the innocent girls whom the artist had tempted with apples and licorice, I felt my face grow warm. I was different from those other girls. I had forced my way into cottage forty-five, and it suddenly seemed my duty to stand up and explain myself, to testify in my own defense. But no one in the courtroom would have wanted to hear what I had to say. Surely whoever knew that I had visited the cottage had already dismissed me as an aberration, the shadow girl of Neulengbach, dour and secretive.

The lawyer explained that little Margaret Wild, the butcher's daughter, had been the first child brave enough to come to the police and tell them about the artist's filthy pictures. Soon other girls had admitted that they too had posed for the artist, and though they timidly declined to say whether or not the artist had persuaded them to stand before him in an indecent state, the pictures were evidence enough. The lawyer directed his argument toward the public, pausing from time to time and nodding to encourage their angry murmuring. When he mentioned the pictures he turned back to the judge, who gathered up the sketches in a pile and leaned forward, concerned now, respectfully attentive. The lawyer demanded—for the sake of the good people of Neulengbach, for the sake of their children—that this man be publicly condemned. Did anyone believe that the sketches in question were art? Only pornography could fetch such high prices, three hundred kronen for a single drawing that in truth was worth no more than a postage stamp.

Did anyone present blame the little girls of Neulengbach for being so trusting? the lawyer continued. Absolutely not, he answered himself. The victims were adequately represented that day by their parents, who waited eagerly to see how the judge would redeem their children. The judge must have decided upon a course of action even while the lawyer spoke, for when he rose he held one of the sketches in his hand. Egon Schiele rose too, casually adjusting his tie, his face so composed that his expression—sly, impertinent—seemed an affront to the judge.

For the sake of the parents of Neulengbach. For the sake of their children. There was only one way to compensate the victims. The judge jerked open the drawer in his table, the woman beside me held out her tin of peppermints, motioning hastily for me to take one, people in the audience strained to see over the heads of those in front.

"You claim you are an artist, sir?" the judge whispered, his voice the only sound in the room, the words sputtering like hot grease. "This is what we think of your art." With that, he lit a match and held the flame steady while he lowered the sketch. The bottom of the paper arched away from the match, fire crept along its edge. Egon Schiele's eyelids drooped in sulky resistance, but his lips curled as the paper burned until he looked quite pleased, his self-possession fueled by the flame.

I gazed at the judge again, at the burning sketch in his hands, at the lines that connected to form a box, a coffin too small for the corpse inside, bent, feeble hocks, hands framing her pubic hair, labia like the fleshy tip of a tongue. What I couldn't see I remembered vividly. I still remember. The judge stared transfixed at the fire, and the artist's amusement grew proportionately as the drawing disappeared.

So the sacrifice pleased all—the judge, the prosecutor, the public, the criminal—all except for me, the girl in the coffin. The flame ate its way through the paper, moving on in a rush toward the upper corner, and when the judge dropped the last tinsel fragment into an ashtray, everyone in the courtroom turned to look at the pornographer, degenerate man, pervert, corruptor of children. He didn't attempt to hide his smile. To him not even this solemn act of immolation was sacred; no one would ever alter his direction or break his pride, and the people in the courtroom must have understood that he had won this contest.

And had I lost? In a sense, I had watched myself die and had felt something akin to terror as the portrait burned. The drawing had made it possible for me to laugh; without me it never would have existed. And as though I really had died, I felt released from myself, released from my desires and from the discontent that had driven me from the room of an invalid. With the image gone, I could return to my mother, I could watch her slow death without disgust or anger. I knew what was involved; I knew what to expect.

Perhaps it strikes you as odd, then, that after all these years I have taken it upon myself to tell the story behind the drawing that the judge of St. Pölten destroyed on May 8, 1912, to describe at such length the piece missing from the retrospectives and catalogues. But there is not much time left. And who, after all—other than Egon Schiele or his minion, Vallie Neuzil—would be better suited for this task? Since they are long dead, it is up to me. What I lack in skill I hope I make up for with accuracy. I have spent most of my inconspicuous life watching and remembering, and there are plenty of stories that I could tell. But none of these other memories involve a man of such importance, a great stone sphinx, so they haven't earned a place in history. There would be no reason.

·

Pleasure. What other excuse does Vallie need? Pleasure is her purpose, and if in search of pleasure she sometimes finds herself in the company of enthusiastic soldiers, she won't stall, she won't act the part of a demure *Mädchen*. She has learned to respect her desires, to take her life into her own hands.

"Thank God," she has said before and will say again, "for vulcanized rubber." But Vallie is "red," meaning that she doesn't go to church, she hasn't even been inside a church since the day she left Egon for good, so when she thanks God for her freedom she can't expect Him to be listening. She doubts that He pays much attention to her at all, especially now with the war preoccupying Him, so she has decided that at least until the armistice, *anything goes*. A nurse taught her that phrase in English, and she likes to say it aloud. *Anything goes*. She likes to hear the soldiers repeat it after her. *Anything goes*. What fun she has with them, these nameless boys, who, as soon as they are released from the hospital, spin for a few days in a whirl of frivolous joys before they are sent back to the front. If they were smarter, these recruits lucky enough to arrive in Dalmatia without permanent injuries would sneak into the forest as soon as they recovered. Instead they wait for new assignments, and while they are waiting they flirt with the Red Cross nurses.

It's no secret in Vallie's ward that she is willing to be almost anyone's sweetheart, especially if courted in the old-fashioned way, with flowers and candy. In October two handsome Magyar brothers are put in Vallie's care. Both have beards—cropped black hair wrapped like a woolen collar across their chins—both wear spectacles and both are over six feet tall, so though their features are quite different, at a glance they appear to be identical twins. Clearly they cultivate their resemblance. Most remarkably, they both have the same injury, three broken toes on the right foot. They had told their commanding officer that they were injured when a shelf in their barracks kitchen collapsed, spilling cans of vegetables across the floor and onto their feet. But they confessed to Vallie that they had broken each other's toes with the butt of an ax. As natives of Budapest, they feel no patriotism toward the tattered remains of the Austro-Hungarian Empire and prefer to spend the war between starched white hospital sheets.

On the day five weeks later when their casts are removed, they surprise Vallie with a special box of chocolates purchased at the hospital commissary, chocolates molded into the shapes of animals. And in return, at the end of her shift, Vallie brings the brothers a single pair of crutches, tightens the bandages binding their tender toes and invites them to escort her to a basement cabaret near her dormitory.

On this particular night, or on any other night for that matter, the cabaret offers no live entertainment. A player piano provides music, and bottles of schnapps keep the customers satisfied. The brothers are generous with their money, and Vallie loses count of the number of drinks they have bought her, she forgets which brother is which, she even forgets that there are two of them and enjoys their attentions without preference. They spend much of the evening setting up a miniature circus on their table, making the chocolate animals perform unusual tricks, tricks that become increasingly lewd—crocodiles copulate in midair, monkeys tangle in orgiastic frenzy, a horse mounts a goat. Before they leave, the brothers hold an elephant over a candle, softening the chocolate until the elephant's trunk can be pulled around its side and inserted beneath the tail. They give the elephant to Vallie, and she delights them by covering the mutilated beast with voluptuous licks, she smoothes the ridges and bumps with her tongue, she licks the elephant along the curved trunk until it is an indistinguishable glob, then she drops the chocolate into her mouth and sucks noisily. The brothers have never met a girl like Vallie, and they tell her so, the odd rhythms of their speech making their German sound ridiculous, endearingly ridiculous, in Vallie's opinion. She asks them if they would like to accompany her back to her room.

Outside the cabaret she motions toward the north and tells her two Casanovas that if they don't want to return to the front then they had better run off before they receive their reassignments. They would have to travel on foot to Zara—they could take the crutches with them—and there they must stow away on a ferry bound for Italy. Somehow they would have to find transportation across Italy to Genoa, where they could secure a berth on an Atlantic steamer. The proposed itinerary merely provokes the brothers to laughter, which indicates to Vallie that they are as apathetic as the rest and will follow the most insane orders, even if it means filling their pockets with stones and walking into the sea. Soon they will be digging trenches again; for a few months they will send Vallie letters full of affected sentiment from the front (*Fräulein, nous vous désirons!*); gradually the letters will become shorter, the silence between each letter longer, until finally the brothers will stop writing at all. The chance of both of them surviving is slim, and Vallie wouldn't be interested in only half of this unique pair. So she will have her fun with them tonight.

When they reach the nurses' quarters, Vallie points to her window on the second floor. A light snow has begun to fall, the flakes as feathery and dry as ash, and the smoke of their breath makes the brothers look as though they were on fire, smoldering inside their pea jackets. Vallie explains that they must enter her room through the window, since soldiers aren't permitted in the dormitory halls at any hour. Without hesitation they fling their crutches onto the ground, and even before Vallie steps inside, one brother has climbed atop the shoulders of the other and is reaching for the sill. By the time Vallie enters her room, both men are there to greet her with smothering hugs that seem unexpectedly brutish. She protests, wriggling free from the sandwich of their huge bodies, and moves behind a bamboo screen to freshen up at the sink. When she emerges, the brothers handle her more gently. The one in front removes her green felt hat; the one behind unclips a barrette and winds a curl of hair around his finger; the one kisses her neck; the other slides his hands beneath her arms and strokes her breasts so softly that a moan ripples up from her throat. Soldiers, Vallie has already learned, usually forget that a girl needs to be encouraged— until she reminds them. But the Magyar brothers are in no hurry, and the novelty of the situation makes Vallie feel especially mallea- ble, pliant, like the melted chocolate elephant.

Their skin smells of winter, their breath smells of schnapps and sauerkraut and cigars. Slowly she undresses. When she has nothing on but a string of purple beads, they step back to marvel at her body, so pale and plump in the darkness. She bats at them playfully, flattered and embarrassed by their admiration. In another life she would have worried about her reputation—it is one thing to be the mistress of an artist, it is another to take strangers, two at a time, into her bed. But Vallie knows that the war will dissolve all rumors and all guilt. *Anything goes*. While one brother pulls off his trousers, the other brother keeps Vallie warm inside the cylinder of his arms. While the second brother removes his glasses and unbuttons his shirt, Vallie leads the first over to the bed, and together they slide beneath the sheets, Vallie gasping at the chill of the cotton and then at the man who has nudged apart her thighs and already buried his face in her pubic hair. The other brother joins them on the narrow bed and covers Vallie's mouth with his, swallowing her gasp.

It isn't exactly the sense of taboo that makes this so thrilling to Vallie, it is more the hint of violence, the suspicion that if she put up a struggle, the lovemaking would turn to rape. More and more of late she finds herself dependent upon such adventures, and although she knows that she would be quick to plunge a knife into a man's chest—or worse—if he tried to rape her, for now she will enjoy the danger. Vallie can't be sure whose buttocks she grips, whose body rocks above her. No names and no future—she wishes all her affairs had been so manageable, dissolving like sugar in water. *Anything goes*.

They are nearly inexhaustible. But just when the friction begins to irritate, the brother on top lets out a long groan, the other pushes him aside and assumes his place. After half a dozen rolling, determined thrusts that bring Vallie to her peak once more, he slips out of her, ejaculates against her thigh as though he doesn't want his seed to mix with his brother's. When Vallie considers this, she can't help but think that a secret discord spoils their intimacy. But tonight all curiosity must be restrained, so she will ask no questions. No names and no future. Their secrets don't matter to her.

Within minutes the brothers are asleep, each with an arm thrown heavily across Vallie's chest, battening her down, their snores like an echo flung back and forth between the walls. She lies on her back, turning her head to the side to examine their faces, mirror images, exact replicas in the darkness, uncanny, unreal. They make Vallie feel unreal, like a chocolate circus animal. She has never asked for jewels or a suburban villa or a box at the opera. Something sweet that melts on her tongue, someone sweet who melts her—this is all she needs. Along with a wider bed, perhaps.

Before daybreak she wakes the Magyar brothers and tells them that they must return to the hospital. They rub their thick fingers over their eyes and fumble for their clothes. Still stuporous from too little sleep, they dress sloppily and head for the door with their boots unlaced, their spectacles awry. Vallie asks them to leave the same way they came in, and they oblige her, squeezing onto the window-sill, throwing both legs over. They lower themselves until they are hanging by their fingertips, and together they drop, letting out a single yelp of pain—another fortunate accident, Vallie thinks as she looks out to see them squatting in the snow, clutching their feet. If they've fractured their phalanges again, they will have to remain in Dalmatia another month. They find their crutches and hobble off, leaving a trail behind them in the snow. Vallie should go out and erase the footprints with a broom, but she doesn't care what malicious stories the nurses spread about her, at the moment she wants only to bury herself beneath the blankets and relish the soldiers' lingering warmth. She is not ashamed. She has no regrets.

By morning she does have an annoying headache and when she tries to sip her coffee she feels nauseous, so she returns to bed. For a few hours she enjoys the torpor of an invalid, the lazy daydreams, ignoring the smirks of the nurses who bring her soup. They pretend to understand everything. They probably assume that she is pregnant. Vallie tries to eat the soup, but the vapors rising from the bowl make her retch.

By late afternoon she has grown unbearably bored. She convinces herself that she could eat something more benign than beef soup—a piece of crustless toast, perhaps, with a spoonful of cherry preserves. But when she stands, the room tilts precariously, and she sinks back onto her bed, shivering as the cool air touches her burning skin, finally accepting the fact that she is sick. Until now she had considered her constitution indomitable against everything except time. Maybe the Magyar brothers had been carrying germs of some rare disease. She wishes they could join her in bed, three invalids, melting together, leaving behind only a chocolate puddle.

The following day Vallie has a rash over her neck and face; her swollen, strawberry tongue makes it impossible to swallow fluids; she is too weak even to brush her hair. The nurses send for the army doctor, who takes one look at Vallie and nods his head as though agreeing with himself. He makes a brief, routine examination and informs the nurses in the room that the patient has scarlet fever and must be quarantined immediately. The patient. She is not a woman anymore—she is the carrier of a contagious disease. Yet she finds the label reassuring, for now she knows what will happen to her. The patient has scarlet fever. Her fever will rise, the rash will spread, and her skin will begin to slough off in small patches. She has seen it happen to others. The patient has scarlet fever. Everyone will die —this has always been a certainty, the one certainty. Her life has been a succession of coincidences, up until this moment. Now she has scarlet fever and must be quarantined while the disease runs its course. Some patients do recover, but Vallie is suddenly tired of hope and is grateful to know finally what to expect.

The nurses cover her with an extra blanket, close the shutters of her window, stand for a minute in the dark, whispering among themselves, and finally leave her alone. Vallie burns. Everyone will burn. Now more than ever she has direction, feels herself to be one among many. In recent years she has felt trapped within her flesh, except during the short intervals of liberating passion. Soon her skin will peel and there will be nothing to separate her soul from the world. This, then, is the purpose: to be free of the body. Does she hear the pensioner playing his hurdy-gurdy? Does she hear the streetcars rattling along the Ringstrasse like carousel horses, going nowhere? Does she hear the snores of a tramp asleep beneath his overcoat on a bench in the Rathaus Park? But how could she hear the sounds of Vienna if there is only bleak Dalmatia outside her window? Vallie has not forgotten where she is or what will happen. She will burn, and men will recoil from her charred skeleton. The patient has scarlet fever. Should she feel betrayed, now that the covenant of life has been broken? Should she feel resentful? Anger has its pleasures, and Vallie angrily considers the dearth of opportunities. She never went to a masquerade ball, never was invited to Katherina Schratt's dressing room after a performance, never owned a string of authentic pearls, never had a child, never . . . the list is endless, and anger in excess becomes wearisome, so Vallie thinks of other things. She hopes that the brothers from Budapest follow her advice and escape to America.

She has always believed that her father lives in America, though she knows nothing more about him than what the single remaining photograph reveals: sunken cheeks, cropped hair, a dusting of a mustache, an unlit cigarette hanging from the corner of his lips. He was just a boy himself when he became a father. Vallie has always expected that someday she would have the chance to introduce herself to him, though she doesn't even know his name. She would recognize him if she saw him. He is a mason in New York, has never married, and Vallie is his only child. How does she know this? It doesn't matter. When her health improves, she will travel with the Magyar brothers to America. But the patient has scarlet fever. Thankfully, Vallie will never become a gnarled old beggar woman, but neither will she become a rich man's mistress. She has heard rumors that Egon Schiele is growing rich from his art. What would be different now if, at the start, she had demanded that he marry her? Her mother never married. Vallie likes to believe that, despite her mother's professed scorn, she continued to love the slender, cocky charmer who is Vallie's father. Now her father works in America, stacking bricks. From time to time he stops to wipe his eyes with his sleeve and to reminisce about the woman and daughter he left behind in Vienna. Be careful, Father, or your eyes will become infected from your dirty sleeve. He doesn't know that Vallie's mother died of apoplexy in 1908. Vallie must find him and tell him what has happened. Maybe she should let her eyebrows grow back. Some fathers don't approve when their daughters pluck their brows and paint their lips.

"Whore! Dirty whore!" A man—evidently crazed—once shouted this at Vallie as she walked on the opposite side of the Lerchenfelderstrasse, minding her own business. It had been drizzling for most of the day, and she was wearing an ankle-length raincoat and carrying an umbrella, not the sort of outfit to incense a man. "Come here, whore!" A girl like innocent Edith Harms would have fainted on the spot, but a girl with Vallie's solid common sense could smile charitably at the man and continue on her way. She remembered another situation, when she had delivered a drawing to a client of Egon's, a lawyer in Grinzing. He invited her in for a cup of the local wine, and before he even poured her a glass he asked her if, for a reasonable fee, she would let him look at her. She knew what he meant. She waited while he poured the wine, inhaled as though preparing to reply, and—ooh la la!—tossed the full glass on his Belgian carpet.

Vallie likes to recall her few triumphs, those instances when she had made a lasting impression. She made an impression on Egon Schiele the day she spit in his face in the Hietzing café. She made an impression on the Magyar brothers. Would they bring her another box of chocolate animals tomorrow? But she is in quarantine and can have no visitors and no chocolate.

Enough of this. The men on her ward must have their supper and their medicines, she has responsibilities, no more excuses, she must put on her white apron and hurry across the yard to the hospital. The men will be asking for her. They will think she has abandoned them. She hopes the Magyar brothers haven't left for America yet —she wants to ask them to take her along. She must find her father in New York and tell him that the woman he loves is dead. Vallie balances against the metal post of the cot, raises herself on the balls of her bare feet for the floor is so cold, ice-cold, cold enough to sear her tough soles. Without releasing the bed frame, she reaches for the knob, only to discover that the door has been locked from the out-side. This doesn't surprise her. If she really wanted to go to work she could climb through the window—the Magyar brothers have shown her that it can be done. But right now she wants to sleep and to enjoy the warmth. She has the doctor's permission to take a holiday. Delicious sleep. She will burn in her sleep, and when she wakes she will be as light as air.

Should she feel cheated because a disease has entered her body? She remembers the day she bit into a raisin bun in a field near the Neulengbach prison and coughed up the tiny bones of a mole. She had felt cheated then. But she can better appreciate that hallucinatory experience now that her own body is transforming. Besides, every-one will burn. Vallie is a patient, one among many. An acrobat. How did the three of them ever manage to cavort on this narrow cot? And what if the seed of the Magyar managed to slip past her protection and into her womb? What if she is carrying more than a disease? The germ would infect the fertilized egg, adding an element of pathos to Vallie's end. She would rather not consider this possi-bility—she prefers to savor the sickness, to take comfort in the certainty. Her bed will become a bier, and the nurses will gather around her, all of them wearing strange folded Bonaparte hats with candles fastened to the peaks. They had better be careful or the flickering candles will set their paper hats on fire and the nurses will burn, the dormitory and hospital will burn, the Empire will burn.

If someone turned on the light, Vallie could see the mirror on the dressing table across the room. She prefers the darkness. But who could be knocking? She remembers the time she snuck into the Harms's apartment and stole Edith's satin graveshoes. Someone had knocked when she was in the kitchen. But she isn't so confused that she mistakes her dormitory room for the kitchen of a fancy Hietzing apartment. The nurses wouldn't bother knocking before they entered. It might be the Holy Ghost. Vallie's great-aunt in Ragusa liked to say, "Any day now, the Lord will come knocking." Someone should inform Vallie's few relatives that the patient has scarlet fever.

She closes her eyes. When she opens them again, the light on the wall above her bed has been turned on, and an awful smell, the smell of a decaying mole, rises from a steaming teacup on the night table. She closes her eyes so that she won't be tempted to look at herself in the mirror. When she blinks again, the tea is gone and the light has been turned off. Soon she will close her eyes forever, and the nurses will gather around her bed and mourn her, speaking in low, admiring voices about Vallie's beauty. Then Vallie will be free to go to America with her Magyar lovers. What about the life she could have lived? Doesn't she deserve another chance? But a girl can't buy innocence; innocence is as much a gift as musical talent or wit, to be nurtured but impossible to feign.

She smells the pungent fragrances of vinegar and snow. Is someone knocking, or has she just imagined the sound? Perhaps she hears the rattling of a carburetor. The brothers have bought an automobile and are waiting for her below the window. Did she forget to erase their footprints? Well, it doesn't matter what slander the nurses trade among themselves, for soon Vallie's bed will be a funeral bier, and the nurses will be obliged to mourn. She has no regrets. But she does have one mean desire that grows stronger as she grows weaker. She can't help it, but a part of her wants the world to die with her. All the patients have scarlet fever and must be quarantined. She would share her bed—there is room for three, at least. As they melted, a chocolate puddle would spread over the surface of the earth. This delicious image on the inside of her eyelids makes Vallie shake with silent laughter, her convulsions cause the little boat to rock, and instead of waiting for it to capsize, she dives into the chocolate, sinks head first, her mouth open so she won't miss the taste as each bubble of liqueur pops at her touch. The surprise of taste. Vallie sinks, one among many. If nothing else, Vallie has been a bud on the tongue, a discerner, evaluating tastes, deciding what is worthy and what is not. The chocolate simmers, and Vallie trembles with laughter. She wishes she could call out to the other nurses to join her, but warm chocolate fills her throat. Everything is so dark here, she can't tell whether she has her eyes opened or closed. Who will miss her? Who will come after her?

But Vallie is not so confused that she really believes in this fantasy of drowning—she knows that she remains on her bed, melting, her skin bubbling like the surface of the chocolate sea, so hot to touch that she can't even clasp her fingers. She remembers how the Magyar brothers puffed white smoke as they stood below her window. They were burning, too, and they shared their warmth with her. If she had the strength, she would write a letter to her father and ask the Magyar brothers to deliver it to him in New York City. Her father is building a house for Egon Schiele—her father, Egon and Edith, and the Magyar brothers will live there together. They will reminisce about Vallie, and she will bang the butt of an ax against the walls to let them know that she is listening. Whoever was knocking earlier has stopped. Vallie wishes that she had invited him in. The nurses are gathering outside her door already—she can hear them murmuring, their satin graveshoes shuffling, their paper hats crackling as they position the candles. They should light all the candles before they enter the room, Vallie thinks, or the effect will be lost. She waits, listening for the unmistakable sound of the head of a match striking flint.

•

There was a time in Egon's life when he wanted to do nothing but invent colors that couldn't be found in the natural world. As a young boy he liked wax crayons better than waterpaints because he could smear the colors, peel them with his fingernails and overlap them until they were as brilliant as flames. Wax crayons were the next best thing to pastels, which were nearly as good as oils. Waterpaints, on the other hand, lacked intensity. Though Egon's teacher had already recognized his student's drafting talents, he hadn't been as impressed by the boy's use of color and didn't have much advice when Egon took up crayons, except to warn him that crayons were a waste of time, that wax surfaces were too fragile to be worthwhile. But eleven-year-old Egon didn't care whether his pictures would last until tomorrow. With his pencil drawings of trains he had demonstrated his skill but with crayons he had discovered how much fun art could be. Since his teacher wouldn't help him, he taught himself to blend and mix and engrave dancing flames in the thick layers of wax with a pin. He would whistle with surprise when, in his experiments, he produced a hybrid not represented in his box of crayons.

His passion for colors was only aggravated by the appearance of a stranger, who came into Tulln on a train from Vienna and set up his easel at the top of a knoll overlooking the town. Egon had watched for an entire afternoon while the man rubbed stumps of pastels over the velvety paper. Egon had stood so close that he breathed in the fine dust of the colors, but he never said a word, not even when the artist asked him his name. The man wore a rubber finger-cot to keep the pastels from staining his hands; he used four different pigments for his wheat fields, blending them together into a gold Egon had never seen before.

At the end of the day the artist put his pastel drawing in his portfolio, folded up his easel and bid his little friend goodbye. Egon followed a few paces behind, trailing the man all the way to the station. He stood on the opposite side of the tracks and stared at the stranger for a good quarter of an hour, until the train arrived. After the train pulled out, Egon saw the man's cigarette burning on the empty platform, so he rushed across the tracks, carefully ground out the cigarette in the gravel between the ties and then placed the half-smoked stick in his pocket. He waited until the next afternoon—in case the man came back to Tulln and demanded that Egon return the cigarette—before he smoked it in an abandoned stable, far from the station house and from his mother's disapproving eyes. He tasted the pastel chalk as he inhaled; he tasted the colors.

The following day he spat and spat and spat into a bedpan in order to convince his mother that he couldn't go to school. When he was alone in his room, he spread his crayons across the bed and began to draw, determined to create for himself a gold even more brilliant than the gold of the artist's fields. Back at school at the end of the week, he refused to use anything but crayons, and his teacher let him have his way. He wrote out his arithmetic problems with crayons. He drew the trains that passed through Tulln with crayons. The colors inspired him so much that he even wrote a few short verses with crayons.

And then, toward the end of the summer, he had a chance to look upon golds far more intense than the stranger's pastel wheat. That summer had been the driest in memory. Marie Schiele gave up trying to cultivate the parched soil of her little garden, and in August wildfires in the hills were reported. Priests were traveling between villages to bless the fields, only to find many of the farms abandoned. Since their crops were doomed, the poorer peasants were wandering north, hoping to find more temperate weather and to sit out the drought. *Bauer* families who could afford it went to spas, for everyone knew that no matter what happened in the plains, the mountain resorts would always have plenty of water. Adolf Schiele's duties as the stationmaster made him one of Tulln's most valuable men that summer—trains transporting supplies to Vienna were often conveniently delayed for an hour in the middle of the night, with a few boxcars left unlocked. The Schiele children were not the only children in town who stealthily collected taxes—in the form of vegetables, flour, beans—from passing freights.

Only the vineyards flourished that summer, and the flavorful new wines kept people giddy and carefree during the scant harvest. But instead of bringing rain and snow, autumn brought the smoldering fires closer to Tulln. Ashes from nearby fields settled on the streets, and people no longer bothered to wash the soot off their windows. Yet as the danger of fire became the main preoccupation of the adults, Egon grew more and more excited. Apocalypse didn't occur every day, and never before had he seen such silken tones in the sky at sunset. So when Adolf Schiele abandoned his post at the station to assist the men in digging a moat around Tulln's granary, and Marie Schiele joined the wives hauling buckets of water from the river to their homes, Egon collected his crayons and paper and set off alone. In the yard he found his sister Gerti building a village with pebbles, and with a shrug he invited her to come with him. She removed a few stones from her precarious tower to ensure that it would be standing when she returned, wiped her hands on her apron and held out her arm for her brother.

They climbed the same road that the stranger from Vienna had taken, but Egon wasn't satisfied with the view at the summit, so he searched the roadside until he found a path leading into the forest. As they walked along the path he thought he heard the sound of crackling flames, but realized that he had heard merely brittle ground cover beneath their feet. And soon, much too soon, Gerti announced that she was tired. When Egon refused to answer she leaned back on her heels and refused to go on. He pulled her forward, oblivious to her caterwauling, intent now on seeing the fire for himself.

It was then that the gold appeared—or at least then that he first noticed the colors around him—ferns, birch and beech leaves, moss growing on the sides of trees, the ivy and grasses: everything that had once been green was now a shade of gold, gold like plaited flax, like jewelry, like brass, like the circles on a peacock's tail, like fire. Egon saw no sign of fire, yet the golds around him were as mesmerizing as the most lively flames. He stared transfixed while his sister tugged to free herself.

"Look at it," he begged her.

"Look at what?" she asked, the taunt of a seven-year-old in her voice, for she understood what her brother meant, knew as well that she didn't share his fascination. "Everything is dead," she said. "I want to leave here, let me go or I'll scream!"

But at the moment that Egon released her hands Gerti threw herself against him, frightened by an abrupt crashing noise and the barking of what must have been—to her mind—a hundred ferocious dogs closing in. The crashing grew louder, as though the trees were collapsing on all sides, the dogs came nearer, and Gerti and Egon could do nothing but clutch each other, for if they ran the dogs would pursue them—everyone knew that dogs loved a chase. And every schoolchild knew the story of Actaeon. Gerti buried her face in Egon's shirt so she wouldn't have to see the dogs before they attacked her. But the dogs (only two of them, as it turned out) weren't interested in devouring a young girl and her brother. A rabbit bounded in a double leap across the path ahead of Egon and Gerti, disappearing into the underbrush, and the dogs dashed in pursuit—small sausage hounds with ears the size of lily pads flapping against their heads, tongues plastered back against their snouts. In a minute the woods were silent again. Egon chuckled at the little coward in his arms.

"You don't need to worry as long as you keep close to me," he assured her. "But you must do as I say." Gerti sniffed and wiped her nose with her apron. Her head hanging, lips pursed in an exaggerated pout, she seemed ready to follow orders. Resistance wasn't worth the effort. So they continued along the path, Egon exhaling wistfully, Gerti stumbling on purpose to show her brother that he was the cruelest tyrant of all time.

They didn't see the flames that day, but the colors in the forest satisfied Egon. Gold—and every other pigment with yellow as its root—was an unnatural color, the color created when light strikes something limpid, something dying—the color of light itself. Sunset improved the sky. Drought and autumn improved the forest. When he was eleven years old, Egon thought it an artist's job to make beautiful pictures, and while Gerti sat cross-legged on the ground and built a village out of twigs and crumbs of soil that she wet with her saliva, Egon made crayon sketches of the forest. He layered color upon color until the texture resembled skin on the surface of scalded milk. Wind carried thin strands of smoke over their heads and rattled the brittle leaves, and for a while both Egon and Gerti were content.

But as the light changed the gold became sallow, and the landscape gradually lost its power over Egon. And then his own wax hues, which had seemed so marvelous a moment earlier, appeared unbearably dull. How could he make beautiful pictures if the beauty of the world didn't last long enough for him to finish his drawing? How could he copy the magnificent shades if they had already faded? In just a few minutes Egon lost all enthusiasm. So many hours immersed in fruitless labor, and every picture was no better than this one of puce and bone-brown. His teacher had been right to insist that crayons were a waste of time. Art was a waste of time. And what did beauty matter anyway?

Beauty is worth this much, Egon thought, tearing his three sketches in half, tearing them again and again, tossing the confetti into the air. *Beauty is worth this much.* He started to kick wildly, spinning in circles, stamping and yelling until nothing remained of Gerti's miniature village. Then he stood panting, hugging himself, staring at his sister, who stared back in disbelief and then with a scream lunged at him. Before he could catch her, she grabbed a fistful of his hair. He forced her fingers open and ducked behind the shield of his arms, let her claw at him because he knew he couldn't quiet her with an apology. Yet Gerti's rage was inexhaustible, and though her arms were weak and the blows fell lightly, the steadiness of the attack finally proved more than Egon could bear, and he overpowered his sister, forcing her to the ground. She struggled beneath him, her small body writhing and squirming, and Egon said her name softly to lure her out of the tantrum, repeated her name until he felt her body relax, whispered her name once more, for himself this last time—merely the sound of the word pleased him.

Even if he could never replicate the exquisite golds of the natural world, he could replicate his little sister. Sweet Gerti Schiele. Why hadn't he ever done Gerti's portrait? With pencils he had drawn trains in laborious detail. With watercolors he had painted groves of trees, rooftops, rainbows. With crayons he had drawn a forest. With pencils and watercolors and crayons he would put Gerti on paper, if she would consent to sit for him. Egon would teach her how to model. But would she be willing? He would have to regain her trust, lost when he had kicked apart her village of twigs. First he would have to convince her that his art was worthy, then he would reveal how desperately he needed her. Without Gerti's admiration, his life had no purpose.

These thoughts rushed through his head while Gerti, with a whimper of protest, began to struggle again. What could Egon say to her? How to begin? He must make a picture so beautiful that she would want to have it framed and hung above her bed. He wouldn't offer to give the finished picture to her—he would have to wait for her to ask. Would she ask? She didn't trust him, and now that he had destroyed her village she despised him.

Egon looked down at her face, pinched and scarlet, even ugly, yet so vulnerable. Dear Gerti. He kissed her on the forehead, was startled by the heat of her skin, felt as though he had kissed a warm-blooded stone, a magical thing that would make his wishes come true. He wished upon Gerti, held her by her ears while he kissed her on the mouth, the one wish turning over and over in his mind: that Gerti would love him as completely as he loved her. He touched her lips with his tongue, tasted the salt of his precious wishing stone. He wanted to swallow her, to keep her inside him forever.

As soon as he released her, she scrambled to her feet, grabbed a handful of crayons that had spilled on the ground during their fight and threw them into the woods. Then she turned and fled along the path, back in the direction of the road. Egon watched her run. He sat absolutely still long after she was out of sight, waiting with the impossible hope that she would come back to him. Every branch that creaked in the wind became Gerti: Gerti stealing toward him through the woods; Gerti climbing a tree so she could drop on him from above; Gerti running like a rabbit from dogs; Gerti flinging herself into his arms.

Eventually he headed down the path after his sister. He ignored the soft colors of dusk around him, ignored the faint smell of burning leaves, thought only of the task before him. He imagined the picture he would draw with his pencils, colored pencils. He would impress Gerti with his precise, elegant lines and he would woo her with his brilliant hues. The conflagration that they hadn't even seen would serve as his subject. A picture of fire, a *grosser Brand* raging across the town, tiny stick figures, twig people in the foreground, some with water hoses, others watching helplessly. A picture of devouring flames.

He never stopped to consider whether this subject might have been too ambitious, far beyond his capabilities—he would try anything to win his sister's love. He would have to make a picture more beautiful than the golden woods, more consuming than the conflagration that was threatening their town. If he showed her that with his pictures he could improve the world, she would surely want to see what he could do with her. Vulnerable Gerti. Vain, vulnerable Gerti. Everything depended upon her consent.

•

Egon Schiele in his diary of May 8, 1912: "Auto-da-Fé! Savonarola! Inquisition! Middle Ages! Castration, hypocrisy!"

About the Author

Joanna Scott is an Assistant Professor of English at the University of Rochester. She has also taught in the creative writing programs at Princeton University and the University of Maryland. She was awarded a Guggenheim Fellowship during the writing of *Arrogance*, her third novel.

Scribners